Winter's Salvation

A Zombie Apocalypse Novel

By
Jason Deyo

Without the people mentioned below my book would never have become a reality.
Thank you
Mrs. Doris Deyo
Mrs. Linda Taylor
Mr. Charlie Phelan and
Kevin Anderson of All Ivy Writing Services Inc.
for all of your constructive criticism and editing.
Mr. C.J. Love of www.clove2design.com for designing the cover and putting my vision on paper.
And a special thank you to my father Robert Deyo (author of *Moon Dancer*) and my mother Deborah Van Ness for supporting me no matter how twisted and disturbed my imagination got.
This book is dedicated to my loving wife and very creative son.

Chapter 1

Best of Friends

"You're not Puerto Rican," Eric said as he picked up a buoy scraper.

"I'm probably the only Puerto Rican you know," Rod responded, slightly offended. He, too, pulled one of the scrapers from a large blue plastic trash can and shook it. The scraper consisted of a long pole with a piece on the end that resembled a thick putty knife, and this one was loose. Rod put it back and grabbed another from the bin.

The smell of dead fish, crabs, and rotting sea urchins filled the thick hot humid air as they fried on the buoy deck of the U.S. Coast Guard Cutter Maria Bray. June was miserable in Jacksonville, Florida, and the worst place anyone could be was on the metal frying pan called the buoy deck of a buoy tender. The crew on the buoy deck, most under the age of twenty, wearing blue coveralls and orange reflective life preservers, were covered in sweat mixed with the crud that covered the five-ton buoy that was lying chained to the deck.

"No, my friend's stepfather's sister's boyfriend Negro is Puerto Rican. He's Puerto Rican, you're not Puerto Rican." Eric attempted rolling his r in *Negro* in a horrible Spanish accent.

"You lie." Rod paused for a second. "What makes him more Puerto Rican than me?"

"He's Puerto Rican and you're not. I didn't say he's more Puerto Rican."

"Why is he Puerto Rican and I'm not?" Rodriquez began to

scrape the side of the green rusting buoy while some of the more senior deckies climbed to the top of the cage to change out the lights and solar panels. The buoy was larger than anyone on deck. Eric walked around and began scraping the other side. With every scrape of the buoy, sea urchins, crustaceans, and barnacles fell to the sizzling metal deck.

"Because he's bad ass," another scrape, "and he has an awesome accent."

"I assume he's black, too."

Eric nodded behind the buoy. "Your point?"

"Yeah, negro means black in Spanish."

"I was very confused growing up," Eric said.

Rodriquez couldn't help but laugh. "You know this is not what I signed up for," Rod grunted as he scraped critters over the green buoy and into Eric's face.

Smiling, Eric clenched his lips tight, but some of the foul black sea mixture had already managed to fall into his mouth. Finding the last halfway decent spot on his sleeve, he wiped his face clean. He finished scraping the side of the buoy to his standards. His scraping wasn't to the standard of many of the other deckies. He was a machinist and cared little for working on buoys, but he had been volun-told to work with the deck crew. A small striped crab made a desperate run across the hot deck; Eric reached down and grabbed hold of it very gently from behind with his thick leather gloves.

Rod had more pride in his workmanship, and was not quite done his side. He was very much aware that he was not going to get away with throwing crud into Eric's face, and watched as his shipmate licked his lips. That was code for *I'm going to get you back.*

"Yeah, the Guard I signed up for showed Coasties kicking in doors and drowning Cubans," Eric said, trying to get a rise out of him.

"Help me grab this chain," Rod said as he stood his scraper up in the trash can.

Eric followed, not saying a word, and followed his lead, tossing his scraper into the bin. He cupped the crab, hiding it from anyone's view.

Rod kicked over one of the chain links that was about the size of a football and pulled it with a chain hook. "I'll pull it out if you can drag it to the other side."

"Yup," Eric said with a grin. As Rod bent over, Eric dropped the mysterious crab into the pocket of his baggy blue coveralls where he kept his cigarettes.

"I can't wait to get home and make love to Julie." Rodriquez licked his lips at Eric, just to drive in the insult of throwing buoy crud in his face.

"Me too." Eric's response was quick. "I mean goin' home and makin' love to Julie."

Rod drove a hard punch into Eric's shoulder, but Eric greeted it with a laugh. Eric was a stocky, five-foot-nine former Olympic wrestling hopeful; the wiry Rodriquez was half a head shorter, but he didn't let anyone get away with trash-talking his wife—not even Eric. Julie, a blond who was gorgeous despite weighing twice as much as Rod, was the type of woman who would do anything for anyone at the drop of the hat. And as Rodriquez reminded Eric often, family is number one to the Puerto Rican people.

After they'd dragged the buoy back into the water, the deck crew stopped to take a break. "So who are you hooking up with this weekend?" Rod asked snidely.

Knowing Rodriquez was about to jump into another of his long-winded *family* tirades, Eric did his best to derail the conversation. "Depends on who Julie's bringin' home," he jeered.

"Being a father and husband are the two greatest things that have ever happened to me." Julie had come with a son from a previous relationship, but Rod treated Drew like his own. They were working on child number two. If ever a couple should have had lots of kids, they were the ones. But Rod could see the men rolling their eyes as they rested on a scuttle. "You all just don't know." He reached deep into his pocket for a cigarette, screamed, and pulled out a crab that was latched onto his right hand with both claws.

The men laughed. Eric rolled hysterically and then was called to the bridge.

****

Later that night Eric and Rodriquez sat on Rod's uncomfortable blue couch. It was the type of couch that sits in hotel rooms and is really there for decoration, not for actual use. The stuffing that filled the cushions consisted of a piece of carpet padding and a blue, almost denim, cloth material. They sat watching the latest movie from Red Box, and Eric migrated to the floor, figuring the carpet was better suited for sitting.

Half way through the movie, the front door's knob shifted and then was thrown open. It was Julie, coming home from work and obviously in a foul mood. "Hey babe, I didn't expect you home so early," Rod said as he paused the movie. "Good day?" He reached up to hug her massive six-foot-tall body.

"Anything but." Julie looked irritated, and beads of sweat rolled down her forehead. She had to bend over to wrap her large arms around Rod's small upper body and give him a quick uncomfortable hug. She pulled the scrunchie from her long blond hair, releasing her pony tail and briefly relieving some stress as the hair stopped pulling at her scalp. She wore the classic nurse's outfit, blue scrubs with white tennis shoes. On her scrubs, just above her right breast, it looked as if she had spilled some wine or something red. "Babe, I really need to take a shower and just lie down for a bit."

"Ok. You hungry? I could go for some Pizza Pizza right now." He skipped backwards in front of her.

From down the hallway Rod's stepson Drew hollered through his closed bedroom door. "I could go for some Pizza Pizza!"

Eric watched and pictured Rod as a little puppy begging for attention from its master. It didn't matter what type of attention it was, just as long as he was attended to. Eric laughed at that thought and was about to say hello when Julie bellowed, "God, Rod, get out of my face already."

Rod shrank back with that warning and stood to the side as she stomped past him. When she closed the door to the bathroom Rod's eyes got big and he whispered to Eric, "I'm still getting Pizza Pizza." Both of them laughed under their breath. The bathroom door opened up again and Julie came out wearing a black short-sleeve shirt and some very short blue shorts. It looked as if she had just stepped out of the shower, but the water had never run. She came back and hugged Rodriquez. "Sorry, I just need to lie down."

"What happened to your arm?" He took her right hand and twisted it slightly, revealing a deep gash and a few light scratches on the back of her forearm.

"This guy scratched me today. He was acting all kinds of batshit crazy and puking everywhere. We actually had to restrain him."

"Did he puke on you?" Rod said, then grimaced, referring to the stain on her scrubs.

Julie, seeing the grimace, was not at all amused. "No, some other guy did. I cleaned the scratches; it should be okay." She started to switch stances and Rod knew she was getting angry. Sweat was dripping from her face and body. Her clothes clung to her body with perspiration. "There were a couple people that came in the emergency room the same way."

"Why don't you take a shower?" He rubbed her large right

shoulder. "I'll order some food."

"I told you I wasn't hungry!" she barked, and Rod prepared to duck an incoming blow. The punch never came, but Julie scowled as if she was going to hurt him. After the outburst she turned and went into their room.

"Looks like you're sleeping on the floor." Eric showed half a smile, but he did not receive the same message from Rod.

"Man, I've never seen her like this," Rodriquez said as he walked to the balcony that overlooked a pond in the back of the third-floor apartment. Eric followed and pulled out a pack of cigarettes. "Something's wrong with her." Rod pondered his statement.

Eric offered the pack to Rod and he took one. Lighting Rod's smoke, Eric answered, "Must have been a real bad day."

"Real bad." The two of them sat on the balcony and listened to the commotion on the street filtered through the trees on the other side of the pond. The sound of brakes and speeding cars filled the streets. This would not have been uncommon for a Friday, but it was eleven at night on a Thursday. Something was going on.

The sound of knocking on the front door broke the silence. Rod inhaled deeply, then flicked his cigarette into the still water of the pond. Leaving Eric on the balcony to finish his smoke, Rod opened the front door. His next door neighbor, Dave, stood on the other side.

Dave was a funny guy who didn't take life too seriously. He was nineteen and relatively new to the Navy, but was very comfortable in his current position. He had grown up in a small town in New Mexico and swore he would never go back. He stood about six feet tall with a very slim build and long hair that was naturally bunched in an Afro on the top of his head. It was considered to be too long for a person in the military, but he managed to grease it down when he decided to play sailor.

He must have been sleeping, because normally he would have

been over at Rod's place drinking or Rod and Eric would have been at Dave's place partying, making jokes about which seagoing service was better. "You have to see this." He mentioned to the front of the complex.

They lived on the third floor of the apartment complex and were happy with where they were, but everyone was jealous of Dave's spot. His apartment overlooked the complex's pool.

Looking over the railing of the balcony that connected the two apartments' front doors, they could see the entire parking lot. Under the beam of light from one of the street lights was a group of people kneeling over something. They looked as if they were picking at or digging through whatever it was.

"What are they doing?" Eric asked as he leaned on the railing to get a closer look.

David, being the excitable person he was, almost screamed, but it came out as an excited whisper. "Dude, you're going to think I'm crazy, but they're fucking *eating* that redheaded chick." Then out of nervousness he let out a small laugh.

Rod and Eric stood staring at him like he was a moron for a few seconds before he spoke again. "You know that good-looking redhead that always wears that white bikini?" Dave only knew this because the weekends he didn't have duty on his ship, he sat on his balcony and watched her swim for hours on end. Neither of them replied, but stared at Dave with the *you really are a moron* look on their faces.

"That's her!" he shouted as he pointed to the crowd, and then quickly covered his mouth to hush himself. A single streetlight shone on the group as if it were a spotlight. Now Eric and Rod could make out a carpet of crimson blood that the people knelt in. As they stared, pieces of red flesh swung around and through the hands of the people kneeling over the red-haired woman. Rod's and Eric's minds wouldn't let them comprehend what was actually happening, and they looked back to Dave.

Eric broke their silence, but was rather confused. He expected that at any second a T.V. cameraman was going to jump out and say they were going to be on the next episode of *Scare Tactics*. "Are you going to do something?"

"Oh my god, are you serious? You haven't been watching T.V.?"

Eric's phone rang, and he looked at the screen and saw it was his parents. He answered the phone, but looked to Dave. "Hey."

Dave waved them into his apartment. His flat-screen T.V. was more like a movie theater in his living room. On it was an emergency broadcast.

A young brunette woman with the look of controlled worry was warning people to stay indoors, lock their homes, and from this point on not to allow anyone in or out. "Be cautious of anyone outside, and if anyone you know has been in contact with anyone from outside your house within the last few hours, quarantine them in a secluded part of your home and wait for the authorities. Do not give shelter to anyone seeking it, including family members if they have been outside."

Eric's face was one of shock and awe, as he focused on the T.V. "Okay, alright, are you guys okay?" he asked with his face pressed hard against his phone. "Well, did you lock everything up?" His left hand pressed hard against his left ear and he hunched over as if that were going to turn the volume down on the T.V. "Dad? Hello, Dad?" He looked at his phone, and a message on the screen read *network busy*.

Rod took his eyes off the screen and looked to Eric. "What did your dad say?"

"He said the same thing the T.V. said. Lock everything up and don't go outside."

"Are they okay?"

"Yeah, so far. He locked everything up, but he's like seventy years old." His voice cracked, but he regained his composure.

The sounds of squealing tires were followed by crushing metal, and then car alarms sounded through the house. Dave looked out the front window to see a baby-blue Toyota Celica crashed across the parking lot about twenty feet from the redheaded woman's corpse. Three people were running behind the Celica. The people gorging themselves on the woman all stood up in unison and took flight towards the wrecked car. Under the shine of the street light was a red mass where the woman had once lain. The mass that was there now was nothing more than a small pile of ripped, blood-soaked clothing. Dave thought he could make out what might have been arms or legs, but the bloody clothes and the lack of anything resembling the beautiful red-haired woman made it difficult for him to fathom what had just happened. All that was left of her was a fan of red hair spread evenly on the pavement above the carnage.

Rod looked just in time to see the crazed people attack the Celica. There were a dozen of them; they all hit the car at the same time, and the driver's-side window shattered. As one reached into the window, the glass ripped into its arms. Rod stood there just long enough to see a man being pulled through the window. He was in his mid-thirties and from his apparel dark-blue button-up shirt and long black necktie he must have been rushing home from work. Rod's thoughts turned to Julie and Drew. *She was at the hospital today.*

Half-consciously his ears picked up the anchorwoman listing the symptoms to look for when in contact with people from outside your home. "Profuse sweating." *Check,* Rod thought to himself as if using a mental clipboard. "Extreme mood swings." *Check.* "Fits of violent rage." *Check.* "Unusual scratches or bite marks." *Check.* "And tight leathery skin with a grayish complexion or skin tone," the news anchor finished her list. *Aha! No grayish complexion.*

"I'm going next door to check on Drew," Rod said as he ran out the front door. Eric was just a few steps behind him when Rod got to his apartment and sent the door flying open. Straight ahead of him, his skinny, pale thirteen-year-old son was standing at the end of the hallway that connected the bedrooms. Drew's black shirt and shoulder-length black curls blended in with the dark hallway behind him. Rod could just make out Pantera's band logo on the front of the kid's shirt. Drew gave him a shocked and confused look.

Rod breathed deep as he felt the anxiety let go for a second. But from the shadows behind Drew, Rod and Eric both saw a mammoth of a figure step out from the bedroom. It wore a black short-sleeve shirt and short blue shorts. Rod looked in sheer terror as Julie's face emerged from the shadows to reveal tight grayish leathery skin. A sadistically playful voice in Rod's head said *check,* and that was followed by a verbal "Fuck!" from Eric.

Julie's small feet sounded like thunder as they pounded her heavy body toward the thirteen-year-old. Drew turned toward his mother fast and took a step backwards just as she fell on top of him. The boy disappeared under his mother's huge body. Julie's head flew up and back with a mouth full of curly black hair. She placed her hands on his head and ripped the hair from it. Eric and Rod both jumped on her as she opened her mouth for another bite of her son.

Drew arched his back and turned his head, screaming, his mother's mouth inches from biting into his cheek. His hands, pushing against Julie's eyes, were small in comparison to her obese face and gaping mouth.

Eric yanked back on her hair as Rodriquez pressed his small forearm against her throat and pushed his body between the child and Julie. Drew tried to push out from under her, but Julie had both her fists full of black curly hair and pulled his head toward her mouth.

Blond hair pulled free from Julie's head, leaving large chunks in Eric's hands and causing him to fall backwards down the hall.

He was up in seconds and back on top of the raging woman, trying to pull her head back. Drew's body was out from under his mother's, but she had him by the hair and was pulling him back in. Eric pulled his small pocket knife from his back pocket and began sawing through the black hair in one of her hands. He quickly went to work on the other hand. Drew was free, but Julie reached for Rod, who had taken Drew's place under her.

From behind Julie, Eric grabbed hold of her right wrist and twisted it up and out to her side as much as he could in the confines of the hallway. "Let go, Julie!" Eric screamed, while he twisted her arm back and up over her right shoulder. Any normal person would have been screaming in agony and trying to be still to stop the pain, but she pressed forward, pulling Rod into her. Eric felt her right arm snap and let go of it in shock. The forearm waved wildly as she used the stump of her arm to get closer to her victim.

Rod pushed up on her face and his left thumb accidently but deeply thrust into her right eye. He tried to pull it out, but his elbow was propped on the ground, and with her pushing against it trying to bite him, he could not pull it free. As his thumb penetrated her eye socket, a greasy black fluid leaked over and into the palm of his hand. She didn't pull back, though, but kept pushing until her face was flush with his palm and his entire thumb was jammed into her eye socket, stopping the leaking fluid.

Eric straddled Julie's back and grabbed her by her throat and pulled back. As her head pulled away, Rod tried to pull his thumb from her head. She turned her head to bite at the hand that was being pulled free from her eye.

Meanwhile David pulled up on her left arm. "Grab the other arm!" he shouted. Eric let go of her neck and her head jutted forward. Rod screamed in pain as he felt his left thumb bend back and a sharp pain shot through his wrist.

Eric fumbled to grab at her flopping right arm. Her hand twisted and spun as she supported her weight on the stump of her right arm. He finally grabbed her between the upper part of her elbow and her armpit.

"Throw her in the bathroom!" Dave shouted over Rod's screams and the growl of the beast that had been Julie.

Eric turned to see how far he would have to pull her to get to the bathroom. It was to his right, a few feet behind him. A couple steps back, he felt her weight being shifted to his side as Dave picked her up.

As they lifted her to her feet, she turned her attention to Eric. She snapped at his face as they began to guide her to the door. She lunged at Eric, ripping from Dave's grip, but Eric was able to sidestep, forcing her to trip and fall face first into the bathroom. She hit her head on the white tub and black blood appeared down the side of the white porcelain. Eric grabbed the doorknob and tried to close the door, but her legs were in its path. She quickly got back to her hands and knees, using the tub to assist her. Dave stepped in next to Eric and kicked her hard in the butt, causing her to fall into the tub. Now that her legs were no longer in the way, a quick pull of the door and she was trapped. The door shook as she beat wildly on it. The sound of her heavy hand beat high on the door, then was followed by a dull thud. She beat the door with her left arm and hit the door with her right stub. Even crippled, she shook the door wildly, and with her large body smashing against it, they knew it would not be long before the door collapsed.

Rod did not say a word. He just sat there with his right arm back to support his weight and his left arm held up in a defensive posture. Looking at his left hand, he realized his thumb had been buried in his wife's eye. His thumb was covered in a thick liquid that streamed red and white with a black tar that mixed the two. The colors and the surreal memory of the incident hypnotized him for a few moments, but then the searing pain of his broken thumb and sprained left wrist shot him back into reality. The pain was great, but he did not show it. He stood up and started to walk to the sink in the kitchen.

Drew stood away from the fight with his back leaning against the kitchen bar. He cleared his throat. "We need to go." He grabbed hold of Rod to shake him out of his shock. Drew looked at him with complete confusion.

Standing over the sink, Rod washed his hands gently so as to not move his thumb. "We need to get out of here," he mumbled to himself.

Eric moved to the door, grabbing Drew on his way out, and Dave followed. As they passed Rodriquez, Eric hollered to him, "Dude, come on!" He pushed Dave and Drew past him. "I'll meet you at my Jeep." He walked to Rod slowly, staring at the stainless-steel sink under his clean hands. "Rod, your son and Dave are going to my car," Eric said softly, "and we need to go with them."

The banging on the bathroom door ended in a loud crack. Eric looked down the hallway to see a bloody hand hanging out of the door, ripping at the hole it had just made. "Rod, the door is not going to hold for much longer. We need to GO!" Eric started talking quietly and ended up screaming.

Rod stared at the distorted reflection of himself in the stainless-steel curve of the sink. Black and red blood slowly drained into the sink and his distorted reflection looked as if he himself were a crazed person covered in blood, staring back at him.

Eric, seeing he was not making any connection with his catatonic friend, smacked his partially clean left hand, turning him into a screaming maniac. "Dude, come on!" Eric screamed back, pulling on the collar of his shirt.

As if Rod had been listening the entire time, he ran past Eric and through the front door. Eric ran behind him and turned as he grabbed the door knob. At the moment he turned, Julie's head broke through the bathroom door. As soon as she looked at him, the front door slammed with no hesitation behind Eric.

Chapter 2

The Road

They took the stairs down to the second level, watching as more wild people seemed to appear out of nowhere.

"I'm going to grab my gun," Dave said and ran back up the stairs. As he left, a low growl that turned into a wild scream came from behind them. Before anyone knew what was going to happen, Rodriquez pushed Drew back against the green wooden railing and stood in front of him. Eric turned to see a man wearing a torn button-up shirt that had been white before his blood completely covered it and a black necktie dangling loosely around his neck. The man turned the corner to run up the stairs and looked directly at the three of them. Its left arm grabbed the railing and its right arm supported its weight as it crouched for a charge.

The crazed businessman looked as if he had been in a car wreck: the right side of his face was smashed in. The charging man's left eye was open wide, its focus fixed on Eric. It stood straight up and revealed an open and exposed ripped-out chest under the torn button-up shirt. Bare and broken ribs were open to the elements for all to see.

The crazed man dashed wildly up the stairs and Eric stood prepared for the impact. He lifted his right leg and connected cleanly with the man's face with his foot. Red and black blood shot out in a spray under his boot.

Any other man would have done back flips down the steps, but the madman's head snapped back violently. It stumbled down one step and continued forward as if it had simply missed its footing. During the creature's charge it lowered its head, mostly to regain its balance, and Eric stepped in front of Rod and Drew and landed a punch square in the creature's face. It flew against the railing and turned with force and speed that flung blood from the right side of its face to splatter over the three of them. It charged wildly back at Eric.

Eric sidestepped it again, tripped it to the ground, and jumped on top of its back. He grabbed hold of its hair and smashed its face into the wooden platform. Again and again he smashed its head into the deck. The crazed man fought to stand up, but was never able to buck Eric off. He continued to drive the man's head into the wooden deck until the smashed right side of his face touched the left side. It may have stopped fighting before Eric stopped, but he could not control himself.

His world had changed. The only people he held dear to his heart were his parents, and they were alone in Maryland. "I've gotta go," he said to Drew and Rodriquez and started to walk away.

By this time David was on his way down to the second level. He looked at the body lying in a running pool of blood that flowed between the wooden deck boards. Eric turned his back to him and Dave could see his fingers were red and black with the creature's blood.

They followed behind him, careful not to step in or on any of the blood the man was spewing. The parking lot was vacant with the exception of a few manic people devouring their victims. A mob had grown around the crashed car, and they were already consuming the crash victim. In a stroke of good luck, Eric had parked his Jeep Grand Cherokee in the darkest corner of the lot, well away from the crash and its crowd. The guys all piled into the car and tried to close the doors as softly as possible. Eric put his phone on speaker and tried to call his father again, but the phone system was not operating. He hung up and tried again, but with each try, *network busy* continued to appear on the screen.

The roads out of the complex were filled with crashed cars, and as the Jeep's lights shone down the street, they revealed piles of bloody corpses close to most of the wrecks. There were a few wrecked cars with no bodies around them, but piles of blood and ripped clothing were close by or hanging from the open doors of the vehicles. The streets were empty of any humans, but as the light passed the balcony of one of the complexes, the guys could see that the balcony was filled with commotion as if the entire floor were having a party. The only difference was that the fun was replaced with horror and the whoops and hollers from games were replaced with screams of pain, agony, and fear.

****

The main streets were filled with racing cars. Everyone was trying to go somewhere else, as if anywhere was better than where they already were. Eric sat and waited for a chance to make it out of their complex. Car after speeding car flew past. There was a car directly across from them in their sister apartment complex across the busy street. Its high beams were on, shining brightly into Eric's and Dave's eyes. The car looked as if it were a van of some sort. Whatever it was, it was perfectly angled so that the lights shined like spotlights to help the frenzied find their way for a meals-on-wheels feast. The van's lights shined directly into the Jeep's passengers' eyes, hampering their vision.

He flashed, then shined, his high beams on the van in sheer disapproval, hoping it hampered the other driver's vision as well. With his high beams on, Eric watched the van pull out of the complex as many other vehicles had, but these lights were moving faster than normal. The van pulled out and turned to the right, the sound of squealing tires following it. The passengers in Eric's Jeep could see four people clinging to the tan van and several more chasing after it. They hardly had time to make out the details of the van and why it had pulled into oncoming traffic before a black truck rammed into its side. The two people who had been clinging to the van's passenger side went flying through the air; the two on the driver's side were crushed completely in half.

The van and truck went spinning into the oncoming traffic in both lanes, while the two smashed-in-half bodies were thrown from the spinning vehicles. The cars that followed the truck slammed on their brakes and slid off the side of the road. The traffic that was coming in Eric's direction slammed their brakes, too, and tried to swerve to avoid the crashed vehicles—with no success. The pileup formed a wall of screaming metal that allowed Eric to pull out.

One of the cars that had slid off the road across from them was trying to free itself from the ditch, but the black car's wheels spun wildly. The torsos of the two crushed people pulled themselves towards the black car, dragging their entrails behind them. The car was halfway down in a ditch, and people started moving from the bushes that blocked the apartments from the street. Maybe Eric wanted to believe these people coming from the bushes were going to push the stranded car out of the ditch, but reality hit hard when the back driver's side door opened and a heavier young woman with black hair, holding a small child in her arms, came running from the car and darted across the busy street. A speeding car slammed the brakes and slowed dramatically, but it still hit the woman and her child hard enough to lift her from her feet and send them flying back. Eric pulled away, knowing there was nothing they could do. The small car that had hit her turned slightly to avoid running her over and continued down the street.

Eric kept an eye on the rearview window, and the other three stretched their necks to watch the mayhem. The stranded vehicle's dome lights were on due to the back door being left open; the interior was lit enough that they could make out people being pulled from the car. The white dome light of the car turned the inside to a crimson glow. The crawling torsos of the two crushed undead reached the woman and child and bit into their flesh.

The Jeep was quiet. All of them wanted to help, they wanted to do something, but none of them knew what they could do. They rode in silence for a minute, which felt like hours, until Dave turned the radio on. It was quiet now with the exception of an emergency radio broadcast. The news broadcaster was giving his report from a helicopter.

He had an English accent and had to speak loudly over the chopping blades of the helicopter and humming of the motor. "All the streets are packed. Bumper to bumper, it's horrible. These raging people are pulling people from their cars. Some vehicles are so close together they can't open their doors. They are trying to climb from the windows but are stuck. They are so close they can't move. The people who can get out are running; they're running in all directions. They look so confused. There's nowhere to go. Oh my God. God help us all. There's nothing they can do. If they run they get chased down. These things don't rest, they don't get tired, they just keep coming. If you are stuck in your car they pull you from it or get in with you. All the victims stuck in traffic can do is wait, wait for help, but I fear by the time help arrives it may be too late." There was a pause in the announcement and they could hear him swallow and breathe heavily. "Please stay home. If you can hear this, avoid the streets. They are all congested. I'm traveling above Jacksonville and I have not seen a single street that was not filled with these crazy people or just jammed up completely, and it does not look as if it will clear any time soon."

Rodriquez put his head between the front seats. "You just want to go to your place?"

Eric answered in a low voice, almost to himself, "That's where I'm goin'." He looked at Rod quickly. "Yeah."

The streets were busy. Some cars still obeyed the laws of

traffic, but as soon as one stopped for a fraction of a second at a stop sign, everyone behind that person jetted out from behind them. These crazy people the radio had spoken of were running wild through the streets.

They turned the radio down low so they could hear what was happening around them on the streets. From the back seat Eric heard a whimper quietly break out, barely audible over the radio. He glanced at the review mirror and saw Rodriquez holding Drew's head against his chest. Rod rested his chin on the boy's black curly hair.

You could hear Rod speaking low, as if he were keeping the conversation between them a secret, but he knew Eric and Dave could hear him. Drew's whimper turned into a sob. He was not Rodriquez's biological son. The only reason anyone could guess this was because of Drew's very pale white skin and Rod's dark naturally tanned skin.

Rodriquez and Julie had been married for eight years and Drew was five when they met. Julie was a single mom and Drew's father had skipped town and was not supporting them in any way. Julie was a hard worker, sometimes shuffling three jobs to give her son what he needed. It may not have been the best name-brand clothing or food, but he got what he needed.

They met while he was stationed at a Coast Guard small-boat station in North Carolina, and decided to get married when he was going to be shipped off to Jacksonville, Florida. Rodriquez would openly admit that he loved Julie with all his heart, but was not ready for that type of commitment. He battled with himself and weighed each option until he came to the decision that getting married only made sense. He was not going to be able to afford to travel back and forth every weekend, and he did not know who he was going to be roomed with. He could have been shoved into a small three-bedroom apartment with two other kids right out of high school, bringing their high-school buddies around every night.

So getting married only made sense to him. The military would give them money to get their own place. Their expenses would be food, medical benefits, and an orthodontist for Drew. Rod had convinced himself that by getting married he was not choosing a long-term commitment so much as helping Julie and Drew out, and in his mind that is how he coped with getting married. After their small courthouse wedding, he never regretted deciding to spend his life with her.

When Rod was not working on the cutter he was with his son doing something. It didn't matter what they were doing, but they were always together. Lately it seemed all Drew wanted to do was play some video game on the computer, which really upset Rod, but as long as Drew was happy, Rod was okay with it. He just missed going out to the festivals on the weekends and hanging out.

Now, in the back of Eric's Jeep, they held each other tight and cried quietly together. Dave turned the volume to the radio up, not to quiet them, but to give them the privacy they needed.

Eric lived in a townhouse on a quiet street. As they rounded each corner, getting closer to his home, the traffic became less and less dense until they rounded the corner a few streets down from their destination and found themselves all alone with a deserted traffic jam. Cars lined and filled the street, but there was no one in them. On both sides of the road, cars were parked parallel to each other, blocking the street. People had been forced to leave their vehicles where they rested and travel by foot if they wanted to get to their homes.

He pulled up to the truck in front of him and sat behind the line of parked vehicles in the middle of the street. Eric turned his lights off, and an eerie stillness crept over them. Rod's phone made them jump as it rang and vibrated. He flipped it open, silencing it, and saw Maria Bray on the screen. "It's the boat." He looked at Eric. "I'm not answering it."

His phone soon stopped ringing, and as soon as it did, Eric's started. He flipped it open, surprised that he had service. He had been trying to contact his father nonstop until he pulled into his neighborhood. Sure enough, it was the cutter. "Hello." There was a pause. "Yeah, I'll be there. No, I haven't seen Rod. If I talk to him, I'll let him know." He hung the phone up and called his parents.

The guys could tell the phone was ringing, because Eric kept the phone close to his ear and didn't let fly any creative curse words of disappointment due to a dropped call. He turned to Rod and said, "We're not going to the boat." The look of surprise and happiness shone on his face as his attention went back to the phone. "Dad!" He turned the radio down and talked to his father as if this were the first time he talked to him in years. "I'm coming up. I'll be there as soon as I can."

Dave tried to contact his family, but could not reach them. The phone just rang and then went to voice mail. A look of worry crept into his face, and with each passing moment and no response from the phone, he got more restless.

"I'll call you back tomorrow morning to find out how the night went. Love yas." Eric hung the phone up and apologized. "I just needed to talk to them. Are y'all ready to go in?" They all nodded their heads.

The street was quiet. Neither Rod, Dave, nor Eric had ever heard this street so quiet. They all stepped out of the Jeep and tried to close the doors as quietly as possible. As they traveled, the sound of a snap, then a moan, echoed off the walls of the townhouses. It was impossible to decipher which direction the noise had come from, but they walked on the sidewalk, cautiously avoiding the spaces in between the cars. The townhouses in the neighborhood sat high on a hill, towering over other structures on the street on this dark night. Each townhouse had a steep eight-foot set of stairs that went to the leveled hilltop, and then another set of stairs that led to the front door.

They heard another moan echo loudly off the walls, followed

by a quarrelling second and third. They slowed, pinpointing the two new voices just up ahead and to their left on the other side of some parked vehicles. Dave was the first to peer around the side of the car from the sidewalk.

He stretched his neck while taking baby steps to catch a glimpse of what was on the other side. On their knees sat four human figures, so badly eaten and torn apart he was not able to make out what sex they were. The two of them had their faces deep in a mound of bloody flesh, chewing. When one would pull free an organ of some type, they would fight over who got that piece. As Dave stepped over a little more, he caught the eye of one of them. Looking up from the corpse with blood and pieces of flesh caked on its face, it let out a scream that was bloodcurdling. It wasn't the moan they had been hearing, but a scream. Dave took off running down the street with no regard to who was behind him. The others starting running too, but couldn't stop themselves from looking at what had made the horrible noise. As Eric passed the figures, he was able to see all four rise to their feet and start to squeeze between the cars towards the guys. The closer they got to Eric's house, the more people started to rise from behind cars.

In his haste, Dave ran past Eric's house. Rod and Drew turned at his stairway and ran to his door, screaming for Eric to hurry up. Eric heard the sound of feet beating the pavement from behind him, but never turned to see how close they were. He screamed to Dave, "Too far! We're back here!" Eric lived in the second house from the end of the block, and David had already crossed the street that started the next block.

Eric ran up the side of the steep eight-foot hill to his house. After his third step cleared the hill, he fell and rolled back to his feet. Reaching the top of the second set of steps, he squeezed onto the front landing in front of his front door. There was a five-foot drop on either side of the landing to the front door, and the landing was only three feet wide or so. Eric had to push Rod and Drew back so he could open the screen to get to the door, but they fought to be as close to the door as possible.

The crazed people were running down the street, now from both directions. There were seven coming from the direction the guys had just come from, and Dave could hear more behind him in the other direction. They were not all running in the same manner, but they all were moving very quickly. Many of these savage people had severe damage to them that would have slowed or stopped any normal human being, such as large chunks of flesh from bite wounds pulled from their legs or broken appendages and feet, but it did not seem to stop them. Some moved slower from their injuries, but none of them showed signs of pain, and they all wanted to move faster, despite their obvious wounds.

Three of them fumbled on the hill right before the steps. Dave got to the steps at the same time these three did. The sound of three gunshots rang between the row houses. Two of the chasing men went stumbling back and the one in back fell to the ground.

Eric, with keys in his hand, stopped to see what had happened. Dave was running toward them with his gun in hand. The first one he had shot was already making its way up the stairs as if nothing had happened. The other five were trying to make it up the hill, working their way toward the stairs.

"Fucking open the door," Dave shouted, turning around and letting another bullet fly into the right shoulder of the man who had just made it to the top of the stairs. This man was wearing a button-up shirt with a nice brightly colored tie. His left side was torn and covered with red blood from a prior incident. His eyes were like white marble with just a touch of black in them. As the bullet knocked him back a step, he snarled. His mouth opened wide, wider than any human could physically open their mouth. Its tight grey skin wrinkled to make way for the gaping maw and to announce the hunger this creature had for its prey.

As the beast screamed, David walked up calmly and pulled the trigger of his 9mm pistol, aiming at its forehead. The frantic man fell backwards down the stairs, making way for the others to climb his body.

Eric watched the whole event, not working on the door at all. He jumped as the gun went off for the fourth time and finally managed to open the front door without any more hesitation.

Chapter 3

The Decision

The door shook as the demented people out front beat on it. Their blows to the front door shook the entire house. Locking it behind them was not enough. Eric frantically searched his house for something to secure the door, but his mind was blank. The sound of the screen door ripping off the hinges was louder to the people inside because they all recognized the extra layer of protection that was no longer there.

Dave ran into the kitchen and started looking at the liquor selection Eric kept on hand. He grabbed a bottle of Everclear and ran past Eric, who was pushing the entertainment center in front of the door. As soon as he pressed the entertainment center against the door, it cracked. "Rod, help!" he screamed.

Dave ran upstairs to the bathroom that directly overlooked the front landing. He looked at the clear bottle and examined the amount of liquor that was left in it. It was just about full and he thought about how lucky they were that they hadn't brought this bottle to Rod's house the night before. He ripped a portion of towel hanging from a hanger and stuffed one end deep into the bottle. Opening the bathroom window, Dave looked outside to evaluate what he was about to do.

Eric and Rod frantically pushed furniture in front of the cracked door. Rod pushed on the sofa and a sharp pain in his left thumb and wrist reminded him of his injury. He continued to pile furniture in front of the door, but was very cautious with his left hand.

They heard the sound of shattered glass, and then the front windows lit up as if it were day. An orange glow lit the front living room, and Eric paused for a second, not registering what had just happened. The heat coming from the cracks in the door and frame snapped him out of his shock.

From the bathroom Dave could feel the inferno bellow. There were six frenzied people on the small landing and more were trying to push themselves onto the platform. He tried to aim the bottle so it would crash right behind the first six, because he did not want to catch the house on fire. For a brief second he thought about the wooden front door, but he dropped the bottle directly on the front six. The flame exploded on them and like a waterfall flowed over the sides of the landing and down the front stairs.

He ran down the stairs hollering, "I need more liquor! I need more liquor!" A pile of furniture blocked the normal way down the stairs, so he jumped over the railing and landed on the couch and entertainment center piled in front of the door. He ran into the kitchen and this time did not care what he grabbed, just as long as it was some type of alcohol.

Climbing over the furniture and back to the bathroom, he looked out the window. The crowd that had started off with fifteen, maybe twenty, turned into a hundred in a matter of seconds. The front six had fallen and the next, already on fire but still in line, ran to take their places in the blazing inferno. None had moaned or screamed any louder after catching on fire than before, and they gave no notion of being in pain or afraid. They just kept coming. The crowd out front was growing, and soon the door would shatter with the weight of flaming people. Dave tossed his next bottle at the bottom of the stairs a few feet past the landing, creating a large spread of fire for the creatures to walk through before they got to the entrance to the house.

Eric, with no furniture left, turned his attention to the flaming door. He ran to the dining room and looked out of the back window that faced the alley. He shared a privacy fence with the neighbor on the end of the block, and now he looked at their two small lots of land. The fenced yard was clear, but in the alleyways he could see people running wildly. These quiet streets were now filled with the moaning and screeching of crazed people. Another sound unfamiliar to these streets was the cries, coming from the row houses behind him, of terrified mothers calling for their children and fathers shouting helplessly as they were being overrun. Down the alley, coming from a house to his right, he saw a woman run from her back door, being chased from her yard. As soon as she stepped into the alley the demented ones turned their attention to the scared woman and attacked her.

Eric had seen too much death and destruction in one night, and the overwhelming urge to run into the alley vanished when he turned and saw Drew standing where his couch once had been, staring at him, hoping he had a solution. He looked back to the alley, and while the creatures' attention was on devouring the young woman, Eric waved Drew toward him and then ran outside.

As Drew got to the door, Eric looked up from his garden's hose reel. "Open the window and grab the other end of this." Drew, completely silent, did as he was instructed and grabbed the hose. "I'm going to feed this through the window, and I need you to give it to your father." As soon as Drew came back to the window, Eric opened the faucet's valve, ensured there were no kinks in the hose, and locked the door behind him as he came back into the kitchen.

"I need more liquor up here!" Dave bellowed from the upstairs bathroom. He was trying to spread the fire away from the house and further down the hill. Now the deranged people had to run through about ten feet of flame and a pile of burning bodies that was building at the bottom of the stairs that led to the three-foot landing before the door. Most of the running ones that made it through the fire got tripped up in the mound of burning flesh and added to the victims.

Rod started spraying the door and was greeted by an extinguishing hiss and a great plume of smoke. Eric tried to look out the two front windows to the left of the door, but the heat of the fire barred him from getting too close.

Dave hollered from upstairs again, "I'm running low up here!"

Eric ran to his fish tank. After years of neglect, it had only one fish still swimming in it. Eric opened up the drawer under the fifty-five–gallon tank. He began to pull out and toss behind him filters and aquarium decorations, until he found what he was looking for. He pulled a long hose and a faucet attachment from the drawer and handed it to Drew. "Take this upstairs and hook it up to the sink."

Eric's mind raced for what he could give Dave. He no longer heard the banging at the door, so the fire was working. The tall whipping flames could be seen from Eric's front windows, seven feet off the ground, but Dave continued to holler for more liquor.

It was then that Eric remembered the red gas can he kept in the shed for his lawn mower. He looked out the back window and saw that the people were still devouring the woman down the street. Running to the shed, he opened the large door as fast as he could, disregarding the noise he made. He took comfort from his six foot tall wooden privacy fence–they could not see him. Grabbing the half empty gas can, he ran back to the house, locking the door behind him.

Entering the bathroom, Eric was hit by thick black smoke that smelled of burning flesh and rubber. The bathroom was small and three people jammed into it made it almost impossible to maneuver. Drew and Dave were both looking out the window, and when Drew looked behind him he stepped back and let Eric in. Out of breath, Eric looked out the window and saw the crazed people moving forward in the flame. They would step in, moving toward the house, but then most of them would start to veer off in wrong directions. He thought maybe while they were in the fire their eyes burned out and then they couldn't see where they were going.

Dave grabbed the gas can from Eric and gave it a little shake. By the look on his face he was not impressed by its contents, but he was not going to give it back.

"That's all I have left," Eric said with a shrug.

Dave pushed it out as far as he could. They watched it land just past the ten-foot section of fire, and when it struck the ground, flame bounced through the air and spread out to the street. Cars caught on fire, and the people who were just arriving, about to run into the fire, were suddenly engulfed in flame. The heat from the sudden burst of fire forced Dave, Eric, and Drew back inside the barrier of the window.

Eric did glimpse what the fire was doing to the front of his house. The only part that was on fire was the trim around the front door. The house was older and completely made of brick, and he took a temporary feeling of comfort that they would not burn tonight. But he hooked the fish-tank hose adapter to the bathroom's faucet, turned the water on, and hung it out the window to put out the fire on the door. Better safe than sorry.

They closed the window as much as possible without stopping the water from flowing and watched the fire from behind the window. The fire looked like it was rolling in waves as the undead carried the fire closer to the house, then bounced back as they hit the mounds of charred bodies that protected the home.

****

The four of them barricaded the back door with a two-by-four from the shed. They pressed it against the set of cabinets directly across from the door and jammed the wood under the doorknob. The windows were set higher and unless the crazed mob started to climb on top of each other, the guys didn't have to worry about them getting in through those.

Eric had two other roommates, both in the Coast Guard, and neither of them was answering his phone. He tried to contact their units and got a busy signal. The townhouse he rented was small, but really no different from any of the other houses on the block. Each house was built exactly the same, and his house was in much need of a rehab. Paint—lead-based, more than likely—was flaking from the ceilings, and there was not a single piece of wood that did not creak as you walked over it. Right now, though, there was no other place any of them would dare to venture. The blaze had died down and moved away from the landing, windows, and front door. The piles of charred bodies created a wall of fire that protected the front of the house. The crazed people continued to feed the wall, making it larger and more impenetrable. The back of the house was protected by a privacy fence. It was poorly made and a child would have been able to push it over, but what it did provide—as advertised—was privacy.

The smell in the house was starting to die down, and the adrenaline they were all feeling was slowly dissipating, but the monsters outside never let them forget they were still out there. Their groaning was unrelenting and constant. The four of them were all sitting in the largest bedroom that faced the alley, because the front room still had the strong smell of burnt flesh in it and was very warm from the fires, even with the A.C. set on its coldest setting.

A few hours later, the sun was beginning to rise and shine a light on the devastation out front. Dave, Rod, and Drew sat on a large bed with messed-up black covers and watched the small flat-screen T.V., waiting to hear any news of what was going on in the world. There was a news anchorwoman who tried to cover her fear and sleep deprivation with makeup and fake professionalism. It would have been hard to believe she had left the news studio at all last night. All they continued to say was that the streets were filled with crashed vehicles and sick people wandering in search of anyone stranded or lost.

Eric sat by himself and rocked back and forth in the rocking recliner, watching his phone, waiting and hoping a message would pop up stating that service was restored.

David broke the gloom with direct orders. "Okay, look, this is what we need to do." He jumped from the bed as if he had rehearsed what he was going to say. "Rod and Drew, I need—" He started over, "We need you to plug the bathtub and fill it with water." With a clap of his hand he pointed to Drew. "Drew, we need you to start grabbing some pots and filling them up."

Reluctantly they got up, but with nothing better to do, Rod waved to his son. Dave knelt in front of Eric. "What's up?" He put his hand over the phone, covering the screen.

"I killed a man today," Eric said quietly, as if it were a secret. "And I think one of the men we burned was my neighbor."

Dave patted his chin up, making him look at him in the eye. Eric did so, but was not happy with the way he got his point across and made it clear by lowering his eyebrows. "You did no such thing. These people are not your neighbors. They're not your friends. These people outside are no longer living."

Eric's angry eyebrows turned into the face you make at a crazy person on the street who is walking and talking to her brown bag of groceries, but Dave continued. "The guy you 'killed,'"—two hands made a quotation mark above his head–"the one that was attacking Drew and Rod. Maybe you didn't notice, but his face was smashed in. And if you were having second thought about its head, oh, I don't know, maybe he was pissed off because he had a *really* bad headache, but maybe you missed the kind-of-unmissable lack of *anything* in his chest or stomach area." Dave rubbed his chest and stomach. "Yeah, he was no longer alive when you smashed his face in for good. As for your neighbor, I have never met this—male or female?"

"Male."

"I have never met this guy, but does he normally just walk into huge blazing walls of fire?" He did not give Eric the second to respond. "No. I'm pretty sure he doesn't, so this individual was ultimately on the same level as the guy on the stairs." Dave shrugged his shoulders. "These people are, for a lack of better word—or maybe it is the perfect word—zombies. You saw me, I put so many bullets in that one, and then for some reason I started thinking about the movies and I shot the fuck in the head and he went down. I thought of those zombie movies and shot it in the head. It worked. He finally went down. Dude, don't feel bad about it, there was nothing you could do."

"I'm going north to my family," Eric said, completely changing the topic.

Dave saw a little light in his eyes. "Cool, let's get into your roommate's gun safe first."

Rod walked into the room with the expression on his face of a person who didn't want to ask for help, but desperately needed some. "I feel bad even asking, but . . . Drew and I want to go to North Carolina to check on Julie's family."

Dave turned to him. "Isn't that convenient," he said, followed by a small smile.

Chapter 4

Naomi

"When do you get off tonight?" the old man asked through the speaker and dropped his deposit slip into the chute.

Naomi was going through her weekly ritual with Mr. Jenkins. "Mr. J., we have already been through this, and your wife would not approve of us riding off into the sunset."

"No, she's okay with it. We have a very open relationship," said the bald mid-seventies retired police officer.

Receiving the deposit, she did not look at him while she counted his money. "Yes, I am very much aware of your open relationship. And she told me I'm too good for you." Naomi smiled as she put his balance inquiry back into the shuttle and sent it back to his rusted green pickup truck.

He took the slip. "What if we just rode off down the street?"

Speaking a little louder, Naomi said, "Get out of here, you dirty old man." But she could barely contain her laughter.

"Have a good night, Sweetie."

"You too, Mr. J." Naomi worked for South Carolina's Trusted Funds Bank. She was the best employee the bank had. She was a paragon of customer satisfaction, and she had never once showed up late. The only time she'd taken an unscheduled day off was when she was T-boned coming in for work and had to be rushed to the emergency room. She knew just who she could play with and with whom she'd better watch her manners. Mr. Jenkins came in every Thursday at the same time, never missing a week, always down to the minute. And every Thursday Mr. Jenkins started his transactions with some comment meant to be a compliment. Most of the time they were something like, "Every day you are more beautiful than the last. I wake up every day waiting till next Thursday just to come down here and look at you. God must have slept at a Super 8 Motel the night before he made you," and the list continues, only getting cornier and cornier. But this was not uncommon for Naomi.

Naomi's mother was a strong-willed black woman and father a white businessman, which left her with a very light brown complexion. Her hair was long, down past her shoulders, ending at the middle of her back in hundreds of small braids that fascinated most people as she walked past them. Her hair was a shiny black and as it moved, a glimpse of dark blue shimmered in it. When people followed her hair to her clean smooth face, they were entranced by her deep emerald=green eyes. She was very tall for a woman, standing a little more than six feet, and her body was perfectly proportioned to her figure. Naomi wore tight clothing that showed just enough cleavage and body to get attention, but not enough to get her in trouble. Today she wore a tight blue dress that hung low across her chest, with a floral scarf that covered her but still showed enough that the men wished she was working the window when they pulled up.

The teller window looked out over a large parking lot that served several different stores in the strip mall. As Mr. Jenkins pulled away, the sight of an ambulance and multiple police vehicles' blue and red lights caught Naomi's attention. In the middle of the parking lot, but on the further end, away from the stores, a circle of cops surrounded a man.

The officers looked as if they were trying to calm this man down, but he kept screaming something. Naomi recognized the young man as being one of the kids who worked at the food mart attached to the strip mall. He wore the white garrison hat, the yellow food store logo on the front of his white apron, and the khaki slacks that everyone who worked there wore. He was screaming wildly, running in small circles, and every once in a while he would charge after one of the police officers and stop inches from him. Just far enough so the officers wouldn't strike him.

Naomi could see that the cops weren't sure what exactly to do. One started shaking a can of pepper spray. By this time a crowd of her coworkers had started to huddle up behind her, asking questions as if she had seen the entire incident.

"What's going on out there?" one colleague asked, truly concerned for the boy. One of the women coworkers told them in a strong southern accent, flashing a sign of warning to the cops and the kid, "They better not hit my car. I don't care what they do just as long as they do it away from my car," she declared.

The boy scratched at his face as if he were in pain, but Naomi saw that none of the cops had sprayed him. He let out a low growl that turned into an intense scream. He bent over with his head up and fists clenched to his sides as he shook his head, screaming at each of the cops. He started running in small circles with his loose apron flailing behind him. The circles started to get bigger until he lunged at one of the female cops from across the circle. She was prepared for the tackle and sprawled back as the kid fell under her. There was a fight, and all the police closed in on the two in a tight group. The group was shoulder to shoulder and the woman who originally sprawled on the boy pushed her way out, holding her right forearm. Everyone from the bank window could see blood dripping from the fingertips that protruded from the sleeve of her uniform.

As soon as the paramedics got to the bleeding officer, another limped out of the tackle, hopping and holding his leg. A few seconds later, the cops started to spread out; everyone from the window could see the boy lying on the ground with his hands cuffed behind him. He was face down and completely still. The police officers spread out in complete disbelief. The boy from what the observers in the window could tell, was unconscious. It looked as if the boy had just stopped struggling. "He musta tuckered himself out," one of the women said.

A few of the officers waved the paramedics over and they started checking the boy's vitals. One started doing chest compressions and another put a mask over the boy's face and started forcing air into his lungs. Another one placed a defibrillator on his bare chest and everyone, from behind the shielded glass of the bank, gasped as the paramedics shook their heads, a sign that there was nothing more they could do.

"He's dead," one of the women said behind them, low enough to sound sad, but loud enough to let everyone else know she was sad.

"Okay, it's quitting time anyway, so why don't y'all count out your drawers and get ready to go?" Their manager was trying to break up the crowd before people started getting emotional. "Okay, move along," he said, waving them away as if he were herding cattle.

****

Sirens could be heard in every direction and cars raced through the streets. Normally for Naomi, traffic on Thursday evenings was not too bad. She got off most days a little before six, just hitting the end of rush hour traffic, but today as she crossed the parking lot she could see a lot of cars rushing through intersections and running red lights as if everyone was hurrying to get somewhere important.

One of her coworkers came up behind her and by her shrill voice, Naomi recognized Darlene. "I just heard there's this big broadcast all over the stations telling people to stay indoors and not to let anyone in their houses. Not even family."

Stories like this were not unusual from Darlene. Once she had refused to eat any of her husband's cooking because, she said, she caught him putting drugs in her food to sedate her so he could run off with his mistress. What actually happened was, he was dropping beef bouillon cubes into the roast he was making for dinner. She wouldn't listen when he pointed out that he was going to eat the same roast. It was not long after the poisoned roast episode that he finally had had enough and got the divorce he desperately needed. Since then Darlene had subscriptions to every dating website known to man and had yet to find a person she could trust not to rummage through her mail. So most of the time Naomi nodded her head and said, "Yup," with the occasional "Really," to whatever crazed fabrication of a helpless victim Darlene played, but this time she found herself listening halfheartedly as she tried to figure out what she was witnessing on the streets and in the parking lot minutes ago.

"I just got off the phone with my aunt and she told me it's all over the radio and everything. People are running around randomly attacking people. The T.V. was saying people should stay inside and lock their doors, don't let anyone inside, not even your loved ones. I hope Tommy lets me in."

Tommy was a new character in Darlene's little world. Naomi had never heard of him, but she already knew that tomorrow she was going to hear about how much of a bastard he was. "Okay," she said, having nothing to come back with, and she just shook her head a little and quickly got into her grey, overly clean, brand-new Dodge Caliber, praying to avoid any details about this Tommy person. She sat back in her seat, wondering how she was going to get out onto the street with all this traffic, and turned her key. She pulled her phone from her purse and checked to see if she had missed any calls. None. She expected the radio to play the modern pop music and was surprised when it was an emergency announcement telling her just what Darlene had told her: *Stay inside, lock all doors, don't get close to anyone, and stay tuned for further information.*

Right away Naomi called her daughter, Sam, who should be home from school by now. She pressed talk, knowing it would take her directly to Sam because she was the last person Naomi had talked to at lunchtime today. The phone showed the message *network busy.* She pulled her car out into traffic, taking no notice of the person waiting to pass through the intersection of the bank parking lot.

Naomi continued to try her daughter, but got the same message every time. She was caught in heavy traffic and knew it was going to take a while to get home, so she tried to relax and listen to the radio. As she tried to take in what the radio was saying, she looked around and noticed everyone was fighting with their phones. All the people around her were receiving the same *network busy* message. She took a deep breath and sat up quickly when she felt her phone vibrate on her leg. The only thing that stopped her from jumping up and hitting her head on the roof was her seat belt.

She picked it up, knowing it was Samantha. "What's going on, baby? Are you alright?" Naomi recognized she was talking at the same time Sam was, and neither one was hearing the other. "Start over, I didn't get that." Once again she realized Sam was just talking and not listening, so she shut up and just listened.

"There's someone trying to get into the house!" Sam hollered into the phone.

Shocked and not sure exactly what to say, Naomi shouted back, "Did you call the cops?"

"I called them and no one's picking up. Mom, I don't know what to do! He's breaking through the door!"

Naomi felt powerless, unable to do anything but sit and listen to her daughter talk, scared to death. She could hear the pounding on the door. It sounded as if she were standing in the same room.

"Can you go in another room? Can you go up to your room?"

Sam screamed at a particularly thunderous slam and said, "I *am* in my room." Sam began to say something else, but all Naomi heard was a bang and the phone was filled with static, then silence, and then the message on her phone again, *network busy.*

She knew that whoever was outside would soon be inside. The door would not last long. Sam's room was upstairs and on the other side of the house, and for her to be able to hear the person pounding on the front door, the person must have been hitting it so hard the house would soon collapse. She dialed 911 and was greeted with *network busy.*

With that, her instincts kicked in, and she determined that she would not be sitting here in traffic. She pulled off the street, jumped the curb and rode to the side streets. Most of them were filled with cars stopped with their hazards on, parked so no one could get by, so she jumped another curb. Now she was driving over people's lawns. Nothing was going to stop her from getting to her child.

As she rode, not paying too much attention to what was happening around her, she did notice there were a lot of people trying to get into each other's houses, and she swerved a little to avoid hitting someone who purposely ran out in front of her, but she was determined to get home.

She was on the street again when she pulled up to her house. She had a long driveway up a steep hill until you got a few hundred feet from her home. Her small Cape Cod house could have been the perfect greeting card picture: white with green shutters, freshly cut lawn that went on forever, and behind the house a mountain of black oak trees. Except now her front screen door was hanging on by the lower hinge and her front door was broken in.

Pulling up to her garage, Naomi felt fear ripping through her entire body. *What if this person had done something to Sam? What if he was still in the house? I have to get Sam.*

She got out of her car, leaving the door open, and ran across the lawn. She ran to the front steps of her house and looked directly into the open door of her vandalized home. The inside was dark, and random pieces of furniture were thrown haphazardly into view of the open door. Pillow cushions from her brown couch were thrown across the room, and she could see the entertainment center was knocked over.

The sounds of talking came from inside the house. There was only one person speaking, but the voice fluctuated up and down. She crept up the stairs and tried to listen to what was being said. Stepping over the screen door, she leaned over, looking into her home. Naomi looked through the living room and towards a long hallway that separated the kitchen from the rest of the house. The stairs that led to Sam's room were in the kitchen. The T.V.'s screen was shattered across the living room floor, as were various cups and vases that had once rested on the entertainment center. The coffee and end tables were flipped over, and as she studied the damage, a microwave from the kitchen flew through the air and smashed against the dining room wall. When it crashed against the wall, Naomi recognized the talking as simply mumbling.

The murmuring sounded very much like guttural babbling, and as Naomi listened, she saw a man turn the corner of the kitchen and stare down the hall way. He stopped and gazed directly at her.

Naomi's legs felt heavy and weightless at the same time. She lost all signals to them and was unable to move. Fear engulfed her body—not the fear of facing a stranger in her house, but the fear of facing her worst enemy in a dark alley. This was no man inside of her home, but a creature not of this world, and this creature's white eyes bored into hers.

The creature had at one point in time in fact been a man, but it showed no resemblance to one now. Its shirt hung in blood-drenched pieces that clung to its body. All the skin from its face was gone, exposing white teeth and muscles that flexed as its face showed complete fury filled with hatred. The skin on the right side of its body was ripped from the muscle it had once covered. Instead of clean lean muscle, the meat had chunks missing where other creatures had torn into its flesh.

The creature's mumbling turned into a violent scream that shot blood from its mouth. Naomi felt the energy flow through her body, and as the beast lunged forward, she lunged back. Her front foot that straddled the screen door got caught, and she fell backwards, losing her high-heeled shoe as she tumbled down the stairs of her porch. She looked back to her home when she heard a crash coming from the house and saw the monster tripping over the entertainment center.

She got to her feet and ran across the lawn to her Dodge, losing her other high heel. The vehicle looked like it was a hundred feet away and only getting further. She turned toward the house and saw the beast fall through the door and down the steps, but quickly regain its composure and continue the chase.

She reached the car and dove inside, reaching for the door behind her. She grabbed it and began to pull it shut, but the creature slammed into it, forcing it closed. Naomi's cries were drowned out by the creature's screams. She reached over and locked the door. She fumbled with the keys, managed to get the right key, and started the car.

The driver's side window smashed as soon as she dropped the car into reverse. Powerful hands grabbed hold of her braids and pulled her head through the window. The car flew backwards down the driveway, and she felt her head getting pulled further out the window, followed by a snap in her neck. At the same time, the car ran over one of the creature's feet. Naomi screamed in agony as she felt hair getting pulled from her head, and searing pain ran from the back of her head down her spine and into every appendage.

The creature, holding onto a fistful of braids, was pulled under the car. Naomi drove backwards a few yards and saw the creature pushing itself up with his arms over the hood. It propped its right leg under its body. It looked up at the Dodge, snarled, and stood up. Its lower left leg was completely mangled. Meat and ripped skin hung through ragged and torn blue jeans. The creature's black-and-crimson shoe dragged behind it by loose strands of muscle and tendon still connected to the foot. The beast began to run, but its leg didn't hold up, causing it to fall. It stood back up and looked at Naomi in the car. Hate and anger stretched across its partially skinless face, and it let out a scream and tried again, only to fall in the center of the driveway.

Naomi reached down for the gearshift, but quickly pulled her hand back as pain shot through her body, starting at her neck. The creature got to its right knee and, using the stump of its left, started to crawl towards the car, growling with each movement. With her back as stiff as possible, Naomi reached down and grabbed the shifter. She pulled it back into drive and pressed on the gas.

The creature soon disappeared from her line of sight and the whole car shook and jumped as she hit the beast head-on. She made sure to run completely over it, and she stopped inches from her garage. Trying to calm down, she took a deep breath and turned her gaze to the rearview mirror. She only moved her eyes, but still felt a sharp pain run through her neck. There was no movement behind the car, but she could not move forward any farther because of the white garage door. She had no doubt that running it over the first time had killed it, but out of the same rage the creature had for her, she backed over it.

Naomi's daughter was still trapped in the house, and Naomi had no idea if she was okay. She got out of the car as quickly as she possibly could while trying to hold her damaged spine straight. She stepped over the broken screen door and walked into the house. The second she passed the threshold, she hollered out for her daughter. "Sam!" She ran through the living room and into the kitchen as fast as she could while maintaining her stiff posture. "Sam!"

She heard a call back, "Mom!" The call came from upstairs, and as Naomi reached for the cherry wood door that lead to Sam's room, the door was flung open. Samantha wrapped her arms around her mother. Searing pain shot through Naomi's neck and back, but she could not let go of her daughter's thin frame. They squeezed each other tighter than they ever had before.

Minutes felt like seconds and they held each other until they both stopped crying, Naomi stroking her daughter's braids. Then Naomi pulled away and studied Samantha's face, a tearstained reflection of her own.

Now that Naomi knew Sam was all right, she was able to take stock of her house. Evidence of the creature's rampage was everywhere. Bloody handprints and larger, body-shaped greasy splotches were smeared all over the white kitchen walls. All the utensils that were thrown and broken were covered in the creature's reddish-black blood.

Sam looked at the walls in horror. The thing had been downstairs just minutes ago, looking for her. If it had done this to the house, what could it have done to her?

****

They sat on the thirteen-year-old's disheveled bed and watched her small T.V.. Pink walls and pink curtains surrounded them, and dozens of teddy bears looked down on them, relaxing them just a little. It managed to give them a small touch of the ordinary. The only thing that changed the atmosphere was the unfamiliar voice and a stranger's face sitting behind the news anchor's desk on the T.V. This was not the anchor who normally announced the news, but this new anchor held his composure and informed the active listener about the events that were happening outside of their homes. The man put his right hand to his ear and looked down at his desk, listening and concentrating intently on the latest information being passed to him.

At that point, the T.V. switched to live footage of the surrounding counties. It showed the highways, the traffic moving very slowly, from the point of view of a helicopter. There were people walking along the cars and keeping pace with them. It made no difference which direction the vehicles went in, because both directions were in the same shape. The unfamiliar voice came over the footage, "We are advising everyone watching us to stay inside. Military and police officials are working together to set up shelters and will be picking up everyone in our listening area." He forced himself to sound sincere, but something in his voice was beginning to creep through: He himself was beginning to have doubts about what he was saying, and it seemed that there was somewhere else he wanted to be. The screen cut back to the anchor. The camera slowly shifted downwards. They were still able to see the speaker, but whoever was running the camera must have let it go.

"Ladies and gentlemen, I regret to inform you that major power outages are beginning to be reported. Some of our viewing area will be losing power within the next hour. The Jasper Generating Power plant and the Urquhart Power Plant have been abandoned. If you have a generator, please prepare for the power drop-off. Please gather all of your batteries and ensure that your flashlights are in working order. We suggest that you gather all of your supplies and keep them close to you. You should avoid your windows and lock your doors."

Naomi had no idea where the plant was that she received her power from, but she lived in Jasper County and assumed she would be losing her power shortly. She made a mental inventory and realized she did not own a flashlight or any of the other equipment she needed to stay here for a long period of time. She barely had enough food for dinner tonight.

The news now started flashing recorded video of other areas outside the county, the state, and all over the world. The videos all looked the same: jammed streets, burning houses, people running frantically. But the report never offered a reason why. The entire listening audience was clueless as to why this was happening to them and to the world. The T.V. flashed to an outside view of the local hospital, and it showed people running out of the front doors. Patients and nurses alike fled from the very place people wanted to go. Another video showed a hallway in the hospital, but the only thing they could make out was people running away from the camera.

Between the frantic shots of herds of people, the T.V. cut to some sort of confrontation that was occurring while people rushed past it. In the middle of the hallway was a boy dressed in khaki slacks, a blood-stained white button-up shirt, and what had once been a white apron that hung loosely around his neck. Now crimson red splashes shone on the apron. Naomi saw this and gasped, because she recognized this young boy as the one who worked at the food mart across from her bank—the same boy they had all watched die less than two hours ago.

His eyes were white and wild, and as the nurses ran past him, he tackled them one by one like a lion jumping on prey forced to run next to it. With every nurse or patient he took down, he would come up with fresh blood layering his face and chunks of his victim's flesh hanging from his mouth. Just as fast as he took one down, he scanned the hallway, his white eyes glowing under a red mask, for his next victim. His victims did not die; freed from his grasp, they got up and ran from the hospital, but they left with painful bites that soaked their clothing with blood.

The T.V. once again shifted to the man behind the desk, and his tanned face became very pale. He tried to say his next line, but he could not find his ability to read the cards in front of him. Each word came out as a short and soft syllable, but he continued to try to report on the news until the frustration of not being able to talk consumed him. He could no longer restrain his fear, and it forced him to his breaking point. Then he magically found his voice. "Sorry, I can't do this anymore." He stood up; the television now only showed him from the shoulders down. He reached up with his right hand, and a set of wires and a hearing device were dropped on the desk. There was to be no more reporting, and the picture on the screen stayed the same. This news anchor had been the last person to stay at the station.

Chapter 5

Mr. Cook

They sat in the pink room holding onto each other until the T.V. screen turned to a solid blue pane. They had watched the empty newsroom for what felt like hours, and they both jumped as the abrupt change shocked them. "We should lock this place up," Naomi said, pulling free from her daughter's grip.

"What about dad?" Sam cried with worry.

"I'll call him, but we need to fix this place up. The front door is wide open." Sam's father was a very bull-headed white man and insisted he always had the right answer, in and for every situation. To Naomi that was the reason they separated. She believed she had the best answer and the one that could get them out of whatever pickle they were in, but Berry could not be convinced otherwise. She actually really wanted him to be with them right now.

The sound of groaning followed by a faint pounding came from the window behind them over the bed. They shifted their positions and looked to Mr. and Ms. Wingate's house, to the right of theirs and directly outside Sam's window. Gathered on the porch at the front of their small blue Cape Cod house were four of those beasts. There was an acre of property between the two houses, but more of the ghouls were lumbering up from the street, some slowly lumbering, others running and pushing. Sam's expression turned to sheer horror, and she looked to her mother. "We need to get out of here," Naomi said calmly. She needed to be strong and prove to her daughter that she could lead.

"I want to go to dad's," Sam cried.

Naomi reached for her phone, but she had left everything in the car. "I need to use your phone."

Sam reached under the bed and started dialing her father. Naomi reached for the phone and Sam retracted it. Reacting to her daughter pulling from her, she grabbed her arm and yanked the phone free.

"God!" Sam hollered, and her voice started to crack.

Network busy, the screen on the phone read. "It's not working."

Sam reached back for the phone; this time Naomi pulled back, and a shot of pain coursed through her spine. "Damn it, Samantha," she hissed. "Look, let's see how this pans out. Let's go and lock up as much as possible and grab the things the T.V. said to get."

"I want Dad. He would know what to do. I want to go to his place," Sam cried and continued to grab for the phone.

Fighting for control of the phone with waves of pain sailing through her, Naomi mustered the strength for one push away from her daughter. "Samantha!" she barked. "We're not going anywhere right now! I mean, we need to get ready." She paused and spoke in a soft voice, "Let's get the stuff we're going to need and start looking at our options. You saw the T.V. Those things are all over the place, and our front door is wide open right now."

Sam didn't reply, but stood quietly and nodded slightly in approval. They traveled down the steps slowly and as quietly as possible. They emerged into the hallway, and a renewed sense of horror at the creature that had invaded their home hit both of them. For Sam it was the memory of the pounding on the doors and walls, while for Naomi it was the image of that beast of a man running through her house trying to get to her daughter, and shivers went through both of them.

Staying as far away from the bloodied walls as possible, Naomi walked in front of Sam, but Sam spared little room between herself and her mother. They passed the bathroom on their left, and Sam stepped to Naomi's side as the hallway got a little wider. As Naomi stepped into the living room, the sound of a gurgling scream erupted from in front of them. Naomi thrust out her right arm in defense of her daughter, stopping her from continuing towards the threat. In the broken front doorway lay the same beast that Naomi had run over in the driveway. It was pushing up with its arms, crawling towards them. Its legs were limply dragging behind it. The left side of the creature's face was smashed in, and a deep black hole existed where an eye had once sat. It reached out toward them and fell forward. It let out another scream as if it were in agony, but showed no other signs of pain. With the yell they were able to see it had no control of the left side of its mouth, as its jaw swung loosely, almost separated from its mangled face.

Naomi pushed Sam back as she stood stiff. Paralyzed with fear, she gazed at the milky white eye that shone brightly within the smashed black-and-red face. Naomi pushed hard against Sam's chest, and Sam caught herself from falling backwards. "Out the back," Naomi hollered to her. The ghoul screamed out, almost as if it understood and disagreed with her.

She stepped backwards, slowly, one concentrating step after another. The slow step turned into a turn and with a forceful push against Sam, Naomi herded her back into the kitchen and out the back door. As soon as they closed the door, they heard something fumbling through their house. This fumbling was not Naomi's hit-and-run victim, but another, faster ghoul that ran in over the downed creature. Naomi and Sam ran down the back steps and towards their neighbor's house. From here it didn't seem that this house had any ghouls climbing over each other to get in like the neighbors on the other side of them did.

Naomi started to think she might be able to get back to her car and drive to her ex-husband's apartment. She told Sam to stay where she was for a second and that she would be right back. They were about thirty yards from their house; she started to run, but she had taken only a few steps when a flailing body broke the glass window in her kitchen door.

A woman thrashed against the kitchen door, trying to get out and go after the two escapees. A large open gash peeled from her forehead, and Naomi believed the woman had just given herself that slash by banging her head against the broken glass. Black and crimson blood oozed from the open wound.

The woman threw herself at the door again and broken glass fell all around her as she flopped out of the window and fell on her face. Unfazed, she stood back up and began to run down the stairs toward Naomi and Sam.

"Run!" Naomi hollered to Sam. "Go to Mr. Cook's!" They both started running as fast as they could.

On a couple of occasions, Naomi had asked the retired teacher next door to help with unclogging a toilet or helping to install a few electric outlets. He would talk with Naomi often, but most of the time she tried to avoid him. Mr. Cook always had advice about her lawn and odd-and-end projects that she had no intention of ever starting. She had grown to enjoy living next to him because of his handiness and willingness to help in any situation, but most days she didn't have time for his endless opinions. Today, though, he looked like a blessedly safe harbor.

Sam had jumped onto the old six-foot chain-link fence that separated the two properties and started climbing to get into Mr. Cook's yard when she saw the old man step out onto his front porch. He was bent with age, and all she could make out of his short, solid, broad-shouldered frame was two skinny, bright-white legs sticking out of blue corduroy shorts and a big gut straining under a dark burgundy shirt. The old man walked slowly along the front porch to the side of his house, and in his hands was a World War Two M1 Carbine rifle—bizarre since Naomi had heard on countless—and what felt like endless—occasions about Mr.

Cook's pacifism.

As soon as Sam landed in Mr. Cook's lawn, Naomi hit the fence and started climbing. Her toes ripped through her black stockings and interlocked, bare, with the fence's steel chain links. She winced, but forced herself to the top of the fence. She ripped her tight blue dress right up the middle when she threw her legs over the top. As she straddled the top bar, the manic ghoul who'd come crashing out of her kitchen smashed into the fence, throwing Naomi over the top, where she landed on her back.

The creature did not climb over the fence, but tried to force its hands and body in between the rusting links. Naomi pushed away with her feet. Her hands were pressed hard against her back, supporting it as she arched it. Sam went to her side and tried to help her up, but Naomi cried out in pain. The zombie gnashed its face against the fence and bit down on the links, breaking her teeth. Thick black and crimson blood smeared across her grey skin as the ghoul smashed her face and forced the rusted links to cut into her flesh.

"Get down," Mr. Cook hollered, and Sam lay over her mother. A shot rang out and the female ghoul was launched backwards and thrown to her back. It was back onto its hands and knees in a fraction of a second. The shot had gone through the right shoulder, but the frenzied ghoul still had function in its right arm. It got to its feet and began moving toward Naomi when another shot rang out.

This time the zombie flew sideways and landed on its left side, facing Sam and Naomi. The shot had gone through the back of the creature's neck, and now it lay looking at the two of them. It let out a scream and ground its teeth, but made no move toward them. The ghoul's milky eyes were fixed on Sam and Naomi, but her body lay motionless. She was paralyzed but still wanted to destroy them. It cared nothing for itself: all it wanted to do was kill.

Naomi got to her feet with the help of Sam, and they started making their way to Mr. Cook. He turned his attention to the front of the house and let out a few more shots. After they were away from the fence and almost to the old man's house, Mr. Cook turned his attention back to the paralyzed screaming ghoul and silenced it with a shot to the head.

Mr. Cook's house was a beat-up old yellow rancher that was as old as he was and looked as if it had been built facing the wrong direction. What was supposed to be the front of the house was facing Naomi's house, and a new front porch was attached to the kitchen. His was the oldest house in the neighborhood, built in the nineteen twenties, and once upon a time a road had run where Naomi's house stood now. The rancher's huge garage was hidden from the current main road by the rest of the house; a driveway led to a garage door on the back of the house.

"I shot those things right in the chest and they just kept coming," Mr. Cook said as he took Naomi's hand and helped her up the front steps to the kitchen porch. The sound of multiple small dogs barking inside followed them as they moved from the once-front of the house, facing Naomi's, to the new front that faced the road. "I saw it on the T.V., these people going crazy and you shouldn't trust anyone, but since they were coming after you I just assumed you two were not a part of the crazies."

Gasping for breath, Naomi thanked him as he led them into the kitchen. He pointed to one of the kitchen chairs with the tip of his rifle. "Grab that chair for your momma, darling." As soon as they took their first steps into the house, three small, fluffy white dogs came running up to them, barking and jumping up, fighting one another for their attention. Mr. Cook tried shooing them away with no results, so he slid one of them with his dirty white shoe, just hard enough to send it sliding across the yellow linoleum. He hollered something unintelligible to it and all three backed away to the edge of the kitchen and sat wagging their tails frantically.

The kitchen was the exact same dirty yellow as the siding on the house. Everything in the kitchen was designed with the same theme, and that theme was the color yellow. Lemon wedges lined the borders of the wallpaper and yellow sun magnets littered the old refrigerator. On the sink was a green ceramic frog with a coarse yellow sponge sticking out of its mouth. Everything in the kitchen had some yellow design to it with the exception of the rolling chairs. The chair cushions were a hard brown plastic material that Naomi heard crack into hundreds of small pieces as the hard chair contoured stiffly to her body.

Mr. Cook looked out the front kitchen window over the sink and said, "They got into the damn yard again. Those first two just pushed in my gate and now I see another one wandering in. That one I shot is getting back up, too." He ran his fingers over his balding head as if he were running them through thick flowing hair. He tightened his black suspenders, snapping them over his large belly, then looked to his rifle. "I'll be right back," he said as he left the kitchen.

"You can't go out there," Naomi said, spinning in the rolling chair.

"Honey, I'm going to kill those things then lock the gate. I saw them on the news, and those things aren't human. They're likely to kill us if we don't kill them." With that, he turned and took a closer look out the kitchen door's window. "I'll be right back." He turned and walked out of the kitchen and down a dark hallway, hollering through the house, "On the news I saw one guy biting people. They said if anyone has any scratches or open wounds not to let them into your house. They even said turn away family." He returned and put a box of bullets on the table and started loading the magazine from his rifle. His hands were shaky, but found a undeniably comfortable skill when loading each round. It unsettled Naomi, and she wondered again what had happened to his pacifist talk—and why he'd kept this gun all these years. Good thing now, though, she figured. "They said they can infect you with their virus if they bite or scratch you. Can you believe that, turn away family?" Smacking the magazine into the M1, he pulled back the action, loading his rifle, and again looked out the window. "I'll be back in a second."

He opened the door and looked out as if he were going to walk across a street; he looked left, right, and then left again. Satisfied with his surroundings, he brought the rifle to his shoulder, looked down the sights, stepped out onto the porch, and fired.

Sam and Naomi thought they heard him whisper after that shot, "Now stay down, motherfucker." That was followed by another shot.

Sam closed the door and locked it. Looking out the window, she saw that Mr. Cook stepped down off the porch just as his second shot sounded. There were three crazies in the yard now and one was in front, walking at a brisk pace toward him, when another shot was fired and Sam witnessed the creature's head disappear into a shower of debris that rained on the two that lagged behind. Sam let out a shriek and closed the curtains. Naomi held her hands out to her and squeezed her—softly, to avoid hurting her back any more.

Multiple shots rang out, and after a few minutes, the doorknob rattled. Sam and Naomi turned to the door and Sam hesitantly reached for the curtains when she heard, "Hey, let me in. I don't appreciate being locked out of my own house."

She unlocked it quickly. He stepped in and wiped his feet on the welcome mat as if he had just come in from the rain. "If I'm out there, at least keep an eye on me, so if I have to come in, I don't have to wait to be let in."

They both nodded, and Mr. Cook pulled a chair up next to Naomi. "Honey, we're going to have to fit you with some new clothes, and we need to clean up your feet. You're bleeding on my floor."

Naomi, completely dumbfounded at his comment, looked down and saw that her feet were bloody from climbing the fence.

"Go use the bathtub while we still have water pressure," he said, loading his rifle again.

"Thank you," Naomi replied.

****

"I know it's not the most stylish thing in the world, but I have to imagine it's more comfortable than what you had on," Mr. Cook said, referring to Naomi's new attire.

She sat wearing a grey hooded sweatshirt bearing a large picture of a bald eagle soaring over a mountain range and, in big letters, *ALASKA*. The blue jeans Mr. Cook had been able to scrounge up were too big for her, as were the pair of white nurses' shoes, but the gauze wrappings around her damaged toes gave the shoes a snug feeling.

They all huddled in dim candlelight in the wood-paneled living room. Mr. Cook sat with his back to the kitchen in an old large brown rocking recliner, and Sam and Naomi sat on the couch, just under the window that faced their house. Sam knelt up to spread the blinds with her index finger and thumb, trying to be sneaky but filled with anxiety, waiting to see something come to the fence. The last Sam could see before it got too dark was more of the ghouls rummaging through the house. She could have sworn she saw a creature moving around in her room, but now she could barely make out the chain-link fence. The moon had decided that tonight would be unusually dark; she could only see the fence when the wind blew, dancing the fence into a faint shimmer of light. Sailing on the wind with the shimmer came the wails and groans of the undead in their house.

"The clothes are fine, and I thank you, so very much. *We* thank you, so very much. We don't know what we would have done if you weren't home." Naomi put her hands in the pouch of the sweatshirt and leaned back gently. The warm shower eased the tension in her back slightly, but she continued to move slowly and cautiously. She looked up and watched candlelight bouncing off the glass light fixture that hung from the ceiling by a chain.

"Well, you are more than welcome to stay here for as long as you'd like," Mr. Cook said, combing his fingers through his thick charcoal-colored beard. "Did you have any plans? From here, I mean."

Sam glanced at Naomi, wanting to hear her response. "I was thinking about going to Sam's father's or heading to my parents' place. My ex doesn't live too far from here, a few miles down the road in the Dunhaven apartments, and my parents live down by the Rail Way Tavern." Sam was happy with the response. She and Naomi's father, whom Sam called Fuzzy Pop Pop, were especially close.

"Those apartments?" he asked.

"Yes."

The old man rocked in his chair slowly, checking the buttons on his burgundy-colored short-sleeved shirt. "The apartments were hit pretty hard. They have the highest concentration of people, and a lot of people were trapped in their apartments." He came to a stop. "It was on the news earlier."

Sam faced him and tears rolled from her eyes, creating flowing rivers that rolled over her small cheeks. "We watched the news, that's not true."

Quickly realizing he upset the little girl, he said, "I could have been mistaken. They didn't show every complex, and I had the T.V. turned down pretty low." Sam didn't say another word, but laid her head in her mother's lap. Naomi ran her fingers through her daughter's long braids, which resembled her own.

They sat in a long silence until Sam noticed a woman in a picture standing next to a younger Mr. Cook. "If you don't mind me asking," she said, "where is Mrs. Cook?" She knew there had never been a woman at his house since she had lived next to him, but had never thought to ask why until now. As she asked, Naomi scowled at her.

He started rocking again. "She passed away years ago." He looked up to the ceiling as if he were thinking. "Eleven, maybe twelve years? No, about ten and a half years now, I would say. Good thing probably, she wouldn't be able to handle this. She passed in her sleep, in the hospital. She caught some type of bronchial virus and it spread to other parts of her body and just got worse. Something like that. There was some fancy name for what it was, but I just chose to forget those details. I focus on the good times we had, and the later days just seemed to happen. As soon as she passed, I started focusing on all the good things and all the news I'm going to have to tell her when I see her again." He smiled a little with the left side of his mouth.

"Sorry to hear that. I'm sure if she were here she would feel safe with you on watch," Naomi said.

"No. She wouldn't." He paused. "She worried about everything that she could do nothing about, but when it was time for her to worry, she didn't. It's fine, though. I will be going up there probably sooner than later now, and if it happens, I'm ready to go. I would prefer not to go out as one of them."

Feeling a little awkward at the path the conversation had taken, Sam decided to change the subject. "You could come with us if you'd like to."

"Ah, maybe, I guess it depends on what happens here. If it gets overrun here, I don't want to be eaten alive, so I may take you up on the offer." He pulled a set of keys from his pocket and put them on the table. "I'll leave these here just in case you need to leave quickly and I for whatever reason can't make it. These are for the truck in the garage"

"Why wouldn't you be able to make it?" Naomi asked, as if nothing outside the house was happening.

"I'm an old man and the ticker just might stop working. You

never know." He raised his eyebrows and shrugged his shoulders, and then there was a long pause. Looking down at his feet while he rocked in the recliner, he asked, "Do you think you would go to hell if you took yourself out? I mean if I were to be bit, and to avoid becoming one of them, I killed myself. Would my soul go to hell?"

"Well, you might actually be saving lives if you did that, so maybe God would think that was admirable," Naomi replied.

"I think you're right." He stood up from the recliner and groaned. "You two take the guest bedroom. The bed is made, and it's pretty cozy in there. I'll be sleeping in the room directly across from you, but I'll check on the house periodically. These days I can't sleep a full thirty minutes without having to use the bathroom anyway." He gave a fake laugh.

Naomi smiled as he walked out of the living room. She cradled Sam, who lay in her lap. "Let's try to get some sleep." Sam rolled over and sat on the couch, rubbing the crusted tears from her eyes.

They both walked into the spare bedroom and got into the queen bed and listened as the wind carried the groans of the undead through the neighborhood. Sam quickly fell asleep pouting, but Naomi stirred as a dull pain traveled up her back to her neck.

The dull moon was shining directly through the spaces between each individual plastic slat of the blinds on the guest-room window. Striped shadows shone across the small room, and the compulsion played on her mind not to close her eyes for fear that a shadow might cross those stripes. When she would close them, she could feel someone standing on the other side of the window. She got up from the bed many times that night just to spread two slats ever so slowly, slightly expecting to see something in the yard. But all she saw was a beautiful scene of the woods at the neighborhood's edge, the leaves swaying in the trees.

Chapter 6

Just picking up a few things

They stayed in the townhouse for four more days. Eric didn't believed what Dave had told him until he saw the woman who had been mauled to death in his back alley start to move. She didn't have much to move, but she moved what she had. Both of her legs were missing; she had lost one of her arms, and the other was so badly mangled that all she could do was roll over to her empty stomach and push herself in small circles. For three days Eric watched as she stayed in the same spot in the alley, spinning in awkward circles, trailing her exposed intestines, screaming. The first day it was a blood-curdling scream, as if she were still being eaten alive. She would turn down the alleyway and start screaming, then just suddenly stop. They would all look out the window to see what had happened and realize she was turning to face the other end of the alley. As soon as she turned completely around, the screaming commenced again.

There were many times throughout the first and second days when they all just wanted to smash her head in, but they did not want to risk being seen. Sometime late the second day the screaming started to die down; it turned into mumbles and low groaning. She stopped spinning as much, and her movements seemed like they were becoming difficult to perform.

Every once in a while, a fellow zombie would walk by and glance at its comrade on the ground—just a glance and nothing more. They were no longer running wildly through the streets, but now moved slowly and clumsily. When they looked down at her, sometimes they would lose their balance and go crashing into a fence. They would fight to stand up, usually with a groan or mumble of some type.

Around noon of the second day, the fires in front turned into embers of burnt flesh and smoking metal from the cars. There were very few walkers on the streets, and the ones who were there walked aimlessly past one another, not acknowledging each other. Many of the townhouses now had broken doors or windows, and from every broken door there led a trail of blood. From the sill of every broken window hung chunks of flesh. This once-happy neighborhood was now dark and full of misery. There were still a few houses that seemed like they were alright, or at least still intact. The windows may have been broken, but there seemed to be furniture pressed up against them to keep the undead out. On occasion the sound of screaming or a gunshot would break the silence, and all the undead would shamble in that direction.

The guys planned to leave the next day, but breaking into Eric's roommate's gun safe quietly took a lot longer than any of them thought it would. It took them the entire day to finally open it up, and to their surprise, the only things that lay in it were a lever-action .22 rifle, two open boxes of bullets, and some rounds that lay scattered in the safe. Eric had seen the rifle before, but expected the .12-gauge shotgun and a pistol to be in there as well. There were no signs that his roommates had been here before them—and why would they have locked the safe if they cleaned it out and had no intention of coming back? Still, in payback for the guns that should have been there, Dave helped himself to the leather jacket Eric's roommate had left hanging over the back of his chair. The jacket was deep brown and buttery soft; Dave had coveted it every time he'd seen it.

The .22 was one like you would see in one of the classic western movies: Wood-grain stock with a golden lever and a gold receiver with the classic swirl engraved in the receiver. Eric had never really held the gun and was disappointed in how light it turned out to be. Dave had to show him how to load and aim the rifle, but they did not fire it. Eric had grown up in the city and had never had an opportunity to fire a rifle, let alone ever actually having to do so. Being stationed on a buoy tender, he never had the opportunity to shoot anything, but a pistol. By that time it had started to rain. None of them were thrilled about starting their journey wet.

They lost electricity in the late afternoon on the third day. The news had notified them ahead of time and said the power plant was abandoned. The plant was now running on emergency generators, and if you were not being supplied by another electricity source, you would soon lose all power. They advised the listening audience on how to conserve water and listed the supplies they should try to gather: candles, batteries, canned food. The news agency must have known that the electricity was about to die, because right before the lights dimmed and power shut off, they told listeners to hang white sheets from their windows so that military and police forces could spot survivors, pick them up, and take them to their secure bases.

As soon as the neighbor directly across the street opened his upstairs window, he caught the attention of a zombie that lay against a burnt car. This zombie had lain in the same position ever since the fire out front had died down, and it seemed somehow to be dead again, but when the upstairs window opened, it turned to face the white sheet. It let out a groan as it straightened its body. This zombie looked in decent shape compared to some of the ones that had passed. There were no marks on it that showed it had been attacked, but then again, David had mentioned that all it took was a small bite or scratch to infect you. The zombie staggered up the stairs to the neighbor's front door and started pounding on it. Its groans got louder, and from down the street, a moan answered its call. Then from the opposite end of the block, two more zombies made their way through the parked cars, groaning as well. They started to show up from nowhere but everywhere at the same time.

Eric remembered his neighbor. He wasn't a nice old man; he was the type of man who just wanted to be left alone. Eric would wave or say hello to him when he passed by his yard on his jogs, knowing he was going to ignore him. After a while it became a game for Eric, and he waved and said hello just to annoy the old man. Every night the old man would don his baggy gardening gloves and khaki slacks, water his garden, and pick and prune his perfect flowerbed. Bright red, yellow, and white roses poured from his yard. Not a single rose was ever out of place or misshapen.

Now the slurred and broken hollering of the old man was louder than the zombies' groaning. His thickly-growing rosebushes, thorns and all, were nothing more than a mild nuisance to the ghouls as they marched over them to his front door. He lived alone, and as far as Eric and the rest of his neighbors could tell, the only care this old man had was his precious flowerbed. Obviously it meant more to him than his own personal safety, because as the zombies pounded on the door, shaking his house, he looked out the front window, screaming with boiling frustration as he watched the crowd grow on his front lawn and destroy his beautiful flowers.

Eric watched, as he knew this man would soon be consumed by the growing horde. All four of the guys watched in despair from Eric's upstairs bedroom window. Rod touched Drew's shoulder as he stood up from the bed and nodded his head. "Let's go somewhere else."

Rod and Drew left the room, and Eric moved closer to the window. He got on his knees and moved as close to the window as possible. A wave of helplessness ran over him. He could not let this miserable old man die or be consumed alive. He had probably lived through wars and fights, been born during the depression, and survived countless atrocities, and now he was going to be eaten alive by his neighbors.

Dave watched Eric, knowing where his mind was wandering. Dave felt his friend's anger and desperation growing and sat back on the bed and waited for him to implode. Eric turned to Dave, sheer fury showing on his face, and he got up to fetch the .22 that lay on the dresser. "Are you sure that's a good idea?" Dave asked quietly but firmly.

"Yeah, it is." Eric grabbed the gun.

Dave leaned forward and rested his elbows on his knees. "You know if you open that window, they will hear it." He ran his hand over his face, wiping away the sweat beads from his brow. The rain was not knocking down the humidity, and the temperature in the house was rising. "If you fire on them, they *will* swarm this house."

"We'll leave through the back," Eric said as he got back on his knees by the window.

"You're willing to risk the lives of three for the life of one?" Dave asked. He leaned deeper over his knees, facing Eric, closer to his level. "You don't have enough bullets to kill them all, and you know they will eventually get inside. If you shoot now they will turn on this house and come through our already weak front door." He paused for a second to let that information sink in. "We don't have supplies ready for the road."

"We're ready," Eric said. "We've been ready for an entire day. The only reason we haven't left yet is because of the fucking rain." He turned away from Dave and unlocked the top latches of the window.

"So what's our plan? Get out and start running north? We haven't even talked about this yet. No cars, the streets are packed. We can't walk up the highway, it's covered with zombies."

Before the power went out, the news had showed pictures and video of the highways and the more traveled roads, as a deterrent to keep the listening audience inside. The streets were full of undead and the highways were worse. Thousands of zombies would gather around cars that had people inside fighting for their lives. Helpless and hopeless, they waited for the windows to break under the pressure of the undead. The news showed women and children being pulled from their vehicles, and it showed the windows shattering and every zombie on the outside trying to shove its rotting body inside the vehicle.

"We go to Carl's place," Eric said.

"Why don't we shoot for the Beach View Shopping Center? We hit the stores and get what we're going to need—food, clothes, and batteries."

"A couple backpacks too."

Dave stood up and put his hand out for the rifle. "I need to check the sights anyway." Eric was reluctant to hand over the gun, thinking David was not going to fire on the ghouls. "We don't even know if this thing fires or not. I'll give it back to you when I adjust the sights and know that it's accurate." He grabbed the barrel of the rifle. "You should tell Rod and Drew to get ready."

Eric let go of the .22, giving it to Dave. They watched each other while Eric left the room. As soon as the doorway broke their line of sight, Dave opened the window. The smells of death, rotting flesh, and burnt bodies mixed with melted rubber assaulted his nose, making him dry heave. This was the reason all the windows were still closed. It did not matter which way the wind was blowing, the scent of the undead was in every direction. When the smell hit him, Dave thought there was not a worse place they could have been. For four blocks in either direction, they were surrounded on all sides by streets of row homes. If each house had three maybe four people in it, there had to be thousands of zombies in this neighborhood alone. They had thought about this before, but faced with getting ready to leave, the thought of actually running out there and facing them struck Dave hard.

With the window open, the groaning and random screaming of one or two in the horde was deafening, and Dave tried to think about where they were going to go after he made his shot. He looked down at the crowd growing from the old man's front step and fanning out into the street. Something in the crowd caught his attention: he saw a line being made in the horde. It looked as if the zombies were parting for a specific individual in the crowd. One closer examination, he saw it was a zombie running through the horde and pushing the ones in front of it out of its way. This running zombie was stronger than the clumsy ones and had more dexterity. He thought back to when he was being chased two days ago and reflected that when people were first infected, it took a while for their bodies to decompose, for rigor mortis to set in. That must be why most of these ghouls were so slow: They were infected in the beginning, but the runners were newly infected.

This running zombie was followed by another from the other side of the crowd. Both pushed their ways through the mass. As the first runner reached the door, it pushed two ghouls over the stair railing and smashed into the door, all in one movement. It was evident that this zombie was incredibly strong. A crack appeared as it pounded on the door, and the old man's expression of anger and disgust turned to fear as he watched. Dave watched him through the window, and from his expression alone, Dave knew he only had seconds to shoot.

He pulled down on the golden lever. His mind flashed back to holding his .22 back when he was a little kid. His vision took him back home with his father, out in the open fields, listening to him say in his rough voice, "Breathe deep and squeeze that trigger when you're good and ready." Looking down the sights of his rifle, the young David had lined up the red bottle cap with his end sight. He had opened his small hands, closed them tighter on the wooden stock of the rifle, and pulled the trigger. The bottle cap had disappeared, but so had the top of the glass bottle it sat upon. He had looked up to his father's clean-shaven face and his high-and-tight haircut. "See what happened? You inhaled as soon as you pulled the trigger. Next time exhale, hold for a second, *then* squeeze the trigger."

With a new cap balanced on the broken top of the bottle, Eric aimed again. He exhaled slowly and squeezed the trigger. The bottle cap disappeared and the air was silent after the rifle screamed out its bang. A heavy hand lay on David's black coarse hair—"There you go, son"—followed by a tight hug.

Now Dave stepped back from the window just a bit to be out of open view of the attackers. A second assault to the front door and the runner was now able to stick its arm into the old man's house. It reached deep, grabbing at air. Dave aimed down from his window, looked down the iron sights, and lined them up with the head of the runner. It was shoulder deep and looking off to the side. The sights were lined up with its temple. Dave exhaled and squeezed the trigger. The runner's head bounced against the wooden door and its knees buckled. It dropped, started to get back up, and then fell once again, its arm stuck in the door. Walkers pressed themselves over the hanging zombie and commenced beating on the door.

He pulled the golden lever down, chambering another round. Two zombies grabbed hold of the wooden door and pulled the top section down. Dave thought if he could fill the front step with undead bodies it would buy the old man a little time. Through the broken front door Dave saw a few pieces of furniture behind the front door. As the two zombies pulled at the top of the door the horde groaned louder with the excitement of dogs at feeding time.

Another shot echoed through the street, and another zombie dropped from the open hole in the door. A third zombie that was climbing through dropped with the third shot. A few more climbed over the three now-lifeless zombies. The fourth zombie was shot square in the temple as it attempted to climb into the house, but only paused and then continued to try to get in. With the next shot, that zombie went down. Shot after shot, undead bodies piled onto each other, making it difficult for the horde to make it to the door. As Dave continued to fire, he noticed some of them did not fall lifeless, but instead continued to force themselves deeper into the door as if not realizing they had been shot at all. David thought that the bullet caliber must not be large enough to destroy the brain in one shot. He pulled down on the lever and fired on another zombie, but no bullet emerged. He had spent ten shots and now had to reload, but Eric had the bullets, and anyway reloading right now would take too long. The zombies would have filled the old man's house before Dave could get off another shot. He looked out of the upstairs window for the other runner. Where he had seen it last, the undead were beginning to fill the path that it made. Initially the path had led to the old man's house, but now it had turned toward theirs.

From deep in his window, Dave could see that half of the horde in the street had turned their attention to his weak front door. His immediate attention was not on the horde of walkers, but on that one runner. For the first time in days he felt a breeze touch his face as he hung his head out of the window just in time to see the runner push its way through the last line of undead making their way to his shelter. Dave pulled his head back in and ran out of the bedroom.

"We got to go!" he screamed as he turned the corner at the top of the stairs. Dave knew the front door would not hold. It was already broken in half and burnt all to hell. At this point the front door might as well been just an illusion, strictly there for show. The only reason it was still upright was because of the furniture that was packed behind it.

Dave ran down the steps, skipping most of them and falling backwards on his heels. He slid to the bottom, maintaining his balance. He could hear the pounding of footsteps running to the door, and as he climbed over the sofa and entertainment center, the barricade shook: the runner had smashed his way through the door and against the piled furniture.

Rod and Eric were waiting downstairs, holding black gym bags filled with as much food as they would hold. They jumped as the house shook with the impact of the running ghoul. Drew looked out the back window and watched the half-eaten woman lying in the middle of the street. He had watched her since the beginning of the attack and believed she might have finally died.

"From here, the alley that runs like this, is clear." Eric made a hand gesture to indicate the alley that ran perpendicular and connected to the alley behind them.

Dave ran past him toward the kitchen and tossed him the .22. "It's empty."

The screaming of the runner was almost deafening, and its endless assault on the furniture was pushing it further into the house with each second. The guys ran out the back door and then through the privacy fence in the back yard. Eric made sure he closed each door on his way out. From the yard they ran to the left, towards the alley that ran perpendicular to the back of his row house. As they ran, peering eyes from every house gazed at them and an undead choir groaned in unison.

The guys reached the alley's end and took a right turn into the perpendicular one. They had all expected the unwelcome company from the houses, but not the mass that was assembled and traveling in their direction. Shoulder to shoulder and multiple rows deep, a horde was working its way down the narrow alleyway. The sun fought through the rain clouds in defiance of the four's desire not to see the hell that awaited any victim of this disease.

Every one of the undead in the crowd was mutilated. Torn clothing exposed their bare muscles and fat under peeled-back skin. Chunks of flesh fell from their faces and bodies as they moved toward the guys. Slow or limping ones were pushed over and trampled so the ones in back could grab at the four.

The guys turned quickly and ran toward the half-eaten zombie that lay in the middle of their own alley. As they ran back in the direction they had come, they all heard the runner crashing through the back window of Eric's house. They ran past the privacy fence, and the runner reached for them as it tried to climb over the weathered and weak wooden boards. The wood cracked in half and splintered into the yard, causing the runner to fall backwards onto its back.

The woman in the alley woke from her undead slumber and came to life as she pushed herself around with her one arm, trying to get a better look and maybe take a bite out of one of them. Her teeth gnashed, reaching for them as they ran past. Eric remembered watching this woman run from her backyard and into the alley. He did not know what the front of her house might have in store for them, but he did know that her back door was still intact.

"This way," Eric hollered as he led them to the woman's back yard. They managed to get through the yard before any of the zombies got to the alley. The house was the spitting image of Eric's. The back door led them directly into the kitchen; they locked the door behind them.

"Try not to make a lot of noise," Dave whispered as he cautiously walked from the kitchen into the living room. The house was designed exactly like Eric's, just decorated differently. This kitchen had roosters on every piece of furniture; they littered every wall in the kitchen and dining room. Framed pictures of roosters with a barn background still hung on two of the living-room walls. Two other pictures were smashed and knocked to the ground. At one point in time, an assortment of rooster and barn knickknacks had been displayed across the dining-room table, but now they lay shattered on the ground next to the broken table they had once sat upon.

There were obvious signs of struggle throughout the house. The broken table and shattered knickknacks were just the first they saw. As Dave moved through the house he was cautious not to touch the walls or any other furniture, to avoid getting any blood on Eric's roommate's luscious jacket.

Eric watched through the back door as the runner ran past the house. Relieved, he pulled the bullets from his pockets and started reloading the rifle. His hands were shaky from adrenaline: this was the first time he had reloaded the gun knowing he might actually have to use it.

The guys all gathered at the front window and saw five undead bump into each other as they wandered down the street. They watched the houses across from them and looked for any that they believed were empty. If they couldn't just walk down the street or alley, they would have to house-to-house their way to the shopping center.

After ten or fifteen minutes, they decided to try one whose door was completely off its hinges. They were able to see through the front window. It looked as if there had been a struggle in the house, because only half the curtains were still hanging, and some of the ones left were ripped. Dave believed that if there were a zombie in there, it would have probably walked out the front door by now. Then again, they might just find a gooey mess that used to be Mister Wilson. *I've got a sick sense of humor*, Dave said to himself.

Rod counted to three, and as quietly as they could they ran across the street.

****

The undead were not far behind them, and from every direction more began to give chase. Eric knew exactly where he was and ran directly for the back of a car mechanic's shop. He knew the shop was completely enclosed by a fence and thought they could climb over. The ghouls that trailed them wouldn't be able to follow. As they made their way, they ran to the large barrier that separated the rows of townhouses from the shop.

They quickly scanned the parking lot, looking for any undead in the yard, and began to climb. Rod was the last over, and as soon as he reached the top of the six-foot fence he fell to the ground inside: the first zombie had hit the metal links. The undead that followed shook the fence, groaning, reaching their fingers through the rusted links, trying to grab hold of Rod, who was now rolling away from his pursuers. The undead bit at the barrier, ripping tight skin from their faces and tearing the flesh from their hands as they forced them through the small links.

The guys ducked behind a couple of totaled cars that the auto-parts store was stripping. The vehicles were all raised, either on jack stands or on cinderblocks. The rusted cars and trucks gave perfect cover and allowed them to look to the street through missing doors and holes in the vehicles. Traffic on this busy street usually moved like a flowing river, but now was filled with cars that had crashed into the vehicles in front of them or were so close they might as well have.

Directly across the filled street was a large parking lot and then the dark Beach View Shopping Center. To their right they saw a few undead rocking back and forth in between some of the wrecked cars. From this vantage point they were unable to tell if the zombies were trapped between the cars or just waiting for the next meal to come wandering past. The vehicles to the right for the most part were still. To the left they could hear the sounds of a random car honking and the sporadic sound of metal grinding on metal.

With his head low, Rod crept forward to the next stripped vehicle. Through the bloodied windows of a few of the closest cars facing his direction, he could see dead passengers sitting in the front drivers' and passenger seats. Further down the line of cars, he could see a few vehicles pointed in the opposite direction that were rocking. From one of the rocking vehicles he could see a pair of hands reaching from the passenger-side window, their owner writhing and twisting in the confines of his seat. The undead passenger reached as if there was a living being taunting him from just outside the car.

They moved to the next car. "There seems to be something going on up there," Rod said as he pointed to the distant left.

Eric looked directly across the street to the grocery store that had been broken into. "That's fine just as long as whatever it wants stays over there. What we want is in there," pointing his finger at the store.

Scanning the street for an open section between the cars seemed impossible. They all knew they would have to climb over some of them if they expected to get across. Getting close to the street was not a problem because many cars had tried to swerve through the auto shop's parking lot to gain a few inches in the traffic, but the drivers had quickly realized that when everyone had the same thought as they did, they all wound up putting themselves in a worse position than they were in before. Having so many cars close to each other gave the four of them plenty of cover to hide themselves.

They had to leap over a few cars, but they always made sure the cars they leapt over did not have any inhabitants. They made it to the double yellow line that separated the two directions of traffic by a few feet that felt to them like an open plain.

Rod led the way down the painted double yellow line. Traveling through the cars had detoured them a little out of the way, and with the yellow path clear, they moved as silently as possible down the narrow open lane. Rod was the smallest of the group and found that he was rather comfortable moving quietly ahead. Drew was not far behind him, then Eric, then Dave.

As they moved closer to the Food Lion, Eric noticed Rod's uncanny ability to keep the canned food in his gym bag quiet, even with his left hand injured and bandaged. Eric felt like every move he made, on the other hand, caused his canned goods to clang against each other in some sort of angry food fight. He tried to hold the bag tight against his body, but that did not help. He pulled the shoulder strap tighter over his neck and shoulder, just tight enough so he was not cutting off the circulation to his head. How was Rod so stealthy?

A few more cars forward, Eric felt a tug on his tight gym bag as he was on his hands and knees crawling. He dropped to the ground and thrust himself as close to the car to his left as possible, making a loud crash of food cans banging against the car and each other. He turned to see a dried, bloodied, skeletal hand lose its grip on his bag as it reached frantically through the car's busted driver's-side window. The zombie's eyes were —at first Eric thought it was extreme excitement, but then he saw that its eyelids had been ripped from its face. It wanted to scream but could not: The ghoul was missing its lower jaw and the front part of its throat. A long fat tongue swung wildly from the top of its chest as it thrashed, buckled in its seat. Blood rained from the zombie's face during its relentless-but-useless efforts to scream; the showers were interspersed with the sound of it sucking the blood back down into its lungs just to let out another bloody shower.

Dave looked sternly at Eric and hit him on the sole of his shoe. "Keep going!" He would have hollered it, but instead gave a commanding whisper. "This one can't harm you." He waited for Eric to start moving, and then continued covering the back of the line.

Rod Peered between two crashed vehicles to see what the commotion was. At the other end of the parking lot, about a hundred yards away and the furthest point away from the grocery store, a crowd of undead was devouring some poor soul. Zombies were ripping the flesh away from something that was unrecognizable anymore. They acted like vultures, reaching in, eating whatever it was that they grabbed, and filling each open space with another undead body. To Rodriquez it looked as if there were thirty bodies fighting over a handful of flesh.

To their surprise, the parking lot was nearly vacant. A few cars were still parked in the lot, but between each car there was a running span. From the right they could see the silhouettes of two zombies walking side by side as if they were a couple, headed in the guys' direction as the sun started to set behind them. There was no way the zombies could have seen the four of them, so they must have been coming to enjoy the feast. At the rate these walkers were moving, the body would be completely devoured before they got to it.

Dave and Eric moved up with Rod to analyze their situation. The feasting zombies to the left would not be that big of a problem if they just maintained their appetite, but the ones on the right were going to see them either way. "I say we run in, get what we need to get, and get out," Dave said as he peered at the couple.

"What is it that we need to get?" Drew asked.

"Canned foods, Spam, cans that have protein in them," Dave said.

"Rice," Rodriquez chimed in.

Eric looked at him and smiled a little. He thought of a hundred things he could say and the way Rod looked at him, he knew he had opened himself up to whatever was going to come his way. But instead Eric nodded to Rod. "Rice lasts forever. Good call. We need to stick together though, we can't separate."

"Power Bars and those body-building shakes and stuff," Drew spoke out.

Dave looked to him and said, "That's what we should focus on." He patted him hard on his back, in a sign of appreciation. "We gather up all that stuff. Power Bars, muscle shakes, and vitamins. We will need them probably most of all. We should rush the health food aisle." They turned their attention to Eric. "You know where that stuff is?"

Eric looked at Dave as if he were speaking a foreign language. "Do you honestly think I know what aisle that stuff is in?"

Dave peered at Eric's stomach and raised an eyebrow.

"When this is over I'm gonna kick your ass," Eric said with a smile.

"Ok." Dave took a breath. "We get the health food stuff. We run on three." He looked them all in the eyes and waited for any disapproval. "One…" No breath or noise rose from any of them. "Two…." They all took a breath. "Three." They all took off in unison down the long stretch of parking lot. Eric led the group and Drew started to fall behind. Rod hung back, but only just enough to encourage Drew.

Dave started to slow, but it wasn't because he was tired. He was looking at what was going on around him. The others did not seem to hear the moans rising from the couple to their right, but their moans did catch the attention of the crowd eating the corpse. Looking into one of the cars as they ran past, Dave noticed movement from inside—and that movement started to crawl out of the passenger window.

Eric slowed when he got to the store window and started to tread on the broken glass. As he turned, he saw Dave pushing the other two to keep them moving. They weren't moving slow because they were tired, but they just could not move as fast as Dave or Eric. To Dave, that was not acceptable and he forced them to move faster.

Dave saw Eric turn his attention to them and could see the expression on his face change from out of breath to absolutely terrified. He could only imagine what Eric was staring back at and was scared to turn to see for himself. "Look inside, see if it's safe!" Dave hollered, breathing heavily. He knew the zombies saw them, and there was no use hiding the fact that he and the others were running across an open parking lot.

Eric stepped over the busted glass wall and entered the store.

It was separated into two halves. The sun seemed to cut into the store like a wedge, leaving dust and fine particles playing and shining back through the light. Directly above the dancing debris, complete darkness enveloped the top of the store like a black curtain. The only light that shone through was from the front wall, which was nothing but broken glass. The store was already ransacked, but random food still lay about. There were plenty of cereal boxes on the ground; fine powders of bright-colored stepped-on cereal littered the front of the store.

Eric tried to look at the aisle signs that hung from the ceiling, but could only read half of each sign due to the lowering sun's casting a shadow through the middle of the hanging signs. Eric thought he remembered that the health food aisle was close to the toothpaste, deodorant, and soap section, so he moved in that direction. The aisle was all the way to the right of the store, and as soon as the rest of the crew got to the window, he waved them in that direction. They all moved without saying a word, but every one of them knew exactly what they needed to gather. The sound of crashing and shuffling broke their silence.

"Come on, you fucking shit-for-brains deadhead." The voice came from a man. It sounded like he had just had enough and wasn't going to take any more. "Come and get me. There's plenty of me to go around." The man had a strong Southern accent.

They were slowed by the voice, and Dave waved them to continue. As they made their way to the right of the store, they could see the undead couple coming towards them. It would not be long before they were on top of them. The four guys had to get the supplies and leave.

They got to the aisle and the sound of a gunshot echoed through the air, bouncing off of every wall in the grocery store. "Did you come to steal from my store?" They were spotted! Rod and Drew ducked into the aisle and Dave and Eric stopped short of it. "This is my store!" the man shouted. Signs hanging from broken windows cast a shadow across his face, leaving part of his chest and his pants the only parts of him visible—and the revolver in his right hand. "You fucking niggers come into my store and steal everything." The man stepped into the light, revealing his face. He had a face full of uncombed salt-and-pepper facial hair; wrinkles lined his facial features from a lifetime of stress and hard living. He wore a camouflage ball cap and a blue collared polo shirt with a name tag on the right breast. This man must have been a manager or some faithful grocery store employee who relied on his position to get him through life.

"This is my store. This is my STORE!" He was infuriated. His eyes were wide and he wildly waved the silver revolver in his right hand. He screamed at them, bending over as if he had just been punched in the stomach.

Dave leaned close to Eric, "Look at his hand."

The wild man was waving his right arm frantically at them, and the end of the revolver shook vigorously. The handle of the revolver was covered in black coagulated blood that stuck to it as thick as maple syrup.

"He was bitten," Dave said in a whisper. "Maybe we should be headed out?" He leaned back and paused for a second. They stood there watching the gunman in his frantic stomping. "We could come back in a few hours. More than likely he would have changed and run somewhere else."

"Or he could be here waiting for someone like us to grab some food."

Rod and Drew quietly emptied the canned food from Rod's gym bag and started filling it with muscle-building bars and vitamins. No matter how quietly they tried to pack them, the pills rattled together inside the bottle.

Eric took off his gym bag, lowering it to the ground as close to the end of the aisle as he could. He slowly raised his hands. "We're sorry, we didn't know anyone was in here." He was quickly silenced by the sound of skin rubbing on glass.

Dave and Eric turned to the glass storefront and were relieved to see that on this end of the store, an intact glass barrier protected them from the two undead that were traveling down the parking lot. The pane next to that one was broken, and the zombies were mere inches from reaching around the glass and realizing they could get in if they just stepped sideways. One smeared its face across the glass, biting at the smooth barrier. Black blood flowed from the ghoul's mouth and smeared in small circles with its face and long hair. The other tried to reach through the glass, not understanding what was stopping it. Reaching hands turned to fists, and it smashed them against the glass.

"We were just coming to get some food," Eric said, taking a step back. "Let us leave through the back and we'll be out of here."

At the sight of the undead couple, the employee started to rock side to side on his heels nervously. His eyes shifted back and forth between Eric and Dave and the two zombies that were now beating on the glass, shaking it, and groaning loudly. "There is no back for you. That is for employees only."

The sound of shifting broken glass caught the attention of the employee, and he turned to his right, looking behind him out through the broken glass wall and into the sun. From behind the gunman, a walker was working its way into the building. This zombie's bare right arm was bandaged as if she had been bitten severely and tried to bandage herself. Long hair covered her face, and white eyes showed through the strands of bloody black hair. She wore a purple sports bra and a pair of bloodstained grey sweat pants. The walking crowd followed many feet behind her. She was faster and had more dexterity than the other walkers. She bent down and balanced herself as she made her way into the store over the busted shelves and random scattered boxes.

The employee's attention bounced back and forth between Dave and Eric and the newly-turned undead girl. The revolver never stopped shaking at the two as he turned back and forth worriedly. He decided to turn his full attention to the girl when she raised her reaching hands for him, followed by a loud hiss that exploded from deep inside the zombie and out through her bloody mouth.

The revolver followed his attention, and Dave and Eric ran into the aisle. Eric grabbed the bag and started loading it with random boxes of food. He was not sure what he was picking up, but he shoved whatever he could over his canned foods. Dave had his back to Eric and with his pistol drawn, watched in the direction of the changing employee. Three rapid shots echoed through the store.

"You motherfucker you! Stealing my shit." The silhouette of a revolver made its way around the aisle shelves, followed by the body of the beaten man. Dave fired two shots, both hitting the silhouette in the chest. It stumbled, fired, and fell backward over some crushed boxes of cereal.

As the man fell, the sound of shattering glass hovered past the second bang. The second bullet had gone through the man's chest and broken the glass that the zombie couple was banging on. As the man lay flat on the ground, the two ghouls fell forward over the half-wall that the glass was attached to.

Drew materialized, feet-first, from the darkness that was making its way into the store. "We found the way out through the back." Drew ran forward out of the blackness and waved to Eric and Dave.

David was still in shock. He walked backwards slowly, looking at the employee, hoping he was going to move or get up. The thought of killing a man was too much for him. To kill the undead was one thing—he never really thought too much about it—but this man had been living and breathing.

Eric found that he was going to have to be the sensible one this time. "He was going to kill us. There was nothing we could have done to convince him. He was changing and going crazy just like Julie."

Dave stepped back a little quicker and turned to him. He looked Eric straight in the eye and raised his eyebrows as if he were giving him a nonverbal "What the fuck," then ran to Drew. With the raising of the eyebrow, it was as if he had wiped his slate clean and was ready to continue moving.

Chapter 7

Mrs. Kim

They walked into Georgia a few days back and on this day darkness fell on them faster than expected. Large single-family houses blocked the moon's light, creating dark shadows on the street they traveled. They hadn't heard any undead groans for quite some time, but they still walked in silence with the occasional small "Watch out behind that truck" or "Don't get too close to those trees."

"Oh, hello there." They all turned to the set of houses on their right, poised and ready to be assaulted in some way. They had not heard another's voice in over a week, and to openly announce their presence shocked all of them. The voice came from a woman, which comforted them for a split second, until they realized she had greeted them loudly enough for a zombie to hear three blocks away.

They looked in the direction of the voice that came from a house they had just passed and could just make out a woman hanging halfway out of her white metal screen door. Shadows surrounded the covered porch, and they were not able to make out any real detail about the woman. They could tell she was wearing something long like a robe, but were unable to see anything else.

The woman stepped onto her porch. "Oh come on over, I'm not goin' to bite ya." She spoke with a sexy not-too-Southern accent, but it lingered with her words. She giggled to herself, "I guess that was a little inappropriate," stepping a little further away from the metal door but remaining on the porch. "You know, the *bite ya* part."

Eric was shocked about the volume at which this woman was talking and commenced to shush her while waving his arms down as if he were landing an airplane. "Good Lord, woman, you're gonna get us all killed," he said in a loud whisper.

"I haven't seen any of those crazy people walking around here in days." She paused. "Look, I have food for ya, if you want it. I just need some company, and I'm willing to cook if I can just have an educated conversation for a night." Dave was already walking toward the house, and Rod and Drew were not too many steps behind him. Eric realized stopping them would be pointless and followed them to the woman.

The woman stepped to the side holding the metal screen door open as they all stepped past her into the dimly lit living room. She wore a fuzzy blue robe that swayed just over the tops of her feet, and her strawberry-blond hair was white at the roots. She looked to be in her mid-to-late forties, but was very good-looking for a woman her age.

They had been about to start looking for a house to sleep in, so this was a welcome surprise. They had seen no signs of life for quite a while, and for a person just to openly greet a stranger seemed kind of odd to them, but this night they would not have to completely clear a house just to make sure they weren't invading a home in which a few undead were trapped.

They had lost track of all time and really were not sure exactly what day it was. When they began to feel tired, they started looking for a house or a secure place to lay their heads, and more than likely they would have found a place on this block anyway. If they were going to sleep outside, someone would have to stay awake as lookout, and if they slept in a house they had to run through all the rooms, barricade all the doors, and cover the windows. This took no less than an hour, and if they ran into some undead, it sometimes would take them several hours: after killing the residents they would have to move to another house way down the road, because they were very seldom able to kill one without it getting the attention of all the other zombies near it.

They had been contemplating sleeping throughout the day in the next house and starting to travel at night; this was Dave's idea, and made sense to everyone. The undead could see them during the day, so they might have a better opportunity to sneak around them at night.

Eric and Rod had started to rely on Dave's advice. A week or so ago this would not have been the case, but because of his obsession with horror and action movies, he had created his own form of education. Back in the real world, everyone saw him as a playful and joyful character, but in a time when the unthinkable had happened, Dave had turned out to be their best commodity. So when Dave started walking into this woman's residence, they all just seemed to follow.

The house was lit by a plate of small candles that sat in the middle of a coffee table, directly in front of a dirty white couch with farm equipment embroidered into it in gold. The dim light shining on the gold embroidery caught Rod's attention. He could not think of a couch more hideous than this one. He looked at the love seat and saw it was of a different color and type: A clean brown suede, the love seat had obviously cost more than the dirty white couch. He thought the couch must have been pulled from a dumpster somewhere.

As Eric and the other three walked in, they were hit by a strong odor of pine, and they all looked to identify the smell. The dim candles on the coffee table were all burning at the same height, and Eric recognized that the candles had just been freshly lit. No wax rolled from them and the pools were not fully developed.

The woman closed the door and rubbed Eric's shoulder. She squeezed between him and the love seat to his right and looked him in the face, smiling. "Y'all must be thirsty. All I got is some water, though." As she squeezed past, the worry lines showed clearly on her face. She tried to cover the wrinkles of worry and her age by distracting them with her big smile, which exposed her pearly white teeth. "I'm sorry, where are my manners? My name's Kimberly."

Dave and Drew sat at ease on the dirty couch, not noticing the disparities in the living room set. Eric and Rod found the love seat surprisingly comfortable, and as the wax started to melt, the room started to fill with different scents that made Eric's throat itch.

The woman came back with four multicolored plastic cups of water. "I got the fireplace going, and I'm gonna start some tea and cook us up some soup. I got some Campbell's vegetable beef left and I'll throw that on as soon as the tea's done."

Eric heard the low moan of a lost zombie coming from down the street. He leaned back and spread two sections of the blinds apart with his index and middle finger. There must have been six or seven undead shambling aimlessly in the middle of the street. "So when did you say was the last time you said you saw a dead person?" he asked quizzically.

The woman smiled and said, "So, y'all have my name?" She walked toward Dave and sat down on the armrest next to him. She looked down at him and handed him the first cup of water.

Dave pulled his arm from the couch and introduced himself as he took the cup. "Is it just you living here?" He took a large drink.

Kimberly grew a small forced smile and looked at Drew. "There were three of us that lived here." The smile disappeared, "My husband, Keith, had just showed up from work a little early and was going to jump in the shower before we went out to that restaurant down the street." She pointed. "God, what the hell is the name of that restaurant? I don't know, it really doesn't matter much anyway. He wanted to jump in the shower and when he was done we were gonna go pick up Li'l Jimmy from the daycare and head off. I had just gotten home a little before him and was gonna do the same thing. I got cleaned up and was sitting on the couch, just watching some T.V. That's when I saw what was going on. Keith got out of the shower and saw it too. He told me to stay here and he'd be right back. He got in his truck and took off." She raised her eyebrows the same way Dave had back at the grocery store.

Drew pointed to a picture on the entertainment center directly across from him. "Is that him?" The picture was of a man with a dark goatee and scruff all over his unshaven face. A large smile was pressed against the cheek of a small, blond-haired boy who looked to be about six or seven and shared the same big smile.

"Yup, that's my boys, Keith and Jimmy."

"He went to pick him up?" Dave said, rubbing the small of her back, trying to comfort her.

Eric and Rod both looked at Dave and knew what he was trying to do. He was trying to comfort her with the intention of doing something else a little more lustful later on that night. To both of their surprise, she looked down at him and squeezed his right shoulder and smiled.

"Yeah. I never saw them again. I've stayed here waiting, but I think I have just about given up completely." She forced another stiff smile. "Until y'all came." She got up from the arm of the chair and grabbed hold of the plate of scented candles. "Let's go into the dining room and I'll put on that soup."

The dining room was dark with the exception of a flickering glow that radiated from the fireplace. Kimberly placed the collage of horribly mixed scented candles in the center of the table, adding to the glow. Flames licked the bottom of a black teapot that hung from a hook in the fire place. "Please sit down," she said as she pulled out one of the dark wooden chairs for Dave to sit on. They all pulled the chairs out closest to them and sat around the dark-stained wood table.

Rod sat with his back to the fire, but moved closer to Eric, who sat to his left, at the head of the table across from Dave. Kimberly pulled the pot off the hook with one of the log pokers and placed it on an oven mitt on the table. She walked into the kitchen and started opening the cans of Campbell's with a manual can opener.

Rod leaned over to Dave. "So what are you planning?" he whispered quietly.

"What are you talking about?" Dave said with a chuckle.

Rod gave him a you're-not-fooling-anyone stare. "Are you serious?"

"Dude, she's lonely, so am I. Kind of. What do you think? You saw the way she was rubbing on me," Dave whispered back.

"I just think it's a little early. You have no idea who or what this woman is."

"No, I know exactly what and who this woman is. She's lonely and needs a man's attention, and you know what? I'm willing to give it to her." He stated his case quickly, sat back against the chair, and crossed his arms as if to say the conversation was over.

Just then the woman walked out with another black pot, which she placed on the poker and then into the fire. "It should just take a few minutes. These pots are actually really good at cooking without burning. My husband was into camping and hunting and all that stuff, so he only got the good stuff." She pulled a stool up next to Dave and sat.

They all waited patiently for the soup to finish. Drew sat thinking about how good something warm and salty would be, rather than a cold Power Bar. He was so excited when Kimberly began to divide the soup that he gripped his spoon in anticipation. As soon as she finished scooping his portion he dove in.

Rod reached over the table, "Calm down and take small sips. Try to savor and enjoy it, a little at least."

After they all had finished their portions of the soup, she began to make more pots of soup. She had a stockpile of all kinds of canned goods. After the vegetable beef, she began to open cans of beef stew. She told them she had been saving this one for a special occasion and believed this was about as special as she was going to get.

Before long they found themselves sprawled out on the living room furniture, holding their bloated bellies, completely comfortable with their surroundings. Eric stretched across the couch, and Rod lay on the love seat with Drew beside him on the floor. Kimberly had given them all pillows and blankets. Dave stood against the entertainment center, knowing where he was going to sleep that night, even though no words had been spoken about where he was going.

Dave kicked his mud-covered white sneakers off next to his backpack by the door. They all had gotten comfortable, their pants unbuttoned and shoes lying neatly next to the backpacks they had found in the random houses they had slept in.

Drew stretched out next to the love seat and his foot rubbed a rough section of carpet just under the dirty sofa. He pulled his foot back and looked at his feet, and the couch's dust ruffle swung back as his foot pulled back. Not thinking too much of it, he tucked his feet up and in seconds was fast asleep.

Eric and Drew were snoring gently, and Rod watched as Kimberly guided Dave by his hand up the stairs. Dave looked to Rod, winked, and smiled as he disappeared behind the wall.

****

Sweat dripped from Kimberly's body and onto Dave's skinny bare chest. He looked up to her, holding onto her large round breasts, as she pushed herself up and down, back and forth, on top of him. She tried to control her moans, but when she climaxed her nails dug into his chest and she let out a roar that Dave knew must have woken up the crew downstairs. But instead of stopping or even slowing down, she thrust harder on top of him, moaning and grinding deeper.

He loved the thought of what was happening. He was fucking this MILF with huge tits and an awesome body. He couldn't wait to tell Rod and Eric what had happened and how great it was, but in all reality, his stomach was killing him. He had eaten entirely too much, and every time she bore down on him to get a little deeper, he felt as though he were going to puke.

He wanted to stop, but she continued for what Dave believed was the same reason he wouldn't stop. Neither one knew when the next opportunity to have sex would be.

He rolled her over and grabbed hold of her hips. She was on all fours, and Dave pulled her hard against him. Every time her behind smashed against his pelvis, he felt the soup and stew slosh back and forth, but with every hard thrust her moaning made him thrust harder.

Standing on the edge of the bed with her kneeling in front of him, Dave noticed an odd smell mixed with the countless scented candles, potpourri dishes, and many different air fresheners and perfumes. He figured it must have been him, because he hadn't bathed in quite a while, and if she hasn't said anything when she was on top of him, she must not care either. The smell wafted past him again. Hidden by the multi-scented room, it now took on a familiarity. For a while he had thought it could be her, but this was not the smell of a woman. It was the smell of undead.

Either they were piled in front of the house and a strong breeze was forcing their smell through the closed window, or one was very close, possibly in the house. Either way, Dave was going to finish. He thrust hard, dealing with the smell and his stomach swashing back and forth, and came inside of her without warning.

She fell forward as if her arms and legs could no longer

support her weight, and David fell over her, then rolled to his back. His legs from his knees down hung off the bed, and he traced a crack in the ceiling from one corner of the room to the other. "Oh my god, that was great!" He breathed heavily and tried to pull himself up onto the bed, but the sheets clung to his sweaty back, preventing him from moving. He gave up and just decided to lie there.

Kimberly breathed heavily and agreed that the sex was amazing. She pulled the pillow out from under Dave's head and rested hers on it. She closed her eyes and gave the appearance that she was asleep in seconds. Dave was unconscious once he gave up the fight with the wet sheets.

The very loud snoring from David gave Kimberly the confidence to move without waking him. His snores sounded like thunder and covered any noise Kim made as she slid off the end of the bed. Opening the top dresser drawer, she dug in between some clothing and found the plastic bag that covered a bloodied ball-peen hammer.

****

Rod was awakened from his sleep by a thud, pounding hard from the upstairs bedroom. The idea of Dave still performing this late was truly astonishing to him, but this was the fourth or fifth time he had been roused from his sleep. It was either a headboard banging, Kimberly screaming, or Dave screaming as the woman clawed into his chest or back. Rod's thoughts of the two still in action were realized when he heard another moan.

An irritated smile stretched across his face, and he repositioned himself on the love seat to fall back to sleep. He listened to the crackling of the wood in the fireplace and started to drift away when he heard a familiar sound. The sound took him back to the buoy deck of the Coast Guard Cutter Maria Bray. It was the sound of chain running through a chain fall. He listened hard, trying to drown out the burning and snapping wood. His eyes opened wide when he heard another moan followed by another heavy and hard thump on the floor. He could hear a chain running across the floor and through a pulley, followed by another moan, but this time the moan was frantic, almost a rough groan, and the thump that followed was lengthened by a dragging sound.

Rod sat up and tossed the covers he was using over the back of the love seat. He was careful not to step on Drew when he got up. "Drew," he whispered, as he gave him a light nudge with his foot.

Drew opened his eyes quickly from a dead sleep.

"I need you to stay awake for a second. I'm going to check on Dave." He crept to his backpack and slipped his shoes on. He looked up the dark steps and could see a light at the top of the stairs. The stairs were surprisingly quiet—no creaks—and he gave himself the credit for moving very stealthily. As he got to the top of the stairs, a light shone from under and over the door directly to his right.

He reached for the knob and opened it slowly; as it opened halfway he could make out a rusted chain lying taut on the ground, stretched from one end of the room to behind a bed frame. He opened the door wide and was hit by the smell that lingered in the house, but was almost covered by the collection of random candles and potpourri. The smell almost made him throw up, but he continued to push it open and saw Kimberly standing with her back to the door in her fuzzy blue robe. The door creaked and she jumped, startled, turning to face the intruder. Kim's hair was wild and her face was no longer happy and pleasant, but now took on a sinister appearance.

She was standing in front of Rod as if she were trying to block his view. "You're supposed to be sleeping," she said with a strong Southern accent that surprised Rod, followed by a half-forced smile and an uncomfortable giggle. She placed her left hand on his chest, grabbed the open door with her right hand, and started pushing him out of the room.

Rod stepped forward, stopping her from closing the door, and followed the chain with his eyes. His heart was pounding, and he knew something was not right, but he had to see for himself. The adrenalin in his body made shoving the woman off to the side easy work. He looked over the soiled, stain-ridden mattress that blocked his view of the chain and saw the end of the chain wrapped around a bare foot.

Stepping into the middle of the room he gasped, as David looked up at his friend with lifeless eyes. Rod's eyes were fixed on the dead emotionless features of David's face, not believing the events that were taking place. Bending over his midsection was a small boy wearing a light-blue pajama set. Rod forced himself to look at the boy and what was happening. The child had long blond hair, and the light-blue pajamas had red fire trucks racing across them.

Rod let out a gasp and stepped backward. The child looked up from David's midsection, grasping two handfuls of flesh, his face covered in red blood. The boy's blond hair was caked thick with blood and viscera, and his large, once-beautiful smile, filled with white sparkling teeth, was now a gaping maw with pink teeth outlined in dark crimson, dripping with guts. The boy's front was completely different than his back. Rod could see a little boy when he looked down on the boy from behind, with his long blond hair and light-blue pajamas, but from the front the pajamas were a dark red that matched his crimson face. Its grey eyes beamed through its victim's blood, and as the kid sat up onto his knees and growled at Rodriquez, it took on the appearance of a demon.

It stood up, holding onto the intestines that were still attached to Dave, and let out another growl. It came out as a groan because it was muffled by the innards that hung from the small ghoul's jaws.

Rod looked back down at Dave as he lay on his back, stomach ripped open, facing up to his friend with a large wound to his head. Time seemed to stand still while Rod looked into his friend's eyes, thinking of all the things he should do. *I should get him out of here. I can't leave him like this. We may be able to save him?* Just then he felt two powerful hands push him forward.

His foot got tripped up on the chain and he fell forward to his hands and knees. He continued to look at Dave for what seemed like an eternity. He felt the fists of the undead child rub across his back as the ghoul refused to release his grip on David's intestines. He knew the boy did not have hold of him, but he knew he was about to feel the demon's bloody teeth sink into his flesh.

The small zombie let go of the intestines that now clung to Rod's back and grabbed hold of his shirt. Rod snapped out of the trance Dave had put him in and with a chill running through his body, he stood up quickly. The demon child refused to let go and lurched forward with its mouth open wider than any human mouth should open. Rodriquez was able to turn his body to face the creature and punch it in the face. The child's face broke inward as its right hand lost its grip on Rod's shirt.

The zombie swung wildly, but maintained its balance by hanging onto Rod's shirt sleeve with its left hand. It came charging after him again with a newfound vigor. Rod broke the child's grip on his sleeve and punched him in the face a second time. This time the power of the punch sent it falling backward over Dave.

Rod turned toward the door and made for it. Kimberly swung wildly at him, enraged after witnessing him assault her son. She connected with his face a few times and as Rod pushed her out of the way, she maintained her balance and instead of falling away from the door, she fell into it, slamming it shut.

He ran to her and tried to push her to his right and away from the door, but she continued to fight and grabbed hold of the soiled and stained bed frame that was just to the left of the door. Now he was not only fighting the woman, but had to move her and the bed. He grabbed hold of her waist, ignoring the pain in his hand, and tried to pull her off the frame, but her hands were fixed to it and now she was sprawled out in front of the exit. Rod grabbed hold of Kimberly's reddish blond hair and pulled her head up from the frame and put his right leg back, preparing to knee her in the face.

He felt a searing pain flow through his body, starting from his right calf as the boy bit deep into him. Rod pulled away and followed through with his knee to the woman's face. When it connected, Kimberly fell limp and into a heap that was piled directly in front of the bedroom door.

Hands wrapped around Rod's right ankle and he felt another pain shoot through his body, starting at that ankle. He tried to pull away, but the grip on his ankle was too strong. Holding onto the bed frame with his back to the boy, he stomped down backwards with his left foot on the zombie's jaw and stood up, pulling his right foot from the powerful undead grasp. His right leg was free, but now the ghoul fought for control of his left foot. Rod jumped up, turned, and kicked the six-year-old in the face.

The boy rolled backwards but quickly managed to get onto its hands and knees. The little beast opened and closed its mouth, as if it were chewing on something, even though its jaw was completely crushed. Rod stepped forward and kicked the boy in the face as it crawled toward him.

Someone was trying to force the door open, but Kimberly's body lay in a ball in front of it. She started to move, and Rod grabbed her by her hair and unraveled her folded body. She slowly reached up, supporting her hair, and started to show signs of a stunned recovery. Rodriquez pulled the woman away from the door by her disheveled strawberry-blond hair, stretching her body.

Eric peered into the room just in time to see Rod kick the crawling boy in the face for the third time. Then he noticed the foot that was just barely sticking out from the end of the bed, stepped completely in, and saw Dave's body lying with his stomach ripped open and his lifeless eyes staring at the ceiling. Rod pushed on his chest and said, "There's nothing we can do for him, we need to get out of here."

"Don't leave me, Sugar." A Southern accent forced its way out of Kimberly. She was trying to get situated, but they could tell she was still very disoriented. She ran her hand through her hair to get it out of her face and tried to hide her naked body, exposed by her open fuzzy blue robe.

Rod looked at her as he shoved Eric out of the door and turned just in time to see her undead son turn its focus and attention on its mother. As they ran down the wooden stairs they could hear the dazed woman pleading for her son to stop. She pleaded for her son to remember her. She pleaded for her son not to come near her. She pleaded for her son not to bite her. She begged for her son to stop.

Chapter 8

The change

They left through the back of the house to avoid the wandering undead, and after they crossed through a few yards in this suburb, the houses started to spread out more and more. After a while, they started crossing multiple acres of wooded land before they would get to the next house. Eric and Rodriquez ran in silence, while Drew asked question after question about David. The only response was from Eric and that was a sharp, "We'll tell you later!"

The morning had an unusual chill in the air, but as the sun greeted Eric and Drew with its warm touch, the chill quickly began to melt away. For Rod, though, the chill was only getting worse. He began sweating even though his body was frigid, and his right leg felt as if he had a hundred bees stinging him over and over again. Frightened that the infection was spreading through his body faster due to his elevated heart rate while running, he suggested that they slow their pace a little and maybe duck into the next house they came to.

His leg was throbbing with wave after wave of pain, and the sting seemed as if it were traveling through his body. As they were cutting through one of the properties, a building that took the profile of a barn took shape on the horizon. "We're stopping in that building up there," Rod snapped. Eric turned and acknowledged his command, but was bewildered at the tone in which it was delivered.

Rod didn't realize his request came out the way it sounded

until he saw the look Eric gave him. "I'm not feeling well," he said. "Sorry about that, I just need to rest for a second."

They had not seen any undead for a while and figured they would play it safe and avoid the house that was beginning to appear behind some trees. The barn seemed like a safer bet. It was a classic red with wood shingles that looked as if they were in dire need of repair. One side of the double doors of the barn was open, so Rod stepped forward and pulled the black pistol that he had gotten from David's backpack. "Let me go in," he whispered as they got close to the door. "Just watch out here and I'll let you know what I find."

Eric pulled his rifle off his shoulder. Drew held a baseball bat at his side and they both took watch outside the barn. Rod carried a bat in his left hand and the pistol in his outstretched right. He walked through the double doors with a mission. A faint hint of death hung in the overwhelming smell of hay. "Come on, you fuck, come and get some." A fury rose up in him that he could not control. He wanted to hurt something. He wanted to squeeze the life out of something. He wanted to feel someone's skin rip between his fingers as he tore into their flesh. He wanted to bite into the flesh of a living creature and feel its blood spurt out through the skin and between each tooth in his mouth. Rod wanted to kill something.

The sun shone through the windows on the right side of the barn like wide laser beams. Fine particles from the dirt floor and piles of hay danced in them. The barn was broken up into separate stalls; chains hung loosely on half of them, and solid wooden doors secured the other half. Large old wooden beams held the ceiling up and attached to them, above the stalls, was another landing. Some of the stalls were used to store feed and hay, and the landing above them was used to store more hay and other farming equipment that hung over the ledge like sharp spears.

Rod walked halfway through the barn, kicking up dried,

powdered dirt. As he stepped through the middle of the barn, adding to the particles in the sunlight laser beams, he heard the sound of rustling on the far side of the building. "I knew you were in here. Show yourself, motherfucker." He began to feel his body tremble. His whole body began to shake with anticipation.

Eric and Drew both could hear him and looked into the double door. They watched as a lone figure stumbled out of the far stall. They were not able to make out any of its features, but with its shaky and clumsy movements, there was no doubt it was a zombie.

The creature walked forward after bouncing off one of the wooden beams with its right shoulder. When it moved closer, Rod was able to suppose that at one time this man had been one of the field hands that worked on the farm. He wore a pair of overalls that hid his muscular lower body, and the straps slung over his shoulders hid his mid chest. This farmhand had died quickly, because as he walked closer to Rod and deeper into the sun light, it became apparent that his throat had several large chunks missing from it.

Rod put the pistol in the back of his jeans and switched his bat to his right hand. He moved closer for a swing, and as soon as the farmhand began to raise its hands, Rod let fly with the bat. The aluminum bat hit the zombie square in the temple, making the sound of a squashing grapefruit pitched at a major league ball player.

The farmhand spun to its right, falling to his hands and knees, and the momentum forced the ghoul to roll onto its back. The undead lay still for a second, just long enough for Rod to observe the damage he had inflicted. The bat had completely smashed in the left side of its face above its mouth. The sight of the damage he had created excited him; the only thing wrong was that the undead did not feel pain the same way he did. He wanted this thing to hurt. He wanted this thing to scream out in agony.

Rod lifted the aluminum bat above his head and brought it

crashing down on the undead's face, then did it again, and again and again. With each hit Rodriquez could feel the bat sink deeper into its skull, past the hard bone and into what felt like a wet sponge. The sound of rustling behind him broke his trance of satisfaction with inflicting such destruction. He turned and saw another body moving toward him. It was another creature to release his anger on, and excitement filled him, sending jolts of energy through his arms forcing him to grip the bat tighter.

Another undead laborer made its way out from one of the stalls. The now-manic Rod ran to this worker and swung, cracking it above the left knee. He did not want to kill this one as fast as he had killed the other one. With the undead's left leg broken, he wanted to find out how many bones he could break before actually having to kill it. The ghoul was on its hands and knees, working its way to a standing position, and Rod was about to swing on one of its arms to knock it back down when he heard a gurgling sound coming from the undead whose head he had just smashed in. He turned and saw it was not dead and was rolling over. The zombie's face looked like a piece of steak attached to a neck. There were absolutely no features on it that would give any indication that at one point this had been a living creature until you saw its body. It rolled over, and Rod brought the bat down on the back of its skull, dropping it finally for good.

A question popped into Rod's head and washed away the need to release his frustration. Dave had always told them to kill the brain, but he had driven the bat so deep into the undead farmhand's head that it would have killed the brain of any living creature. Hitting the back of the head seemed to be the important thing. He thought to himself he needed to hit the new one in the back of the head, just for experimental reasons. His rational thought made him angry. He had finally been releasing his anger and it had felt so good to him, and this thought had snapped him out of it! Rodriquez turned to the undead that had just fallen again because it had tried to put its weight on its broken leg. The back of its head now faced Rod as if it were bowing down to him. He swung straight down on the back of the head and the zombie dropped face-first into the dry dirt.

Rod felt the sunlight hit him in the back as he heard the groan of another zombie entering the barn from the opposite double doors. It swung one of the doors wide enough to get its body through and was making its way into the barn and straight for Rod. This one was faster and moved with an excited purpose.

Rod was now angrier than before, frustrated by the conflict in his mind between his raging emotions and the need to test out his theory. He walked to the double doors to meet the uninvited guest.

Eric signaled for Drew to follow him after he saw the zombie come through the northern door. They ran around the western side of the barn so that the sun would not shine in their eyes. They took a couple steps around the corner to the northern end of the barn, then hastily ducked back, but it was too late. They had seen what had to be about twenty undead stumbling toward them, just a few feet from the double doors. Some were beginning to stand after kneeling around something that might once have been a cow. As the zombies stood, Eric and Drew could see that the animal was still alive, and with the zombies moving away from it, they could hear it cry out in pain.

Most of the ghouls turned their attention to Eric and Drew; only a couple were already halfway through the door after Rod. "Go back to the bags!" Eric hollered to Drew and started to run. They ran back to the south side of the barn, shaded by the sun, just as the first set of undead made it around the building.

Eric pulled the lever down on the .22 and chambered the first round while he was running. Lifting the rifle to his shoulder he looked down the iron sights. He thought back and replayed Dave's instructions in his head, as if he were there, coaching him through his first shot. *Take it easy. There is no point in pulling that trigger if you're not going to hit it. I set this up so you can see where your shot hits. Look through the V of your closest sight and focus the green dot in the middle of the V.*

He breathed slowly and focused on bringing the green dot into the middle of the top sight. *Now place that green dot directly under the middle of the zombie's eyes.* The undead was moving slow and blessedly not wavering side to side too much. Eric focused the green dot just above the bridge of the undead's nose. *Now FIRE.* He squeezed the trigger and a small dot appeared directly between the eyes of the undead. It completed the step it was taking and then fell face first to the ground. Eric pulled the lever down, chambering another round, and focused on the next zombie in line.

Multiple shots rang out, every shot hitting its mark, dropping another ghoul. The screaming from inside the barn got louder with each zombie that entered the double doors. They knew it was Rod screaming, as if he were conducting a strange march to his own deadly swings.

After Eric's tenth shot and tenth slain zombie, he lined his sights up on the next in line and pulled the trigger. Fear gripped his body as this zombie did not fall, but continued to move forward. The absence of the small kick and loud explosion shocked him. The rifle was empty.

The five remaining undead worked past their fallen companions and reached out for Eric and Drew. Eric backed up and reached out to ensure that Drew was moving backwards. As he stepped backward and was about to turn to find Drew, he saw one of the zombies in the back get spun around, and black blood showered the undead in the front of it.

After Rod had destroyed his now-welcome visitors, he had walked out of the north doors of the barn just in time to see the little bunch turn the corner where Eric was shooting. After giving it a second to ensure Eric was finished firing, he greeted the last one to turn the corner with a swift swing of his bat. The next closest zombie turned to Rod and was greeted in the same fashion as Rod's last victim: a solid blow to the face. Knowing this was not a killing blow, Rod followed it with a hard swing downward to finish the creature. The last three were finished in the same manner, each suffering one or two hits to the head.

Blood was splashed across Rod's body as if someone had randomly drawn black, brown, and crimson paint strokes across him; speckled blood spots littered his face. He breathed heavily, standing over the pile of undead, and his small-statured body now looked ten feet tall.

"How you doin'?" Eric spoke with a slight playful cue in his voice to hide the concern he felt. He had just witnessed his longtime friend go through a manic episode and was not sure what he was going to do next.

Dropping the bat and running his bloody fingers through his blood-caked hair, he snapped out of his daze and turned to Eric. "Who's Puerto Rican now? I need a cigarette."

"You are definitely Puerto Rican, and you and I both need a smoke." Now knowing his friend was back, Eric counseled, "We drew too much attention here. I say let's make our way up to the house," he pointed to the large house on the horizon, "and see if we can find some decent food and a place where you can get cleaned up."

Rod picked up the bat and turned to retrieve the gear they had dropped as the mauled cow called for someone to put it out of its misery. Pulling his pistol, Rod stepped up and silenced it.

****

They walked up a set of old painted stairs that the blue paint was beginning to peel off of. The stairs led to a matching rotting-wood deck. As they traveled across the creaking deck, the sound of swarming flies grew louder the closer they got to the door. The front door of the house was hanging open like the doors on the barn. Rod was the first to enter the house and stopped suddenly as he saw the half-eaten remains of what he guessed was the owner of the property. A pool of blood had dried into the light-blue carpet right in front of Rod's shoes; it had poured from a set of legs still in their blue-jean bib overalls.

Rod stepped in and felt the fibers of the carpet crack from the dried blood. He grabbed the boots of the legs and began dragging them out the front door. "Check the rest of the house. I'll take care of this." The house was void of any undead visitors, but it had been ransacked. Nothing edible was left but the rotting, molding remains in the freezer.

The blood and dried pieces of guts from the farmer made the first floor reek of death, so they moved upstairs to let Rodriquez get his rest. He shook under thick covers, pulled up to his chin as he lay on a queen-sized bed in the front bedroom of the farm house. Drew waited in the back bedroom, looking out the window, down on the barn and the undead they had just killed.

Eric sat on the bed in the room with Drew, pulling the protein bars from his backpack, trying to decide what flavor he wanted to eat. Cookies and cream or chocolate peanut butter? Either way, none of the bars they had tasted like what they advertised, so he gave the choice to Drew. "What flavor do you want?" he asked, trying to pull the boy's attention from the window.

"I really don't feel like eating any of them, to tell the truth."

"Same here, but I'm hungry and we have to eat something." Eric had decided he was going to stick with the chocolate peanut butter if Drew didn't want it.

"It doesn't matter, cookies and cream I guess." He turned just in time to catch it as Eric tossed it to him. The farmhouse was getting increasingly hotter, as the sun was now directly overhead. Eric watched Drew try to peel the melted bar; finally he gave up and began eating it off the wrapper.

"I used to work on a farm like this one back in Maryland. Some of the coldest and best water I ever tasted came out of an underground spring. I think I saw a spout out there where the trough was." Eric waved his hand. "Would you mind filling up our water bottles while I check on your dad?"

Drew nodded and grabbed his and Eric's bottle. Eric reached into Rod's backpack and pulled out the pistol. "This here is the safety." He pointed to the lever that was above his thumb. "If anything happens out there, you fire this at its head. Understand?"

Drew grabbed the gun from him and aimed it at a light switch on the wall. "I get it. I've shot before and by now, I would hope I know how to take one of those things down."

Eric shrugged the comment off, walked to Rod's room, and stood to the left side of the bed. The sun was shining brightly through the window of the master bedroom, and Rod's face was turned away from the beams. The sun's rays reflected off of millions of small dust particles suspended in air or swirling with Rod's small and shallow breaths. The right side of his neck was exposed to the sun, and Eric could see his bare skin glisten from his profuse sweating, but that was not what caught Eric's attention.

His tan skin was now lighter, almost pale, and a black vein stretched from below the covers, up his neck, and behind his right ear. Eric reached for the window shade and looked out to the front of the land. A few undead walked aimlessly, searching for the location of the gunshots and Rod's screams from three hours earlier. He lowered the window shade just enough so the beams would not directly touch Rod's skin, but high enough so Eric could study his features. "How are you holding up, bud?" He hoped Drew was not going to be confronted by those few walkers.

Rod struggled to face Eric, but did so only after realizing the sun would no longer be in his face. Every movement caused him severe pain, so he moved very slowly and only enough to be able to see Eric with his eyes without moving his head. "I'm cold, but I can't stop sweating. I hurt all over."

"What can I do?" Eric asked.

Rod clenched his teeth in agony as he tried to face him a little more. "I need you to do me a favor."

"Anything, you just ask it and I'll do it." Eric jumped at the opportunity to help his friend.

Rod turned his head till he was facing him, but closed his eyes, trying to adjust to the radiant light. Hundreds of sweat beads rolled off his forehead and drenched his hair. "You're going to have to take care of Drew."

When he turned his head, he revealed three large black and red veins running up the left side of his pale face. "You're going to be just fine after you get some rest," Eric said. "Drew is getting some fresh water and we're going to crash here for the night and take off as soon as you're good and ready."

Anger started to swell in Rod, and he clenched the heavy covers and let out a cry as he threw them from the right side of his body, exposing his right leg. "Look at what that, that *thing* did to me," he roared. His leg was pale at the thigh, but at the knee the pigment started to blend into a spider web of black veins, and the skin got darker until it turned into a heavily infected black at the calf. The veins crisscrossed and got thicker at the knee and seemed to stretch up his thigh, changing the pale into a darker black. In the middle of his calf was a swollen bite mark that oozed a mixture of yellow, green, and black pus, and his right foot was covered in the same slime from the bite on his ankle.

Eric was in shock and could not stop looking at it. "What happened?"

He threw his head back onto the wet pillow, "When I found Dave, I tried to help, and that boy bit me."

"You just need some rest and you'll be fine." Eric wanted to believe it, but knew his friend was in bad shape.

"No. I'm dying and I don't want to be one of those things, so you're going to have to put me down."

Eric laughed softly, "What are you, some sort of dog? We're gonna put you down?"

Rod tensed his body and slammed his fist on the bed. "Goddamn it, Eric!" he screamed, causing Eric to duck and get off the bed as if something were being thrown at him. "You're not fucking listening. I'm turning. I'm changing into one of those things out there. Soon I'll be looking to kill you." He started to cry. "I'll look for my son"—he couldn't bear to say it—"I'll look for him too."

A pain was coursing through Rod's body, and he knew that he had to eat. He was suffering from severe hunger pains, and he had a craving for something, but he didn't know what exactly it was. At least, he did not want to admit to himself that he knew what it was. He wanted flesh. Rodriquez wanted to bite down on something and make it bleed. The thought of piercing flesh, the warm taste of iron spurting into his mouth, made him desire that feeling more. He could smell the blood and he could taste the meat that was under Eric's skin, and that yearning made him livid. He he wanted to lash out at Eric and hurt him. Not for the feeling of biting into him, but just to physically hurt something. Killing those ghouls in the barn had given him a feeling of completeness, killing those creatures had made him feel complete ecstasy, and he knew that the only way he would feel that again was if he hurt someone. That someone was Eric.

Eric sat back on the bed next to Rod and laid a hand on his arm. Rod opened his eyes a little wider, adjusting to the light, and revealed to his friend his cloudy eyes. The whites of his eyes were filled with dark veins, and the brown of his iris had turned to a milky grey, while his pupil turned to a bluish grey. Eric stood up in shock and stepped back.

Rodriquez calmed down after seeing the fear and shock of his friend. He forced himself to take control over his body and lowered his voice. "Look, I'm becoming that guy in the store. I can't control my anger. I just want to"—he clenched his teeth, straining his jaw muscles down and forcing them to show through his skin—"sink my teeth into something. I just want to bite into something and eat. God, I am so *hungry*."

Eric stepped back from him until he was pressed against wall next to the window. "You need help, my friend."

The pain and anger coursed through Rod's body and weighed on his mind. Each time Eric said something, it felt as if his head were being pressed in at the temples.

"We can go to town. We can get some antibiotics or some type of anti-infection shit." Eric wanted to help, but knew he couldn't do anything. The closest town was miles away, and even if there was a chance of making it, neither one knew where it actually was. Eric realized that he would have to be the one to eliminate his friend, and he believed he would have to do it soon.

"You can't go to town. You don't even know where it is. Besides, you need to be here for Drew."

The sound of light footsteps walking up the stairs stopped Rod from speaking, and he turned to the door.

"Do you want me to tell him to go away?" Eric offered, still pressed against the wall.

Rod paused and thought about what could happen. He thought, *What if I feel that urge and hurt my son?* Covering himself back up with the heavy covers, he decided, "No, I would like to see him one more time before I have to go."

Just then the door opened and Drew stood in front of it with the two water bottles. "How's he doing?" he asked with deep sympathy after seeing his father moving under the covers.

Eric walked toward him and grabbed one of the bottles and took back the hand gun. He began to answer, but Rod spoke before he could. "I'm doing," he paused, "okay," Rod said as he repositioned himself under the covers.

Drew walked over to him and knelt down on one knee next to the bed. "Do you want some water? It's real cold."

Eric started walking back toward the door to give them some privacy, but the wide-eyed, worried look on Rod's face told him he wanted him to stay.

"I'm actually not doing well at all, bud. I got bit back at the house and I am getting sick, real sick."

Drew and Rod had never had a relationship that was truly emotional, and they never hugged, but Drew leaned over the bed and squeezed his shoulders while he hugged Rod's face with his. Rod felt the urge again, but he was able to fight it. His eyes started to sting as the tears that rolled from the corners of his eyes clung thickly to his eyelids. He wrapped his arm around his son and wiped his eyes the best that he could. Rod thought about the pus that was coming out of his wounds and thought the fluid coming from his tear ducts was the same.

"What will you do?" Drew asked when his father finally released his grip from him.

Rod looked at his fingers, which now had the yellow pus on them. His grey eyes started to burn, and it was difficult for him to open them due to the thick pus holding them shut. With every blink it was a task to open them again.

Drew watched his father looking at his fingers and wiping his eyes. He was clearly disoriented and thinking of his current situation. "What are we supposed to do?" He paused, waiting for a reply. "What are you going to do?" he asked, putting his hand on his right shoulder to give him support.

Rod could not open his eyes due to the yellow glue leaking from his tear ducts, sealing them shut. Anger filled him and he felt the muscles in his body tense. Panicked, Rod started to kick his feet under the covers and with every movement, the pain from his infected leg darted through his body. "What if I just cut it off, will that save me?" he said loudly, forgetting Drew was kneeling in front of him. "What if I just fucking cut it off?" He screamed out as loud as he could, "Would that save me!?" The pain that flowed through Rod's body only escalated with each move he made. The stress of not being able to see started to scare him. He was falling into a deep panic, on top of his anger.

Drew stepped back away from the bed when Rod hollered. "What's he talking about?" Drew asked as he looked at Eric, desperate for an answer.

Rod wrenched at his eyes, pulling his eyelids away from his face. He did not hear Drew speak, but when he was able to see, he saw Drew staring at him with a worried look on his face.

Eric stepped up close to Drew and took a protective stance next to him, not knowing what Rod would do. Rodriquez took offense at Eric's posture. The covers on the bed flew up in a wave as Rod jumped off the bed, releasing a strong stench of ammonia from his wounds and threw his chest out at Eric. "What are you going to do? Do you think I'd hurt my son?" He pushed Eric against the wall and turned his attention to Drew. "Do you think I would hurt you?" He put his face right up to his son's. The pus lined his cloudy eyes, and his eyelids were red from being rubbed raw. Rod's breath smelled of rancid meat, and a look of disgust lined his features.

Drew backed away from the assault, wishing he had never entered the room. He didn't know what to say, and no matter what his reply was, he didn't believe it would please his father. After he put some distance between them, he saw his father's infected leg.

The only clothing his father was wearing was his blue boxers, and they clung to his body from his sweat. Feeling as if they both were teaming up on him, Rod pushed Eric back against the wall. Eric had always been stronger than Rod, but he had never been physically pushed that hard before by anyone. The shock stunned him, and Rod stomped out of the room.

After a few seconds, Eric and Drew were able to take in what had just happened and followed behind him. The back door slammed shut, shaking the house. Eric went running down the stars when he heard Drew holler for him.

"Eric, you have to see this." He was pointing to the window that faced the front of the house, the one on which Eric had pulled the shade down earlier.

They stared out the window, which looked out over green acres of land, and on that land were the roaming zombies from earlier, making their way toward the house. Behind that small group was another, larger pack, following behind them. "They must have heard Rod screaming," Eric said. "Go get our stuff and get ready to go. I'm going to get your dad."

Eric turned back to the steps and when he got halfway down, a loud bang silenced his footsteps on the stairs. At the bottom of the steps was the front door, and staring at Eric through one of the three square windows at the top of the front door was the face of a zombie, mashed against the window. It could see him through the small window and began frantically banging on the door as it got more and more excited by his presence.

"Hurry up, we're leaving now!" he screamed as he ran back up the steps and into the bedroom. Grabbing his backpack, he tossed the energy bars into it and glanced at the back of the farm, toward the barn. Rod was pacing the front of the barn, scratching at his head, trying to pull his short black hair over his face. Drew entered the room with Rod's shoes and backpack in his hands and grabbed his own pack.

The tops of a few more ghouls' heads could be seen from the other, smaller windows of the door as the undead started to pile onto the front porch. Eric and Drew ran through the back door and both of them made eye contact with Rod by the barn at the far end of the property.

"I'm gonna get him. I'll meet up with you on the other side of the fence." Eric pointed in the opposite direction of the barn. "Try to stay quiet."

Drew took off, first running away from the farmhouse to get as much distance between the zombies and himself as possible, then headed north away from the barn. Eric jogged toward the barn, holding Rod's backpack.

When he got within talking distance, Rod turned from him and entered the barn, leaving the double doors swinging. The barn was lit by beams of light shining through cracks in the roof and walls in the high-noon sun. Particles danced in the rays of light from the dust that was kicked up from Rod moving quickly through the barn. He was crouched over a body in the middle dirt aisleway. The body was lying face down, and Rod grabbed hold of the hair on the back of the ghoul's head. He pulled up on it, forcing the dead body to bend backward, and twisted the creature to face Eric.

"See this?" Rod said.

The face of the body was a boy's, no older than fifteen, with no bruises or blemishes, but the complexion was a shade lighter than just pale. Eric was not sure what to say, but let out a whimper of "Yes."

"What's different about this one than the others?"

Eric looked down at the dead bodies that Rod had slain earlier that morning. All the bodies were twisted and broken. They all were farmhands, and Eric could not tell any true difference other than that one looked very young, so he stood there silent.

"This is the first one I killed when I truly found out how to kill them." He twisted its head the opposite way with a snap that would have killed any living human and revealed to Eric a bashed-in bloody imprint at the back base of the head. "You can shoot these things all day and you can smash their faces in, but the only way to destroy them is if you destroy the back part of their brains. I figured this out by taking my bat to this one's head after killing a few of the others." He threw its face back into the dirt. "Look at what I'm going to be." He circled, looking at the other ghouls. "I can't do it, Eric. What if I come back for you or my boy? I'm done, I'm going to change. I can already feel it."

Eric moved closer to him and Rod screamed, "Stay back! Don't come any closer, I'm a monster." Rod stepped back a few steps while he was talking, and then he stopped and looked directly into Eric's eyes. "Give me your gun."

Now Eric was confused. He could not bear the thought of giving his best friend a tool that he knew he was going to use to kill himself. He reached for the gun that was sitting in his deep pocket. "I don't know about...."

He was quickly silenced as Rod rushed to him and grabbed hold of the gun that was still in Eric's hands. "Leave me," Rod said quickly, as if he were in a hurry and his words came sharply. His once-tan face took on the lightest shade of pale, and black veins traveled up his body. Rodriquez looked at Eric sympathetically with his eyebrows pulled together in a sign of sadness for just a second and said, "I need this."

Eric's hands released from the pistol. He turned his back on Rod and walked out the swinging barn door. The undead were gathering around the house, the majority piling up around the front porch. He began to walk away from the barn and down the small hill away from the farmhouse. He knew he was running out of bullets for his rifle and had what would equal a whole box full of 9 mm ammo inside one of the back pockets of his book bag. Eric was slow to move further away from the barn because in order for him to make it, he was going to have to have that pistol. Turning to the barn, he watched as the zombies circled and crawled at the farm like bees swarming over their nest. Their groans were loud enough that he did not have to worry about how much noise he made at this distance.

A shot was fired, and light flashed between the red boards of the barn. Not being worried about how much noise he was making made him comfortable with his movements, but the loud bang of the pistol forced him to jump and cringe, because he knew they all heard it. Every mouth that was seething with anticipation to get into the farm turned its attention to the barn and Eric. Quickly, instinctively, and with everything they had, they began to move toward him. Most of them were clumsy and stumbled at the start, but some started to move smoothly and methodically, one foot after another, with control. These were quicker and would soon be at the barn.

He ran back into the barn and saw Rod leaning against a stack of bailed hay. He ran over to him, trying not to see anything above his chest. He tried not to look at his face and to focus on the gun that was still grasped in Rod's hand, resting on his bare left thigh. He could not help himself and had to see what Rod had done.

The shot was not to the back of the head. The bullet had traveled up under his chin and out the top of his head. Rod had known this shot would not kill a zombie, but he did it this way because he did not want anyone to know he was a zombie. Rod wanted whoever it was that was going to move him and clean the mess up in the barn to know that this body, *his* body, was not a zombie and that he had taken his own life before he changed.

Removing Rod's loose fingers from the pistol, Eric picked up the smoking gun. The sounds of constant footsteps and groans were coming down the hill toward the barn. Running out the opposite side from the footsteps, Eric ran down the hill, away from the farmhouse. He ran so the barn was between him and the mass of ghouls, and when he hit the tree line, he broke north to catch up with Drew.

Chapter 9

Nightmares and Shadows

The wind was picking up when Naomi finally fell asleep, and the sound of the leaves rustling against each other drowned out the moans of the undead. The air was cool in the house, and a breeze from the barely-open window brushed her cheeks.

Naomi finally fell asleep spooning up against Sam with her arms folded over her, protecting her from the things that wandered outside. The cool breeze traveled down her left ear, across her smooth jawbone, and down her neck. It blew again, but this time the wind had a weight behind it and tickled her. She brushed her jaw and cheek, swatting away the invisible force and some of the braids that wrapped around her. The feeling came back, except this time she opened her eyes just a little and adjusted to the light coming in the window and reflecting off the wall.

Within the striped shadows of the blinds stood the figure of a person on the other side of the window. She spun around quickly and saw the creature she had run over in her driveway, falling on top of her. The left side of its face was caved in and its jaw swung loosely on the left side. The crimson-faced creature reached for her as it fell through the window.

Naomi sat up with a hard gasp, waking Sam up as well. She reached for her face and then reached for the window. Naomi had been having nightmares every night since everyone had changed. She had lost track of time, but knew they must have stayed with Mr. Cook well into their second week. The sun was shining brightly this morning, and when she looked at the wall, no shadows were visible.

"You scared the crap out of me," Sam said, getting up and letting out a stretch. She pulled her shoes from under the bed. "I'm going to see what Mr. Cook is going to make for breakfast."

"Leave Mr. Cook alone." Naomi adjusted her shirt and bra and ran her fingers through her hair, trying to wipe away the nightmare. "We'll fend for ourselves and maybe get back into the house to get some of our own food."

Samantha heard her mother, but did not want to go back into their home. Their house was infested with the undead, and she did not want to have to deal with them again. She was very content with staying here for as long as possible.

Just then, a small knock interrupted them, and Mr. Cook's rough morning voice spoke through the old wooden door of their bedroom. "I got some sausage, bacon, and a few eggs, ready to be eaten."

Sam looked to her mother, raised her eyebrows, and widened her eyes as if to say, *see*. She opened the door and followed the old man towards the kitchen. The smell of cooked meat filled her nostrils, and her stomach responded with a low growl of appreciation.

Mr. Cook had a wide display on the dining room table. Their plates were already set, and in the middle of the table was a serving dish with more pieces of bacon, sausage, and some toast. On the far end of the table, a sizzling Coleman stove was cooling down from preparing the feast.

Upon Naomi's entrance to the dining room-kitchen area, she was struck again by how yellow the room was and had to give her eyes a second to adjust. She opened her eyes slowly and was shocked at the amount of food that was prepared.

"Now, I know what you're going to say before you say it, and I have a good reason for cooking all this food," Mr. Cook said as he sat next to the green Coleman stove. "We have to start eating some of this, because this food will start to go bad. I threw some of it in the deep freezer in the garage, but that's only going to keep for so long. This was mostly stuff that was in the fridge."

Naomi wanted to come back with some kind of solution, but it was too early in the morning and she did not have an acceptable one at that moment. "Thank you," was the only thing she could think to say, then she rubbed her eyes again.

"Yeah, I always wanted to paint this room another color," he responded to her squinted, adjusting eyes while she scanned all of the yellow knickknacks littering the walls. "I have gotten used to walking around this place with my eyes closed until I have my first cup of coffee. You know, it has got to be about twenty-two, maybe -three years now that I have had to squint for about forty-five minutes before I can actually fully open my eyes in the morning. I have told myself time and time again, as soon as she passes I am painting these damn walls and getting rid of these damn knickknacks."

Blushing, Naomi apologized. She did not mean to offend Mr. Cook, but he would not accept her apology. He knew the walls and décor were horrendous, and he jokingly made fun of them. "I have the paint in the garage just waiting. It's been sitting there ever since she passed. I just always find something better to do when it actually comes time to paint. Either that or it's too cold and I can't keep the windows down, or it's too hot, so I keep the AC running and I don't want the house to stink." He ran a piece of white bread through the bacon and sausage grease that was starting to thicken on the Coleman stove.

They sat and ate the largest breakfast they'd had in a long time, and Naomi started to wonder what they would do when all the food was gone. "We have more food at our house, if you wanted to run over," she paused for a second, "or I could go over and get it."

"Hon, you look like your back is giving you more trouble than my old decrepit one is, so I think it's fair to say you should probably just relax a bit." With that, she sat down on the plastic-covered chair and began to make a plate. "I set up a generator in the garage this morning." He said.

Naomi looked at him oddly and was about to say something as soon as she finished her mouthful.

"I ran an exhaust line under the garage door, so we won't get gassed out. I figured we could run it an hour or two every night just to refreeze some of the stuff in the deep freezer. I have two five-gallon gas cans filled and another one that has two, maybe three gallons in it, so that should last us a few days," Mr. Cook said with a raised eyebrow. He always tried to stay positive.

After they had finished their plates, seconds, and forced thirds, Mr. Cook stood up from the table. "If you have to leave take the keys, and" he waved his hand in a follow-me gesture "come with me, I'll show you how to open the garage door."

When he opened the door that led to the garage from the kitchen, a quiet moan stopped them from moving forward. Mr. Cook put his arm out to keep his guests from entering the garage. That did not stop the three small dogs from rushing the door, barking in protest. Mr. Cook forced the first one hard across the linoleum with his foot and jumped at the other two. They stayed back just out of kicking distance, but were at attention, waiting for the first opportunity to speak their objection.

The white aluminum garage door was not closed all the way, and the only light came from the small opening—about six inches, more than enough to allow room for the generator's exhaust hose. Two pair of feet could be seen walking just on the other side. The garage was filled with clutter with the exception of a small path that led to the driver's-side door of his blue Chevrolet pickup truck. Mr. Cook had never bothered with cleaning the mess because he was the only one that had to get to his truck. Ms. Cook's car was next to his, but boxes and garbage bags filled with various household knickknacks lay on top of and surrounding her cream-colored hatchback; now a small generator was piled amongst the debris. He had never gotten around to cleaning the garage after she passed. That was one of the many things he had always said he was going to do.

The two pair of feet were walking past the rolled-up door, and then the sound of rustling from a trash bag caught Mr. Cook's attention. The old man walked down the two wooden steps that led into the garage and grabbed a shovel that was hanging on the wall next to the steps. It was a tight squeeze between the back of the bed of his truck and the aluminum door, but he sucked in his large stomach and moved between them. When he was halfway out from behind the blue truck, he could see a bare grey arm covered with dried dirt swinging back and forth under the garage door, reaching for anything it could grab. The black bag it was touching was in front of the hatchback, just out of its fingers' reach, and each time it swung its thin arm, its finger tips just barely brushed the bag.

Mr. Cook turned to the open door of the house and looked at the two women standing in it. He did not want them to see, but his truck blocked their vision and it was too dark in here to make out what he was actually doing anyway. He grabbed the top of the bag and tossed it on the heap on top of the hatch back. The creature under the door began to moan, as if it knew something was happening. Another hand reached from under the door and the swinging arm moved its attention to Mr. Cook's feet. He stepped back and came down on the new arm with the shovel, and metal rang against concrete as it cleaved the ghoul's arm just below its elbow.

It let out another moan, but no louder than before, and continued to reach for his feet with its now black, bleeding stump. Mr. Cook came down again on the other arm.

"Mr. Cook," Sam said and pointed to the opening of the garage.

Two more sets of hands were reaching under the garage door. The two that had been walking away came back, responding to the calls of the first reaching zombie, which was still trying to get to Mr. Cook's dirty white shoes. Instead of squeezing between the door and the truck, he stepped on the back tire and crawled over the bed of the truck.

"Naomi," he cried out in a loud whisper, "come pull down on that chain!" He pointed to the chain connected to the roll-up door. Naomi knew exactly what he was talking about and pulled on the two chains, ensuring she would pull the proper side and not open it instead of closing it. Naomi could now see the two sets of arms swinging under the door, and she tested the chain with a light pull, ensuring the door was not going to open even an inch.

Unlocking the chains, she pulled as hard as she could without putting strain on her back. Mr. Cook was off the truck and at her side in seconds, taking her spot at the door. The ghouls' constant reaching was putting pressure on the door, and it was shifting up slightly with each push of the undead hands. Mr. Cook leaned back on the chain and pulled down hard. The door smashed down on the reaching arms, pinning them to the concrete. He leaned back more and then slid the chain onto the latch.

He walked up to Naomi and Sam, and they both looked at him, confused. "I'm going to take care of them," he said.

They walked through the house and looked out the windows for any undead that were in the vicinity of the fence. Sam pulled the shades back from one of the windows and looked out of it just as a ghoul passed. She was startled and let go of the blind. It was walking in the direction of the distressed zombies. "I got one," she whispered loudly, so everyone could hear.

Mr. Cook walked to the front door, passing the kitchen table and grabbing the M1 that lay on it. He looked to the women. "So, don't lock me out. Okay?" he said jokingly, but deep down inside, he was very serious.

Naomi caught his sarcasm and agreed she would not lock him out.

With rifle in one hand and the shovel in the other, he stepped out of the house. There was a small group of about six or seven walkers outside the long driveway fence, wanting to get inside the yard. He scanned the perimeter of his fence and counted six more that had been walking aimlessly, but turned toward Mr. Cook now that he had revealed himself. As he turned the corner toward the garage of the house, he heard the sound of his garage door being beat on. He could see the zombie that was walking had stopped at the garage and was pounding on it with its bloody fists.

The ghoul was pounding with both of its fists simultaneously and was moving back and forth, spreading smears of black blood across his white roll-up door. He knew he could not get a clean shot, so he took aim and hollered "Hey!" He used this method often when he was hunting deer to make them stop in their tracks and figured it would work well in this situation. He spoke just loud enough so it would hear him and turn to face him. As soon as he spoke, it stopped and looked directly at him. It opened its mouth and Mr. Cook pulled the trigger, dropping the zombie in a heap.

The other two that were being held down by the garage door crushing their arms turned to him, but could not move. He stepped over the top of each in turn, straddled it and drove the shovel into the back of its neck. It took two chops to each, but their heads were severed. Now all he could think about was the black blood leaking from the stumps of their necks, spreading onto his garage floor from under the opened garage door. The heads moved slightly even though they were severed from their bodies. He turned over the head of the first zombie and saw the creature's eyes and jaw were moving in such a way that it appeared the head was trying to draw closer to him.

He picked up the shovel and raised it over the first one's head. The decapitated head opened its mouth, reaching out with its lips, snapping at the air. Mr. Cook thought about driving the flat blade into the side of the head, but the thought of it turned his stomach. Instead he slid the blade under the head, causing the metal end of the shovel to scrape against the cement. Cook began to walk through his yard to the fence. The head rested on the blade facing him, stretching its broken and chapped lips, trying to take a bite out of its carrier.

The undead around the perimeter of the yard started to move toward Mr. Cook and crowded the section of fence closest to him. Six undead walked the outer edge of the fence apart from the horde at the main gate, but while he had been outside the number of ghouls seemed to be growing. With careful precision, Mr. Cook swung the shovel up and launched the head, sending it spinning high into the air over the growing crowd at the fence. The undead paid no attention to their ally, but squeezed and forced their fingers into the chain links.

Cook looked across his multi-acre property to the front fence and watched as more undead gathered there. From this distance they looked small and appeared to be moving very slowly, but he knew their sheer numbers would soon be overwhelming.

****

The following morning Naomi was greeted by another breakfast, but a little bit smaller. The smell of instant pancakes made her feel slightly at home until she was assaulted by the horribly bright-colored kitchen.

"Good thing we still got water pressure," Mr. Cook said, turning to her, taking his attention from the propane griddle and the pancakes. "At least until we still have water up there." He pointed up as if the tower were right above them. "We'll have breakfast in just a couple of minutes."

Sam, kneeling on the couch, was looking out the window that

faced her house. "Is it ever going to move?" She got up from the couch and sat at the set table ready to eat. "There is one of those things standing at the window. Just standing there." She paused as Mr. Cook slid a large platter with three massive, perfectly round pancakes down to the end of the table. He slid another smaller dish, filled with sausage links, next to that. "It has been standing there since before you started cooking." She was taken aback by the size of the breakfast that was placed before her. "Wow," she said, responding to the pancakes.

"We used to always try to make the largest pancakes possible. My son and I would always make these ridiculously huge pancakes that never turned out right. They always burnt right on the edge and never fully cooked in the middle, but" He threw his finger into the air in a little celebration. "I have perfected the largest and best pancake ever."

"Is there syrup?" Sam asked.

Cook looked around and then answered, "No. I didn't even think about it until they were just about finished."

"I'm sure they don't need syrup and are perfect just the way they are," Naomi was quick to interrupt and scowled at her daughter.

Naomi made her way to the window and glanced out at her house. The broken glass from the kitchen door's window was scattered over the small porch, sending shimmers of sunlight reflecting at her. She looked through the window next to her kitchen door, and a lone figure stood with its back to them, standing completely still in the middle of the kitchen. It was hard to be sure, but it looked as if it were not wearing a shirt; long, stringy, unkempt hair flowed from its head.

"What are we going to have for dinner?" Sam asked after swallowing a large mouthful of pancakes. She had realized the pancakes didn't need any syrup on them after all.

"Why don't you go out to the garage and pick something out?

We got all kinds of meats out there, but the ones on top should probably be eaten first."

Sam chewed another mouthful and got up from the table. Naomi watched as she left and followed close behind her. Sam was hesitant to open the door at first and did so very slowly. She peeked through the slightly-open door and tried to listen closer than any human could. She expected to hear the sound of a bag rustling or of claws trying to dig through the concrete floor, but it was silent.

She opened the door wide and ensured it was not going to close behind her before going any deeper. Once again, the only light that was shining through was coming from the three-inch gap under the garage door and from the kitchen, surrounding the silhouette of her mother standing in the door way.

The freezer was old and showed its age from the dirt and rust that streaked the once-white surface, and as Sam opened the freezer, she looked at the rubber seal that was peeling away from the lid. Like Mr. Cook said, a wide variety of meats presented itself, but some of the meats and poultry looked as old as the freezer. A turkey was buried under a mountain of boxed fish sticks and packaged ground beef. She poked at the ground beef and the tips of her finger tips dug into the red meat. She pulled the package out, then grabbed a box of fish sticks and felt the cardboard go limp in her hands from the moisture.

She looked to her mother. "I don't think this meat is going to last much longer? I think the freezer is no good."

"I was thinking we should probably test the generator out today anyway, so we'll let it run for an hour or two just to refreeze the stuff that is thawing," Cook said, approaching the garage as they were talking. "It looks like it is going to rain, so as soon as she opens up, we'll run her."

The rain didn't come for many long and boring hours. Mr. Cook talked about his son, who died during Operation Desert

Storm, and his lovely wife, and all Sam could think about was what her friends were doing. For the first time in her life, she missed school and actually would have preferred to be sitting in her classroom right now. Every once in a while she would glance at the lone figure in her house and then look out the windows at the fence line. The ghouls that had been surrounding the fence appeared to have moved on, and at the southern end of the property she was able to make out a few figures. They looked to be moving and would soon be away from the house.

For lunch they ate the thawed fish sticks, and then at dinnertime, while forming the thawed ground beef into hamburger patties, they heard the first sounds of rain tapping on the roof. They looked at each other with mild excitement, and Naomi quickly realized how sad it was that they were looking forward to the rain, just so that they could do something different.

The rain began to pick up as they finished dinner. The sound of thunder shook the house and Mr. Cook addressed them: "I think we could run that generator now." He nodded for Sam to join him. The generator was in between his truck and the junk pile on his wife's cream-colored hatchback. Mr. Cook had to walk on top of fallen bags in order to get to the small generator, and for each one that he stepped on, another fell off the vehicle. The bags he stepped on, he tossed back on top of the pile.

Sam watched him from the kitchen as he shuffled through the trash bags and pointed into the bed of the truck to three red five-gallon gas cans. He disappeared behind the passenger's side of the truck and then Sam could hear the pull start of the generator's engine.

The roar of the generator sounded as if the small house was falling in on itself, and Sam began to panic. The generator was too loud. Cook reappeared and walked back from a cleared path. Sam's mother was leaning over her shoulder in agreement that this was a bad idea. He waved them back into the kitchen and closed the door behind him. "They can't hear over this rain." The crack of thunder overhead agreed with his analysis. "As soon as the rain begins to die down we'll turn it off, but the meat will spoil if we don't keep it frozen."

"How long will it run for?" Naomi asked.

"About six hours on the gas that's in there. This rain is not going to stop for a while yet. We will be okay." Mr. Cook pulled back the curtain of the kitchen door's window. The rain was coming down hard, and the moon was blocked by dark clouds. The fence line was just barely visible through the grey wall of rain. "See, there are none of them out there. If we start to gather a crowd I'll shut it down."

Naomi didn't like the thought of running it, but they had to eat, and the food was beginning to spoil. She walked to the couch and looked towards her house. All she could make out of her home was its dark silhouette against the darkening sky. There was a figure standing on the other side of the fence, walking the fence line as if the pounding rain had no effect on it at all. "Are you going to stay awake while the generator is running, just in case?"

"I don't think we're going to need to, but if you want me to I will." Mr. Cook sank into the large recliner. "The generator will die out before the rain does," he predicted. Mr. Cook turned the dial on a grey battery-powered radio, looking for some sign of life or just something to listen to. He did this periodically throughout the course of the day, but never had any luck. Time after time he scrolled through hundreds of channels of white noise.

Naomi didn't like the thought of no one being awake, but did not want to stay up nor ask the old man to do so. The generator gave the house a consistent hum, and Naomi began to feel comfortable with the rumble of the engine. She believed she would quickly fall asleep once she was able to relax and lay her head down. The shadows in the house began to stretch across each room as the rain clouds became thicker and darker. "I think someone should definitely stay awake while it is running, though," she said.

"I'll stay awake, and if I begin to tire I'll come and wake you," Mr. Cook said to Naomi. She didn't want to be awakened, but it was the best thing for everyone, and she responded with a half-smile and a nod.

In the guest bedroom, no light shone through the windows, and the constant low hum of the generator put her at rest. The feeling of her daughter climbing under the covers with her topped off her comfort, and she felt herself falling into a deep slumber. As she rested on the pillow next to Sam, she felt her daughter breathing softly, but she was restless as she wrestled with the passing events and how her whole world had changed in a matter of a couple days.

The dark clouds covered the bright moon and hid the shadows of the blinds on the wall. Even though she did not have the shadows to play tricks on her mind, the undead on the other side of the fence still lingered with her. Naomi closed her eyes and for the first time did not have to strain to keep them closed.

****

"Damn it, Coco, I'm going to kick you in the face!" Mr. Cook hollered out from his room, and the volume of his voice traveled directly into Sam and Naomi's. This was a very popular saying here at the Cook residence. He never actually kicked any of the dogs in the face, but he threatened quite often. Naomi and Sam both often wondered if at some point in time he actually did kick them, because normally, whatever the dogs were doing, they immediately stopped.

The first time they heard him say this, Coco was sitting on the end of the couch with its legs open, licking itself, and they were both surprised by the speed with which the dog stopped. If the dogs stayed too close to or under the table waiting for falling scraps, the threat was thrown out again, and all of them left with expedience.

This time the threat was used because one of the dogs was running on the kitchen floor, and the constant pitter-patter of prancing nails tapping the linoleum was very loud in the dark and quiet rancher. Tonight Naomi thought she might actually kick the dog in the face if it would help her fall back to sleep. *Sleep.* It had felt like only a second, but the house was quiet and the sound of the dog's feet seemed louder than the generator. *How long was I asleep?*

Naomi pulled the covers off her and rolled over, facing Sam. *Was Mr. Cook awake? It sounded like he had hollered from his room.*

"Are you ever going to stop moving?" Sam snapped. She was obviously agitated by her own thoughts. Her mother must have been tossing and turning, but she could not tell. This had been the sleep she was hoping for and needed, but now it had been stolen from her.

Naomi sat up. Her tight back sent a spike of pain through her body, reminding her that she couldn't move as quickly as before. She watched Samantha put her shoes on and walk toward the door. "Where are you going?"

Sam let out an irritated sigh. "Getting a drink of water." She did not offer her mother any, but Naomi did not feel the need to ask and instead was going to join her.

Naomi scooted to the end of the bed and gripped the edge, squeezing tightly to release some of the tension in her back. With her back forced straight, she slid her feet into the white nursing shoes Ms. Cook used to use and pulled the grey Alaska hoodie over her. She listened to the sound of a drop dripping onto the window sill. The rain must have stopped a while ago, and there was no telling how long the generator had run. *He must have shut it down if he was in his room.* With that thought she began to feel better about the situation. She wanted to believe Mr. Cook would have shut it down before he would have gone to sleep.

One of the dogs started to bark, and nails frantically scratched the linoleum kitchen floor as the two other white dogs ran to the barking one's side.

"God damn it, dogs!" Mr. Cook's bed groaned as he tried to get up. "Toto, if you're in my blinds again, I am going to have you for breakfast!"

"I'll get them, Mr. Cook. I'm getting a glass of water anyway," Sam said with a completely different attitude than she had had seconds before. All three white Bichons were barking now and tearing at something.

Now that the rain had stopped, Naomi was physically forcing her eyes away from the wall. As she sat straight up in bed, she was startled by the shadow she cast along the barred wall. No longer could she feel the comfort of the clouds covering the moon, hiding the shadow that plagued her thoughts. The moon shone brighter than ever through the window behind Naomi.

She sat and looked at her shadow, trying to force herself from the bed. The moonlight shone through perfectly on her back and she could see every piece of braided hair that was out of place on her head. She thought about giving up and lying back down, but with the dogs' constant barking and now that she was filled with worry, she knew sleep would not take her again. Naomi thought about going out into the living room, sitting back in the same position she was in earlier that day, tracing out the images that were engraved in the wooden paneling that covered the living room.

Sam stepped into the living room and saw one of the white Bichons Frises standing with its rear legs digging into the back cushion of the sofa, trying to hold itself up while it raked at the living room blinds. The dog had a few of the slats pulled out from the blind, and where it focused on digging there were none at all.

The other two dogs were fighting for position on the back of the couch. Samantha pushed the digging dog on its right side, sending it flying off the back of the couch and onto the sofa seat cushions, but not without the dog showing its disapproval by snapping at her hand and grabbing the tip of her fingers. "Bitch," she said softly, holding her left hand close to her face, trying to study the damage the dog had done.

Sam brushed the fighting dogs off to the side and they fell to the yellow floor, jumped onto the love seat adjacent to the couch, and began fighting.

The dogs were fighting for the same piece of window Sam had used earlier that day to watch her house, and now she moved closer to see if she could see her house through the hole the dogs had made in the blinds. Even though the moon was bright tonight, Sam could not see very far. She moved closer and began to feel a little queasy in her stomach, but she wanted to see if she could make out anyone in her room.

She put both knees on the couch and looked out of the hole the dog had made for her. There was a brown blanket swaying on the other side of the window. The blanket started to move, and she realized it was not swaying in the breeze, but rocking back and forth. The cloth appeared to move down as if someone were removing it, and then a man's face appeared, looking through the hole in the blinds.

His cheek was ripped from his face in a perfect circle, revealing a set of white molars. He let out a groan of excitement as he made eye contact with Sam. She knelt there on the couch and screamed as she watched the creature's tongue roll in anticipation of its next meal.

Naomi had just pulled the knot tight on her shoes when she heard Sam scream. She looked up and stood, but her shadow never moved. Her dark shadow was engulfed by a larger, ominous one that was created by the same moon that created hers.

Two large, shadowed hands pressed on the window, its fingers spread, and then pulled back and hit the window, now in the form of two fists. Glass fell and landed on Naomi's back and covered the bed. She scooted to the door as the ghoul reached into the room and tore down the blinds. It reacted to Sam's scream, but when it thrust its head into the room, it saw Naomi and let out a groan of its own. Strands of bloodstained cloth hung from its mouth, stuck between broken and bloodied teeth.

Naomi backed up until she was in the hallway and bumped into Mr. Cook. He looked into the room just as the creature climbed over the windowsill and landed on the bed, rolling off to the floor. Naomi was forced to the side as Cook reached into the room and pulled the bedroom door shut.

A plethora of noises came from the living room. The sounds of hands banging on the kitchen sliding-glass door mixed with the sound of the windows being beaten; these were followed by the shattering of glass across the linoleum floor. The three dogs' barking added to the chaos coming from the front of the house. Sam came running down the hallway toward them, followed by one of the white dogs.

Cook ran into the living room and picked up the rifle and the set of keys on the table. Naomi was not far behind him and the keys were thrust into her hand. "Go get the truck started." This was a demand and Mr. Cook had a very serious look on his face. He did not show worry or fear, but his eyebrows formed a stern V that met between his eyes. He gave the command firmly and blocked her view of the ghoul that was crawling through the window and onto the couch. His plan worked, because Naomi turned as if she were conducting an emergency drill that had been practiced hundreds of times until it was flawless. She turned without question and went into the garage.

Sam was not as obedient and witnessed the zombie climbing in. She also turned and saw Mr. Cook make a quick adjustment to the rifle and take aim on the ghoul.

The garage was dark, and only the outline of the truck could be seen from the door. Blindly feeling for the door handle, Naomi found it and opened it, allowing the truck to illuminate the garage with its interior lights and cast ominous shadows on the wall. Naomi whipped around to the door of the house when she heard the first pop of the M1 Carbine explode in the house, but was denied her ability to see what was going on by Samantha slamming the door that separated the house and garage behind her.

Sam spoke to her mother with her wide and fearful eyes of what was happening behind the door, and Naomi told her wordlessly to get into the truck.

Naomi unlatched the garage-door chain and began to raise it. When the rolling door opened to about three feet, she realized this was the only boundary separating her from the undead outside. She ran back to the Chevrolet and hands began to reach for her from under the door, and then a body was crouching its way into the garage.

Naomi jumped into the truck, pressed the clutch, and turned the ignition, making the garage roar from the truck's engine, but one sound stood out amongst it all. Sam could make out the distinct sound of scratching paws at the garage's house door over the undead's groaning and pounding.

Sam felt a strong urge to get out of the truck and rescue the dogs. She held onto the truck's door handle and cracked it open as soon as her mother put the truck in reverse. Light from the interior lights shone on their faces, and Sam opened the passenger door.

The light confused Naomi as they looked at each other. "Close the door!" she screamed, and the truck jumped into gear, backing into the roll-up door. The door bent outward and the Chevy stalled. It quickly roared back to life and lurched forward. The lights stayed on in the truck, and Naomi turned back to Sam as she was about to climb out of the vehicle. "Close the fucking door!" Naomi screamed. Three shots were fired in the house, and then the scratching stopped. The truck moved forward, crushing two plastic trash cans, as Naomi tried to get as much room as she could to ram the garage door. Sam stepped out of the truck. "Get your ass back in here!"

"I'm getting the dogs!" Sam hollered back in defiance. Then she looked at her mother and screamed as she noticed one of the undead walking past the truck's bed and reaching into the driver's-side window of the Chevy.

Naomi turned just in time as the ghoul reached for her face. All she could make out of the undead was the filthy hand that reached for her. A grey palm, covered in its other victims' blood and caked with dirt as if it had been crawling in the mud, grasped for her face. Behind that hand was a gaping maw filled with broken teeth that needed to be filled with the flesh of its victim. She felt herself being pulled to the window toward the open mouth that exuded the stench of death and decay. The ghoul had her grey hood in his hand and was pulling. She braced herself against the door and the steering wheel, but the power of the zombie pulled her closer. Naomi tucked her head and pulled her arms through the sleeves; the ghoul began to pull the hoodie off of her. Her arms were out of the sleeves, but she had to wrestle to get them out of the hoodie. The hungry and frenzied zombie grabbed hold of a portion of her braids through the sweat shirt and pulled the hoodie into its mouth.

The teeth bit into her long black braids through the grey sweat shirt, and she could feel the creature shaking its head back and forth like a pit bull playing tug-of-war with a piece of rope. Two ghouls were making their way under the bent garage door and crawling toward Samantha. Sam covered her face in fear, not knowing what to do as she watched the ghoul rip at her mother. Her feet were made of lead and her legs, Jell-O. She wanted to do something. She wanted to pull her mother out, but her feet would not move, and she could not pull her hands from her face. Her mind raced with hundreds of scenes that she could not comprehend. Thousands of thoughts jammed into clouds that fogged her mind as she watched her mother being pulled towards the ghoul's mouth. Then the sound of groaning blew the clouds from her mind, and she turned in the direction of one zombie beginning to stand and another one crawling, inches from grabbing her leg. She forced her heavy feet and weak legs to jump into the truck. Sam slammed the door and then began to scream. It was a bloodcurdling cry that made all other sound impossible to hear. It was just then that one of the undead smashed its shedding skin up against her window.

A loud pop and then a deafening ring sounded in Naomi's and Sam's ears. Naomi fell back against Sam as she was released from the grasp of the undead. She pulled the rest of the hoodie off over her head and looked up to see Mr. Cook with his rifle in his hand.

He had walked to the side of the ghoul as it shook the grey hoodie wildly, placed the barrel against the side of its head, and eliminated the mad beast. "Get out of here, I'll open the garage." He mouthed out the words, but Naomi only heard two things: the low tone in her ears from the gunshot and the piercing sound of Sam screaming.

Cook began to pull down on the chain to open the roll-up door, but the truck had knocked it out of the track, making it very difficult to raise. It was moving, opening, but very slowly. With each forced pull on the chain, the old man had to reach higher for another pull. Every effort moved it slightly, popping the door back into the track.

More undead began to crawl under the door as it reached a little more than a quarter of the way open. Mr. Cook backed away from their prying and clawing hands, trying to work the chain. He could not move away from them any further and work the chain, so he let go. He backed away from the door and drew his rifle. "You have to go! You have to get out of here," he screamed as he lined his sights up on the closest ghoul, crawling on its hands and knees. It did not take the time to stand up, and it reached out with excitement as it got closer.

Naomi heard Cook scream something as the tone in her ears started to fade, but Sam's screaming muffled any coherence from his voice. Through the rearview mirror she watched him move closer to the truck, and then she was able to make out one of the white dogs running from the kitchen toward the garage. Behind the white dog was a horde of undead that had filled the house shoulder to shoulder, making their way toward the fleeing animal.

One, two, three shots rang out one after the other; the crawling zombie dropped. Cook was at the driver's-side window now and turned to Naomi. "Get out of here! Go!" She was able to make out what he screamed, but only because she was able to read his eyes and lips. Sam was still screaming, her legs pulled up to her chest and her hands cupping her ears.

Naomi pulled the shifter into reverse, and that made Mr. Cook believe she had finally snapped out of the daze and was actually going to leave. He lined his rifle on another undead and fired dropping the next one that was behind the crawling zombie. He was walking backward toward the garages house door when he noticed a white blur shoot out from around his legs. He turned to the door to see a wall of undead making its way toward the garage.

Naomi looked into the rear view mirror and saw nothing, except for the upper torsos of undead that had made their way under the roll-up door. She floored the gas as she released the clutch, and the truck jolted backward and jounced up and down as the tires ran over whatever undead were behind her. Shards of glass flew all around Naomi and Sam's heads as the cab hit the garage door, breaking the back windows and stopping the truck.

The wheels spun out under them and smoke from the tires began to fill the garage. The undead around the truck now focused on Mr. Cook, who was standing in between two walls of undead making their way toward him. Undead were piling under the garage door and now fighting to get out of the house door and into the garage.

Naomi pushed the blue truck into drive and moved forward next to Mr. Cook. He made eye contact with her. He stood perfectly still as Naomi pushed the truck back into reverse and began to move backward. The old man looked at Naomi and said as if he were saying a prayer, "God, please forgive me." He put the barrel under his chin.

The truck moved backward as Naomi watched Mr. Cook pull the trigger. Nothing happened as hands came within inches from grabbing him. He looked panicked. She saw him pulling the trigger over and over, hoping the gun would fire and relieve him of the death he was about to experience. Hands covered him and pulled him down to the ground. He screamed in fear, pain, and agony as the undead began to eat him alive.

The Chevy hit the bottom of the roll-up door again, pulling it further from the tracks and then releasing them from the garage. They flew backward, running over the rough ground as they drove off the drive way and over whatever ghouls happened to be behind them.

Naomi stopped the truck in the middle of the yard and turned the headlights on, which revealed hundreds of undead wrapping around the house. The only clear area was the path the truck had made, full of undead that were crushed, writhing, trying to get back to their feet.

Hundreds of glowing eyes turned towards the vehicle and focused on the lights. The undead that were walking around the house and not trying to get into the garage turned to the truck. She spun the wheel away from the house and toward the main gate. The headlights shone on the open front gate, and Naomi felt relief wash over her. She saw no undead by the gate, and as she made it onto the street, she saw that it was clear.

Chapter 10

Trust

"Just over the bridge is Good Hope Landing," Eric said as he swung his heavy backpack over his shoulders. "I know a guy from there. We could stop by and hopefully get some rest."

A cool breeze on the bridge blew over their faces and gave both of them a sense of relief from the hot September sun. The first few steps on the bridge were easy. The bumpers of the jam-packed cars were either touching or so close they could not shimmy between them, so they walked on top of them. A quick look through the vacant vehicles and Eric began to imagine all the people trying to move closer to the car in front of them, honking and hollering at each other, thinking that they could move a little bit faster. He thought about the people trying to leave, looking at their rearview mirrors, seeing waves of travelers fleeing their cars and a mob of undead running or shuffling relentlessly after the fleeing travelers. Some of the vehicles were so close to each other they would not have been able to open their doors, making climbing out the windows the only option. They peered into a few cars with interiors covered with random body parts and blood. No bodies were left in them, but by the looks of the broken windows, Eric could picture zombies reaching in with gnashing teeth and grasping claws that grabbed at anything alive.

"We'll stick to the right side of the bridge. That way we only need to watch straight ahead and to our left," Eric said as he guided Drew to the right side of the bridge. He thought of everyone leaving their possessions and running straight ahead, away from the mob of undead. How many families were separated during this time, and how many families were trampled by the retreating travelers? The road was relatively clean, meaning there were no bodies and too much bloodshed on this part of the bridge. They had become used to the bridges and main roads filled with mutilated corpses with hardly any muscle left on them. As they passed a light-blue Saturn, they noticed a blue cooler left in the back seat.

"Score," Drew said and reached for the cooler. He struggled a little bit to remove it, but pulled it free from the hot car. Upon inspection, the cooler contained a few sandwiches that were green with mold, a couple bags of chips, and a couple plastic-wrapped oatmeal cookies sitting in a puddle of dirty water. Drew grabbed one of the oatmeal cookies and tore open the wrapper. This was the first time Eric had seen him smile since before his mother's death. Drew looked up with his cookie in his hand, and the smile on his face reached from ear to ear. Eric smiled at him and opened one of the bags of chips.

They were coming to the top of the bridge, and the wind began to pick up. It was a beautiful morning, and while they enjoyed the cool breeze, a foul odor of decay hung in the wind. Eric took note that they were downwind from the rest of the bridge and knew they might encounter some unwanted travelers. Drew took note of this as well.

He looked at Eric and held his nose, indicating he could smell the dead. In the panic of the waves of running people, the drivers of the cars had pulled to the shoulder of the road to move up in line faster. The idea had backfired here just like on the road between the auto mechanic's and the Food Lion back in Jacksonville. Eric and Drew approached the first car that blocked their path. It was pulled in front of them on an angle. Eric climbed over the sedan and stood on its hood. From here he could see most of the bridge with the exception the northbound lanes, which were blocked from view by two tractor trailers. From the looks of it, they were standing at the cleanest and most organized part of the bridge. Beyond the sedan lay pools of blood and broken glass from every one of the vehicles, and off in the distance a few zombies could be seen wandered back and forth between the cars.

Eric grabbed hold of Drew's arm, pulled him onto the hood of the sedan, and knelt down on one knee. "We're gonna have to start walking in the middle of the bridge." He pointed to a path between cars down the center. "We can't keep climbing over the cars."

They had to climb over a few cars to get to the middle, and each time they climbed, they timed it so the ghouls were turned away from them. On the down side of the bridge there were obvious signs of a fight with a lot of casualties. They started making tracks in the coagulated blood between the cars, checking every vehicle they passed while trying not to be seen.

In their slow-moving caution, they both jumped when a gnarled hand darted from the front bumper of a car just three feet from Eric's foot. It grabbed a piece of intestine from a lucky corpse that was too badly eaten to become animated. If not for standing next to the tire, Eric might have been spotted.

He signaled Drew to step backwards and move between the two cars on their right to go around this undead passenger. They moved slowly, never turning their backs on the zombie. As Eric stepped in between the cars, he could see the ghoul with the organ shoved in its mouth. The back of its skull was exposed, and part of its grey skin was pulled up over the top of its head.

Moving between the tight squeeze of the cars to the right, Eric focused on getting behind this one and putting it out of its misery. With bat in hand, he moved forward toward the eating undead. Just then Eric felt himself lifted off his feet, and he was pulled back to the car on his right. He slipped on the coagulated blood that was spread in deep puddles next to the car and was forcefully pulled against the car, making the horn go off.

Drew saw the hand reach out from the red Impala's window and pull Eric's backpack into the car. With each pull of the backpack, the ghoul inside the car hit the horn, making it blast. He recognized that Eric was in no immediate danger. His backpack was large and the zombie would not be able to fit it through the window, so Drew quickly scanned the bridge. Undead appeared in every direction, twisting around cars or peering from behind them to see what the commotion was about. One walked directly in front of them from down the bridge. No cars were between them and the surprised undead, and the ghoul took off in a sprint up the bridge toward them. It had been a while since they had seen a runner, and as it ran, it let out a screech.

The horn blasting with each pull acted as a dinner bell for every zombie on either side of the bridge. Drew thought that the undead from the town on the other side of the bridge were leaving their houses just to visit this dinner. He took his hatchet from his belt and tried to get a shot on the unbreakable hold of the ghoul's hand, but the backpack was pulled too far into the window . Eric struggled to get the pack off, but every time he went to stand, the tug of the backpack made him slip on the coagulated blood. Drew opened the back door and climbed in behind the undead driver.

The ghoul, still buckled into the driver's seat, was reaching across its body and grabbing hold of Eric's pack with its right hand. The ghoul looked as if zombies had eaten his entire left side. He was missing his left arm, with nothing but loose, ripped clothing left to cover the exposed left side of his body. The ghoul opened and closed its mouth, trying to groan, but was silent from its throat being ripped away.

Drew raised his hatchet as much as he could in the confined space and swung it down on the ghoul's head. He connected, but did minimal damage because the headrest blocked most of his swing. The undead driver let go of the backpack, though, and twisted in its seat to grab at Drew like an angry parent reaching to slap one of his kids. Drew flinched back, hitting the back seat hard, rocking the car.

Now that Eric was not being pulled back, he shook his backpack off. To his right he saw the running zombie moving faster and the crouching zombie behind the car stand up, the organs it had just eaten falling from its ripped-open stomach and flopping onto the car's hood. Eric saw that this undead could eat the same meal over and over again, simply picking up the contents that fell from its stomach.

Shaking, Eric reached into his belt, trying to pull the pistol from the front of his pants. The running ghoul was getting closer. It wore black pants with no shoes or socks and had a bare chest that revealed multiple deep gashes that spewed lines of black blood. It tore at the cars, pushing itself forward in an attempt to reach its victim faster. Blood and gore sprayed from its mouth as it continually bellowed out its piercing screech.

Eric began to skip backward while trying to pull his stuck pistol from his pants. Finally freeing it, he lined the iron sights of the pistol up with the ghoul's face and pulled the trigger. The hammer fell, but no bullet fired. Eric skipped faster, creating more distance, pulling the trigger frantically, but got the same result and the creature got closer with each step.

Eric turned and began to run. He knew the ghoul was getting closer because the sound of his feet hitting the concrete was getting louder. He tried to examine the pistol while he ran, and he hit a crashed car parked in front of him. He began to climb over the car when he felt two powerful hands grab hold of his shirt and pull him down off the hood of the car. Eric saw that the gun was missing something and finally realized the safety was on. He flipped the safety, revealing the red dot, arming the pistol, and pulled the slide, loading another round.

The ghoul pulled at him as if he were weightless, sending him flying whatever way the zombie pleased. Eric tried to slip from his shirt like a sleeve, but his right hand holding the pistol got stuck in the sleeve.

Drew dodged the flailing ghoul strapped into the driver's seat. It reached behind into the back seat, trying to twist itself free, but the shoulder strap and lap belt kept it tightly in the driver's seat. It arched its back, attempting to break the strap, trying to scream, but black and crimson bubbles gurgled from its mangled throat.

Drew swung his silver hatchet at its face, but most of the swings were stopped by the headrest. Only a few actually connected, and the ones that did dug deep into the creature's skinless face. Drew took another swing with the hatchet and noticed something moving toward the window to his left. Multiple ghouls were making their way toward his window.

They hit the window, making him jump back to the passenger's side while hugging the back seat to avoid the wild swings and reaches of the almost-blind driver zombie. He pressed against the back door and then heard something shuffle behind him. Drew was too slow to react to the hands that reached through the window and grabbed hold of his shoulders. The bony, cold, dead fingers dug deep into his slender shoulders and began to pull him out of the car. Drew tried to slide down into his seat, but the ghoul's deathly tight grip kept him from getting away.

He swung the hatchet above his head and connected with the ghoul as it tried to bite down on him. He pulled the blade out and felt thick blood of the consistency of syrup pour over his head. The ghoul's blood slowly rolled over his eyes. He shut his them as tight as he could and began to wipe frantically. He knew he could not get the blood in his eyes or mouth or he would change. He shoved his axe straight up to the car's roof, connecting with the ghoul again. With his eyes closed he pressed up with his axe, creating some distance between the creature's hungry mouth and its grip. Drew slid to his back and tried to raise his legs in an attempt to press them against the ghoul.

He pressed his feet up to the roof of the car and found the creature's head. Drew could feel the ghoul fighting the pressure he was putting on it. He strained his legs, trying to crush its skull between his feet and the roof of the Impala. The ghoul in the driver's seat grabbed at his legs and tried to pull them toward it. He pressed hard, ignoring the driver, and felt the cushions of the back seat compress under the force of his pushing. He ducked his head under his shirt and strained to crush the zombie's head. He felt a snap, and suddenly his left foot got a little closer to the roof of the car. The creature continued to struggle, but Drew let out a grunt, released the pressure, and pressed hard again. The skull of the ghoul felt like a soda can compressing under his feet, and then cold, thick blood began to crawl down his pants legs.

Blood was still on his face, and he used the bottom of his shirt to remove as much of it as he could, but he was still hesitant to open his eyes. Squinting through loosened eyelids, he looked to the driver's-side windows and saw a sea of bodies banging at the back window and more reaching through the driver's side, climbing over the buckled driver. Hands were reaching around the ghoul that Drew's feet, pressing on the roof, now held up.

The ghoul scratched at Eric, and he continued to swing around, keeping his distance, and pulled the pistol up. He let a few shots out and they all hit the ghoul, but all landed in the stomach or the chest. This slowed the ghoul, but not enough. Quickly the zombie regained its composure and continued to wrestle its victim.

Eric stumbled backward, trying to get out of his shirt, as the ghoul grabbed a handful of blond hair from the top of his head. The creature pushed down on Eric's head, causing him to fall, and then it picked his head up, trying to pull it into his mouth. Eric twisted to his back and grabbed hold of the creature's neck. Every muscle in the ghoul was firing, and Eric could not come close to matching its strength. He pulled the pistol up and fired it above his head wildly. Eric found the ghoul's face with the end of the pistol and then pushed the barrel into its mouth.

The zombie pushed on the pistol, trying to get closer to Eric's head, caring nothing of the gun being pushed down its throat. The metal of the gun's butt dug into Eric's scalp as the ghoul pressed closer to his skull. The rough metal began to scratch his scalp. He fired and recoil of the pistol struck him in the head; the slide caused a deep gash on the top of his scalp. Then he felt the full weight of the beast lie on top of him.

He pushed the ghoul off of him and rubbed his head. The tips of his fingers were lined with bright red blood from his scalp. Blackness started to close in on him, but he forced himself to sit up and look around to see what was going on around him. Ahead of him a group of undead were trying to force themselves into the red Impala that Drew was in.

"Hey! Hey!" Eric screamed at them, trying to get their attention. Then he realized he was still sitting on the ground. Forcing his feet under him, he attempted to stand. The bridge and cars spun in front of him, but he hollered out again. Drew was in that car, and he could not let Rod down. He had been left in charge of Rod's son and he could not let him down.

The few walkers behind the horde hanging in the Impala window turned their attention to Eric. Now he knew he had to do something, so he crawled to the closest car to his left. He stumbled, but when he grabbed the car he climbed over and rolled off the other side, hitting the concrete hard. The undead behind were moving quickly, but he stopped to shake his head, trying to stop the bridge from spinning. The thought of the few undead turning their focus toward him gave him a slight relief, knowing they were not going after Drew. He stood up just in time to see the ghouls reaching over the front of the car.

Feeling his blood make its way back into his legs, he jumped up onto the car behind him and then began jumping across the hoods from one car to the next, making his way back to Drew. The growling and moaning coming from the angry mob made it impossible to hear anything from inside the car, and none of the undead turned toward him except the few chasing him. He began to travel to the car in front of the Impala and noticed bodies quickly making their way up the bridge. Standing on the car in front of the one Drew was in, he was able to make out a body stuck in an awkward position in the back seat.

There were three ghouls on the driver's side of the car, and two of them were trying to squeeze through the front window past the driver. The third was beating on the glass of the rear window. On the passenger's side, one was trying to shove its body past the dead zombie being held up by Drew's feet in the back passenger's side window. The only clear shot was at the zombie looking through the back window.

Eric walked up behind the ghoul and pressed the gun against the back of its head. Pulling the trigger, he dropped it at his feet. The two in the front window began to recoil from the car. Eric grabbed hold of the first one's dirty brown collar, and as soon as its head was free from the opening, he pulled it up and dropped it with a quick bullet to the brain. He grabbed the next one just in time to control its body and executed it the same way. The ghoul in the driver's seat continued to grab at Drew's legs, and as soon as the hot barrel touched the back of its head, it turned. Eric waited until it was completely facing him, pressed the barrel between its eyes, and pulled the trigger.

The slide of the black pistol opened, indicating it was out of bullets. The ghouls he had ducked just moments before were quickly making their way toward him. Eric opened the back door. "Come on!" he screamed, but Drew continued to hold the dead ghoul at bay with his feet. Eric reached in, grabbed hold of Drew's leg, and pulled, but he was no match for Drew's fight-or-flight response, currently in overdrive. His legs were as strong as iron beams holding the ghoul's crushed skull against the roof of the car.

Eric jumped over the car's trunk and kicked the hips of the climbing ghoul. It fell out of the window and onto its back. He tried to force the back passenger door open, but the zombie stuck to the roof stopped it from opening fully.

"Drew, you have to let go!" he screamed. He forced the door open again with a grunt and looked down at the boy. Black blood, as thick as syrup, covered his face in smear marks, and he had his eyes shut tight. Eric leaned close to his face and talked softer and a little calmer. "Drew, it's me, Eric. Let go so we can get out of here." With this, Drew was able to understand, and he released his grip on the crushed zombie.

The door opened fully and jammed into the door of the car next to it. The ghoul Eric had kicked got up and grabbed hold of the door. He grabbed Drew's feet and pulled him out the passenger side. Drew wiped his face franticly. "I can't see. I can't open my eyes!" he finally said after attempting to clean his face again.

"Come with me!" Eric had to scream over the groaning of the reaching ghoul. He took hold of Drew's arm and climbed back over the trunk. The ghouls were close now, and Eric had just enough time to grab his backpack with the rifle tied to it and Drew's bag.

He guided Drew over the next car and looked at the wave of undead coming up the bridge. Between every other car were two or three ghouls making their way up the bridge, and in spots where the cars created barriers, they pooled and began to climb over the obstacles. Every one of them was attracted by the noise and commotion the guys were creating. The boy spit into his hands and tried to clean his face more, but the thick blood just continued to spread, now covering every inch of his face. He spun his backpack around and reached in, looking blindly for his water bottle.

"You're just gonna have to trust me," Eric said. "We're gonna have to jump."

Drew tensed his body, remembering they were at the top of

the bridge. "From up here?"

"No, we can make it down a little, but." The ghouls behind them caught up to them and reached at their feet, banging on the car they were standing on. Eric pulled Drew closer to him, out of reach of the zombies, causing him to drop the water bottle he had just found. "We gotta move until we can get to where we can jump from the bridge." With that, Eric pulled the boy down the front window and onto the hood and then hollered "Jump!" to get him to the next one. They did this until a clear row made by the cars presented itself. Eric held onto Drew's hand, and Drew made sure he was directly behind him. They got to the side of the bridge and were stopped by another set of parked and wrecked vehicles. Eric took this moment to climb and look for another clear path, but no path was available that was free of any undead.

"We're going to have to jump from here," Eric said and then jumped down from the car onto the bridge's surface.

"Give me some water so I can clean my face." Drew patted at Eric's backpack, fumbling for the zipper. Eric was about to give him his water bottle when they both jumped as a ghoul banged on a closed car window next to them. Eric put his backpack back on, fighting off Drew's prying hands.

He pulled him close to the side and looked over the guardrail. The bridge was not as high as he had figured, and then, looking back, he had made it further down the bridge than he thought.

"I need to clean my face, I can't jump," Drew said and then grabbed his pack again.

"We're, like, twenty feet up." Eric was lying and looked back at the water. It was closer to forty, possibly fifty feet. "I'll scream *hold your breath* right before we hit." He stepped up on the side and straddled the guard rail. He helped Drew guide his legs over.

The boy's fingers dug into his arms in sheer terror. Eric put his legs over the side and Drew felt his movements and did the same. Eric looked over the side again and now believed he may have grossly miscalculated the distance to the rolling water. The sound of shattering glass made it easy for Eric and Drew to get over this sudden fear and they both fell. Just before they splashed Eric screamed out, "Now!"

Chapter 11

Here Kitty Kitty

The road was quiet except for the blue Chevrolet's engine and Sam's relentless screaming. Her knees were tucked into her chest, and her hands gripped tightly together, holding her legs close to her body as she continued to scream. "Sam, you're okay now. We're far from that now." Naomi tried to soothe her, but nothing seemed to work. Only when Naomi took a corner a little harder than she normally would have and it knocked Sam off balance, causing her to lean toward her mother, did she momentarily catch herself.

Her screams were turning into hoarse cries by the time she regained her self-possession, and now she sat silent and looking off into the black side roads, past the head lights.

They drove for almost an hour along old side streets and dirt roads that were only traveled by the local community. Naomi had decided to go to Fuzzy Pop Pop's house instead of her ex-husband's. After seeing the news broadcast and witnessing firsthand what the undead could do, she had decided that going to her father's, Sam's grandfather's, would be safer than heading to her ex-husband's apartment.

There was no traffic nor any abandoned vehicles between Mr. Cook's and Fuzzy Pop Pop's neighborhood, but the closer the houses got together, the more abandoned vehicles started to pile up. They didn't see any undead until they were forced to drive onto someone's grass to get around a car that was stopped in the middle of the road. There were no vehicles in front of the house, but both of the front doors were open, and it looked as if whoever was in the car had just jumped out in a hurry and left it behind. That was, until they got around it and saw multiple mauled bodies lying in a heap of bloody body parts. In the middle of the heap something was moving. Sam quickly looked away and breathed in rapidly and deeply, as she had seen a hand reach above the bodies as if trying to escape its fleshy cage.

Fuzzy Pop Pop's was just a few more blocks ahead, and Naomi was able to make out a group of cars that were stopped, facing in every direction. Naomi thought that the congestion was just past the street where her father lived, or at least she hoped it was. This was the house where she had spent most of her high school years. She was very familiar with the neighborhood.

As they slowed and approached the clogged street, she realized that the congestion was right before her father's street. She decided to turn down the one before that. Her plan was to drive down the block and come up the other way. Making the left down the street, she glanced at the houses on her left and saw four undead with their arms outstretched making their way across the corner lot's lawn. The engine roared a little louder now as her foot pressed the gas a little harder to put more distance between herself and the approaching undead. The streets were eerily quiet, but as she moved down the block, dark shapes began to appear from the shadows of open doors and low hanging trees. Curse this old Chevy's loud engine!

At the end of the block she instinctively turned her right blinker on, as if she were driving in normal traffic. She came to a stop when her right turn was blocked by vehicles parked in the middle of the road. "Fuck," Naomi said under her breath, but it was loud enough to wake Sam from her trance.

Samantha had looked straight ahead for the entire hour they were on the road, but had never once acknowledged the fact that they were not going to her father's. Now she looked back and forth, confused as to where they were. "Where are we?" she asked with her sore throat and raspy voice.

"Fuzzy Pop Pop's is the street next to this one. I think we may have to cut through one of these yards to get to it." Naomi was hesitant because she knew the backlash Sam was about to give her.

"I thought we were going to Dad's?" She cleared her throat and each word was forced.

Naomi expected Sam to explode, but did not know how to tell her any other way: "Your father's place has too many of them."

"No! You just don't want to go there. You don't want to go because you think he would fucking take me with him instead of you." The last words were barely audible.

"You need to start thinking about who the hell you're talking to." Naomi's anger swelled in her. "I should leave your spoiled ass here. I'm trying to get us someplace safe and all you can do is curse me and give me a hard time."

"You hate him, you want him to die!" Sam was screaming as loud as she could, but it came out as a raspy, barely-audible whisper.

When Naomi faced her livid daughter, something caught her attention out of the corner of her right eye. She turned and looked out the broken back window to see ten undead walking down the middle of the street. Then there came a groan that seemed to be louder than their argument. Sam was still ranting in incoherent whispers as Naomi slammed the old Chevy into reverse. "You need to shut up now," Naomi barked, and Sam turned around, terror halting her barrage of insults.

Naomi turned the wheel to the left and crashed the truck bed into a parked car behind them. She turned the lights off as the undead stumbled closer and began to groan with excitement. Each zombie's groans made the others try to move faster, though they kept bumping against each other. The zombies' shadows reached into the passenger-side window and wrapped around Samantha.

The moon was low and shone on the ghouls' backs, elongating their shadows down the street and into the truck.

The interior lights shone and shocked their eyes for a split second as Naomi opened her door, then fumbled with the radio and looked for a CD button. She tried to stay calm, but years of not having had a cassette player in any of her vehicles confused her until she was able to recognize the play button. She took a leap of faith that Mr. Cook would have some type of tape in the player. She pressed the button hard, and the old familiar sound of the tape winding and beginning to play filled her with hope. Quietly inside the truck, "Let It Be" by the Beatles began to play. Naomi turned the radio up as loud as it would go and slid out of the vehicle. She held her hand out for Sam's and felt her daughter squeeze it as she turned to look behind her. They both slid from the driver's-side door and jumped into the shadows of the parked vehicles.

Zombies from the parked cars and from deserted houses started to emerge like hungry undead Beatles fans, making their way towards Paul McCartney's voice. Naomi and Sam crouched between the bumpers of two vehicles as ghouls walked past them, focused on the music coming from the truck. Sam held onto her mother tightly, breathing loudly. Naomi tried to maintain her own breathing and was glad she had turned the music up. She was hoping the volume would drown out her daughter's frantic breaths.

Naomi pressed her face against Sam's and whispered, "We are going to run between the houses and cut through one of the yards to get to Fuzzy Pop Pop's." She held onto her daughter's hand. "Are you ready?"

Sam did not respond, but looked up at her.

"Ready. I won't let go." Naomi got up to a squatting position and looked over the hood of the car in front of her. What she saw shocked her and made her legs weak. When they had run from the truck, only a few undead could be seen—the ten from down the street and the few that passed them between the cars. Dread washed over her and clung to her when she saw that the small group had turned into a horde of undead that easily numbered in the hundreds, clawing and beating on the truck. She lost hope after seeing the mass in front of her. Sam squatted as well and felt the same anguish as her mom did. Naomi looked toward the houses and then to their left. Sam pointed in that same direction, indicating that it was clear.

Naomi acknowledged her and said, "It's, like, the fourth or fifth house." She got up, ignoring the pain in her neck, and began to run. The undead on the outside of the swarm turned and began to groan. Sam and Naomi were sprinting past the horde, and something caught their attention and sent shivers down both of their spines. A sound from the groaning mass resonated louder than the entire horde's groaning. A shrill, high-pitched screech that sounded as if it had come from the bowels of a demonic harpy came from the crowd.

They continued to run, but both of them turned to look behind them. Pushing over the undead that now faced them was a woman with blood-matted hair that had hardened and formed to her face. She pushed her way through the crowd and took off in a crazed sprint toward them. Naomi turned her attention to the houses and saw an open gate on a white-picketed, six-foot privacy fence between two houses. It was short of their destination by a few houses, but it was going to have to do right now.

The screaming ghoul was gaining on them quickly as it made precise steps over the ground; whereas the lumbering zombies would easily stumble on any small hole, this one quickly regained its balance and continued the pursuit after every misstep.

Once inside the yard, Naomi turned to close the gate, but Sam held tight to her hand and wanted to continue running. Naomi pulled her arm away, but her daughter's strength had grown tenfold, and she had to peel her hands off. "Let go!" Naomi hollered just before she pried her fingers loose. Reaching out from the yard she began to pull the gate shut. It scraped the rough ground and got caught on some of the earth, making Naomi pick up on the fence in order to pull it closed. The crazed ghoul swung wildly in a strange balancing act as it lurched forward with each step. The door was still a foot from being fully closed and was held open by large tufts of unkempt grass. Naomi lifted and pulled, but was unable to free it. Just then, the woman threw her body against the door slamming it shut and locking her out of the yard.

The creature pounded the white plastic fence and screamed in frustration. Naomi did not test the door and was not sticking around to find out if it was going to hold up against the assault. Instead she took hold of Sam's hand again and turned her focus back to Fuzzy Pop Pop's. They had to clear one small chain-link fence before getting to her father's, but as they got to their destination, they saw the back door was ajar.

The back door to Fuzzy Pop Pop's single-family home was partly open, but the house was the same as Naomi had always remembered it. As they entered the back door, the odor of old cellar desperately trying to be covered by the scent of potpourri filled their nostrils. The house was in the same shape it always was in: organized chaos.

"Stay here." Naomi moved into the next room, trying to be as quiet as possible but fast at the same time. She checked to make sure the front door was locked and was surprised to see that it was not. She locked it, pulled back the front window's curtain, and scanned the street, searching for her father's teal-green Nissan Sentra.

There were a few scattered vehicles in front of some of the houses, but none was her father's. There was a car parked in front of the house and she recognized it as one of the neighbors'—or at least she believed it to be.

Across from the front door, behind Naomi and to her left, was the stairway that led to the second floor. She stood on the burgundy carpet at the bottom of the stairs and talked softly up them. "Hello?" She waited for a reply. "Hello?" No sound came in reply, so she waved Sam deeper into the house.

Sam locked the back door behind her, sat down on the grey recliner next to the steps, and began to cry. Naomi walked over to her and got on her knees. She reached forward and pulled her head against the side of her face and hugged her. They both cried for what seemed like hours, until both of their eyes were bloodshot. Sam broke from the hug first and sat back in the recliner and quickly fell asleep. Naomi pulled a blanket from the back of the couch and lay down watching Sam. She was curled up as tight as she could make herself. The tighter she made herself into a ball, the less body exposed to the atmosphere, the safer she felt. Her panting began to relax and her tense body began to unfurl itself as the sound of the screaming ghoul died out. Naomi watched as her tired daughter finally submitted to the sleep she desperately needed.

They both awoke as the sun beat down on the front of the house. The window over Naomi welcomed the sun and allowed a small sliver of light to shine directly on her eyes. Sam was already up and acted as if last night had never happened. She sat in the brown recliner scribbling on something that was hidden behind her pulled-up knees. Sam rocked the recliner back and forth by the simple up and down movement of her toes. *How could she go through something like this and not be affected by it the following morning?* Naomi thought. She also wondered how she herself would have acted when she was thirteen. Maybe now that she had to support her daughter, she had more to worry about—she was forced to make the decisions.

Sam seemed to be just fine and began writing on a notepad that she had found in the house somewhere. Sam had started a diary in the few days that they stayed at Mr. Cook's, but because they had to leave so quickly, all the writing she had done was left behind.

Naomi tried to sit up, but her body wanted no part of it; her back tightened to the point that she could not physically move, but she did manage to position the blanket to prevent the light from blinding her.

She looked to Sam and saw that she had just pulled something from her mouth; it looked to be a clear bottle. "What's that?"

Sam looked at her as if she were asking a stupid question. "Water."

"Where did you get it?"

"The fridge."

"Is there more?"

"Yes."

Naomi now knew she would never be as carefree or calm as her daughter, because already first thing in the morning she was getting sick of her one-word responses. She felt her temper begin to flare, but she breathed and quickly calmed herself. "Could you grab me one?"

Sam scribbled one last thing and got up. Naomi listened to the refrigerator door open and then slam shut. Sam returned with a clear bottle of water in her hand. "You have to hold your breath to drink it. The fridge smells horrible."

Naomi chuckled and it sent small spikes of pain through her. "Don't make me laugh."

"It smells like something died in there."

"Because something probably did. All that food is rotting away." She opened it and began to drink. "You were right, it does smell bad. Tastes good though. Thank you."

"Are we going to leave today?"

"I don't think so."

****

The door was open, but it was getting late, and Eric and Drew needed somewhere to rest their heads. The temperature was dropping and the humidity seemed to be dissipating, which was a huge relief. They both thought they might actually be able to get a good night's sleep for once.

The house was in complete disarray. The trinkets that normally sat happily locked in a glass cabinet now lay smashed with sharp edges pointing up, waiting to impale the feet of an undead passer. The scent of death was vague, but lingered in the breeze of the broken windows. It seemed as if just recently the undead had visited this house looking for dinner.

Walking to the back of the house, Eric cautiously stepped into the kitchen. The first cabinet he opened was full of canned goods: beef stew, canned peaches, pears, peanut butter—he was in heaven. It was like looking down on a freshly-laid Thanksgiving table.

Drew stayed close to him, and Eric gave him one of the cans of beef stew. "We're gonna eat good tonight."

Eric was ready to dive into the cabinet and open a few cans for himself right then and there, but he knew they needed to secure the house first.

The main floor and upstairs were zombie-free. There was one closed door upstairs, and Eric thought this could be a child's room. He had already been through two rooms, one a master bedroom and the other one obviously a spare, judging by the drab décor. Eric thought back on what he had witnessed at Kimberly's house back in Georgia. A sweet middle-aged woman had lured them in to feed her undead son. Every time he came to a closed door, the image of a dead, blond-haired, blood-caked little boy seemed always to be standing on the other side.

He stood now in front of a white door that had a splintering crack down the middle like a lightning strike. Eric held his breath and moved his ear up to the door. The beating of his heart seemed to rise up against him, and he thought it was pounding louder this night—more than normal, at least. He exhaled slowly, trying to maintain the volume of breath flowing from his mouth. He ran his bat down the door, just loud enough for something inside to hear.

After listening for a few seconds with Drew waiting patiently with signs of exhaustion showing on his face, Eric stepped back with his bat at the ready and opened the door. To his relief, it was a child's room minus any undead children. The room had been destroyed. Scattered clothing littered the floor and ripped World of Warcraft posters hung from the walls.

These caught Drew's attention, and he started to inch closer to get a better look. After Eric looked under the bed and ensured that nothing was in the closet, Drew came in and started sorting through the scattered clothes. Coincidentally, this kid was probably about the same age as Drew, and most of the clothes looked as if they would fit him.

In the kitchen there was a door that led to the basement. Opening the door, Eric saw that a set of stairs led to a pitch-black abyss. Drew agreed to stay at the top and keep lookout. Eric pulled out a Mag Lite from his backpack. The light was beginning to dim, so batteries were going to be the next priority. As he crept into the basement, he saw a classic man-cave. On one of the walls were posters of beautiful half-naked women, and directly across from them were a set of medieval weaponry and a suit of chainmail armor. A computer desk sat in the corner of the room, and next to that was a brown suede couch. Eric pulled a battle axe off the wall. It was very sharp, but very heavy. Most of the other weapons, he could tell, must have been picked up from the local flea market. Eric knew if he were to swing them at any of the undead they would more than likely fly apart; besides, they all were stamped *Made in Pakistan* along the blades, indicating they were for show and not for actual use. Still holding onto his aluminum baseball bat, he thought it would probably still be his best choice.

From the corner of his eye, Eric saw a large wooden shaft protruding from behind the arm of the couch. He pulled the handle from behind the arm and found a handmade axe with a blunt hammer on one end and, opposite the hammer, a handmade crescent-axe head. The handle was lined with black metal buttons that made gripping the axe easy.

It looked as if this weapon had been handmade by the owner of the house, or whoever stayed in the basement. With a handle made of wood and about three feet long, the axe definitely beat his bat. "Gonna get medieval on their ass," he whispered in his best tough-guy whisper.

The chainmail, from the looks of it, was roughly his size. The idea of walking around in a suit of armor made him think back to his younger years, sitting around a table, playing Dungeons and Dragons with his friends. *This could prove useful,* he thought. Someone took a lot of time to loop these small rings together, and he could guarantee they never thought *this may become useful during the zombie apocalypse.* The armor was heavy. It weighed between forty to fifty pounds and Eric was determined to try it on, but first it was time for dinner.

****

Empty cans littered the cluttered wooden dining-room table. Beef stew was still evident on Eric's face, and the red tomato sauce from the canned ravioli covered Drew's lips and up his cheeks, extending his smile. They both sat back in their seats with their stomachs swollen. In front of each of them was a clean white plate that the food had never actually touched. The excitement of actual food and not a leathery protein bar had made the act of pouring the food out excruciating. They could not bear to spend those few seconds on postmodern politeness.

Eric opened his bag and placed a couple cans of peaches and

ravioli into it. "I suggest you do the same." He nodded to Drew's bag, which sat on the chair next to him.

"I think I'll sleep in tomorrow. It's supposed to be nice," Drew said from his food coma as he struggled to raise his arms to reach for his bag.

"How do you know the weather's gonna be good tomorrow?"

"Because I want it to be."

"Sounds good to me." Eric stood up with a groan and stretched his back, then followed it with a yawn. "Did you want to take the upstairs bedroom? I was going to crash right here on the couch."

"I think I'm going to take the master bedroom," he said proudly. Drew felt the need to prove that he could be independent now that his father was no longer with him.

This came as a shock to Eric, for he did not like the thought of sleeping alone, but was not going to argue with him. "If that's what you want. I'll be down here if you need me," he said trying to hide his disapproval.

As Eric closed his eyes and Drew had just made himself comfortable directly above him. They both heard a series of "PSSTs!" from outside, as if someone were trying to coax a cat to come to them.

****

Naomi lay on the couch watching Sam at the front window. "Get back from there before one of them sees you," she said as she pulled her covers up to her chin.

Sam was looking out the large front window from behind a slightly opened curtain at all the other houses on the block. This night was brighter than most of the other nights and she wondered why the sun couldn't reflect off the moon like this every night.

Fuzzy Pop Pop, Naomi's father, was known for his sense of

humor, the impossibility of embarrassing him, and his pepper-colored beard. His house was littered with pictures of Naomi and Sam, his only daughter and only granddaughter, but now many of the frames were broken and scattered across the house. Naomi planned on cleaning up the house and collecting some of the pictures and some sentimental items as soon as her neck and back felt better.

Most of the other houses on the street had been broken into. Either their doors were smashed in or the windows were broken. Sam thought about her friends who used to live in those houses and play on these streets. Her mind raced with the thoughts and memories of the kids playing on the sidewalks, and she wondered what they were doing now. The thought of her friends being zombies crossed her mind, but because she had not seen a child zombie yet, she was able to convince herself that children did not become zombies. She wanted to believe they were all together in some safe area playing and eating all the foods she was craving.

She watched the house directly across the street from her, thinking that soon she would see a ghoul pass one of the upstairs windows. The house looked as if it were a ghoul itself. It was a red-brick single-family house with broken windows darkened by shadow and a black hole where the door had once stood. The open doorway resembled a sad, elongated moan and the dark upstairs windows resembled the black eye sockets of the undead. If there was any place one of these undead would be hiding it would be in that house, she thought. Sam did note, though, that one of the houses across the street had its front door shut. She believed that the door had been open when they had arrived, but now it was closed.

Even with this strange opening and closing of doors, she had to admit that this area was pretty quiet, with the exception of the random groan off in the distance. The truck's battery had died many days ago, and since then, not a single undead had been spotted on the streets. She pulled away from the window as her mother asked and opened up her notebook. With immense boredom setting in deeper and deeper, she decided to start keeping a new diary. She propped a flashlight between her cheek and shoulder and began writing.

Sam continued to write, sitting on the recliner, until she heard a familiar sound from outside. The sound was from a cat outside of the house meowing. She quickly weighed the risk of getting caught looking out the window when her mother had just told her not to. She looked to her mother, who was fast asleep on the couch, and decided the risk was worth it. As Sam leaned out of the recliner, a small snore escaped her mother's closed lips, confirming her decision. She crept to the window and pulled back the curtains just enough to see out through one eye. Huddled next to the front passenger-side tire of a car just to the right of their driveway was an orange tabby cat with white paws, meowing.

She got up and slowly opened the front door, very carefully so it did not make a sound. Lowering her body, she called for the cat quietly in a low, repeated, "Psst!" The cat acknowledged her presence with a stare, but did not move from the tire. She rubbed her thumb across her fingers, acting as if she was holding some sort of treat, and called with the same "Psst!"

From behind her, she heard her mother get up from the couch and call her name. Sam knew she only had seconds, so she stepped out to the front porch and began to walk towards the cat, rubbing her fingers and making the *Psst* sound, trying to lure the cat to her.

"Sam." Naomi was standing at the door and saw her daughter leave the front porch.

Samantha turned and saw her standing just inside of the doorway, with nothing but the screen door separating them. Naomi did not open the screen door or move out to the porch, but stared at her, feeling rage build up inside her.

Sam moved faster towards the cat, thinking if she got the cat quicker she might not be in as much trouble. She moved out to the front lawn, further from the house, getting closer to the orange tabby.

Naomi walked out to the end of the porch, looking back and forth through the neighborhood as if she were walking across a busy street. "Samantha, I swear to God, if you don't get your ass back in this house..." The threat was real, but she didn't know what she could do to punish her. Staying in the house was no longer a punishment—that was just what they had to do. There were no computers or iPods, so Naomi truly had no idea what she could take away, because everything had already been taken away.

Sam knew she was going to be in trouble, but she was almost to the tabby. She was already thinking about names she could call it and what they had to eat that she could feed it. As she got within a foot of grabbing the tabby, the hair on the cat's back stood at attention and it let out a hiss, showing its yellow fangs. Sam recoiled, but then recognized that the cat was not hissing at her. Sam turned in the direction the cat was facing and saw an undead man come walking through the bushes that were planted against the side of her house. The man was bald with a short black goatee. His blue coveralls were caked with blood and dirt from the roads he had traveled, which made them look bluish grey, matching the complexion of the ghoul's skin. Black veins spread up his neck and stretched across its face. The ghoul was fixed on Sam and easily pushed the last little bit of brush out of its way.

Naomi heard the bushes rustling and turned to the end of the porch in time to see a bald-headed man moving along the end of the porch. It was enthralled with getting the small girl and did not notice Naomi.

Sam saw the cat dart from the shadow of the tire and run out into the street, and the zombie opened its mouth and looked as if it were going to scream, but nothing came out. Moving closer, it inhaled and let out a bellowing groan that echoed off of every house in this quiet neighborhood.

Naomi ran to the edge of the porch and kicked the zombie through the railings and connected with its temple. Not flinching from the impact, the ghoul turned its attention to Naomi and reached through the railing, trying to grab her legs.

Sam ran back up the porch and grabbed her mother to pull her back into the house. The sound of moaning rolled down the street as one ghoul answered the next. Sam turned as she tried to pull her mother and focused her attention on the eerie house directly across the moonlit street.

The bald zombie continued to groan, and with every noise that came from it, Naomi was quick to kick down on its face. The ghoul reached clumsily up through the bars, trying for her legs. Naomi, standing on the porch, had a huge advantage in dodging his grasps, and continued her barrage of kicks.

Never taking her attention off the nightmarish house, Sam watched as a figure emerged in the open doorway. "Mom, we have to go," she said as she pulled on her waist. Naomi was deaf to her daughter's command. Filled with adrenaline, she no longer felt the pain in her back and wanted this creature to suffer for being what it was. Holding onto the top railing and keeping her left leg back, she kicked furiously at the ghoul with her right.

Sam watched as these quiet streets quickly began to explode with excitement. The figure from the nightmarish house was now moving toward them, and lone bodies made their way toward them from both sides of the street. The moon cast shadows of these ghouls in the middle of the street, making them appear much closer to them.

"Mom, they're coming!" Sam yelled, snapping her out of her trance of rage.

Naomi, now conscious of her surroundings, was horrified at the sight of multiple undead lumbering down the middle of the street. There was a large crowd walking almost shoulder to shoulder coming from the south side of the street. From the other end of the street they were scattered, and if Naomi briefly thought about running through them, once Sam interrupted her aggression-filled trance she quickly began to feel the pain of her injury.

Sam stood on the porch and watched the undead begin to circle around the railings of the deck.

Naomi quickly had the idea of running out the back. Sam, still holding onto her, pulled her through the door. They ran through the house, through the kitchen, and to the back door. They opened the door and, to their surprise, looked down on a dozen undead that were at the bottom of the back porch steps. The undead were being drawn to the front of the house, but quickly changed direction toward them. Naomi's stomach rushed up her throat and her knees got weak as hopelessness cloaked her. She thought this was how she was going to die. She was going to be eaten by her father's neighbors. Sam pulled her mother back around just in time for her to hear the first undead in the front of the house run into the screen door.

The screen door was almost as loud as the undead that surrounded the house. The sheet metal quickly began to fold in on itself as the weight of the zombies pressing against it tore it down and pulled it from the hinges.

Like a beacon of light, the stairs that led to the second floor caught both of their eyes. Naomi slammed the back door, not making the same mistake twice, and ran to the stairs. The horde of undead lunged at them as soon as they reached the first step. The first ghoul missed and fell forward, causing the ones directly behind it to fall on top it.

They ran to the first door they saw and closed it behind them. Naomi locked the door and Sam began to push a dresser behind it. This room was Fuzzy Pop Pop's master bedroom. Pictures of Sam and Naomi fell from the dresser as they pushed it to block the door.

The heavy footsteps and bodies that crawled up the steps

shook the small house. The undead groaned with excitement, knowing their meal was within their grasps. Their moaning was becoming louder as more and more began to pile up the steps.

The women stood with their backs against the wall opposite the door, staring at the dresser for a second, and then Naomi tried to pull the bed closer to the door. The room was plain with white pull-up blinds and pink rose-petal curtains. A thick, loose, green carpet carpeted the entire room. After Naomi's first tug at the bed, the muscles in her body refused to let her inflict any more pain upon her body, and she could not muster the strength to even try. Sam pressed her body into the corner of the queen-sized bed and moved it two inches before the carpet grabbed hold of the bed's legs, preventing it from moving. The dresser was lighter, and by picking it up from underneath, Sam and Naomi were able to position it in front of the bedroom door.

The sound of scratching, followed by a thud, signaled that the undead were at the door and wanted more than anything to get in. The thuds became more rapid as more piled against the door. The pounding slowed to a stop as the first few to arrive were being smashed against the door under the weight of the hundred. The door broke from the hinges and the door and dresser started to push forward. Bloody fingers reached through the opening as they tried to force it open more. The carpet started to fold up, creating a small curb that kept it from opening any further.

As soon as the dresser stopped, a crack appeared down the center of the door. Sam and Naomi looked frantically for a place to hide. The closet or under the bed crossed their minds, but quickly vanished. Sam opened the curtains and pulled the white blinds down and began to open the window. She pulled up as hard as she could, but the window did not budge—until Naomi unlocked it. Then the window flew open with ease, and Sam looked out at the horde of zombies, which roared out all at once as if she were some rock star making her first appearance at a concert.

****

Eric moved to the window and slightly pushed the curtain to the side, just enough to peer out with his left eye. He scanned the street, looking for the source of the "Psst!" noise. Across the street and two houses down, a woman stepped out from the front door and onto the front porch. She appeared to be trying to talk to someone, but no one was there. Then from behind a car a figure stood up, and a cat ran from the car and across the street.

Something was moving from the side of the house toward the figure behind the car, and he recognized it, from its jerky movements, to be a ghoul. As the person behind the car ran to the porch, Eric was able to see that it was a second woman. One of the women was very thin and smaller than the other. The one that had come out of the house was tall, a little thicker but very toned. The thought crossed his mind that they might be a mother-daughter duo, because in the moonlight, their long individual braids matched each other's exactly.

As the two women stood on the porch, the ghoul groaned and then more began to answer its call. Drew came running down the steps with his shoes in his hand. "Are we going to help them?"

Eric thought about this for a second in silence as he watched some undead walk past their house. He also remembered promising Rod that he would take care of Drew. "Let's see what happens. They should have a man in there."

"What if they don't?" Drew's voice was filled with excitement and frustration.

Eric felt an anger rise up in him, because Drew was being loud and giving their position away, and also because he was a little scared about having that be them. He had witnessed the old man's house across the street from his get broken into, and when they had attempted to help him, they had almost become victims themselves. "Let's just see how this pans out."

Drew was slipping his shoes on. "You fucking wait. I'm not going to sit and watch two women get eaten." He got up and marched to the front door, but Eric stopped him a little more forcefully than he had intended to.

"Grab my flashlight and grab those liquor bottles downstairs," Eric said. He looked him in the eyes, and Drew instantly knew what he was going to do, but remembered him saying there was no liquor in the bottles. Still, Drew nodded in agreement.

Eric ran to the back of the house and looked at the garage. It seemed so far away, and in fact, it was. It sat in the corner of the lot to his left, at the furthest point from where he was in the yard. He had not paid much attention to it before, but a paved driveway ran from the street and into the yard to the single-car garage. His plan was to run to the garage, grab the gas can for the lawn mower, and make Molotov cocktail bombs with the liquor bottles. He understood that this plan of his would not work if there was no gas can in the garage. He opened the door that led to the large yard and looked around at the other properties. A large wooden privacy fence enclosed the yard, and those surrounding his had the same. He could see the heads of a few undead to his right that were walking in the street to join the growing crowd out in front of his house.

When Eric came back in with a red gas can, Drew had already lined six bottles up on the kitchen table and was cutting up one of the shirts he had collected from upstairs. Eric made a mess filling the bottles, but managed not to get any gas on himself. He reached for a lighter, and then he began to tell Drew what he was going to do. "I'm going to run out and head up the street," he pointed in the direction of the street with a couple zombies walking down it. "I plan on running around the block, since I didn't see any in the other yards and cutting through the yard just behind us."

Eric grabbed the chain mail and picked it up. He was still

breathing hard from the forty-foot dash from the garage and quickly decided he was in no physical shape to be carrying a fifty-pound suit of medieval armor. He did, however, put the pistol in the back of his pants and slide the axe down the right side of his belt. They both looked out the window again, just in time to see the two women climb out the front upstairs window of their house onto a small section of roof and slide away from the window as far as possible. They both tucked their legs close to them, but the toes of their shoes still hung off the edge of the shingles.

When Eric stepped out onto the porch, the undead marched past him, not seeing him and only focused on the meal that was now in plain view for all to see. The street to Eric's left had a small crowd that was bunched together, but the rest of the street, he knew, was maneuverable. The other side of the street was filling rapidly, and he was glad he had planned to head the other way. Eric walked out with four bottles and placed two on the curb just outside the house. He lit the first bottle and walked out into the street. The undead to his left turned their attention to Eric, the closer prey. He held the second bottle to the lit rag of the first and watched it ignite.

Eric took one step, pitching like a professional baseball player, and broke the bottle on the crowd to his left. Instantly they caught on fire. Ten of them moved toward him with outstretched flaming arms. He ran to the house with the two women on the roof—just close enough that he knew he could hit the closest part of the hungry mob—and let the second Molotov cocktail fly. The crowd went up in a flaming inferno. He ran back to the curb where he had set the other two bottles and held the rags close as he attempted to light both at the same time.

Naomi and Sam were both startled to see the middle of the street, just a few houses up from them, go up in flames, and then saw a single man weave past a few ghouls, running toward them with something on fire in his right hand. The man threw this ball of fire toward the horde in front of them. Naomi instantly recognized it as a Molotov cocktail and watched as it shattered, igniting a large number of undead.

By the sound of it, the scattered undead were getting closer, but Eric held his ground, refusing to move until the bottles were lit. He knew once they caught fire he was within grabbing distance and was elated when they finally flamed up. He tossed both of them into the middle of the mass in front of the two women and then turned to look for his escape. The once-scattered horde was now closing ranks, and he looked desperately for a way to get around them, but none opened. He knew he could make it back into the house with Drew, but the flaming group of ten were pushing together. With the closing crowd lighting each other on fire, he did not want to draw any attention toward Drew—especially from the undead that were on fire. He made a break for it, away from the house and toward the houses across the street.

Drew lost sight of Eric when he ran past the high flames of the burning undead and thought about what he was going to do if he were alone. He watched as the undead in front of his house turned away from him and back up the street. This must mean that Eric had made it past them and was making his way away from the house. Eric was the last person Drew knew in this world, so he unlocked the front door just in case Eric couldn't make it and had to come back this way and into the house.

Naomi and Sam both were happy to see that the crowd in front of the house was burning up, and the flames were only getting higher and spreading. As the ghouls moved they would bump into each other, lighting the next one, adding to the heat and size of the inferno. They both watched as the scattered ghouls closed in on their single hero, and they watched as all of the holes that once existed in the crowd began to close. All the undead that were initially going after them turned their focus on this one man. A wall of fire moved toward him from one direction and a closing

171

horde from the other. They watched him run until the trees next to the house blocked their sight of him.

Their thoughts of being rescued quickly went away as the first undead reached out the bedroom window and clawed at them. It leaned out the window and tried to grab at Sam's legs and then began climbing out the window, just to fall into the crowd of undead that was beginning to catch fire. As the fire grew, intense heat began to burn the women's exposed skin. The high flames changed the smell of rotting flesh into that of burnt skin and hair.

Drew watched as the fire began to spread amongst the undead. He wanted to help Eric, but he didn't know what to do. He pictured himself under the roof, hollering for the women to jump, and then pictured them falling into his arms as he rescued them one by one and saved the day.

The house was filled with undead, so going in to rescue them was out of the question. The fires in front of the house were growing rapidly, and he wouldn't make it anywhere near the front before he was consumed. He didn't have an answer, so he ran to the back and watched for Eric. He saw from the open garage door what he believed were the legs of an extension ladder.

Drew kicked the bottom of the driveway's fence to jolt it from the broken concrete slab that held it from swinging freely. The burning ghouls lit the right side of the street, and as he left the back yard, the back of the ladder dragged across the concrete driveway. He took the last two glass bombs sitting on the kitchen table and worked his way toward the stranded women.

The heat on the street was intense, and it was becoming hard to breathe. The closer he got to the house, every breath he took filled his lungs with burning air. Drew faced the house and could see undead moving around from the back side of it; by the time he was able to set up the ladder, they would be exactly where he wanted to be. He dropped the ladder and struggled to get close enough to the burning bodies to light the bomb, while keeping far enough away to keep himself from catching on fire.

The heat on his hand started to bite at his skin, and right before the cocktail bomb's cloth took flame, a figure moved toward him in the inferno. The creature's arms were outstretched, reaching for whatever would land between its fingers. Drew fell backward, spilling the fuel from the first bottle on the street. The ghoul let out a scream, and fire swirled from its mouth as it bellowed. The creature's eyes were open, but all that remained were pits in its burning head. It inhaled to let out another scream, and the fire from around its face and clothes was pulled over its peeling skin and into its gaping maw. It let out another breath of flame, but no sound traveled with it.

Drew crab-crawled back to avoid the contents of the spilled bottle just in time for it to light up. The ghoul dropped onto the newly-lit flame and remained still. Drew took the last bottle from his other hand and lit it on the still zombie. Running to the women's house, he threw the Molotov cocktail at its side into a group of undead that were making their way toward the street. The flame exploded against the zombies, the side of the house, and the bushes along the side of the home.

Naomi and Sam watched this boy risk burning alive while avoiding the undead all while trying to drag an extension ladder toward them. Naomi shuddered when he threw the bomb toward the house, as she knew her father's home would surely catch fire. As the thin boy moved out of sight from the roof, she moved to look over the edge. Over the groaning of the burning ghouls she could barely make out the sound of the extension ladder banging against her parents' house as it was extended.

The top of the ladder almost struck Naomi as it was propped against the house; it caused her to flinch backward. "Climb down!" came from the out-of-breath boy. "I'll get them away from the house!"

Naomi grabbed the ladder, looked over the side, and saw a

burning body lying face down just three feet from the bottom of the ladder. The boy was guiding the rest of the undead into the fire and then trying to lead them away, but as they caught fire, they seemed to lose their direction as their eyes began to burn.

Naomi took hold of the ladder, trying to maintain her balance, and stood off to the side to let Sam climb down. Sam cautiously began to climb down, taking one cautious and concentrating step after the next. Excitedly, Naomi urged her daughter to move faster as one of the zombies made its way onto the roof. It was on its hands and knees, trying to stand, but another zombie crawling onto the roof from the window pushed the kneeling ghoul off the roof and onto the horde below.

Many undead reached for Drew over the porch railing as he led the undead nearest the ladder through the flames, then away from the escaping women. Naomi and Sam made it to the ground as the flames on the side of the house climbed up the siding. Naomi knew the home she had once lived in was going to burn. All of her memories from that house were going to burn up with the undead in it. She wished she could have grabbed a picture of her parents, and for that split second, she realized that she would probably never see her parents again.

The fire was spreading rapidly, and the sky filled with grey and black smoke. They began to cough as the thick smoke hung heavy next to the house. Drew came running around the fire with a look of confidence. He jumped over one of the burning, motionless undead that lay face first in the dirt. Naomi and Sam both watched him run toward them and waited for instructions. "Run!" was the only instruction he gave, and even that he shouted as he passed by them.

They both followed and saw that the fire from the street was spreading amongst the ghouls, jumping from zombie to zombie, and stretching toward the house. The undead on the porch reached for the women as they ran past, and the orange glow of the flame was beginning to lick the underside of the roof that they had just been sitting on.

Drew ran across the street and glanced back to ensure they were behind him. As he looked back, he saw that the wall of fire to his left was gravitating toward him as the undead were pushing through the flames. The zombies were scattering to other houses on the street, and many bushes that lined the street were beginning to go up in flames with the undead bodies lying in them. He ran to the driveway and watched as Naomi and Sam caught up with him. The fire on the street had spread just shy of his driveway, and the few undead that managed to follow the escapees were moving too close to the fire and were completely engulfed and falling before they reached the sidewalk.

When they got to the tall wooden fence, Drew closed it behind them and guided them through the back of the house where he and Eric were staying. Quickly he went to the front window to see how far the fires were actually going to get. The undead that were hit with the first Molotov cocktail were lying in the street with their bodies still aflame. There were no more coming from up the street, but the groans of the undead were still loud coming from the direction of Naomi's house. He heard the back door close and ran back toward it.

He stood next to Naomi and watched her twist the padlock on the door. Drew grabbed hold of the lock and twisted it back before she could let go. "I have to keep this door unlocked. I have a friend who will be coming through, and he can't be out there waiting for one of us to unlock it. He should be back anytime now." From across the street and as they were running, Drew had never realized how tall Naomi was. He had to look up to her as he spoke, and the girl, whom he assumed was Naomi's daughter, was just as tall as he was.

A sudden movement from the back yard startled all three of them as they peered through the windows in the door. Falling from the six-foot privacy fence, a figure of a man was made visible by the bright rays of the moon.

Chapter 12

The Beach

Eric was breathing heavily by the time he got inside the house. "Wow, *that* was interesting," he said as he bent over and put his hands on his knees. He took a large deep breath, stood up, closed the curtains to the back door, and took a look at the two visitors Drew had welcomed in. Eric was taken aback by Naomi's height and then caught a glimpse of her deep-set, dark, emerald-green eyes. For the first time in weeks he found himself thinking about his hygiene. He began to think of how he must smell and whether he was clean or not. He had been bathing when he could, but hadn't washed himself with a wet cloth in a few days, and this meeting with a beautiful woman made him uneasy.

"We can't thank you enough," Naomi said, feeling out of place. She felt Eric's awkwardness and wanted to fill the few seconds of silence. "My name's Naomi," she said to both Drew and Eric. "This is my daughter Sam."

As she spoke Eric put his hand out to welcome her into the house. She accepted the hand like the professional woman she was and squeezed it firmly. "Eric." He threw his hand to Drew. "This here is Drew; if you haven't introduced yourselves yet."

"That was my parents' place across the street." Naomi nodded her head and raised her hand to the front of the house. "They weren't in there. They probably got stuck on the street somewhere going to our house." She looked down at Samantha, who was staring at her, hanging on every word she spoke. Naomi continued to talk, but the volume of her voice trailed off to a whisper. "I don't believe my parents will ever come back to that house." She began to distance herself from her old home. "Their car is gone and now their place is on fire." That broke her composure for an instant, but neither Drew nor Eric caught it. Samantha, however, did, and that caused her to lose hers. "Even if they did come back, they have nothing to come back to." Tears were now pouring from Sam's eyes and rolling over her light-brown cheeks.

Eric was unaware that their house had caught fire and wanted to comfort the two guests, but was not sure how to do it. Naomi didn't give the impression that she was the type of woman that would welcome a hug or even any type of helpful pat. He was not going to approach her daughter, because the vision of an angry mother bear popped into his mind. Instead he took the sympathetic, mournful approach. "I'm truly sorry about your parents." He paused. "I didn't mean to damage their house."

"No need to apologize." Her eyes were glassy as tears continued to well, but she fought them from pouring from her deep emerald-green eyes. "They weren't coming back anyway. I am not going to hold my breath waiting for them."

Eric and Drew thought this was odd, maybe a little heartless, but Drew turned on the part of good host. "Are you hungry?" Drew waited for any reply. "We have all kinds of food in the cabinets."

Naomi refused politely and made her way to the front windows. She watched as her parents' front porch collapsed, sending spirals of burning embers dancing high into the night sky.

Sam joined her and they watched with a long, silent, hypnotic stare as the fire grew larger. Naomi snapped out of it and turned to Eric, who was trying to think of what to say about catching her parents' house on fire. "Whose house is this?" Naomi asked.

Drew looked around the living room, studying his surroundings, looking for an answer. Eric paused, thinking of his reply. He didn't know exactly how to answer and not offend her. He thought about her fragile state of mind and whether she would blow up on him after he told her they had just decided to break in, eat all the food, and sleep in the comfortable beds. "Um, I have no idea. The door was open, and we needed a place to stay until morning." He thought about how he answered her question and continued with a little more buffer, "We were just making our way north and needed a place to stay for the night."

"Where up north?" Naomi asked evenly. With the sudden destruction of her old home, she was swiftly building a new shell around her emotions and learning to adapt. She felt inside that the best way to get over her missing parents and new homelessness was not to care about anything else. She had only one thing she could not turn her cold shoulder on, and that was her daughter.

Eric expected a little confrontation, but it never materialized. "We're going up to Maryland."

"You have a long way, then. Were you planning on walking all that way? The news showed the highways, and they're completely shut down. All the busy or major roads are blocked, and a lot of those things are on them."

"So far we've been traveling by foot. I would really love to find a bike or something, though." Eric looked to Drew. "Maybe we should start looking for some." Drew responded with a shrug. "About a month or so ago, when this first started, I got in touch with my folks, but the phones died, and I haven't heard from them since. I have to see for myself that they are okay."

"What if they're not?" she responded coldly. Naomi was trying to find comfort in her new persona.

Eric was taken aback by this question. It was legitimate, but he didn't know. He had never really thought about the outcome of going home and his parents not being there. Even worse, what if he made it there and they greeted him by trying to eat him? "I don't know. I guess I will travel somewhere else." He didn't know what he was going to do. All that he had ever known was what he has always done, every day waking up and going to work. Every day he would go out with his friends, or go to the local fast food or grocery store to grab a bite. He was used to having some type of agenda that normally consisted of doing something normal. Yes, he had been adjusting to eating on the go with every house that they stopped in, but what was going to happen when he wanted to settle? If he got to his parents' place and they weren't there, was he going to move on? The canned foods would eventually run out in the surrounding neighborhoods, and he now realized that he had no skills to survive on the road or out in the country. Eric did not respond to the question and fell into deep thought about how he was going to be able to survive and what he was going to do after he got to his parents' house.

A few seconds passed by, and they all could see that he was in deep thought and angry with the question. Drew was the first to break this silence. "Are you planning on staying here? You can come with us if you like."

Naomi had some doubts about traveling, but Sam did not. Sam wanted nothing to do with traveling to Maryland. Her thoughts were on her father. They had wasted more than a month staying at Mr. Cook's and Fuzzy Pop Pop's when they could have been out looking for her father.

Sam responded quickly without weighing the options. "We are going to be headed back to find my father."

Naomi was insulted that her daughter would speak for her (knowing she wanted to do nothing of the sort). She responded with, "I think we could go with you." She had to make the decision, not her daughter. Sam wasn't thinking rationally. The more people they had, the better they would be able to survive. Naomi knew that in her state she was no good to Sam and they were going to need someone to get the things they needed. Plus Drew and Eric had proven that they could hold the dead off better than Naomi ever could.

"God! You hate him so much that you want him to die!" Sam

screamed at her mother.

"You saw the news. The apartment complexes were destroyed," Naomi screamed back.

Drew stepped in, in an attempt to lower the noise level and also to justify the mother's not wanting to go to the apartment complexes. "The apartment complexes are in bad shape. There were just too many people living so close, and so many were infected and didn't even know it. My mom came home infected. From the time she walked into the door until the time she turned was a matter of minutes. I don't know when she got bit, but that was just my house. My apartment complex was in complete and utter chaos just before we escaped.

Naomi liked his answer and agreed with him, but Sam didn't care what the excuse or reasoning was for not going to rescue her father.

"I promise we will go back for him, but there are just too many of them out there right now." Naomi swore.

"If you would like, you can travel with us?" Drew asked.

Naomi smiled, Samantha grimaced, but they both agreed to travel with them.

****

Traveling with two new sets of eyes and ears had its benefits, but bringing along different personalities also brought some tense moments. It took them a little longer to get through South Carolina than Eric originally wanted because apparently women need specific items that men generally don't. Eric, Drew, and Sam would use the bathroom outside most of the time and just take toilet paper with them, but on one occasion they had to stop into three different houses so Naomi could find the perfect bathroom to use. She would go outside sometimes, but they had to stop so she could find personal hygiene products. Apparently, to Drew and

Eric's surprise, toilet paper does not always suffice.

Traveling at night was a little different as well. Eric and Drew did not like to travel at night and only did so when they had no choice. Securing buildings in the dark was difficult and they tried to avoid it, but sometimes they would have to push the envelope. Having two extra bodies, one of which was generally in pain during most of the time they traveled, forced them to begin securing a building or house two, sometimes three hours before nightfall even crept over the horizon. Because of this it took them a month of travel to get through South Carolina and partway into North Carolina.

One good thing about having Naomi around was that she knew exactly where she was going and how to get there. Originally Eric had been thinking about following just to the side of Highway 95, but Naomi convinced them to travel east to the Outer Banks and then north. This would take them through a vacation spot that would more than likely be deserted. Once people had found out what was happening, they would have rushed to get home, and more than likely most of the people on the Outer Banks would have left.

Naomi continued to talk about how it would be more than one hundred miles of peace and quiet once they got onto the main road of the island, but getting onto that road proved to be rather hair-raising. Naomi was right about everyone trying to leave the island, and apparently they had all decided they were going to leave at the same time. The bridge off of the island was a maze of cars that filled both lanes and were pressed against one another, so tightly packed that the travelers walked from hood to hood across the bridge.

There were no signs of any physical struggles with the undead on the bridge, but although Eric crouched down and looked through the front and rear windows of each car they walked over hoping to see a cooler or maybe a bag with a few canned goods, these cars held almost no useful items.. Still, in the past, every time they'd encountered a traffic jam, bloody handprints had covered the vehicles and shattered glass had littered the road from the zombies beating their way into the undead's canned goods. There was something comforting about these wrecks' lack of gore.

As they came to the end of the bridge, the cars started to space themselves out a little more, and there was evidence that people had already looted these vehicles. To think that no one else was doing the same thing Eric and Drew normally did was ridiculous, but until now there had been little evidence of others looting vehicles. Eric was disappointed to find they had competition, but he kept it to himself. He glanced back at Drew and saw that he was on the same mission, looking in the windows, searching for food.

After crossing the bridge, they passed a set of stores and began to make their way north up the main street of the Outer Banks. Eric thought about the other people looting the vehicles, and what they must look like filled his head. He saw images of people with wild hair and pieces of metal and rubber tied to their bodies with ripped pieces of old leather belts like in a post-apocalyptic movie, but then he caught a glimpse of a shiny black Mercedes in the driveway of one of the huge beach houses and lost that thought.

He had never been one for camping, or hunting, or scavenging for food, but he believed he could probably do it better than the lawyers or doctors who were the likely owners of that car. Then something occurred to him: *All these cars have been ransacked and left to sit for however long, but this vehicle hasn't been touched.* It was at that moment he glanced at the upstairs window and saw a small figure dart behind the curtains. He believed it was a child in white clothing, but it moved so fast he could not be sure. One thing he did know was, it was no zombie, because it did not start bashing its head against the window to reach them.

He walked silently for a few moments and then said quietly, just loud enough so the other three could hear, "We're not alone."

Naomi moved away from one of the cars on the side of the road and joined the rest of the group walking in the middle of the street. "What do you mean?"

"I believe some people decided to stay. There are people in the windows," Eric said, looking straight at the road to avoid the group looking up into the windows. "Don't look, but the house back there had a little kid in it."

"All the windows are open in most of these houses," Naomi said after a few seconds of looking around. Not all the houses had cars in the driveway, but in a lot of the houses, curtains could be seen blowing with the sea breeze through the screens of the open windows. This was another thing Eric could add to the list of things Naomi was good at: She was very observant. Another thing Naomi pointed out as they walked was that one house had the bottom-floor windows secured from the inside with wood that was either pressed against or nailed into the frame work of the window. "People use the AC over here, they don't open windows. If people left when this first happened, they wouldn't have taken the time to open them."

The wind was picking up, and the evening sun was beginning to hide behind dark clouds. The wind picked up sand that was lying on the ground, and all of them had to squint as they walked forward. "We're going to have to find a place to stay pretty soon," Naomi said as she studied the sky.

"I don't like this area, let's travel up a little more. Every once in a while I see something in the windows," Eric said as he kept focusing on the road in front of him. "At least we know they're not zombies."

"Really? How do you know that?" Sam asked.

"They're not falling out of the windows," Drew answered quickly for Eric.

After all of them began to feel uneasy, they decided to walk along the shore until they found a place they wanted to stay tonight. They were all amazed at how empty the beach was. For as far as they could see, there was not a soul on the sand. Eric studied one of the houses, and as he looked up, a drop of water landed on his cheek, and then one of the children made the obvious comment of how it was beginning to rain.

Eric looked up at a three-story beach house and watched the clouds move quickly above the building, giving them the illusion that it was falling over them. Naomi was looking to see which house seemed to be vacant, but Eric was looking to see which was the biggest and most luxurious.

The clouds were turning from grey to a deeper black, and Naomi began to get impatient with Eric's search for the perfect house. "Eric, we're staying in that house there." She pointed to the house just past the one Eric was inspecting. The windows were closed and there was no vehicle in the drive way. Naomi figured more than likely the buildings whose windows were open were the inhabited ones. She assumed the buildings that were closed must have been that way since the beginning.

A set of wooden stairs led from the beach to a balcony attached to the second and third floors of the house Naomi had selected. They looked into each of the ground-floor windows and saw no traces of life. There was a front and back door on the main level and then two sliding glass doors that led into two large bedrooms. These were all locked, and Eric thought about how easy it would be for a zombie to just come walking through one of these doors and how much safer one of the more luxurious houses would have been or at least that's what he wanted to believe.

After trying each of the doors and windows, the group found that the third floor door on the back balcony was open. This floor had a large vaulted ceiling with large windows that faced the beach. A big kitchen was opposite a large sliding glass window that led to a balcony with three plastic reclining chairs. A master bedroom featured its own bathroom and a sliding glass window that opened onto the large balcony. A huge T.V. over a fireplace and three oversized grey and blue couches sat in a large entertainment area. The first thing Drew noticed was the X-Box 360 under the T.V. and a large assortment of games.

This house would have been Eric's and Naomi's perfect getaway if the situation were different. Now, with stairs that led to each floor and the many large windows, this could be a deathtrap if a horde of undead were coming in their direction, but this building was an older one and built to last: it had survived many hurricanes and the windows, though old, were sturdy with multiple panes. The back of the house butted up against a thickly wooded area, and only the tops of a few houses past the woods could be seen.

After making a round of the house, Eric and Drew secured each door and window. On the main floor, Eric gazed into the woods from one of the bedroom windows. Even though they hadn't had any contact with any undead here on the islands, he just could not feel comfortable with the thick forest behind him. The entire time they were securing the windows, he avoided looking into the woods, and now that the clouds were turning and covering the sun, the shadows of the tall trees played tricks on his mind. Growing up in the concrete jungle of Baltimore, Maryland, being surrounded by woods was not natural to him, and no matter how hard he tried to convince himself that there were no undead in the area, the snapping of a twig or the movement of a bush sparked images of a gnarled zombie reaching out to grab him through the glass. With these images playing on his mind he quickly pushed the beds mattresses up against the window.

The first and second floors were now pitch black; no sun entered the two bottom floors. Upon arriving on the third floor, Eric could hear that the rain was still maintaining a slight drizzle, so he had just enough time and felt secure enough that he sat out on the deck on one of the plastic chairs and enjoyed the cool sea breeze as it brushed over his face. He focused on the sound of the rolling waves and tried to drown out the sound of the branches rubbing together and moving in the sea breeze and the thought of something crawling out of them.

The sun was staging its last fight to stay above the horizon and shine through the dark clouds. Just as Eric sat and got comfortable, a lone figure broke the plain of the beach. He watched as an undead vacationer shuffled over the sand. As it lumbered up the beach, Eric could see the tattered, loose clothing hanging from its flesh, and it looked as if its skin were crawling. He leaned over the edge of the railing a little more than he should have, just to examine this zombie. The skin of the ghoul was crawling with crabs. They hung from the chunks of loose rotting flesh, trying to eat him as he made his way through the sand. The ghoul seemed not to care about the shellfish eating it and paid no mind as they whittled him away. As each wave crashed against it, it struggled to maintain its balance, and more crabs seemed to grab hold of it with each wave of the sea. Eric knew that this ghoul would surely disappear as the crustaceans ate it while it looked for its next meal.

The night came faster than expected, and the rain started to pick up. Eric called Drew and the girls out to see this sight, but the women wanted nothing of it. Drew, on the other hand, was just as fascinated as Eric was, but the night fell quickly and the rain fell faster and heavier, just as the undead vacationer was passing under the balcony. Neither one wanted to get soaked, so they fled for shelter back on the third floor. Naomi and Sam had taken the master bedroom and closed the door, so the boys chose to sleep on the couches close to their bedroom.

Eric drifted into a deep sleep, listening to the rain beat on the beach house. He sat up quickly when the soothing sound of water tapping the windows turned into the sound of pounding feet running up the wooden steps. He listened quietly, trying to determine whether the thudding feet belonged to undead or to an actual live human being. The steps were consistent, and as they passed the second floor, Eric made out a second set of footsteps. He stood up and reached into his open backpack, instinctively grabbing hold of the black pistol.

He ran past the couch Drew was sleeping on and slapped him on the head. "Wake the girls," Eric whispered as he ran to the side door. He arrived at the door at the same time the pounding feet did; the door knob began to turn and then stopped abruptly. Once the house was cleared, Naomi had gone around every door and ensured they were locked. The doorknob shook vigorously as the intruders wanted to get in.

"Did you lock the door?" a male voice from the other side asked. There was no response to the question, but Eric imagined a person shaking their head no. "Then some son of a bitch decided to make themselves comfortable in our house." There was a short pause as the intruders thought about what they were going to do.

Eric never thought of himself as the intruder. After the many houses they had stayed in, the sense of actually breaking into a person's house had left them a long time ago. Never once had they been confronted about being in a vacant house and there was nothing in here to indicate this house was taken, but apparently they were now the intruders.

"Are we going to break in?" the second voice asked.

Eric turned to the bedroom as the outlines of Drew, Sam, and Naomi made their way through the door frame, engulfed by the deep darkness of the master bedroom.

The first voice whispered in response, "They're probably sleeping."

Eric had no idea what they would do or who these people outside the door were, but he felt that these people were not the type to shake hands and accept them into their home with open arms, so he decided to respond in his own way. He grabbed the slide and snapped it back. The sound of the pistol arming was louder than either their pounding feet or their conversation, and his response to the intruder's statement was heard loud and clear through the door.

The new intruders stood, not moving, and then one of them spoke a short reply, "Oh." The sound of two sets of feet traveled back down the stairs and could be heard making their way to the ground floor, but much more quietly, without the enthusiasm they had when they traveled up.

Eric looked to the three in the doorway and Naomi said quietly, "We leave at the break of dawn."

****

Eric and Naomi didn't find sleep the rest of the night and were ready to leave hours before the sun rose. The following morning was cool, but the humidity from last night's storm lingered over them. They picked up four beach bikes as they passed some of the beachfront houses and made their way away from the resort area. They pedaled quickly to avoid last night's visitors, and within a few hours they were pedaling into what Naomi believed to be Virginia Beach. Their food supplies were running low, but they began to feel confident that they would find something to eat, as they were heading into another resort town. They pedaled up the sandy streets that lined the back side of the beach houses.

The beach houses in this area were not as luxurious as the homes they seen in the Outer Banks, and they were a lot closer together. They passed a few undead sitting on the side of the road against a car or in between houses, just standing there, rocking or walking away from them on the street. Every ghoul they passed bellowed a low moan to alert their fellow walking dead.

The vast majority of the side streets were clear, but every once in a while they were forced to squeeze around a car that was stopped in the middle of the road. It was when they slowed to swerve around a few parked cars in the middle of an intersection that Sam looked down the adjacent street and noticed a grocery store in a little strip mall. Hunger was beginning to make their stomachs rumble, so Sam suggested they should stop.

Cars were cluttered on the main roads that lined the outer edge of the strip mall, so they parked their bikes across the street and made their way towards the supermarket on foot. As soon as they got off their bikes, they heard a once-familiar sound they hadn't heard in a long time: The sound of a large vehicle making its way down the street, crashing into everything that was not secured to the concrete.

Soon a red pickup truck could be seen racing down the sidewalk and over the grassy median. The large truck had three people seated in the cab and four people riding in the bed. The four in the back were holding on effortlessly and moved expertly with the rough rocking of the vehicle. Their heads swiveled, watching and looking through dark sunglasses for any undead that they were riding up on or had passed. They pulled to the front of the grocery store, and all at once, the four in the back jumped over the sides of the bed and ran into the store. The four that ran in were wearing all-black clothing and exchanged their sunglasses for clear face shields as the dark shadows of the store swallowed them. They had nothing in their hands, but each one carried a weapon of some sort. Two had machetes hanging from their sides; one had a small axe and the other a baseball bat slung over their shoulders by looped pieces of rope. As the four ran into the grocery store, a heavier man jumped out of the passenger's side and stood at the front door with a bat in his hand. The driver stood by the driver's side door and watched over the random parked cars in the lot. The one man who sat in the middle was shorter than the others and very wiry, but what really made this man stand out were the long blond dreadlocks that hung over his dark-tinted face shield. He pulled a large machete from a green scabbard attached to his hip and stood with the driver.

The groaning of hungry undead echoed from the street they had just traveled down. Eric pushed the crew out of eyesight of the ghouls making their way down the street. Then undead began crawling from the parked vehicles and rounding the corners from the direction the red truck had come.

Crouching down between two cars, they watched these mysterious men. As the undead made their way through the parking lot, four men came out of the supermarket with their arms full of groceries. Cereals, boxed pastas, and canned goods were thrown into the back of the truck. The dreadlocked man scanned the parking lot then turned to them and screamed, "One more trip!"

The parking lot was beginning to fill with lumbering undead, and Eric didn't like the number that began to fill in between the cars. He felt that his escape routes were beginning to close.

They watched as the zombies began making their way closer toward the strange men. The man with the dreadlocks and the heavier one who stood watch at the door ran out to the closest ghoul to the left of the store. The heavier man stood in front of the undead that reached wildly for him. Its mouth opened and closed as if it were already eating his thick flesh. The smaller man ran wide around and behind the undead, taking the machete to the base of its neck. The ghoul dropped instantly and lay still. As soon as it collapsed, both of the men ran to the next one that was making its way to the store. They repeated this same act again and again, and with each undead that fell, they moved on, confident that it was not going to get up.

Eric was amazed at the accuracy and confidence these men had, but was very upset that his group would not be visiting this grocery store anytime soon. They were all hungry, but they could not risk running into a store that was quickly becoming overpopulated with undead. The four men ran from the store with another load of boxed and canned goods, tossed them into the bed of the truck, and jumped in. The driver honked his horn and the large and dreadlocked men ran back to the truck and jumped into the front seat.

Seeing their escape routes closing, Eric and the rest of his crew got up and began running up the street perpendicular to the one they were on. The heavier man was the last to enter the truck, and he caught a glimpse of them running. Eric turned as the man hollered, "Come with us." The four in the bed of the truck turned, and then the truck started to move slowly forward.

Undead were quickly gathering around the strip mall and the truck would not be able to make it to them without battling a few obstacles. A series of cars divided them, and between those cars lined scores of undead. Eric did not reply, but forced his crew up the street and the truck rode away with no attempt to reach them. Eric did, however, hear one of the men holler as they drove away, "Keep traveling up the beach!" Then the message was drowned out by the groaning of undead that now turned their attention to them.

The streets were full of movement now, so they decided to make their way back to the beach houses. The main street was crawling with the undead, answering the calls of other ghouls. They ran down the beachfront, passing a few small duplexes, and ran up to the first one that they came across with the front door open. They barged in, hoping no undead were able to actually make out what house they had gone into, and closed the door as quietly as possible.

This house was unoccupied, or at least it had been vacant during last night's storm. The reason they knew this was because the windows were open and the couches under the windows were saturated with rainwater. The carpet bubbled and pooled around their feet with each step as they walked over it. Eric made a quick inspection of the house, and by the time he came back down the stairs he found Naomi, Drew, and Samantha digging through the cabinets.

There was enough food here to last them a few days. Most of

it was junk food such as potato chips and little snack cakes, but it was something to fill the void in their stomachs.

Chapter 13

The Village

They set out the next morning and agreed they would follow the beach up and continue to travel north. There were more undead on the beach now since yesterday's rendezvous, but the ghouls had a harder time traveling through the sand than living people did. A few would get excited and try to trudge their way through it, but the most decomposed zombies no longer picked their legs up to give chase and wound up falling face-first over the piles of sand their shuffling feet made.

They traveled the soft sand beach for almost an hour before the strain on their legs became unbearable. They moved to the wet sand to alleviate the burn in their legs, but their shoes and socks started to become sodden with ocean water. Even though it would be a little more hazardous, they came to the unanimous decision to travel the street just beyond the first set of beach houses.

The further they walked on the streets, the fewer undead began to emerge from the houses and buildings. When they first decided to walk on the main street, the cars were packed tightly due to vacationers' haste to exit the beach resort. The further north they traveled, the more sporadic the vehicles became. Soon the vehicles began to be positioned in an organized manner, as if someone had taken each car and purposely pushed it off to the side of the road. The vehicles were positioned with the trunks facing the road and were parked so close to each other that nothing could squeeze between them. The houses and side streets petered out, and the clean paved street they were traveling on turned into an unkempt asphalt path. The street still existed, but no one would ever have known it until they stood on the road itself.

Two distinct tracks were visible on the path: A vehicle had traveled this road on a routine basis, and they all had the feeling it was the red truck they had seen the day before. Random weeds grew up to Naomi's waist from sand-covered cracks, and brush reached from the sides of the road into the middle of it, brushing all who traveled down it. No stores were built in front of them; to the left they could see a few old dark buildings off in the distance, but they seemed to die down as well the further they walked this old road. The path began slowly to turn away from the beach, but the sea wind continued to touch their cheeks.

They traveled down the sandy road, which changed to dirt, for what felt like ever. It was beginning to turn to dusk, but they all felt at peace. They were all very comfortable and at ease; even Eric was relaxed, despite being surrounded by tall grass and the unknowing of what lurked in it. Sam was the first to realize what it was that made her feel contented: "I can smell the ocean and the grass. It smells clean." She was right. For the first time in weeks, the lingering stench of rotting flesh did not assault their noses. They all inhaled the fresh air.

Even though they were all calm, none of them wanted to stop on this road, so they continued to travel well into the night—or possibly the morning—until something peeking over the grass caught their attention. A solid structure was up ahead, and the moon shone on two larger wooden structures separated by a large fence.

As they approached the chain-link fence, a lone figure stood guard on the opposite side. The guard held some sort of assault rifle. It was one of the guns Sam believed she had seen some action hero in a war movie firing. If Eric had to guess it looked as if it was something like an AR-15. The man raised his rifle to prepare himself. The moon was shining on their backs, revealing to the guard nothing but the silhouettes of four humans traveling down the road. As they approached Naomi suggested they should wave their hands over their heads to show they were living and not infected.

The guard lowered the barrel of the gun, almost touching the dirt, when they began to wave. The overweight guard wore a red-and-black flannel shirt with a beat-up John Deere hat that sat loosely on his head. With his fingers intertwined in the fence, he recognized them as human. "What do we have here? Y'all are a long way from home, I bet?" Walking up to the fence, the overweight hillbilly wiped something from his scraggly brown beard. Staring at Naomi with what could have been mistaken for awe, he said, "We don't have any of your type here." He paused, thinking about how that might have come out, then seemed content.

Upset, but knowing they could use some help, she half-smiled, "I'm pretty unique." She wanted to give the benefit of the doubt that he was joking or playing, so she decided she would maintain her temper until she found out if this person could help them. For the sake of feeding her daughter she was able to withstand some ignorance.

"I mean pretty ladies," the guard said, smiling as if to court her where she stood.

"We were looking for a place to stay and maybe get some food," Eric butted in before this conversation could continue. "Just for a little while; we just need a place to get a decent night's sleep."

"Yeah, sure, we can accommodate you." He looked at Naomi as he slowly pronounced every syllable in the word accommodate, following it with a grin that would have scared a horde of undead, but was apparently meant to be more than friendly toward Naomi. "Let me run go get the Doc and see what he has to say 'bout y'all." With that, he walked between some make shift lean-tos and some old tents.

"If he tries anything I swear I will cut him." Naomi spoke softly, but very seriously.

From their side of the fence, the village looked to have multiple structures to house many residents. What Eric guessed was the main road was lined with variously-sized tents of all kinds and colors. Behind the tents were small houses raised about ten feet or so off the ground. The houses were supported by planks of wood and pieces of construction staging. They looked as if they had been thrown up with whatever pieces of wood could be found and nailed, screwed, or glued together just to make them stand. As Eric examined the village and its houses, they took him back to a memory of when his friends and he would build forts out of whatever they could lash together and make a huge mess of his father's back yard. Thinking back on it now, the bases he used to make looked like they were constructed better than many of these shelters, but he would be happy with just about anything right now. Just the thought of talking to more people, hearing their stories and telling his, excited him immensely.

Eric and Naomi stepped back a few steps and looked at the fence that appeared to surround the entire camp. Just as they started to take in the entire scene, the hillbilly came strolling back with a man who wore a beat-up white lab coat that hung down to his knees and an orange hooded sweatshirt under it. The hood covered his face, and the man's head was angled to the ground. The four travelers had lost track of time, but the way the Doctor hung his head and rubbed his face gave them the impression he had been awakened by the guard and it must have been very late or early in the morning.

The overweight guard smiled at Naomi, presenting his rotten front teeth almost as if he were proud of them, and opened the gate. He pushed the gate open, and it swung freely till it crashed against itself, making half of the front wall shake. The metal fence played a loud tune against each link.

"Good Lord help us all!" the sleepy Doc shouted in a whisper. His head was straight and his once-tired eyes now pierced the guard's soul. "You're going to lead them right to us. Or did you forget they can hear just the way we can?" The Doc looked at Sam and Drew, then back to the guard. "I'm going to lead them right to *you*, so they get their fill and they won't bother with the rest of us, you fat…." He glanced back at Sam and Drew and held his tongue. His words came out in a stern whisper strong enough to let the guard know he had messed up. His ego bruised, the fat man started to hold up his chest and argue back, but just as soon as he opened his mouth—"So help me God, if you wake up any of these kids," Doc continued, waving his hands to the tents, "next time you come in for a headache, I'll give you something to make your dick fall off." Looking at the four guests, he tilted his head in a *Follow me* gesture before the guard could think of a reply. They trailed behind Doc, passing under some of the houses, ducking and stepping over the support beams of the staging, passing quite a few tents. As they passed one of them, they could make out the silhouette of what they thought was a child readjusting a sleeping bag.

Doc pushed back the flap of a large white canopy and lit a lantern that sat on a wooden desk on the left side of them. The lantern lit the entire tent, revealing a massive dark oak desk engraved with deep carvings of flowers. It was one of the desks Eric imagined a high-class lawyer would put in his personal office. Someone had spent hundreds of thousands of dollars for this desk, and now it supported a Coleman lantern in a large tent. Straight ahead of them was another desk, but this one was plain and bare. To the right of them against the nylon wall were eight cots covered by thin white sheets.

Clearing her throat, Naomi asked, "Are you really a doctor?"

Doc pulled a plain metal folding chair from behind the expensive desk and sat down, fumbling with the lower drawer. Not looking up from the drawer, Doc answered with a snicker, "No, I showed up in this coat and got the name. It seemed to fit, though. I wouldn't want any of these people looking after me if I got ill, so I just played along."

"Do they know about this?" she asked with some concern.

Looking up from the drawer, he revealed a pad of paper with a few pens. He looked directly at Naomi. "Yeah, I told them I wasn't a doctor, but that's what they kept calling me, so I just, like I said, played along. I could be out there hunting." He snarled his lip. "I could be building houses up on stilts." He snarled his lip and crinkled his forehead. "I could be digging holes, burying shit out in the fields." Doc grimaced. "Yeah, I'll play Doctor for a while." Flipping over the first page of the pad of paper, he instructed, "Y'all have to undress down to your skivvies." Feeling the evil look Naomi gave him, he followed that statement with, "I have to look for any type of bites or signs of infection."

Sam looked up at her mother for guidance. "It's alright, he's looking out for his people," Naomi said as she unsnapped her pants.

"I'm not wearing anything under my shirt." Sam told her with a scared look on her face.

Doc stepped toward her and bent down in front of her to get to her eye level. "Let me see your belly and your arms."

She pulled her shirt up, then held her arms out to her sides. "I've never been bitten, I promise."

"You know what? I believe you," he said with a smile. He got up and examined the rest of them. "Have you had any encounters with them in the past twenty-four hours?"

"No. We saw a few on the beach, but we avoided them," Eric said as he was being inspected.

"We're going to set you up in a tent; it's going to be tight in there, but it's all we have right now for people who just got here." He sat back behind the oak desk and started writing on the pad of paper. "What did you do before Z day?" He pointed his pen to Erik.

"I was a machinery mechanic for the Coast Guard."

Doc shook his head and shrugged a nonverbal *And that is what?*

Eric recognized the look and explained. "I worked on engines, hydraulics, and pretty much everything mechanical."

Looking down at his paper, Doc scribbled something on his pad. He scrolled down his paper as if he were looking for something, "Naomi?"

"I worked at a bank."

He stood up. "So you're good with math, I assume?"

Naomi nodded in agreement.

"Okay, follow me." Doc led them to a small grey tent directly next to the large tent they'd just been in. "I won't be far from here, and if you need anything.... You know, just wait till morning. You'll be safe. Dan is on duty tonight. He's an idiot, but the one thing he takes seriously is standing watch. We don't really trust him to do much else." Showing a small smile followed by a yawn, Doc said, "I'll see you in the morning."

The tent was as small as Doc had warned, but they all slept well that night.

****

Eric was awakened by the sound of a child crying. As he rolled over and opened his eyes, he saw that he was the last to wake up. The others were sitting close together in the cramped tent and talking quietly amongst themselves. Eric realized he was taking up half of the tent by lying sprawled out and quickly moved to the far side of the tent. "Sorry."

He sat up and opened the tent flap. The morning breeze was crisp, and he felt good being able to sleep through the night, not having to worry about a door being broken down or glass shattering. They had all needed this night to sleep soundly. For the first time in months, they all had closed their eyes and been able to get a few hours of rest without the fear of being attacked in their sleep.

He poked his head out from the tent. "Good morning." Eric heard a familiar voice and shielded his eyes from the sun as he looked up. "Hope everything went well last night," Doc said. He wore the same clothes from just a few hours earlier.

Stepping out of the tent, Eric answered, "Yeah, everything was great. For the first time in a long time I actually managed to sleep." He let out a big stretch, standing on his toes and extending his arms.

"Sorry for the–" Doc pointed to the tent across from them, referring to a crying baby the grateful sleepers hadn't even noticed. "When you guys are ready, come see me in the canopy." He turned and walked away.

The four of them walked into the large tent. Doc sat behind the oversized, elaborate desk, and across from him sat a large man with a huge white beard that came down to his chest. He wore a brown sports jacket and a pair of black corduroy pants.

"Good morning, did you sleep well?" the large man said as he stood up and reached his right hand to shake Eric's. "My Name's Elijah."

Eric reached out and felt his hand crack under the strength of Elijah's. "Eric," he introduced himself, "nice to meet you." He pulled his hand away. "Thanks for your hospitality."

"Oh, not a problem, we're just happy to see new faces, and especially those that can possibly help our li'l town grow." He took one step back, and the smile on his face never left. "I'm the sheriff of the town, and if you have any problems, I have an open-door policy, so please come see me and we will find a way to settle any and all of your problems. Eric, I hear you are a mechanic."

"Well, that's what I did in the Coast Guard."

"Great, we need some good hands." He turned to Samantha and Drew. "We actually have a school set up for you two, as well." The smile on his face was uncanny and never faded. He turned to Naomi. "We have jobs for you, too. We would love for you to teach the math department in our school. Doc tells me you're real good at math. Playing with numbers has never suited me."

The self-appointed sheriff had created this town. Originally, it was him, his wife, and their daughter, living out of an old R.V. Over time, another couple showed up asking for food, and Elijah welcomed them into the camper with open arms. They hunted and made the best of what they had. Then another small family appeared—father, mother, and two boys—looking for shelter. The camper was only big enough for the sheriff and his family, but he gave them his tent to use just for the night, and they pitched it right next to the R.V. It seemed people just started to flock to Elijah's because it was so deserted, and once people got here they wanted to stay, so the tent that was on loan turned into the family's permanent residence until new developments were made, and it still stood today to house any new traveler who needed a place to stay for the night.

More and more travelers had begun to show up and wanted to stay, so as the population had grown, so had the need for security. They had begun traveling to the local cities to pick up supplies and hardware to begin working on a fence. At first the fence was just an early-warning system for the occasional ghoul, and over time it had turned into the structure it was today. With even more people showing up, the tents had begun to be replaced by wooden shanties and structures made from construction staging.

"I. We were actually going to head off," Eric said. "I have to get to Maryland and find my parents."

Running his hand over his white beard, Elijah mused, "Well, why not stay for a little while? I imagine WoJo probably has some breakfast still, so why don't you go eat and we'll discuss this later?"

For the first time since the beginning of the walking dead—since these were the first living people Eric and his crew had seen in two months (he guessed—time had escaped him), he felt compelled to ask, "How did all this happen?"

"The zombies, you mean?"

"Yeah."

"Well, that depends on what story you want to believe." The sheriff spread his fingers and ran them through his thick frost-colored beard again. "How do you think it started?"

"I have no idea? I was watching a movie when all this went down," Eric shrugged.

"Every person who has come to this village has a different story. I have heard that a meteor struck and started this. I was told that some kids found a barrel of military-grade toxic waste and when they opened it, some smoke came out and infected them, but I'm pretty sure I saw that in a movie. One paranoid family that left rather quickly told me the CDC was doing experiments on monkeys and one got out and just started biting people."

"CDC?" Naomi asked.

"Something disease something. Some government agency that studies diseases and viruses," Elijah responded quizzically.

Drew spoke out, "Center for Disease Control and Prevention."

They all turned to the young boy and were impressed by his knowledge.

"Very good, little buddy." Elijah put his large hand on his head and gave a little shake, ruffling his black hair. "I personally believe a story that was told to me by some military guys who passed through a long while back, but let us go eat first. You have to be hungry, and I don't want WoJo to start putting everything away for dinner."

"There is no lunch?" Samantha asked.

Elijah started past them, opened the flap to the village, and waved them out. He held the flap open for them as they walked past and started guiding them to the dining area. "We really fend for ourselves when it comes to lunch. Food supplies are running low. If we get lucky enough to find some flour or some meat, we do have lunch, but lately we've had not much luck."

When they arrived at the dining area, a generator had just been silenced. The dining area consisted of four picnic tables lined up in a row and a classic-looking meals-on-wheels truck adjacent to the benches. The food truck was made of brushed chrome, but was covered with dark-colored sheets to prevent the sun from reflecting off of it and giving away their location. Also, the morning sun reflecting off of the roach coach would have blinded all of the villagers.

Elijah walked up to the window on the side of the covered food coach and put his head inside, looking back and forth. Finding his target, he called, "Hey, WoJo, good morning."

A very peaceful voice came from the window, "Good morning to you. I noticed you didn't eat, so I put a plate off to the side for you." A plate of food appeared on the window sill, and then a head over it.

The cook, with his very skinny neck and oversized head, looked distinctly like a giraffe. He wore a blue hat, and a very dirty white apron was tied tightly around his thin neck, hugging his body. "Ah, some new visitors," he said cheerfully. Wiry, short, pepper-colored hairs covered his face, and as he talked they stuck out coarsely.

Elijah introduced WoJo to them, and then WoJo greeted them all with plates of food. Each meal consisted of what looked like canned yams and some form of white-meat substance. They carried their breakfasts to the closest bench and began to eat.

"So anyway, the story I believe is," Elijah said with a mouth full of bitter yams, "these two army guys came down headed south.

They told me, after they gave me some M.R.E.s and I gave them a solid shelter for the night, that DARPA was doing experiments on how to make the soldiers not need as much oxygen to function. Without dying, of course."

Eric looked at him curiously.

"Yeah, I did the same thing," Elijah went on, responding to his look, "but over in Iraq or Afghanistan, if they were to be hit by some toxic or poisonous gas and did not have their gas masks on, they would all succumb to the gas and die, so I could see the point of it."

"Who's Darpa?" Sam asked not touching her food.

"I asked the same question. DARPA is the company that makes up all the crazy stuff that you would see in the sci-fi movies that you think could never happen, but they make it work. You know, like eye scanners, laser guns, teleportation beams, all the crazy stuff in *Star Wars*." He let out a little laugh that made a piece of white meat stuck in his beard swing back and forth. "Well, so, for them to make a chemical or a pill that would limit the human body's need for oxygen, to me is not farfetched.

"The scientist that started this study was named Thomas Wielder," Elijah continued. "He started with rats, dogs, cats, monkeys, and he could not get the formula right. He started this during Desert Storm and really got into it when Bush Junior took office. Anyway, that's not important. The first side effects were extreme cramping, loss of hair, tightness of skin, crazy mood swings, and the pigment of their skin turning to a dull grey. Years and years passed until he finally got it right."

"How did he know he got it right?" Sam asked again.

"You know, I asked the same question; great minds think alike. They told me they tied a monkey up and threw it into a pool of water," Elijah said very quickly.

Sam gasped and scowled at him, "That's so cruel."

"Can we PG-13 this," Naomi said as a statement, not a

question.

"Sure, sorry, but it did survive. The next time they did it, they used electrodes to monitor its vital signs. The heart still pumped and there were no negative brain wave readings or anything like that. So it was a good thing." He half-smiled at Sam to make it better. "The brain did not need nearly as much oxygen as it needed before, and it still functioned normally. They monitored the monkey—I think they said it was a chimp—and it acted normally. It ate normally, breathed normally when it wasn't in the water, and still flung poo at the scientists as they walked by." He looked to Drew and Sam and laughed. "The next step was to test this on some volunteers, and they had some side effects initially with the human specimens, like the tight skin, cramping, and mood swings, but wouldn't you have mood swings if your skin all of a sudden got tight and gave you cramps?" He laughed at that statement. "But ultimately it worked. The human test subjects no longer needed to breathe oxygen on a regular basis. They could stay submerged for ridiculous amounts of time. I think they told me they could stay underwater for almost an entire day. After they fixed the side effects, they started with a few military members. They gave it to a squadron or platoon or whatever they called it that was going to Afghanistan. Then they gave it to a few others that were going to some more hostile places, and then he gave it to himself. Life was good for a while, but Mr. Thomas Wielder started noticing some changes in his daughter and son. He started running some tests on them, and he started noticing they were acting the same way his initial test subjects had acted. Then they started getting reports of the families of military members acting the same way."

"How was it being passed?" Sam asked.

"Well, that's the thing. Mr. Wielder figured he must have passed it on. Maybe from eating after his children and kissing his wife? His wife started acting the same way, so he rushed them into his lab. He gave them the same antidote he had given the first volunteers and waited. More and more reports came in from all over the world. Eventually his family's pulse started to slow and they started to turn violent. He rushed them to the hospital and saw that many other children and adults with the same symptoms were in the emergency room. Then the cramping started. He realized that he had passed it to his family, and they passed it to their families, and so on. This all happened at once. Everyone started to change all at once."

"That's the story I believe," WoJo said, cutting in and sitting down next to Elijah. "It makes more sense than 'Hell is too full,' or some kind of crazy stuff like that. Besides, I think that was in some movie or something."

Elijah finished his yams in one huge bite. "So, when would you like to start helping out with our village?" He emphasized *our* as an invite into the village.

Eric forced the white-meat substance into his mouth and spoke sensitively. "We were really just looking for a place to stay for the night. We were intending to head north. I was going to find my family. I lost track of them the night all this happened and have to go to them." Naomi and Sam looked at him inquisitively.

Eric saw them from the corner of his eye, but said nothing and did not acknowledge their stare.

"Well, I'm sorry to hear that. I was really hoping you could have helped out around here. We are in need of a mechanic and the li'l school we have set up sure could use a good math teacher," he said sadly. "But I do understand you have to find your family. I do hope you find them and everything is okay." He stood up from the picnic table and extended his hand to them. "I have to be going, but please stay as long as you'd like, and if you come back round these parts you are always welcome." They all shook his large hand. "If WoJo has any food left over, maybe he could get you guys a doggie bag or something."

WoJo nodded, "I don't have much, but I can scrounge up

something."

"That would be awesome." Eric smiled.

****

They finished their food and began their trek back to the tent. They passed rows and rows of makeshift shanties that butted up very close to the boundary fence. There was only enough room for a guard to walk a muddy path in between. In the center of the village, sections of tents and small wood huts circled open areas with either campfire pits or fifty-five gallon drums that were used for fire. They passed the old wood-paneled RV that the sheriff lived in. It was built into a section of the perimeter—two sections of the fence were tied into the front and back bumpers of the RV.

They heard the sound of laughing and carrying on, and as they walked closer to the ruckus, they saw a pavilion made of wood staging and painters' tarps stitched together and draped over the top. At the stage or front of the exhibition area, a blond-haired woman was trying to talk louder than the groups of children talking and carrying on. She was writing on a small chalkboard a basic multiplication problem. Her audience consisted of twenty-five youth. The youngest had to be five or six, and the oldest looked to be about fifteen. Most of the older children sat on plastic chairs, and the younger kids sat on wooden logs lined up in rows. The older children who did not have plastic chairs pushed and shoved their peers for their seats. Naomi saw this and thought that this woman couldn't possibly teach all of these children with such a wide range in ages.

Eric was the first to crawl into the tent and begin to gather his things. Naomi stayed outside and looked at her surroundings. She saw a village that had potential for a new start. She saw a village in which she could make a difference, and she felt a sense of security, and that was what she needed right now, for her and more importantly for Sam.

She heard rustling inside the tent, and Eric tossed his orange backpack out of the small flap. Eric looked up to her from his hands and knees, wondering what was she waiting for, and realized she was having second thoughts about leaving.

"I think Sam and I are going to stay here," she said to him, looking down on him. She liked looking down on people; she felt it gave her power over the people she was talking to. Sometimes she would stand on a curb and look down on the people she was with just to give her the satisfaction of being higher than everyone else. Then Naomi realized what she was feeling was the reason most of the men in her life had left her, and she did not want Eric to leave her. She knelt down to look him level in the eye. "I would like to give this place a chance. These people could use your help—our help—and I need to stop running for a day or two at least. My neck and back have been killing me ever since this all started."

"I really need to know about my parents."

She brushed her hand across his face and cupped his cheek. "I don't want you to leave without me, but I need a couple days just to stop running. We are all tired and need a sense of peace for a little bit."

Eric stared deep into her dark-green eyes and then turned to Drew, who was standing behind her. He hesitated for a few seconds, breathed deeply, and said, "We'll give it a shot, for a little bit at least. We all could use a break."

Naomi smiled and leaned closer, kissing him on the lips, then hugged him tight against her body. "Thanks."

Chapter 14

Getting Comfortable

They walked back to the paneled R.V. and Eric knocked on the small door. Two black rusted steps led up to the door, but time had sunk the tires into the ground, and the bottom step was now resting on the overgrown grass. The door opened quickly, and Elijah squeezed his broad shoulders out, then took a step out of the R.V. He had a smile on his face, and they could tell he knew what they were going to stay.

"So, what do we do now?" Eric said.

Elijah let out a roar of a laugh and gave him a hug. The sheriff was like this with all the people in the village. He could not resist the urge to ruffle kids' hair as they ran by, and he purposely ran into everyone in the village at least once a day, just to ask them if they needed anything. "That is outstanding. We will start first thing. I'll set everything up and show you exactly what you need to know. Let's go find Doc. He keeps track of all the paperwork and all that stuff."

"Paperwork?" Naomi asked.

"Yeah, just so we know who is living where. Doc takes care of that as well. He's not only the doc, but the local real-estate agent as well." He said that jokingly, but thought for a second about it. "Maybe we work that man too hard? Yeah, we have to get you situated with a new place. That small hole is not going to work for y'all anymore. That's guest housing. You'll be moving into one of the circle communities."

Eric and Naomi were both rather concerned about their new

roles in the village, but decided they would keep quiet until they found out exactly what was in store for them. They met up with Doc, and he showed them to their new home. It was a yellow-and-green domed tent, just big enough for the four of them. Eric could see that one side of his body would be pressed against the side of it, though. It was located on the left side of the path that led into this semicircle, so anyone who entered this community could see their shadows if they had the lantern lit. In the middle was a campfire; one of the residents had taken great care in decorating the fire pit. Every stone was specifically placed and stacked around the fire. Around the fire pit were logs for people to sit on and roast their own food.

Doc explained, "When someone leaves the more desirable tents, they will be filled in order of seniority in the community."

Doc stopped by the school first and then asked Elijah to continue the tour because he had to make sure the latrines were being dug and maintained properly. They could tell they were getting close to the school by the volume of laughter and chatter from the pavilion. As they got closer, they saw Dan, the redneck guard, leaning against one of the pavilion's support beams and talking to a few of the older students in the back of the class. Whatever he was talking about had them enthralled, as they laughed and carried on, pushing and shoving one another.

"This is Miss Unthank." Elijah motioned to the blond-haired woman at the center of the pavilion, trying to be speak louder than the teenagers. The older children stopped carrying on when Dan saw Elijah and fell silent, then turned his attention from Elijah and looked toward the teacher.

Elijah acknowledged Dan's presence, but did not greet him. "I'll leave you here and you can get situated with your new coworker and your new class." He looked down on Sam and Drew and shook his hand on top of Drew's head, then let out a welcoming wave to the teacher. She waved back, but with only a fraction of his enthusiasm.

Naomi, Drew, and Sam walked down the middle aisle of the class towards Miss Unthank, who extending her hand. They greeted each other, then Miss Unthank waved to the class, dismissing the children for a few minutes. She was a short, heavier woman with long blond hair. She wore a very neat grey turtleneck sweater with a black skirt and black low-heeled shoes. She looked to be in her early forties, but she could have been younger and just showing her stress.

"You are the best-dressed person in this entire place," Naomi said, trying to lighten the mood.

"I try to give them a little remembrance of what an actual school was like." She rubbed her hands down her skirt as if to press out the nonexistent wrinkles.

"So you were actually a teacher?" Naomi asked happily.

"No. A teachers aid in college many years ago, though. I guess that was enough to put me here. Victoria, by the way." She put her hand to her chest.

"Oh, Naomi," Naomi returned. "We just arrived here last night, and Elijah offered us a place to stay. Who can resist a decent place to stay nowadays?"

They talked for some time before the children started to funnel in. "So, how did you want to do this?" Victoria asked.

"Do you have some type of curriculum?"

Victoria laughed, "Yeah, trying to keep the older ones quiet while the younger ones, who actually still have some manners, count the seconds until I have a nervous breakdown."

"Why don't I take the older kids? I will start teaching some basic math to them, and you can take the kids between five and ten."

Victoria agreed, wrangled them up, and left the pavilion. The ones that were left ranged in age from eleven to sixteen and were scattered in the back of the class. They were all at the highest part of the pavilion and fighting over the few plastic seats. Drew and Samantha sat in the front of the class on the first set of logs. "Hello, everyone, my name is Naomi, and I will be instructing this class from here on."

Most of the kids ignored her and continued to banter amongst themselves. "I am not going to scream over you all day, so would you please come to the front of the class?" The youngest in the class moved closer, but the older ones continued to take no notice of her. She stared for a few seconds at the eight students who were talking amongst themselves.

She walked up the middle dirt pathway to the top of the pavilion, where two of the teenagers were trying to force themselves into one white plastic chair, and without hesitation Naomi grabbed it out from under both of them. Neither one of them wanted to give it up, so the momentum threw them both forward over one of the wooden logs. With chair in hand she walked to the other two occupied plastic seats. She grabbed the back of the closest one and pulled up on the back of it, forcing the kid to stand up and out of it.

She looked at the other student, who had already stood up and put his hands out as an offering. "Take that one to the front of the class"—she paused—"please." Her back was coursing with pain, but she resisted the urge to show it on her face and never let her movements show her discomfort.

The teenager stood up and walked behind his new teacher, listening to his peers snicker and call him obscene names as he walked down the dirt path. He turned and smiled to them as he took the calls and sat next to Drew and Sam.

The gang in the back continued to carry on as Naomi put the plastic chairs behind her. "Now, you-all can go find Doc, and I'm sure he can find you a place with the current toilet-hole diggers."

They all stopped and acknowledged her with a stare.

"Do you have a problem? Can you not hear? I said go find

Doc and go dig some shitholes so we all have a place to relieve ourselves after class."

None of them moved. They stood staring at her and waited for her next reaction. Was she serious? They all stood in amazement. The teenager who was now standing by himself, since his friend was now voluntarily sitting in the front of the class, broke the stillness, made his way to the front, and sat on the log next to his friend. The other students followed shortly thereafter.

Now, with the entire class sitting in the first two rows, Naomi continued, quite happy with her accomplishment. "My name is Naomi," she looked at her daughter, "And this is my daughter Samantha." She looked at Drew for a second. "And this is my son Drew."

Drew sat back, gave it some thought, and decided to accept of the title. He was happy to officially be part of a family again. Sam stood up and gave a wave, and Drew stood up, nodding his head to the class, affirming Naomi's gesture and showing her that he welcomed it.

****

Elijah and Eric walked towards the opposite end of the village, passing a few more circles of tents and a few makeshift houses shaped like lean-tos. Periodically they would pass a wooden structure built on top of metal staging next to the perimeter fence.

"What are those for?" Eric asked, pointing to the staging.

"We have guards watching the camp twenty-four/seven. We have not had any undead enter the village since we put the fence up, and since the guard towers went up, we have not had one touch the fence." He seemed rather proud of himself. "We are very safe and secure here. I assure you, you will not have to worry about being woken in the middle of the night by the undead biting at your feet here."

They walked the rest of the way in relative silence, aside from Elijah's shouted greetings to every other person they passed. The far side of the camp was beginning to make itself visible: a series of vehicles stood near two buildings that were built from the same staging as the towers, but constructed with better materials and visibly more structurally sound. Both buildings were very close to the perimeter fence, one very close to the fence's swinging gate and the other about twenty yards further along the fence. There were more people walking around in this area than any other section of the village, and the vast majority of them were men and older boys.

"Everyone here in the village helps out in one way or another." Elijah was working his way up to telling Eric what he was going to be tasked with. "We have over eighty working-class people here in the village, and from the age of sixteen until you become incapable of performing any task, you have to assist us in your trade. Since you are a mechanic, we would like you to assist us in maintaining our fleet. Also, since you were in the military, we would like for you to put some of that expertise into assisting in defense and acquiring supplies. All the mechanics are assigned these extra duties."

Eric was not the greatest car mechanic in the world and in fact despised working on them, but he agreed to help. "I don't know about the whole expertise thing." He looked up at the large man. "I was in the Coast Guard." He laughed, "Now, you put a buoy out there and I could scrape the shit out of it, though."

Elijah laughed a good hardy chuckle and then spoke calmly. "Maybe we could use some of that discipline you must have received to motivate and keep the village running properly. Sometimes the younger kids try to be heroes and go off and almost get themselves killed, along with the people working with them."

Eric thought about this for some time and continued to walk toward the busy section of the village. "I'm not making any promises, but I will do what I can for the duration that we're going to stay."

"That's all I can ask of you, then." Elijah was pleased with his response.

As they made it closer to the motor pool, Eric saw that the red Ford truck they had seen the day before was parked next to the swinging entrance gates with its hood up and someone working in it. Next to the pickup were a few cars and S.U.V.s, but this was the only truck. The back part of the village butted up against a thick section of woods, and the same road they had walked on to get into the village led completely through it and out the opposite side. They walked to the building closest to the swinging gate.

When they got up to the truck, Eric could see that the man working on it was the blond-dreadlocked man he had seen the day before. Today his long, thick locks were tied together with a piece of twine that held them stiffly down the middle of his back.

"Jacob," Elijah said as he tapped the man on his back.

Jacob pulled away from the car and stretched. He was very thin, thinner than he had appeared when he was fighting the undead in front of the grocery store, and his dreadlocks appeared too thick for his small frame. He looked at Eric and then to Elijah. "New guy?" He had a slight Boston accent that to Eric just did not seem to fit his clean–shaven, tight face.

"Yes, this is Eric. His wife and his two kids are going to be here for a little bit," the sheriff responded.

"You're the guy we saw at the supermarket," Eric stated. "We thought for sure you would all be stiffs by now." He turned to Elijah. "Has Doc seen them yet?"

Elijah just stared at him.

"You never know." Jacob got the point. "Look, no offence, but we have to look out for our own, and you were just not in a position where we could get to you and ensure we weren't going to get bit ourselves. I hope you can understand?"

"I understand. We were about to hit that store and get some supplies for ourselves when you and that loud-ass truck came barreling through. Have you ever thought about silencing that thing?"

"Yeah, we just haven't taken the time to actually put another muffler on it." Jacob's attention was focused on something else. He hollered to one of the men passing by, "Joe, they fucking made it!"

Eric recognized Joe as the heavier-set man who had distracted the undead for Jacob at the grocery store. The heavy man came strolling over to them. "Wow, I thought for sure you were going to be creeper food. How did you make it out of there?" Joe was very tall , and his body frame matched his height. Red patches of stubble outlined his jawbone as if he were desperately trying to grow a beard, but having no luck at all.

"I did what anyone else would have done. Ran," Eric was short, but apparently everyone in the motor pool had talked about the poor family who had just gotten eaten.

Elijah stepped into the conversation. "Eric is a mechanic in the Coast Guard. He's going to be joining us, so please make him feel comfortable, because you know we could all use the extra help." He looked to Eric, "If you need anything just come up to the R.V. and see me." He patted his shoulder and walked off.

"So, where do I start?"

"You brought your wife and kids? There were two of them, right?" Jacob responded to his question while he wiped his hands with an oily cloth that hung from his back pocket.

"Well, I'm not married, and they're technically not my kids." Eric felt as if he was being quizzed or being given some sort of test, so he answered the question openly. "No ring on this finger."

"So how did you meet up with the lady and the little ones?"

"Well, I met Naomi and Sam when I burnt their house down with them in it." Joe and Jacob's eyes widened, and Eric could see their brains spinning with questions. "Naomi is the taller woman and Sam's her daughter. I've known Drew for about four years now. His father was with us originally, but he wasn't able to finish the trip."

"Elijah said you were married and they were your kids." Jacob fired this statement off quickly and Eric knew he was going to come back to the *I burnt their house down* comment.

"Well, he never asked if I was. He just assumed we were."

"So I have to ask, you burnt her house down?"

Eric laughed, and Jacob and Joe just looked at each other. "Yes, I did. An entire street of undead was trying to knock down their front door, so I threw a couple Molotov cocktails into the middle of them, and a couple managed to make it to the porch and light the house on fire. The boy that's with us, Drew, actually pulled an extension ladder out of his ass and rescued them."

"So, what can you do?" Jacob responded, wiping his hands again with the same oily rag from his back pocket and just managing to smear the same grease evenly on his hands.

He was not ready for this one and had to switch gears and think, pausing for a few seconds. In the Coast Guard he had done a lot of different things, but most of it was just basic preventative maintenance. He did consider himself a jack of all trades, though. "I can do just about everything that you would really need, I guess."

"Do you think Jesus was a zombie?" Joe tossed a curve ball into the conversation.

After all the random and quick questions, this one really stunned him. Eric had never been the type of person to attend church regularly, but he was a reverent Christian and believed there was a heaven and a hell. "I believe a lot of things, but that is not one of them," Eric said in response.

"Think about it. He died on the cross; they buried him, and a few days later he was up and walking around."

Eric could tell Joe had thought about this for a very long time and had this same conversation countless times. This must have been an idea someone had brought to his attention, because Eric got the feeling Joe had probably never even opened a Bible, let alone actually read one. "You know, everyone is entitled to their own thoughts and opinions, but that is one thought I am not going to entertain, so no, Jesus was not and is not a zombie."

"There is a reference that says all men will seek death, but death will escape them."

"Where does it say that?"

"Revelations." He continued with his scripted conversation, "So people would actually try to kill themselves, but can't die. They would jump off of buildings or shoot themselves and just continue to live all fucked up, like the zombies do now."

"A lot of things happen in Revelations, and I am not familiar with that passage, but if it is written in Revelations it may have something to do with when the end times do get here and Jesus has already left the earth with all of his people. Then the demons probably will not allow the people left on earth to die." He thought for a second and added, just to confuse Joe, "What if the zombies aren't actually dead and they are actually wishing for death, but death has"—he made quotation marks out of his fingers—"escaped them? What if they are conscious of everything they are doing, but this is the sentence they were dealt because they were not believers?" Eric laughed to himself, as he saw Joe's red eyebrows reach his thinning hairline.

Jacob reentered to steer the conversation back to the practical. "Do you have any weapons?"

"I have this," Eric said, and he pulled his pistol from his back belt, "and an axe and a .22 rifle in my tent. Why?"

"We may actually need somebody religious next time we go out, so you're coming with us. Keep the gun, go get that axe, and come back—we're getting ready to bounce." Just as Jacob turned to walk away, he turned back around. "Don't ever call me Jacob, I hate that name. Everyone here calls me Jay."

Eric nodded and left to get his equipment.

Chapter 15

Conflict

The road led north and then took a sharp turn west, following the coast past a curtain of thick woods. During the trip, Eric studied and took note of everything they passed. He pictured himself and his three companions eventually traveling these same streets. They passed through the woods and over a few open fields that eventually led to a paved road that didn't have grass growing over it or large mud puddles. He sat in the bed of the red truck with Joe, Jay, and another man who introduced himself as Mike.

Mike had a muscular, slender frame and was a little taller than Eric. The black beard wrapped around his face was meticulously trimmed. He was a quiet man, but what he lacked in communication skills, he made up for in his ability to design and weld. All the permanent staging around the village was his work and it all was very sturdy—it would have taken a truck to knock them over. The huts on top were another story. Mike wanted nothing to do with building the huts.

They began to slow when they started passing streets that were filled with large single-family houses and vehicles lining the sides of the road. The cars they passed all faced away from them on both sides of the street. They were parked so closely that no living or undead creature could have squeezed in between them. As they continued down the street, the large single-family houses turned into rows of small storefront buildings and small town family restaurants.

"So, how does this picking-up-the-fuel thing go?" Eric asked.

Jay grabbed a clear hose that was about five feet long and one of the many red plastic fuel cans that littered the bed and bounced around their feet. "This one is yours." He handed a plain hose to him. "You stick this end into the car's gas tank and you suck on this end until you see the gas come out. Once you see it you put it into the gas can until nothing else comes out."

"I'm very much aware of how to siphon, thanks." Eric pointed to the cars with one of the bitter ends of the hose. "I mean the cars, why are they parked like that?"

"Well, if we can, we push the cars off the side of the road and park them as close as possible. That makes it easier for us to travel to the next location later on and also makes a wall against any undead that may come out of the stores later on. They can't fit in between the cars, and they can't hide in them if they can't get in them."

"So, my job is going to be to siphon. And then what?"

"Then we all push the cars where they need to be, so next time we can travel a little bit further," Jay stated. "You'll see. Nothing to it, really."

They traveled the vacant-vehicle-lined street for a few miles until the road ended with a single green car blocking the road. The truck slowed to a stop, but just when Eric was about to jump out of the bed, the truck swung into reverse and did a three point turn so that it faced the direction they had just come from. "Just in case we need to bounce in a hurry," Jay said, answering Eric's confused look. "It also helps us push the cars."

They all jumped out. Jay was the first to the car and Joe was right behind, looking into the windows of the vehicle, standing guard over him. Jay acted as a skilled professional—quick, fast, and in a hurry. The red gas can was open before he placed it on the ground under the car's gas tank and he pulled a clear hose from his pocket. He had a squeeze pump on it, and after shoving the hose into the car he began to pump gas into his can.

"Why do you get a pump?" Eric asked, holding his clear hose.

"You find one, you can use it." He pumped until gas began to flow freely. When the car's tank was empty, they pushed the car to face the sidewalk, and then the truck pushed the car off of the street and up against the curb.

Joe wiped the sweat from his forehead and tapped Eric. "Now we just keep on until we fill the rest of the cans." He moved on to the next car, which was only a few feet from the one they had just pushed.

Three cars emptied, three cars pushed and five cans filled, two undead were alerted by the noise of the truck pushing the cars off the road. Their groans called out with enthusiasm, and from an alley between a shoe store and a restaurant, another pair of moans could be heard. The man behind the wheel of the truck hollered to the people filling the cans, "You better pick up your shit or start sucking a little harder."

Joe and Mike grabbed the weapons from the truck bed. Joe picked up his bat and Jay's machete, while Mike grabbed the two axes—his smaller one and Eric's medieval handmade battle axe.

Mike leaned Eric's wooden-handled axe against the car he was siphoning. "I'll watch over you."

Eric felt, with Mike watching over him, nothing was going to get close to him. Even though he had just met this man a few hours ago, Mike's confident demeanor would not allow him to fail. Just as the flow of fuel bubbled and slowed to a stop, the two undead traveling down the alley stepped into the street. A dozen undead had answered the call of the first two and were moving between the unorganized cars up the road in front of them; those were faster than the first two. Twisting the cap on the gas can and making it click closed, Eric picked up his axe.

"We got a runner!" Ronny screamed. Ronny was the full-time driver. He had been with the village for a month and had been working in the motor pool ever since he got there. He was not capable of doing much of anything, and almost immediately after being assigned to work in the fields, he had sustained an ankle injury. No one was sure which ankle it was, because he had been spotted favoring both legs and was not able to run, so he was restricted to driving the trucks. When he was asked to perform any physical activity he got a flare-up in his ankle, and according to Ronny, it was a disabling pain. Due to this he received very little respect, but Jay's crew was stuck with him because no other crew would entertain the thought of even watching him for the slightest period of time.

Everyone's head turned to see how fast the runner was coming down the street. From the direction they had come from, a skinny male, covered with crimson blood from its last victim, came running up the middle of the street. As soon as their attention was turned on the runner it let out a shriek that bounced off all the storefront windows, echoing from every direction, sounding as if there were multiple undead running from all directions.

The driver realized that four undead would soon be on them, with another dozen moving between the cars on the street and catching up quickly. He pressed down on the gas and floored the red truck toward the frenzied undead to make a little bit of distance between them and the runner. The bloody ghoul ran toward the truck as if to attack it. It ran wildly, ripping at the air with its torn button-up shirt waving behind it like a small cape. The truck collided with the zombie, sending black tar-like blood splattering across the windshield when its head smashed on the hood of the truck. The truck skidded to a stop, and the ghoul was sent flying back, tumbling head over heels down the road. The windshield wipers were in high gear as Ronny tried to clean the windows, but he only managed to smear the ghoul's thick blood evenly across the glass.

Mike ran to the walkers traveling down the street, and Jay ran toward the two from the ally. Joe stutter-stepped, but ran behind

Jay. Eric looked at both and then at the truck. A mixture of black blood and windshield-wiper solution was being thrown from the sides of the windshield. The zombie that the truck had hit stopped rolling in the middle of the street. The ghoul rolled to its knees as purposely as an acrobat, then stepped forward into a full-blown sprint back toward the truck. When it looked up and broke into a sprint, Eric could see the ghoul's forehead was smashed in, black blood pouring from the gash and down over its face.

Ronny had no idea that the zombie was back on its feet because the thick blood blocked his vision. Eric sprinted toward the truck, hollering for him to back up. The undead ran to the driver's side and reached into the window, grabbing at Ronny. The truck started to drift forward as Ronny's attention turned to the crazed creature trying to pull him from the window. Eric ran toward the ghoul, but the truck was drifting away from him. He switched his grip on the axe and was preparing for an awkward swing when the ghoul spotted him and turned its attention away from the driver.

With a sharp scream, it let go of Ronny and ran at Eric in mid-offhanded swing. The axe's neck, just short of the blade, connected with the zombie's head, knocking it sideways into the red truck, but it continued forward toward Eric.

Eric stepped to his left, but not fast enough—the ghoul grabbed hold of his shirt. The zombie was incredibly strong and pulled him toward its gaping maw. Eric thrust the wooden axe handle into its mouth. It bit down and teeth, mixed with blood, fell from its lips. Eric was pulling back, and as the ghoul pulled him close, he was able to side-step and create a small space between them. Eric's back was now toward the truck, and he pulled the axe handle from the creature's mouth and pushed the axe head under its chin. The zombie pushed forward, and Eric felt the butt of the weapon smash against the red truck. The weapon created a barrier between them, but the ghoul pulled at his clothing, and Eric ducked his head, sliding out of his shirt.

The frantic ghoul reached and clawed at Eric, but the axe kept it just out of reach. Eric pressed himself against the truck and held onto the handle, keeping the head against the creature's neck. He pressed against the truck as if he were trying to mold into the Ford. The wide, curved axe head and long hammer end stopped the zombie from getting around the barrier. Eric focused on keeping his weapon straight and level with the undead's neck. He turned to Ronny just in time to see him make his way out of the passenger's-side door and run from the fight.

Eric screamed for him. He screamed for him to come back and help, but Ronny ran down the street in the direction of the village, away from the other battles. The zombie snapped its mouth and screamed in frustration, but as the butt of the axe dented in the metal panels of the truck the tips of its fingers started to scrape at Eric's face. Just as the ghoul was able to paw at Eric, off in the distance Eric could see Jay making a wide turn behind the undead.

Eric turned his head and pressed the side of his face against the truck as the cold, wet, and sticky fingertips of the ghoul scraped his cheek. Jay ran up behind the frantic zombie and embedded the end of his machete into the base of its neck, severing its spine and paralyzing it . Eric felt the axe head get forced down, and he lost his grip on the handle, letting it fall to his feet.

Jay looked at Ronny running from the fight. "It looks like his ankle is a lot better."

****

Days turned into weeks, and those weeks turned into a month or more. The atmosphere in the village began to change. Eric was welcomed into Jay's crew and was now running his own missions scavenging for building materials, gas, and food. Naomi was able to maintain control of her classroom just as long as Dan stayed on the other side of the village and as far away from her as possible.

Eric managed to convince Mike to build a new set of staging next to the garage that overlooked the vehicles and even influenced him to build a shelter on top of it big enough for Eric, Naomi, and the kids to live in. Eric fit perfectly into Jay's crew and with the extra set of hands, they began making some improvements to the motor pool. The first thing Eric did was change the muffler and make adjustments to the red Ford to make it quieter; the second thing he wanted to do, with Mike's help, was make a wind-powered generator. This powered a few car alternators they picked up along the way; the alternators, in turn, charged a battery bank and provided power for all of the motor pool's tools and the roach coach.

With the temperature beginning to drop in the village, Eric and his crew had to start looking for autumn items in the houses and grocery stores they raided. They began to look for warmer clothing, which was a challenge, because when the world as they knew it ended summer clothing had just been put out on store shelves. They began to look in people's closets and to search through plastic bins in garages for thick coats, boots, and blankets. They began to collect and store children's toys. They believed they were in October, and Christmas was something every child looked forward to, so they were asked by many of the parents of the village if they could look for specific items their children had wanted before the end of civilization as they once knew it.

The colder temperatures got a lot of the crew looking for covered vehicles. Jay's crew put a cover on the bed of the red pickup, but one trip of any length, cramped and bent over under the cover, led to some hurt backs and some not-too-happy scavengers. The answer to that was to find something bigger. Eric found and brought back a cream-colored Ford Explorer S.U.V. The Explorer was large enough for the crew to pile in and out of when they needed to. The vehicle was big and strong enough to run over a few undead without risking too much damage, but the best thing about the Explorer was that it had heat. After the cream-colored vehicle was welcomed into the village, more people wanted to work with the motor pool, just to sit in a little bit of warmth.

****

Naomi taught her class from a series of school textbooks and a few added small blackboards the scavengers happened to find on one of their expeditions. She had a system in place for teaching each age group of children. The younger children, eleven to thirteen, were now working on basic math that most of them were already somewhat familiar with, as well as fractions and decimals. The fourteen-to-sixteen-year-olds were working on beginners' algebra.

She carefully thought about the math problem she wrote on the black board today, and she paused slightly, questioning herself. Naomi was not a teacher, but taking this position had made her feel needed again, and she had begun to find it rewarding. That was until she started entering the higher-level math. As the math became tougher and more complex, the older children started to fight what they were learning.

The tallest and always the best-dressed teenager asked, "Why do we have to learn this?" Brandon was sixteen and the oldest kid in the class. He had blond hair and fair skin, and he always managed to get the newest and best clothes whenever the village went on a scavenge because his adoptive father ran his own scavenger group. He didn't attend class every day, and when he did show up, he generally didn't stay the entire time. Naomi dreaded seeing Brandon sitting in the back, because he never had anything constructive to add to the group and always created a distraction. Today he wore a dark blue-button up shirt, very wrinkled but clean, and a brand-new pair of blue jeans.

Before the zombies had begun walking and destroying everything she ever knew, Naomi was working on becoming a loan officer with Trusted Funds bank. She had just started working with interest rates. Most of the time she just dealt with adding and subtracting, and the vast majority even of that was done by computer: She punched in what was to be added or subtracted from an individual's bank account, the computer told her what to put in or pull out, and then she printed a receipt. To this day she still had a hard time performing long subtraction problems by hand.

"Because someone is going to have to start this world over again, and you may just find a reason to know this." She was annoyed by the question because she thought about that very same thing and couldn't truly think of an answer that didn't begin with, *"If you were creating a rocket ship or were working on a nuclear reactor."*

The older group fought learning math that they believed they would never have a purpose for, and Naomi had a hard time persuading them otherwise, but because she had already started, she was not going to let them persuade her not to continue. She spent many hours scrolling through the textbook Victoria had given her under a flashlight late at night, studying the math she would teach the next day, but found that her best resources were Sam and Drew. But after that question, she decided this would be the last time she taught algebra.

"Why aren't we learning how to build fires or find shelter?" Brandon asked. "That's the stuff we should be learning." He began to get a rise of agreement from the rest of the class. "Who cares what X equals? We should be learning a trade like welding or working on trucks. This is stupid."

"How do you think we got engines and alternators and the ability to use hydraulics? People used math. They used the theories that we have today to create running, working machinery." She began to raise her voice a little more than appropriate. "These are the basics for creating and doing anything remotely intelligent. What if you run out of welding wire? Are you going to weld with just that . . . thing?" She waved her hand in the air, searching for the term *welding stinger*. "You could create the new form of welding or find a new system for welding. Or you could just help WoJo in his RV. I'm sure he has some dead cats that need to be served. "

Brandon was not one for being talked down to and insulted, especially in front of the kids he believed were looking up to him. He was the oldest and toughest and by far the Alpha. "I don't see the mechanics writing math problems to change the oil, and I sure as hell don't see the scavengers running out there thinking of the proper angle to get back to the village." He stood up from the log. "This is bullshit!"

"He's right, Ms. Naomi," a deep but comforting voice boomed over the class. At the top of the hill behind them stood Elijah in his lumberjack flannel shirt.

A smile appeared on Brandon's face and he felt his chest stick out a little farther, filling with pride. His confidence exploded now that Elijah had come in support him over the time this woman was wasting.

"We are obviously not utilizing this young man's ambition. I'm going to take him from your class and put him to work in a respectable trade." Elijah nodded to Naomi after seeing the frustration on the teachers face.

The rest of the children in the class broke out into an uproar, pleading for Elijah to take them as well.

"No, you all will sit and chew up everything Ms. Naomi is trying to feed into your brains."

As Elijah and Brandon left, the other children stirred in their seats, and Naomi, quite confused, had a hard time finding her rhythm again. She began to return to the existing problem on the chalkboard, but could not find her place to figure out the next step.

After spending a few long seconds studying the equation, she continued to draw a blank: Brandon was flooding her thoughts. She erased the problem and wrote a new one on the dirty blackboard, but her motivation was not to be found. "It is getting close to quitting time anyway, so why don't we just pick up here tomorrow?" Without hesitation, every one of the children except Drew and Samantha stood and left the class.

"What's Elijah going to have Brandon do?" Drew asked Naomi after the rest of the children had left.

"He's probably going to have to clean the Port-A-Potties or something like that," Sam replied quickly.

Naomi watched the students walking back to their tents, laughing and carrying on, every one of them wishing they were doing whatever it was Brandon was doing right now "Y'all should go get cleaned up and get ready to eat. I don't want to be the last ones to get there this evening," she said as she gathered her books and notes.

****

When Naomi showed up to the covered food truck, a line of villagers was already starting. Her hunger was growing and she believed she had showed up early, but the villagers had begun arriving earlier and earlier to ensure they would get their share of food. Standing at the back of the line, she scanned the villagers in front of her and at the tables, looking for Drew or Samantha.

With six people left in front of her, she finally saw them standing close to the end of the growing line. She hesitantly stepped from her place in line and walked to them, smiling at the villagers who gave her any acknowledgement. Many of the people she passed paid her no attention, and it was not happenstance. Some of them appeared to purposely look away from her. She couldn't help but think this all stemmed from her kicking Brandon out of class today.

"I thought you would be here earlier?" Naomi said to her children and stepped in front of them, joining the line again. She turned and said to the man standing behind them, "I was up at the front of the line, but jumped back here to be with my kids." She smiled at him and was taken by his relatively clean-shaven face. He was a tall man in his mid-thirties with a very pronounced chin and new stubble covering it. His hair was well groomed, and she was surprised that she had never met this man. More and more people were coming to the village, so she understood he must be new, but his demeanor was one of comfort in his surroundings.

"No, it's fine, just jump on in. It's all good," the man said under a smile.

"Thanks." She began to talk to Sam when he interrupted her.

"*We* all have to stop what we're doing early to get a good spot, but apparently not enough people are busy here anymore, because this line continues to get longer and longer every day." He showed his seniority by his comment, and also began to grab the interest of the people behind him.

Naomi felt she had created enough bad publicity today, and she was exhausted from replaying Brandon's and her argument. To stop any hostility, she spoke very politely and slowly. "I am sorry it appears I butted in front of you, but I was already in front of you up there." She pointed to the head of the line. "I stepped back here to be with my children. Sorry for the confusion."

"There's no confusion. I'm quickly realizing if you have any type of responsibility, you will get screwed." He threw his hands up and began talking in third person. "I guess you just won't eat today, Jason. Who cares if you work all damn day for this shit-ass village? If a pretty face decides it wants to step in line because her kids saved her a spot—"

Drew was quick to stop him and pushed him into the people behind him. "Fuck you!"

Naomi, completely drained pulled back on Drew's arms. "Don't worry about it, honey. He's just as angry as the rest of us. I got some food at our place."

"You can get in front of me," the woman in front of them offered. Naomi thanked her and put the children in front of her.

"I'm not hungry after all, but thank you so very much," Naomi responded and walked over toward Elijah, who sat in the middle of the filling tables. The grass in this area was dead from all the feet traveling on it. She sat across from the sheriff as he put a large amount of white meat into his mouth.

"Did you get your food yet?" he said after the food in his throat had fallen into his stomach.

"No, not yet. —I am beginning to see that I may not have been your best choice as a teacher."

He pulled his eyebrows together, making creases in his large forehead. "Explain. I think I am a decent judge of character, and I believe you are the best person to teach our youth, but what seems to be bothering you?"

"If I am unable to explain to an adult that if there are fifteen people in line in front of you and one person decides to step out of line to join some people behind her but still in front of you, there are still fifteen people in front of you—" She threw her arms up in the air in defeat.

"No, I believe you explained it perfectly well, because I'm not the brightest star in the sky by any means, and I understood perfectly. The problem you are faced with is, some people are just stupid." He stood up from the table. "Hold on." Elijah walked to the roach coach and went to the back. After a minute Naomi saw him walk back around the mobile cafeteria with a plate of food in his hand.

He placed the plate in front of her. She looked at the plate and then at the man that made her get out of line initially. He had watched Elijah carry the food to her, and now she gave the man a look of triumph. "Thank you. I appreciate it. I am absolutely starving."

"You're welcome, Ms. Naomi."

"So, what are your plans for Brandon?"

Elijah put a piece of cut meat into his mouth and chewed it while he thought about her question. He chewed it for a long while, not saying a word, and Naomi got the impression he didn't have any plans for the boy. "You know, Brandon is a good kid." He swallowed and then began to cut into the meat again. "Some children are just destined for other paths than the norm. He will conform to our society, but it is going to take some remedial discipline." He put another piece of meat in his mouth and began to think again. When he swallowed he picked up his conversation. "I had a dog once named Jasmine that basically destroyed everything. It didn't matter what it was." He started to chuckle to himself. "My mother's brand new shoes, my dirty old ones, my mother's handbags, even her new set of pot and pan handles. Now that I think about it, she might have just not liked my mother." Elijah was laughing even harder now, and it got the attention of everyone at the other tables. "Jasmine was a great dog after a while, though. A year or two it took until we finally figured out what to do with her. She had so much built-up energy that she would have to displace that energy onto whatever she could, and she generally did it by breaking and destroying anything in her path. The way we got her to stop her path of destruction—a path that was leading her back to the pound, I might add—was to make her use up all that energy." Elijah paused for a beat and looked Naomi directly in the eye. "And also beat the shit out of her."

Naomi did not really like the comment, and it was evident on her face.

"Things were different back then, and we weren't so touchy-feely with everything like we are today. Or at least, were, past, recently. Or recently past. You know what I mean. Anyway, I would strap a book bag onto her back, and I filled it with rocks. Small ones and light ones until I found what she was comfortable with and what she could handle without hurting my girl, and then we would go out back, and my brother and I would throw the football back and forth. The whole time Jasmine would run back and forth between us, trying to get the ball. In just an hour she was completely worn out, and she would pass out until we came back from school, and then we would do it all over again. The moral of the story is, my shoes and my mother's items were never bothered again. Brandon is like Jasmine. I just need to find out what I can do to displace that energy and whip him into a model member of the village."

"Thanks for dropping Brandon off to us. We really can use that extra hand," Eric broke in as he sat next to Naomi, straddling the bench, surprising her, and jumping into their conversation. "Jay told us to give him the shit jobs that no one else will do."

"I guess you know where I placed him, then," Elijah said facing Naomi, smiling as if she had just found out a big secret.

"Yeah, Elijah said Brandon needed a little motivation to get his act together. So he could join the rest of the village."

Elijah leaned over to Naomi and talked quietly to avoid any ease dropping. "I placed him in the care of the motor pool and Doc. When the motor pool is finished with him, or at sunset when they shut down, he will be dropped off to Doc."

Eric moved in closer to the two. "You could not have dropped him off at a better time, and we are actually really glad you did. We were about to draw straws about who was going to be the unlucky S.O.B. to pull the corpse out of the wheel well of the truck."

"He might learn his lesson sooner than we thought, then." Elijah let out a chuckle.

Naomi was distracted and disgusted by his job assignment, but was even more curious. "So you actually have to do that? Pull stuff out of the trucks like that. And what happened that one of them got hung up in the truck?"

"Well, nothing special, really. We were on our way back and one of them walked out between two parked cars and we hit it. Nothing special about it, other than getting hung up in the tire. It's done, I mean no longer moving, but it has to be removed. We were literally getting ready to figure out who was going to do it *right* when you walked in and called for Jay."

"I wonder how many times he is going to get stuck doing jobs like that before he comes back to class?" Naomi asked both of them.

"What? He did something in your class today to get him kicked out or something?" Eric asked Naomi.

"He was being a pain and a distraction, and Elijah just happened to be walking by and pulled him from the class."

"I imagine he is going to play it up for a week or so and then find a way or a reason to get sent back to class. Brandon is not the type to apologize, and he will tough it out for a while until he thinks he can keep his dignity." Elijah put the last bit of meat into his mouth and swallowed. "You will never get an apology from that kid, but he will be a different kid when he comes back. I can assure you of that."

Eric responded, "Yeah, Jay said to make his visit as miserable as possible. We already have a few jobs designated for him. Once he's done with the stuck ghoul, he's going to clean the chimney vents in the shops. And of course he will be in charge of custodial services."

Naomi was pleased with the repercussions of Brandon's actions, and as Drew and Sam sat with them, she changed the subject to other village issues and began to eat the meal Elijah had gotten for her.

****

Darkness came quickly that night, and the wind started to blow more strongly with the darkening of the clouds. They brought a little bit of rain, which everyone knew was only going to get stronger. When the sun set here at the village, most activities stopped if nothing was going to be cooked on the fire pits; and when it rained, the village turned into a ghost town.

With a crack of thunder, Naomi shot up from her dream. She felt the urge to use the bathroom, but was hesitant because of the rain. Eric rolled over, opened his eyes, and saw she was sitting up.

"You alright?" he asked.

"Yeah, the thunder woke me. I think I should use the bathroom, though, before this gets worse," she responded and pointed to the sky.

"I think that might be a good idea," he said and thought he could make out a smirk of a smile while she slipped her shoes on.

The rain was beginning to beat faster on the wooden roof, and Eric could feel the scaffolding shake and could hear the sound of her feet traveling down the metal ladder. The dirt paths were beginning to fill with mud, and her shoe sank deep into a puddle when she stepped off the ladder. Eric could hear the sound of her cursing but couldn't make out what she was saying. He looked out the plastic sheeting that acted as a window and watched the dark figure run to the makeshift latrines.

She ran to the main road, trying to avoid the gathering puddles by jumping from dry spot to dry spot. Naomi saw two people throwing a tarp over one of the tents in the circles, and as she watched the two men, she recognized one of them as Brandon except this time instead of clean-cut and well-dressed, he was wet from the rain and covered in mud from the duties he had been performing. Brandon met her stare and watched her as she got to the main road and jogged up it.

Eric was about to lie back down when he saw the two dark

figures move behind her after she ran past.

The bathroom area of the village had a battery-powered lantern hanging on a stick next to each one of the latrines. Naomi grabbed it, turned it on, and stepped into the blue temporary bathroom facility. She turned and locked the door, and just as she unbuttoned her pants, something hit the plastic side of the bathroom, causing it to shake.

"Hello, Ms. Naomi," a young voice traveled through the screened-in window of the plastic enclosure.

Naomi looked up to the screen and could see eyes peering in. She recognized the eyes as Jeremy's and the voice as Brandon's. Jeremy was Dan's right hand man. Wherever Dan was, Jeremy was soon to follow. Other than Dan being almost double Jeremy's weight, they could have been fraternal twins.

"Oh, I can see you," Jeremy said as if he were overly excited about seeing her in the bathroom. His voice was extremely raspy from years of chain smoking and drinking hard liquor and moonshine.

Naomi unlocked the door and tried to push it open, but was met with resistance, keeping her trapped. "Let me out, you fucking redneck."

"That's not very nice for a teacher to say, now is it? I was always told if you don't have nothing nice to say, you shouldn't say nothing at all," Jeremy said from the other side of the door.

"What kind of math are you going to do now? A guy on the other side holding the door closed and you trying to push it open. I don't see it happening, but maybe if I give you a pen and paper you could figure it out." Brandon said mockingly and then hit the side of the plastic bathroom, causing it to shake again.

Naomi heard a loud yell and then the door flew open as she pressed against it. The door was stopped short again, not from someone pressing against it, but because she had hit someone with the door.

Eric had run down the street and witnessed Jeremy, dressed in a beat-up, holey red plaid jacket, pressing hard against the door; he could only assume Naomi was on the other side. He jumped and kicked Jeremy as hard as he could in the ribs, and then the door flew open and hit Jeremy on his side.

Naomi came out angry and fuming. Brandon looked at Eric; no longer was he neat and clean, but now cold, wet, and dirty despite the black Carhartt coat he had on. He moved to Eric and took a wild swing. Eric easily stepped to the side and took his knee to the angry delinquent's thigh, just above the knee. This dropped him to that very same knee, and then Eric kicked his other leg out from under him, sending him face-first into the growing mud puddles.

Jeremy came running back after he regained his composure. Eric prepared himself and took a step back. Jeremy came lunging at him with a wild right-handed haymaker. Eric stepped inside and threw a straight right punch that connected squarely with his nose. Once again, Jeremy fell backwards into the mud. Eric paused, standing between his fallen opponents, waiting to see if either one was going to get up, but neither one did.

"Do you still have to go?" he asked calmly; Naomi stood shocked.

She didn't answer for a few seconds, and then replied, "Yeah."

"I'll stay out here."

****

News of the night's events didn't take long to spread throughout the village, and just about everyone knew before breakfast was served. Women came to Naomi, wanting to know in detail what had happened and hoping their men would do the same in that situation; men came to Eric wanting to know what it was like to finally shut Jeremy's loud mouth. Instantly, overnight, Sam and Drew had become the most popular kids in the village, and the way they found out was from the other children telling them what had happened.

The main road was wet from last night's rain, and Naomi took caution when traveling down the hill to the front of her class. There was someone waiting for her when she got to the stage, but he did not walk from behind the set of black boards until she arrived.

"Hi," he said, startling Naomi. A very stout man, slightly taller than Naomi, made himself known. By the way he was dressed, she assumed he was Brandon's adopted father. He had short dark hair and wore a very clean dark-blue jacket that perfectly matched his clean blue jeans.

"Hello," she responded nicely, but she did not like his approach. "Can I help you?" She backed away from him.

"I want you to take my son back into your class." This was not a request, but a demand.

"I don't have any control over that. He is going to have to want to come back, one, and he needs to talk to Elijah. He's the one who took him out of my class."

"Just because he sees things differently is no reason to kick him out. He should not be punished because he has a different viewpoint. You're not even a real teacher, so you don't know how to handle kids." The man began to slightly raise his voice.

"Once again, sir, I did not kick him out, and I am more than qualified to take care of any of these children; I have two of my own. And he needs to talk with Elijah before I let him come back, and then even if Elijah allows him to attend school, if I don't believe he actually wants to be in this class, I will send him back," she snapped.

"You obviously don't know who I am."

"You obviously think I give a shit," Naomi fired back.

"I run my own team. We are the best scavenger team this

village has, and I'm sure if it came down to losing me and my team or getting rid of some know-it-all bitch who doesn't play well with others, you would be run out."

"Get the fuck out of my class room!" Naomi screamed and pushed him into the chalk board he had hidden behind.

"And tell your boyfriend if I ever see him, I'm going to fuck him up, too, for hitting my boy," the man said quickly and began walking away. When Naomi raised her voice and pushed him, many people passing by had stopped and looked down on the class.

"You know where he is. Go tell him yourself, you coward!" The onlookers began to whisper amongst themselves, and Brandon's father began to feel increasingly more uncomfortable, so he picked up his pace, leaving the class.

The teenagers sat, very interested in everything but the lesson plan. Naomi wrote the pages she had read for today's lesson plan on the chalkboard and said, "Read these pages, and then do the exercise at the end of the chapter." She sat for a while staring off into the distance, thinking about last night and this morning. She continued to daydream, and then she stood up. "Continue reading, I'll be back in a second." And then she ran off, away from the classroom.

****

"You know, if we could get these to cover the wheels, we might actually be able to stop any more undead from getting caught in them again." Eric was holding up a makeshift shield that covered the entire wheel well of the red truck, trying not to kneel in the fresh mud from last night's rain. He was pressing it up against the frame of the truck for Mike to see what he could do as far as welding it or creating some other form of attachment.

"You should really learn to control your woman," Brandon's father said as he passed Jay's section of the motor pool and addressed Eric, but neither Eric nor Mike were really paying attention. It was very common for the other scavenger group to walk through their section of the motor pool because theirs was the closest to the main road. Most of the time, as they walked through, the common courtesy of a "good morning" or "hello" was given; there had never been any real controversy between the groups other than small gambling debts or friendly competition.

Mike looked down at him quizzically, "What he say?"

"Not sure." He stood up and yelled to him, "What?"

"You heard me. Fuck you," Brandon's father hollered back as he walked into the other motor pool's building, just past theirs.

Mike and Eric looked at each other and shrugged their shoulders. "Must be having a bad day?" Eric said.

"It's probably because you beat up his kid last night." Mike said.

Eric's eyes got wide. "Oh, is that him? I knew he was in the other pool, but didn't know who it was. I didn't hurt him bad. Actually, I never laid a hand on him." He laughed a little. "Just my feet." He mimed a kick. "What's that guy's name, anyway?"

"John, I think? Something like that. I think they call him Johnny?"

They continued to discuss the idea of the wheel well cover, and then Jay opened one of the sides of the double door to the motor pool. He had a smoke in his mouth and shook the pack, making the filtered ends of the cigarettes protrude from the box. He held the cigarette box out as an offering, and Eric took one, but Mike refused.

"When did you get these?" Eric said as he leaned into Jay, lighting up and then inhaling deeply. The warmth in his lungs made him want to cough, but then his old habit took over and relaxation washed over him.

"I save these for special occasions, and last night was a good one, so I can indulge a little with everyone," Jay said with a lascivious wink.

"Do you have to stick your dick in everything that moves around here?" Mike said.

"Look, if it's going to come my way and I don't have to work too hard for it, then…" He was stopped short in his sentence by Naomi storming down the main street toward them. "I think you might have fucked up," he said to Eric, then pulled Mike back from him, creating a wide berth so Naomi could enter the circle.

"Have you seen Brandon's father?" she asked Eric, loudly and out of breath.

"Yeah, a few seconds ago."

"He said he was going to fuck you up."

"Really? He mumbled something, but we couldn't make out what he said," Eric said and Mike nodded his head in agreement.

"He walked up on me first thing this morning, making all kinds of demands, calling me a bitch and making all kinds of threats. He threatened you and made a big scene right in front of the kids. He came at me right before class started, when he knew no one was going to be around." Naomi was very worked up, and her eyes were glassy with frustration.

"Sounds to me like you got to do what you got to do," Jay said after her rant.

Eric took another drag from his smoke, snuffed it out on the truck, and then gently placed it on the dash inside the vehicle for safekeeping. He pulled his pants up and walked toward the other scavengers' building with Jay and Mike following.

Joe had overheard the whole story and began following, too. He had seen two other members of their group showing up late for work and hollered for them to follow. Shawn and Brian were new members of the village who had joined Jay's crew. Both of them were very large men, and their physical prowess had been proven on many runs against the undead. Even though the morning air was chilly, both of them showed up in tight t-shirts, showing their muscular definition. Neither knew what was going on, but seeing the speed and attitude with which their crew was moving made them eagerly join the march.

Eric was the first to open the door. Six men sat at a round table directly in front of the door. With a quick scan, Eric quickly recognized Johnny sitting on a metal chair. The other men sitting at the table were beginning to stand, not sure exactly what was going on, but Johnny had anticipated this.

In a few steps, Eric ran past three of Johnny's men with his fist clenched and rage boiling in him. John was used to intimidating people with his size and loud voice, and as Eric ran to him he started demanding that they get out in his meanest tough-guy voice and with his angriest, most intimidating look. Eric was not buying it and lunged at him. He kicked John's chair, forcing him to spread his legs and flail his arms to maintain his balance, and then Eric grabbed a handful of John's clean, groomed hair. He pulled his head back over the metal chair and came down on his face, hammer-fisting his nose.

John fell back over his metal fold-up chair as the barrage of fists rained down on whatever they could connect with. Johnny's men stood and began to make moves, but Jay and his guys spread out in the room and screamed for them not to touch them. In sheer confusion and shock, they all stood back and watched.

"This is *their* fight!" Jay screamed. Johnny's men started to move around the table until Jay pulled a knife from his pocket. "No one will jump in!" he demanded, and they all stopped.

John spun when he hit the ground and tried to move at Eric, but Eric controlled John's movements by the hair on top of his head. When John spun, the raining hammer fists turned into waves of uppercuts. John stood, but every time he began to make a move, Eric pushed him back down by his head. He reached at Eric's hands, trying to pry them from his hair, but every time Johnny tried, he left a portion of his face unprotected and a fist managed to find it and connect.

John managed to grab hold of Eric's foot and pulled it in, hoping to pull it up to gain some form of control, but Eric dropped his shin on the top of John's neck and began hammer-fisting the side of his face again. John pushed up, letting go of the leg, and the uppercuts began again. One uppercut connected cleanly and made his body go limp.

The full weight of the large man fell from Eric's hand, and he let go of his hair. John was still moving and was still conscious, but barely. Eric rolled him over to his back and began making connections squarely to the front and sides of his face. John was no longer protecting himself and was clearly unconscious, but something had hold of Eric and wasn't letting go.

"That's enough!" one of John's guys screamed, and Jay's crew agreed. It took Shawn and Brian both to pull Eric off of him, and even they were having trouble stopping the onslaught of blows.

"You're going to kill the man if you don't stop!" Brian screamed into Eric's ear, finally making him calm. John's crew pushed the chairs and table out of the way and one guy ran for Doc as soon as they had made space and pulled Eric off.

****

Eric worked in the shop the entire day. Jay didn't want him leaving the motor pool and walking through the village by himself. Jay even assigned Joe to sit in class and keep an eye on Naomi and the kids for the rest of the day, even though Joe quickly fell asleep sprawled out over one of the log seats.

During dinner Naomi joined Eric in the motor pool's building, and Jay came in shortly after. "How is John?" Eric said to both of them as they sat at the white plastic folding table.

Naomi didn't know, but Jay responded. "He'll be okay, but he definitely knows he got in a fight." He laughed a little. Eric thought it was humorous, but Naomi didn't find it as entertaining.

"You know, there's a lot of shit going around right now," Naomi said, annoyed. "Dan is all kinds of riled up and talking about getting back at you. And me too." Now she was angry. "What are we going to do? All kinds of rumors are being spread."

"I don't know," Eric responded.

"If you wanted, the four of you could stay here tonight," Jay suggested.

"Where's the kids?" Eric asked.

"They're with Victoria and Joe. They'll be alright, for now, but I wouldn't put it past Brandon and Jeremy to do something to them if Joe wasn't around."

"Jay, could you give us a minute?" Eric asked.

"Yeah, sure, anything you want." He began walking out the door. "Did you two need anything?"

They both shook their heads no. Eric reached over the table and grabbed hold of Naomi's hand. "It may be time we consider leaving." He entered this topic gingerly, remembering Naomi's initial reaction to the idea of leaving when they had first gotten here.

"It's fucked up, we are talking about leaving when these hicks are the ones who are starting all the trouble." She was getting upset. "Why don't you, Jay, and the rest of them just handle those people?"

"You know it's only going to get worse. Once we go after them, they are going to come right back even harder. Someone is going to get severely injured if we keep doing what we're doing." He leaned in, talking lower. "You *know* Dan and Jeremy are sitting with Brandon somewhere right now, talking about how they are going to get back at us. And it's not just us they are going to try to get back at. They may bring Drew and Sam into it."

"I'll fucking kill them first," she said pulling back and

becoming enraged.

Eric pulled her back down and close. "Before we have to do anything crazy, let's leave. I'll drop a car off so we can walk out the gate and it will be waiting for us. I can do it tomorrow night."

"Why don't we just leave during the day? Tomorrow afternoon or something, won't they give you a vehicle?"

"Jay would, that wouldn't be a problem, but the other groups may say something. Besides, if people know we are going to leave, Dan and his crew may try to do something sooner. I can get that Explorer over there. I'm the one that does all the maintenance on it, so I can test drive it and drop it off a few hundred yards down the road."

"I really don't want to leave this, though. We have a good thing right now."

"No one is going to kick them out of the village. Elijah is only a figurehead now." Elijah's power was all for show now. As the town got larger his power slowly dwindled away. The motor pool now controlled the village, and Dan and Jeremy were friends with Jason's crew, so they were not going to be kicked out. "So this is kind of like the Wild West right now." He squeezed her hands. "This was only supposed to be temporary, anyway. The winter is soon coming, and if my parents are alive, they won't make it through a winter in Maryland."

Naomi didn't want to agree, but was scared for the children. "What do we tell the kids?"

"Nothing. We don't let this get out. We can't let them know until we are getting ready to sleep. That way we will have everything packed and we can take off without anyone else knowing."

Naomi agreed. "Then tomorrow night, we leave."

"We'll be okay. I promise I won't let anything happen to you or the kids."

Chapter 16

The Escape

Eric had the hood to the Explorer open and was leaning over it, pulling the oil dipstick out. They had just came back from a run and gotten some more clothes, warmer blankets, and a bin of random toys they kept hidden in the motor pool so that next month Santa could drop them off in front of the tents for all the good little boys and girls of the village.

"What's up?" Jay walked behind him and then studied the dipstick. He was carrying a thick rolled-up blanket in his hands.

"It was running rough earlier. I just wanted to take a quick look, see if there were any obvious issues I was missing." Eric wiped the dipstick with a dirty cloth and put it back in, just to pull it back out and examine it once more.

"Joey forgot his blanky," Jay said as he held the blanket up. Joe had made it perfectly clear that he was going to keep this blanket, and on the way back to the village he had sat in the back seat and taken a nap on it. He had drooled all over it to seal his ownership, knowing none of the others would want it after he had lain on it.

There were only three groups that would go out scavenging, and they all tried not to claim and keep the best stuff for themselves, but all the groups sometimes did, on a small scale at least. Everything was supposed to be given to Elijah, and he was supposed to distribute all of the goods evenly. That way no one could accuse anyone of getting the better items, but in practice the scavengers had the best choices as far as clothing, covers, toys, or really anything they picked up and snuck into their pockets.

"So it's running rough?" Jay looked at him quizzically.

"Yeah, it wasn't running right, so I added a little transmission fluid to it and checked the levels. I was going to take it out on a little run, real quick, just down the road and back."

"I'll go with you," Jay said as he tossed the blanket into the back.

Eric put the dipstick back in and dropped the hood. "You don't have to. I'll only be a minute or two."

"Nah, I'll go with you," Jay said. Eric was about to argue, but Jay looked at him and insisted. "I'm going with you."

Eric had gotten this vehicle for one initial reason many weeks ago. It wasn't because it was large and had a big enough storage area to hold a lot of stuff. It was because he had intended to claim this one as his own when he did decide to leave. The current situation had only expedited his departure. The Explorer could also easily drive over undead and a curb or two without getting stuck. They didn't want to have to worry about having their vehicle turn into a coffin.

Eric got into the S.U.V. and turned it on. "Did you feel that stutter?"

"Nope."

The guard at the back gate opened it as they approached, and once they broke the perimeter of the village Jay turned to him. "Okay, so what's really going on? There ain't nothing wrong with this truck."

Eric believed Jay already knew. He just wanted to hear it from him. "We're leaving tonight."

"Where you going?"

"We're going north to Maryland, like I was originally planning when we first got here."

"You're *still* going to look for your folks?" The statement came out slightly sarcastically.

Eric thought about this and knew Jay didn't mean for it to come out the way it did, but he was serious about the question. "To be honest, I'm not." He searched for the proper way to say it, but could not think of any way that wouldn't make it sound as if he had given up hope.

"You need to see for *you*," Jay finished his statement for him. "So you're going to take the Explorer?"

"Yeah. I found it and I'm the one that worked on it to make it run." He was telling the truth. He had removed the parts that had to be replaced from the Explorer on one of their excursions, and as he found parts from other vehicles, he would exchange them. On every trip he would fix another item until the S.U.V. could be driven back to the village. "No one in the village can know. We haven't even told Sam or Drew yet."

"So how's this going to work? You're going to take off in the middle of the night and not expect anyone to know?"

"Something like that." Now that Jay knew, it put Eric in an awkward position. If Jay went back to the village and told someone they would watch over the Explorer and not let him take any of the vehicles. "You can't tell anyone."

Eric could feel Jay's eyes staring through him. "Are you serious? Do your thing." Jay spoke loudly and from the heart. "You got to do what you got to do. Everyone knew that you wanted to leave, but you're not leaving 'cause of those rednecks, are you?"

"Fuck no. That was just what pushed Naomi over the edge."

"I don't think anyone believed Naomi wanted to go. How did she take it when you told her?"

"She's cool with it. She thinks it's better that we go before I burn their tents down while they sleep, or they do the same to us, so we think it's just time for us to go. We really only stayed here for as long as we did because Naomi hurt her neck and back pretty bad and we were all tired from running."

"We could take care of that other gang and those Hillbillies if you wanted us to."

"I'm not worried about them."

"So you're going to start running again? You're going to travel up through some of the most populated parts of the country to find your folks? That sounds pretty stupid, risking your life and the lives of the others to go make sure your parents are dead."

"Fuck you," Eric snapped back, "We're leaving tonight, with the Explorer."

Jay sat back and fell silent. They had traveled this road many times before and never seen a ghoul on it, but now one stumbled toward them in the middle of the road. The sun was just overhead and shone down on the slumping figure. Eric slowed the vehicle and stopped in the middle of the street about thirty yards in front of it. "What are you doing?" Jay asked.

"I made this thing up the other day and wanted to know how it would work." They both stepped out of the car and scanned the bushes and trees. Jay strapped his machete to his side and Eric pulled something from the hatch of the Explorer that resembled a long silver pitchfork. "Remember when that runner got me against the truck?"

Jay nodded in response.

"It wouldn't push or pull the axe off its throat, so it wasn't able to grab me. I created this to see if they all would just keep coming like that." He stumbled back on his words, "I had the idea and Mike welded it up for me. I didn't really want to do it on a hunt, because this is a prototype. I just wanted to see how it would work." He grabbed the six-foot pole with both hands and started walking in the middle of the street.

The wind blew in their direction and the tattered clothing that hung from the ghoul waved in the breeze. The smell of rotting flesh attacked their nostrils. The zombie moved very slowly, having to struggle to maintain its balance, and took slow, concentrating step after step. This undead was just about rotten to bone. The first ones that had gotten this disease, or virus, or demonic possession, or whatever it was, were the ones that were the most decomposed. Even though they continued to function instinctively, their muscle tissues were being eaten by bugs and literally rotting off of their bones. This ghoul's skin was taut on its face and sculpted around each bone, creating sunken temples and jutting cheeks. As it opened and closed its mouth, the skin was pulled tight like a stretched balloon. Its eyes were smaller, wrinkled, and appeared to be sitting loosely in its eye sockets.

Jay and Eric walked closer to it and it stopped, standing very still to listen for its welcomed visitors. They both stepped to the side of it to get out from downwind of it. As they moved, a skin-covered skeletal hand fanned out for them with stretched-out fingers that resembled dull spikes. The bony undead could see them when they got closer to it, and as it went for them, Eric positioned the ghoul catcher. He placed the silver U under its bony chin and pressed firmly against its neck.

Its arms were as thick as a chair's leg, but it reached out for Eric with growing enthusiasm. Eric did not have to plant his feet or even try to push to hold this one back. This zombie was falling apart in front of them. The weight of the tool itself could hold this one back. "Well, since our specimen sucks, this is how I was planning on using it." The ghoul tried to move forward, twisting its head back and forth. The U was ripping into the skin and parted it, creating a gap in its throat three times the thickness of the catcher. The taught skin pulled the slice apart and as it moved the cut grew larger. "We could either hold it like this, but if we had a runner, I made it long enough, so if we put the butt end on the ground it will continue to walk up and not be able to get to us." He put the butt end on the ground in front of him and secured the butt with his foot. The ghoul walked forward and the hook continued to raise its head, outstretching its neck. "When you got them like this, this would be the perfect time to bury that machete." As soon as he paused, the ghoul lost its footing from being forced up and fell to the ground.

It lay, trying to get up, rocking back and forth on its back. Jay chopped through the front of its neck, severing its spine. Eric laughed and tossed the catcher back in the Explorer. "Are you going to tell anyone?"

"Really? No. You're going to need me anyway." Jay pulled himself into the passenger side of the Ford.

"You want to come?"

"Hell, no! There's this new Miss in town and I just haven't had a chance to hit that yet. I got too much of a good thing here. We're going to park outside the gate, about a hundred yards from the fence, and walk back. This way no one will dare go looking for it, and secondly, if they see us walking back from it, none of those other slugs are going to know how to fix it."

Eric put the truck in gear. "Thanks."

"I do hope you find your family."

"I know you do."

****

The weather in the village had turned from cool to wet, cold, and extremely windy. A stiff breeze smashed against the high house on the staging and caused the scaffolding to rock, but with the exception of Eric, the rocking caused everyone inside to drift into a deep sleep. The rocking of the staging encouraged him more and more that this was their time to go. The reasons not to stay were weighing on his mind, and one reason was, how was this place going to look after a major storm came through? The scaffolding they slept on was secure just as long as a strong storm didn't collapse it or tip it over while they were in it. A piece of clear plastic taped to the sides of the window came loose in one of the corners and began to flap, causing Sam to stir a little.

From behind the clear plastic, Eric watched the guards at the back exit next to the motor pool that separated him from the Explorer. From this window he was able to face the guards and also the main dirt road that lead directly to the back gate. There were a few people walking around the village, but most of the villagers were fast asleep in their tents or wishing they could fall asleep with the heavy wind.

The rounds the guards made consisted of walking to the two corners of the village on their side and glancing down the long fence. After looking down the fence, ensuring nothing was clinging to it, they would turn and walk back to the back gate.

"Naomi, it's time to go." Eric shook her shoulder gently and whispered to her.

Already being packed, she gave a quick stretch and woke the children. She pressed her index finger against her lips and shushed into it. Eric had watched the guards and was anticipating that they were getting ready to make their rounds, so he began to pack the kid's pillows as they lifted their heads.

"Did you see the atlas?" Eric had given up looking for it a long time ago, but in desperation started searching the small room again.

Naomi, shocked by the noise he was making, pointed out, "You said you didn't need it once we got to Baltimore. We can just head north and run into Maryland, it's not a big deal. We'll make do without it."

Without saying a word, his body language gave in to her logic. "It would just be nice if we had it, that's all."

Eric put the pistol in the front of his jeans and wrapped Drew and Samantha up in the blanket they shared. He ensured they had all the best coats and blankets he had come across, even though it violated the village rules, but then again they made the rules as they went now. Naomi wrapped herself in a blanket and then handed one to Eric.

They climbed down the staging and moved closer to the exit. Just as he had planned it, the two guards left the gate to patrol the sides of the fence. Eric removed the chain carefully from the two swinging doors that made the exit, but in the cool air the clanging of links rubbing across metal fence sent echoes down the vacant dirt street.

Leaving the swinging gate open, they ran from the village. They did not take the time to close it, but ran as fast as they could. Their bags beating against their backs, they breathed heavy plumes of breath into the air. Just a few steps away from the village a voice rang out. "Eric, don't make me run afta'yahs." Dan's voice and horrible use of the English language were very distinct.

"Keep goin', I won't be far behind." Eric stopped and the three others traveled on just a couple steps beyond him. He kept his blanket tight over his body, hiding his body features. With the moon behind him, the light shone bright on the guard, but the moon hid Eric's own features in mystery.

The fat guard walked up, slowly shuffling his feet. He pointed the AR-15 at Eric at his hip level. "Y'all jus' thought y'all were gonna get up an' leave without saying goodbye?" If his horrible red-and-black flannel jacket didn't give him away, his even worse ability to talk sure did. "I believe you an' my buddy have a little disagreement, an' he wants to show you his side of the story."

"Look, Dan, we're leaving. We thought it would be best if we did it this way."

Jeremy was the other guard on watch this night, and he came running behind Dan with a baseball bat in hand. A bandage covered his nose, making his voice gruffer than it already was. "We're not just going to allow you to leave. You are going to have to ask us nicely and maybe even give us a little something before we allow you to leave." As he ran up, Dan lowered the tip of his weapon.

"Yah know, I could give two shits about where it is you are going, but I could really use a bit of nigger lovin'," Dan said as he waved the gun in Naomi's direction. "What do you think, Jeremy? She gives it up, we let them go."

"That's what I was thinkin'." Jeremy smiled, showing two missing front teeth. Eric couldn't help but think that he had done that.

Naomi and the children were standing less than fifteen feet behind Eric. She pulled the children in close and then forced them behind her, using her body as a shield.

Standing between them, but up the road to the village, another figure walked toward them. Eric recognized Jay from his long hair and also saw the machete swinging from his side. Something he had never noticed before from him was the shape of a pistol in his right hand. "Hey." Jay said just loud enough to get Dan's and Jeremy's attention.

Dan began to pick up the AR-15 to point it in Eric's direction. Now that Dan's head was turned towards Jay, Eric had the chance to do something about it. In one motion, Eric grabbed the barrel of Dan's rifle and, letting the blanket drop from his shoulders, pressed his pistol against Dan's forehead. "We just want to leave," Eric barked, forcing the redneck to arch his back backward from the pressure of the gun.

"Hell, you probably don't even have any bullets in that gun, you fucking pussy," Dan's partner said confidently as he started to step closer, wrapping his hands tighter on the bat. "And this don't concern you, Jay."

"He's got bullets!" Dan hollered out.

With Jeremy's first step closer, Eric threatened, "Do you really want to find out?" After a short pause, Eric added, "We are leaving."

Jeremy took another step.

Eric took a side step to widen his stance and looked Jeremy in the eyes. "Jeremy, you will die today."

"I think you should listen to him, Jeremy," Jay said, trying to be the voice of reason.

Jeremy took a half step. Before his foot touched the ground, Eric pulled the trigger and fired the shot into Dan's head, never taking his eyes off of Jeremy. As Dan's body fell lifeless to the ground, Eric turned the gun on Jeremy and pulled the trigger. A single shot went into his chest and another quickly followed. The three bullets rang loud throughout the dirt streets of the village.

"We cool?" he asked Jay.

"You my boy." Jay nodded his head and walked over to the two bodies. "Take it easy out there. I hope you find what you're looking for."

Eric nodded in appreciation, and then they ran the short one hundred yards to the Explorer. The S.U.V. started quickly, and they began the journey to Maryland.

Chapter 17

Don't Wait Up Too Long

Maryland always had a smell and feel about it that felt like home to Eric, and as soon as he stepped from Virginia into his home state, a feeling of elation washed over him and a smile spread across his face. They began walking after reaching the furthest point the Scavengers traveled due to the obstructed roads. Taking one step closer to home made him smile, but that step was greeted by a bitter cold sting over his face as a strong breeze filled his hood like a balloon. The wind in Maryland was constant and strong. It felt to them as if there was an invisible wall that stopped the wind from entering Virginia.

They spent two nights' travel in Maryland before making it to Eric's home. They arrived at the single-family house in the suburban development just before sunset, and Eric debated with himself about going in when the sun was beginning to go down. But after traveling months to get here, the thought of not walking in when the opportunity was right in front of him was overpowering. The thought of his parents meeting him at the door with open arms passed through his mind a couple times while they were traveling through Maryland, but then again, the idea of finding them dead, eaten alive, also continuously ran through his thoughts.

The streets were quiet, but a still silhouette of a figure at the end of the street stood statuesque from the setting sun, and passing shadows moved between a few houses, putting them at full attention. They traveled in trained silence and were able to make it with no unwanted encounters, but night was falling, and Eric could feel Naomi beginning to become uncomfortable with the falling sun.

His house had been broken into and was no different from any of the other hundred or so different houses they had slept in, except that he noticed that his father's cream-colored Nissan was parked in the driveway. The open red front door had a large crack through the middle of it and was broken off its top hinge; the screen was ripped off, and most of the windows on the first floor were broken from undead trying to crawl in or out. There was a small porch with green outdoor carpeting slippery from the wet and cold weather; dirty white lawn furniture had managed to stay on the porch, but was now thrown haphazardly around. Walking up the steps leading to the front door revealed something to Eric that instantly broke his heart, but also gave him a strange form of relief.

A body lay on the living room floor, but not in one piece. It was so badly mauled, it could not complete the change to a zombie. Torn and ripped jeans were close to the front door, and what looked like the chewed remains of a torso were hidden under a knocked-over end table. This body Eric recognized as being his father's. He was able to put together the ripped and paint-stained blue jeans and the shamrock belt buckle as the same ones his dad had always worn. If not for that, he would not have been able to identify the body.

He stood looking down at the corpse for a few moments, trying to convince himself that it was not his father, but there was no denying it. Eric began to truly accept the feeling of relief, knowing his father had died quickly and not wound up as one of the undead. He turned to the three who waited just outside the door. "Come in" he said as he stepped over the pants and deeper into the living room. Just then, something moved upstairs as if responding to his voice.

Naomi, Sam, and Drew stepped lightly into the living room

and carefully over his father's remains. He did not have to tell them this was his father, because they all looked to him with sympathy, knowing from his melancholy facial expression that this person on the ground was a family member.

Eric began to walk deeper into the house. "I'm going upstairs." Naomi began to follow, but he held out his hand, stopping her. "I want to go alone."

After he walked to the kitchen and turned a corner, the sound of creaking footsteps followed every soft step he tried to make. Naomi walked quietly to the back and turned the corner, looking upstairs to see Eric standing very still and looking through a railing at the level above. His hands hung by his side in defeat, and not moving a muscle, he stared at something on the second floor. Eric peered down at Naomi, and a clean line over dirty cheeks escaped his welling eyes. The tear rolled down his right cheek and then got caught in his unshaven face. It continued to shine on his cheek until the last glimpses of light remained in the house.

He turned and walked down the steps, no longer trying to be quiet, and when he got to Naomi standing at the foot of the stairs, all he said was, "Let's go."

****

They stayed in a house directly across the street from Eric's. Everyone knew he had seen something on the second level, and everyone guessed that his mother was up there, but no one knew for sure. The house they stayed in was a mess, broken glass littering the floor and the smell of mold from months of open windows lingering in every room, but the front door's lock worked well. They secured the house, closing the windows and ensuring there were no surprises in any of the closets, and then Eric went up the stairs to the master bedroom and stared across the street to his parents' house.

Naomi wrapped her arms around his waist from behind and laid her chin on his shoulder, looking through the window at the broken house with him. "What are you thinking?"

"My mom is up there." He moved just a little to wipe a tear from his face. Naomi was silent and decided she was going to let him speak when he wanted to. "I used to work on a farm a few miles from here. We should probably head that way. At least there, we won't have to worry about too many undead."

"Sure, that sounds good." She squeezed him through his thick coat. "You are our leader, and we need you." Naomi could not believe what she was saying, but it felt good to let go. "I don't think we could do this without you." Letting go of the weight of being in charge and making all the decisions felt good to her, and she turned his head toward hers and put her cheek against his, matching the curves of their faces. After holding it there for a moment, she kissed him. She kissed him again, and he returned it with deep emotion.

Eric felt Naomi's invisible guard drop, and he embraced her, pulling her close to him. He grabbed her by her hips and pulled her warm body against his. His hands slid up her shirt and coat, pulling them over her head, revealing her soft, mocha-colored body. She unzipped his thick coat and let Eric lead her to the bed. He spread open her legs and leaned over her, kissing her thick lips, and then all thoughts of his family left him as they caressed and let passion take over until they both drifted away into full ecstasy.

Eric woke to Naomi spooning and rubbing her nude body against him from behind. This served two purposes, Eric thought; one was that she was still passionate about the events of last night, and the other was that it was cold and she was trying to get them both warm. The temperature had dropped below freezing, and white vapor churned from his mouth when he welcomed her with a moan of satisfaction and comfort.

"Do you really want to head out in this weather?" Naomi said with a little chatter of her teeth.

Eric smiled as her teeth rattled together and was surprisingly comfortable with Naomi's body heat wrapping around him like a warm blanket. "Roll over," he said as he rolled toward her and wrapped around her. He did this to warm her, but feeling her firm body fit perfectly against his excited him. He tried to maintain his composure.

"What did you see in the house last night?" Naomi grabbed hold of his arm as it caressed her curves.

Eric didn't hesitate in his reply. "My mother."

"Was she dead?"

The word *dead* now could be used in a couple ways, and Eric had never thought about having to call his mother anything but his mother. "She is one of them now. So, she's"—not wanting to call her anything else—"dead, I guess."

"I didn't mean the way it came out."

"I knew what you meant. I just don't know what I'm going to do now."

"With your mom?"

He fell silent for a few moments. "Yeah." He knew that his mother would not want to live the way she was now, but he could not kill her. The thought of taking a bullet to his mother, or even his axe, was just not possible to him. That was something he could see on anyone else, even other people's mothers, but not his own. "I can't leave her the way she is right now."

"How is she? What do you mean?"

"It's like she never stopped waiting. She is at the top of the stairs waiting for me to come home." Eric could not have his mother suffer until the end of time. He knew he had to kill her. He had to kill it. "*It*," he said, emotionless. "It was waiting for me."

"It?"

"That thing upstairs is not my mother." He slid from under the covers and quickly stepped into his clothes, rubbing his arms up and down on his sleeves and pant legs, trying to use the friction to warm them. The light shining through the window was extremely bright, and as he stepped closer to look upon his old house across the street, he noticed the black pavement of the street was now covered with white snow. Blades of grass were protruding from a white blanket that lay evenly over the ground.

Eric looked down on a human figure standing still next to a snow-covered car on the sidewalk in front of the house they were staying in. The figure wore what looked like surfing shorts and was standing barefoot in the snow. It wore a short-sleeved shirt covered with dried blood that sparkled from the snowflakes and shimmered off the morning sun.

Naomi joined him at the window and looked down on this young ghoul. "It looks like he froze there last night," she said quietly.

"Let's go check this out." After putting on his clothes, Eric went to the room Drew and Sam shared and woke them up. He walked out front with his axe in his hand and walked up to the boy. The ghoul slowly turned its head to him. The zombie was young. It must have died in its early teens. Its eyes were gray and a large wound from a bite was on its right forearm. Eric walked behind it and the boy tried to turn its body but seemed to struggle with the movement.

Eric pushed the ghoul with the head of his axe, and it slowly rocked forward, then fell face first, flat on the grass. The zombie was still in the position of trying to turn when it landed. When it hit the grass, a low groan escaped from deep within its chest. Its mouth did not move, but the moan was loud and clear. This ghoul was almost frozen. Eric raised the axe and brought it down on its neck, severing its head with very little mess. No black blood or gore splashed on him, and the cut was clean.

By this time the other three walked out and noticed a body lying in the grass to the left of them. The body was a woman's, fully clothed but missing a portion of her right cheek. She looked as if she were trying to crawl, but could not. Her left leg was bent to the side as if she were trying to push with it, and her arms looked as if they were reaching forward. She had long black hair that hung into the snow, and she looked straight ahead in front of her in an endless stare. The ghoul tried to turn its head, but its stiff hair seemed to be frozen to the ground, inhibiting its movement even more.

"I think we could probably cover some good ground today," Eric said with a smirk, louder than he had talked outside in over six months. "Go get your stuff ready. We'll take off in a little bit."

He walked to the back yard of his parents' place and went into the large blue shed. It was exactly how he remembered having left it. The white door that never closed properly was still hanging loose, and blue paint was chipping and falling off the walls. Stepping into the shed with the familiarity of having done it for years, he reached in and grabbed the red gas can.

The back door was open, so he let himself in with the gas can in tow. Walking up the stairs, he looked onto the second-floor hallway through the railings of the steps when he was almost at the top. His mother had not moved much from the night before. She had only moved maybe two feet forward. As Eric took the last couple steps up, his mother slowly turned her head down toward the sound of the creaking steps.

She was holding onto the second-floor bannister, looking toward the top of the flight of stairs. She was extremely skinny, with her bones protruding through her skin. Her skin was no longer the pale snow white that it had been in her life, but now a dirty grey complexion like all the other ghouls out there. She had been was one of the first to change, and rot and decay were eating away at her muscle tissue. Her eyes were smaller and wrinkled, with a shriveled grey-blue dot where her pupil and iris used to be. The eyes themselves were falling out of their sockets from the amount they had dried and shriveled. The only way he was able to tell it was his mother was because she wore the small silver cowboy pendant that now seemed huge compared to her skeletal figure. He had gotten it for her when he was very young.

He placed the gas can at the top of the steps, walked toward her, and stood silently in front of her. She did not acknowledge his presence, but continued to look down toward the top of the steps. He reached for the clasp of the pendant without fear, removed it from her neck, and placed it into his pocket, and then felt the outside of his jeans ensuring it was in there and safe. Then he took a few steps back. "I love you," he cleared his throat, "Mom."

She looked up to him, opening and closing her mouth as if she were chewing or wanting to chew, but she did not move. She could not move. If she lost her grip on the banister or a stiff breeze blew through, she would fall or possibly just float away.

He took the gas can and began dumping it around her feet, then down the steps, into the living room, and out to the front porch. He pulled the junk drawer in the kitchen, found the lighter he knew would be in there, and stood back from the house. Drew, Samantha, and Naomi were standing on the sidewalk across the street. Sam was holding Eric's backpack and they were all watching in silence, waiting for him to say his goodbyes.

He looked at the house that he had grown up in and began thinking of all the fun times he had in his home and all the things he had done with his mother and father. He thought about him and his father building a fort in the back yard out of the old shed and a beat-up tent; he thought of the memories of his mom cooking dinner and putting a juicy, moist roast in front of him and his cousins. He remembered his first kiss with Katie McCloud on the front porch swing and a few years later, playing with his friends and breaking that same porch swing.

Then he stepped back onto the first step and lit the trail of gas. He watched the fire travel into the living room, and a blast of warm air bellowed from the front door, then traveled up the stairs, and then he imagined the fire wrapping around his mother's feet and engulfing her.

"Goodbye." With a half-hearted smile and tears in his eyes, he walked across the street toward his new family.

Chapter 18

The Peeping Tom

"It's just one," Naomi said as the afternoon passed and the temperature rose. They had been walking for hours, and the temperature was beginning to increase rapidly. They were not sure when they had gotten the attention of this lone zombie, but they assumed it must have been in a house and sheltered from the freezing temperatures of the night before. The undead walked with a limp and was missing its right arm from the elbow down. At this distance they were not able to tell exactly if it was male or female, but it had long hair disheveled into millions of knots on top of its head.

"Yeah, but you know one can turn into a hundred," Eric responded.

"How much farther do we have to go before we actually even get to this place?" Samantha did not like the thought of going to a farm. She was a city girl, even though the city was no longer an option. She could not imagine herself living on an actual farm. The thought of chickens, hay, cows, and blue-jean overalls had never crossed her mind as even an option for a living arrangement. Sam convinced herself she was very content with digging through pantries, searching for food every night, if her only other option was trying to catch chickens. "Why don't we just go back to the village?"

"The village will soon be torn down, as soon as the real cold weather sets in. Those prima donnas are going to look for houses once they begin to freeze in those tents they got set up. Those are all well and good when it's fall or spring, but not when snow is turning your tent into a freezer," Drew answered.

Eric was happy someone else was siding with him. "We're going to have to stay somewhere tonight maybe, or we might show up really late, and I don't want to be walking those twisted roads in the dark. There are houses close by the farm, just not as many as here, so there may possibly be walkers on the streets." He turned to the ghoul behind them. "If this one continues to follow us I'll go take care of it, if we decide to stop for lunch."

Another two hours passed, and the temperature increased. causing the snow to melt. The undead following them had been left behind many streets ago, and they had no concerns of that one finding them, but down many of the streets they crossed, new undead began to move in the roads, and the sound of their groans called to the travelers as they passed each street.

They were all hungry, and the children had begun to complain about their hunger pains. Turning down a street to avoid a few undead moving between some vehicles a few yards in front of them, they walked up to the first house on the corner. It was a small white two-story house with pink shutters surrounding the front windows. Eric ran to the first window to the right of the front door and looked into it, examining the living room. The front door was closed, and Naomi believed it was going to be locked, but the knob turned and it glided open invitingly. The white two-story house was clean and appeared to be in the same condition as if the owners of the property had just cleaned or it had been vacant since Z day. The furniture was clean and set up perfectly; not a single trinket from the entertainment center or Lladro porcelain figurine on the end tables next to the flower-printed, cream-colored couches was out of place. Naomi was very excited about the house—as soon as she stepped into it and felt her feet sink into the thick, light-green carpet, this house was home to her. The smells of a clean house filled her with warmth in the chilly temperatures. The only thing she thought this place needed was a good dusting.

Eric had believed this house was zombie-free when he looked into the window and saw its pristine condition, but once they stepped in the first thing he did was to start making his rounds, clearing the residence. From the middle of the living room, Sam looked out of the side window and saw one of the ghouls they had passed standing in the street.

This undead was a bald man who wore a purple Baltimore Ravens football jacket and had a clean-shaven face that looked in the direction they originally had been traveling. Naomi ran to the window and pulled the blind down. Drew took the hint and began pulling the other window blinds as well.

As everyone was securing the house, Naomi went straight into the kitchen. She opened the wood-stained cabinets and began inspecting the contents. Canned and packaged food filled the cupboard solid from front to back and bottom to top. She turned the corner to the living room and faced the children, who were kneeling on the couch, peeking through the same blinds at the undead that now walked the streets. "Look at all this food," Naomi said with excitement as she held a variety of fruit, oatmeal, and candy bars in her cupped hands.

They jumped from the couch and grabbed the bars from Naomi. The bars were devoured and fruit and oatmeal covered Drew and Sam's mouths before Eric could make his way down from upstairs. He let out a laugh, hugged Naomi. and ran into the kitchen, where he pulled out some soups and instant white rice and looked at the stove, hoping it was gas and praying there was some left in the pipes. Within a few moments, a blue pot full of soup was being licked by the flames of the stove.

This was the first hot meal they had eaten since the village, and they savored each spoonful of chicken noodle and rice, dessert sitting just a few steps away in the full cabinets. After dinner they lay sprawled out on the clean couches, but Eric was getting antsy about getting back on the road. There was still a lot of daylight left, and Eric thought they would be able to make it to the farm well before nightfall. There was four hours of sunlight left, and it should take them just roughly two and a half to get there, if his memory served him well.

"We should be heading out in a little bit," Eric said as he rearranged the items in his backpack to fit some extra canned goods.

The thought of traveling on a full stomach didn't sit well with Naomi, but Drew was the first to object. "I just need thirty minutes," he said as he positioned himself across the love seat with his feet hanging off the side and rubbed his stomach.

Samantha turned on the couch and pulled the blind back slightly from the window so she could see what kind of activity was going on out in the street. The same ghoul stood outside the window in the street, looking away from her. She glanced over at Drew and smiled, agreeing with the timeline. She looked back out the window at the ghoul, but now it had turned and was facing the house. Sam looked through the blinds and made direct eye contact with its cloudy, dead eyes. Her heart dropped when she realized the zombie had looked directly at her. Sam could see that its purple jacket covered a bloody torso, and the undead let out a loud, energized groan and began to move toward the house.

"Oh my god," was all Same could say, and then she slammed the blind against the window.

Everyone responded slowly to her initial phrase due to their food comas, but after her quick movement to close the blind, everyone was up and on edge. A loud bang shook the house, and then something hit the window.

Eric got up and opened the blinds. A small hill led to the side of the house from the street, and from just a few feet below the window, the bald, undead Ravens fan reached up for Eric and scratched at the glass. Behind it, the undead from the street moved toward the house. "We gotta go. We gotta go!" Their moment of relaxation turned to frantic hysteria. Eric tried to maintain his composure, but his hands trembled as he attempted to zip up his backpack.

Naomi opened the front door and a groan of excitement came in along with the breeze from outside. She slammed it and fumbled with the lock. When she had opened the door, a horde of ghouls traveling out front had turned toward her.

Eric ran to the back of the house, toward the back door. The sound of banging on the siding got louder, and then the back door shook from the pounding of an unwanted visitor trying to break in. Eric ran back. "They're coming from the back, too!"

Samantha had moved to the floor and sat with her back to the couch. With each scratch and bang she shook violently, her legs held tight against her chest, frozen with fear.

They all could hear the back door crack, and then the groaning and banging in the house fell silent for what felt like an eternity while they all anticipated the next sound. The back door broke from its hinges and fell to the kitchen's linoleum floor. The open back door let in a wave of groans and then the dragging sound of undead feet making their way into the house. Eric grabbed hold of Naomi's arm and pushed her up the stairs, then screamed for Drew and Sam to follow, but Samantha was not moving.

Drew pulled at her arm, trying to pick her up off the floor and onto her feet, but she fought him, scratching and clawing at his attempts. He tossed his bag and hers toward Eric and pulled at her again. Naomi tried to squeeze past Eric down the steps, but he would not let her past. She screamed for her daughter and reached for her over the railing of the steps.

The sound of items crashing against the floor from the countertops and of the kitchen table and chairs being shoved across the linoleum indicated that the ghouls were making their way closer to them.

"We have to go, Sam!" Drew screamed and then slapped her across the face. It seemed to stop Sam from frantically fighting, and she looked up at him, dumbfounded. "Sam, we have to go!" They both turned toward the kitchen just in time to see undead pushing each other over and reaching toward their newfound meals.

Drew pulled her to her feet, and Sam wasted no time running past him and then up the stairs. Naomi turned and ran into the first door she came across, and they all followed. They closed the door just as the horde reached the bottom of the stairs. A few seconds felt like hours as they stood in the middle of the small room looking at each other, and then Eric thought about his axe and rifle. "Fuck!" he screamed, and then opened the door.

The undead were crawling on top of each other, pressing down, each crushing the ghoul under it to get to their trapped victims. Eric could see his axe and the golden-lever-action rifle leaning on the love seat next to the front door. Naomi and the children called for him to come back into the room. He closed the door with defeat showing on his face.

He looked around the room at the Disney characters smiling and looking down on him in his moment of helplessness. The room was obviously a small child's room. A small red racecar bed and various pictures of Disney characters lined the walls, and at this moment, Eric felt every one of them was mocking him.

The moans of the undead got louder as they thumped up the stairs. The heavy, dragging footsteps fumbled on each other with no order, but the volume of their excited groans indicated they were getting closer. Eric pressed his body against the door as soon as the first ghoul assured them with a loud bang that it was just outside this barrier.

A shriek from one of them came from down the stairs, and Eric knew a runner was on the first floor. He could not hold this door against a runner, and he was fully aware of it. The door would surely buckle under the newly-turned undead's attack. Drew and Samantha looked out the window at the horde, trying to force themselves towards the back door, as Naomi frantically pulled items from the closet, looking for something that could help them. But all she found were neatly-organized piles of clothes. She pulled a box from the top shelf and was showered with baby shoes—but then she saw it: the small outline of a square made from floor-molding on the ceiling.

She was overcome with relief: she had finally found what she was looking for. A second later she had pulled the wheel-well portion of the racecar bed into the closet and was pressing the middle of the square. The plywood lifted easily, and the attic presented itself as a means of escape.

Eric had pushed a dresser in front of the door and pressed his back against that, but the pounding on the door got harder to hold against as more and more undead pressed their bodies against the weak obstacle. With more bodies applying constant pressure and as the ghouls beat on the door, it began to open. The shrieking got closer as Eric pictured a lone zombie pushing other undead down the stairs to make its way to the door. The top of the door cracked just above the dresser, and he looked at a toy chest and played with the thought of grabbing it, but as soon as he let go of the dresser he knew the undead would storm the room.

"Come on," Naomi hollered to the two children, who were looking down at the mass of undead trying to squeeze into the house.

Drew was at the closet first, but he stepped aside to let Sam climb. Drew and Naomi both pushed her into the attic and then started handing her their backpacks. Naomi began to push Drew, but he refused. "I'll push you up."

Naomi didn't like that idea. "No, you go."

"I can't pull you up. Besides, I can climb up faster and better than you."

She was about to reply, but Eric chimed in. "Naomi, get your ass up there. Drew can make his own way, and then I'll be behind him."

The top of the door let out a loud crack, and Eric had to press against the top to prevent it from folding over, which would have allowed the ghouls to climb in. In order to press the top of the door, he let some of the pressure off the dresser, and that allowed the door to open more. Now dirty, cracked fingernails, caked with blood and filth, were reaching around the door frame. The ghouls reacted to the snapping door by groaning louder in anticipation of their next meal.

Naomi stood on the wheel well of the bed and grabbed onto the attic's ledge. She pulled with her arms and Drew cupped his hands under her feet and lifted with everything he had. In seconds her feet were being sucked into the attic.

"Eric, I'm going up," Drew screamed, trying to be louder than the excited ghouls.

Eric turned and watched him, and they locked eyes. Drew's expression showed worry, not because of what he was going through himself, but because he did not believe that Eric was going to make it. Drew believed this was the last time anyone was going to see Eric alive.

Eric could feel his emotion and reassured him, "I'll be up, just go!" With that, Drew grabbed hold of the attic opening's edges and pulled himself in.

The door cracked and a visible split appeared in the door. The runner was making its way closer, and Eric knew he had to make it into the attic before that one got to the door, so with no time to waste, he let go and ran to the closet. The top of the door split right above the dresser as soon as he released his grip, and it folded over, revealing the mass of undead. Bloody faces with gnashing teeth growled and snapped at him as he ran. What appeared to be hundreds of hands reached out toward him all around the hungry mouths.

He pulled the red racecar bed out of the closet and jumped up, reaching for the opening to the attic. His first attempt failed, but he backed up and took a few steps before he jumped. He grabbed the edge of the opening and kicked off the closet wall, picking himself up to get a better grip. Drew reached for the top of Eric's pants and belt as he was pulling himself in just in time to see a ghoul round the corner of the closet.

Drew pulled up harder than he ever would have believed he could, and Naomi and Sam grabbed under his armpits, lifting him up into the attic. He was in the attic to his waist when the undead grabbed him and began to pull him down. Eric felt the strong, icy grip squeeze through the skin and muscle of his left calf, pressing hard on his bone.

He flailed his legs and kicked wildly, but the undead would not release its grip. Eric screamed. This was the closest one had ever been to him. He had never been touched by a ghoul and now could understand why they were so effective: A single person couldn't get away from their grip. This was what Rod had felt before he was bitten. Eric began to think of the bite that was sure to follow. He anticipated rotting teeth piercing his skin, and he counted the seconds before it happened.

The pain he felt in his calf was excruciating, but the fear of becoming one of the undead was worse. Then panic set in as he felt that sharp pain in his left foot. Eric had been waiting for this bite, and it had just happened. His scream was tinged with a sob, and then it was hard for him to hold onto the ledge any longer. The muscles in his arms became weak, and he felt that he could no longer hold himself up. Then a loud bang, and the pressure on his calf was gone.

He was lifted into the attic by his pants and laid on a thin piece of plywood with pink fiberglass insulation coming up around the edges. Naomi had squeezed the pistol between the attic opening and Eric's body just enough to get a shot on the ghoul. The one shot had been enough to destroy its brain, causing it to let go. Same managed to replace the plywood over the attic opening just before the rest of the undead made their way into the small bedroom.

Eric pulled his left boot off and saw a bloody sock. He quickly pulled it off and saw that the side of his foot, just before the small toe, was bleeding from the bite. Teeth marks were indented into his skin, and the side of his foot was bleeding from the pressure of the bite.

They could hear the mass of undead pacing and circling in the bedroom below them, tripping on their recently deceased dead companion. Eric examined his foot and his boot in a single sunbeam that shone through the attic's screened, vented window. A clear bite mark was imprinted on his boot, but it had not ripped through the leather or torn it. His foot did not have any tears or bleeding punctures that he could see, but the blood coming from the side of his foot filled the punctures and he was unable to clean them completely.

He was reaching into his bag for another sock when Naomi reached over to put his pistol back into his bag. He pushed the gun back at her and looked at her, but Naomi already knew what he was going to say. "You should hold onto it for a while," Eric said.

Drew shone his flashlight on the wound to better examine it as Eric cleaned the bite marks. The indented teeth marks were red from his bruised skin, but no blood filled the sunken teeth marks. This set them all at ease, but still Eric insisted Naomi hold onto the pistol.

The rubber sole of his boot had stopped the zombie from piercing his foot. He wrapped the bloody sock around it, putting pressure on the wound, and then slid his other sock over that. He unlaced his chewed boot to make room for his bandage.

The children were now focused on their surroundings, and the beams of their flashlights frantically swung from one end of the attic to the other. The attic was completely empty with the exception of a row of eight-foot-by-four-foot pieces of thin plywood that spanned the middle of the attic and long nails that jutted down from the roof in rows every six inches or so.

Eric pulled his flashlight out and crawled across the plywood to the closest corner. A breeze picked up and blew cold air into the attic through the vented windows. They were going to have to stay up here, at least until the undead downstairs decided to leave or until they figured a way out. Eric thought of his mother and knew waiting for the undead to leave was not a viable plan. They would have to crawl back over the dresser to get out of that bedroom, and there was nothing to motivate them to do so, so the four were stuck in the attic for now, at least.

"Sam, Drew, start putting some insulation in those window vent things." Eric shone his light on both of the windows, one each side of the house, and they went to work.

Hundreds of large nails held the shingles in place and all Eric could think about was, why did they use such long nails? He started banging the nails with the butt of his flash light so they would bend safely and not jab straight down, but he couldn't see, so Naomi used her flashlight to assist him. He commenced banging the nails sideways and then started kicking the roof at the corner of the house with his right foot. With a few solid and hard kicks, light shot through the attic.

After about an hour of bending nails and kicking the roof, one section of plywood was loose enough to be bent back from the frame of the house. Eric pushed the plywood up, laying it on top of itself. He climbed out onto the roof and looked down the street to see the hordes of zombies that lined the road. Every square foot of space on this property was taken up by a ghoul, and every one of them was trying to jam itself into this house.

Eric climbed back into the house and pulled the broken section of roof back onto its rafters. They used the insulation from the rest of the ceiling to box themselves into a shelter with four walls made from pink fiberglass in the far corner of the attic, away from the broken roof. The sound of shuffling was still audible below them, especially when one of them dropped a flashlight or spoke too loudly. It was still early in the afternoon, and the moaning of the undead, mixed with claustrophobia, began to make them feel very uncomfortable and agitated.

Naomi and Sam held each other close and cried into each other's arms while Drew and Eric stumped each other on how to spell words like *ascorbic acid* and the eternal question, *Why does a can of diced peaches need this to "Promote color retention"?* For most of the rest of the day and night, they sat in the darkness and waited for the following morning. Eventually, in the late evening, rain began to beat on the roof, and they all drifted away into a very uncomfortable sleep, only to be awakened each time one of the undead felt the desire to let out a loud groan.

"I think it's morning now?" Sam whispered as quietly as she could to Eric, and he was instantly wide-eyed. Eric believed he hadn't slept at all and was startled by her whispering in his ear. His jumping slightly woke Naomi and Drew as well.

"Have you heard any of them?" Eric whispered after clearing his throat as quietly as he could.

"I hear a knock or a shuffle every once in a while, but it's pretty quiet," she responded.

"How do you feel?" Naomi whispered, feeling the same way Eric did.

"My foot feels like shit, but other than that, I feel the same way I've been feeling."

"So that's a good thing, then?"

"I didn't say that." Eric followed that with a smirk, trying to add a little humor, but none of them found it funny. While they were eating yesterday afternoon was the first time he had seen any of them smile, but he could not criticize because he knew he was the same way.

Eric crawled out of the insulation refuge and moved toward the attic opening. He used his fingernails to pick up the attic cover, which sat almost flush with the ceiling. After he had it picked up, he began to twist his body to put it off to the side, but Drew took it from him.

The closet below was empty, and Eric did not see anything in the room. From this angle, hanging upside down, the only thing he could see was the big bubbly black shoes from one of the characters on the wall.

He lowered his head down from the attic, and then something caught his eye in the closet just below him. It was out of the usual, but he could not place it until grey smoky eyes opened and locked onto him.

The ghoul slowly moved toward him and began to let out a groan. Two hands slowly reached up toward his head. The zombie had been standing perfectly still in the in such a way that he was camouflaged by the hanging clothes. Eric reached back for the cover, but as soon as he pulled his head into the attic Drew was already securing it.

"Back through the house is not an option," Drew announced to Naomi and Samantha. "How many do you think stayed around the house last night?"

Eric crawled on his hands and knees and tried to keep his left foot from touching anything. Just the natural swing of his foot sent bolts of pain through his body. Light filled the attic when Eric lifted the loose piece of roof, and they all shielded their eyes. Immediately following the insulting light came a wave of frigid air that made them shiver.

It took a few seconds, but Eric was eventually able to stand and look at what awaited them outside. The top of the roof was covered in a thin, evenly-layered blanket of ice. He looked down at what remained of the horde. Hundreds of undead lay on the grass in the same positions as if they were standing. There was a ghoul every few feet from the house, lying either face-down or -up, and the further from them, the more spaced out they were. There were a few that were standing, but they were holding onto or leaning on the side of the house. Eric was able to see that the ones directly under him, holding onto the siding, had the same blanket of ice on them as the roof had on it.

He pulled the rope from his backpack and tied one end onto the same backpack. Lowering it down he bounced it off one, then another of the standing zombies. The bag bounced on their heads, but none moved or even flinched. He excitedly turned and said, "We're getting out of here."

The zombies outside had frozen due to the rain and cold, but the ones inside were not exposed to the same environment. The undead inside the house were almost frozen, and that was why the ghoul in the closet had moved so slowly. Eric tied his best knot around one of the rafters. Not very confident in his knot-tying abilities, he agreed to go first only after he pulled on the rope with everything he could muster.

He stood up, heaved his left leg over the wall carefully, and straddled it. The siding of the house had a thin layer of ice covering it. Eric rubbed his leg on the siding, trying to get a grip on it, and figured he was going to have to slide down the rope. He threw his right leg over and pain shot through his bleeding foot when he put the smallest amount of weight on it, causing him to spin on the slippery siding.

He grabbed hold of the rope tightly, but was spinning and falling fast. His body hit the ghoul he had bounced his bag off of, breaking his fall. The noise he made flailing on the aluminum siding was incredible, and it echoed down the quiet street. Eric shrugged his shoulders in angst, knowing if there were any undead *not* frozen on the street, they would soon be here. He looked up to the roof and saw Sam, Drew, and Naomi looking down at him. Eric could tell by the look of concern on their faces that he had been too loud.

Eric pressed a flat hand to them, telling them to hold on, and then hobbled to the front of the house. He looked down both sides of the street, watching to see if any undead were leaving the houses or making their way toward them, but none showed. He limped back, nudged the zombie that had broken his fall, which was now lying face down in the frozen grass. After getting no response, he waved for the rest to come down.

Chapter 19

Beauty is not skin deep

The trip to the farm was excruciating for Eric and Naomi both. Naomi's back and neck were beginning to bother her again, and Eric's foot was throbbing. He knew if he did not get some peroxide or something to clean it out, it would surely get infected. Most of the trip up to the farm was on back roads, and they passed very few houses; the ones they did pass were many yards away from the main road.

These roads they traveled were quiet. Eric remembered that these back roads had been populated by people riding horseback or random pickup trucks riding through, kicking up stone and dust, but a lot had changed in the three years he had been away. These back roads were now paved with blacktop, and stop signs had appeared at each intersection. Yellow lines marked two distinct lanes. The closer he got to his old farm, the less familiar the roads looked. More houses had been built, and they were moving closer to the road to make room for bigger houses behind them.

Eric had imagined they were just going to walk right up to the old farm where he had once worked, but now they darted between unkempt bushes and overgrown tufts of grass to avoid being seen by anything moving within the dark houses. They finally made it to his farm, and an iron fence with the warning "DO NOT ENTER" plastered to it greeted them. Beyond the fence, directly in front of them, was a new white horse stable just as large as the houses they had passed. To the right, on top of a hill, was the farmhouse his boss lived in, or at least used to.

The house was exactly how he remembered it: very tall and slender, with a very steep roof and a chimney that topped the tallest peak of the roof. The house had always reminded him of the typical haunted house you would see on any creepy cartoon. The things that caught Eric's eye were the new, huge single-family houses built just beyond it. They were so close, Eric believed they might actually be on his old boss's property.

Drew pressed on the gate, and it was locked, but no *Do Not Enter* sign was going to stop them. They had not stopped at the hundreds of other warning signs they had passed. The only thing that made this warning sign different was that Eric knew everyone out here owned a few guns and more than likely would not have hesitated to fire off a few at some strangers trespassing through their property, even before the recent trouble had started. Worse, if some strangers were mistaken for ghouls trespassing on their property, then they wouldn't even think about whether to shoot or not.

They dipped through the fence and walked up a dirt driveway that led to the new stable. "I thought we were going to the house?" Sam asked.

"There's a way to get to the house back here. No one ever drives up that driveway. If we did, and my old boss was home, he would get real suspicious."

"What's your old boss's name?" Naomi was tired of him referring to him as his old boss.

"Rick." Eric imagined the horses that would graze in the fields as they crested the top of the hill that the stable was on. "He's a great guy. I guarantee when he sees me he's going to say something like, *How's it going, hawse?* or something like that. I guarantee it."

They were in the main ranch area, and directly across from the stable stood a large, classic-looking red barn that Eric informed the group was used to store hay. Across from that, another one housed

Rick's farm equipment tractors, Bobcats, and hay-baling equipment. Eric walked toward the stable and was about to go in. The white stable had two large doors that swung open to allow the horses to come in and out and directly next to the large double doors was a smaller door that looked like it might lead to an office. "He would more than likely be out here if he were going to be anywhere." Eric was excited to see his old boss again and had seemed to forget what was going on everywhere else in the world. But as he grabbed the large handle to the double door, a shuffling was heard from inside.

He let go of the handle as if it were on fire. Naomi grabbed hold of him and shushed quietly with her creased lips. She shook her head no, and they walked backward together. This put Eric back in sneak mode, and they made their way around the large farming equipment and toward the creepy house.

They walked up the three dry-rotted stairs that led to a rundown front porch and to an open, matching front door. The paint had disappeared from years of being bleached by the sun. Naomi handed Eric the pistol and said, "You can go ahead."

Rick had had company. The company may not have been wanted, but someone or something had come through the house. They entered a front living room that was not much different than those in the houses they had gone into before. No scent of undead, but the house was completely ransacked. The people that had come through here had even flipped the couches over. A staircase led upstairs directly to the left of the front door. Eric gave the three a hand signal to stay here and watch the steps while he cleared the rest of the house. The kitchen was completely empty. Rick was a bachelor farmer, so he did not have much as far as stored food. He had been in the habit of taking Eric to the local tavern to get some dinner or lunch after a hard day's work, so his not having food in the house did not come to a surprise to Eric, but he was beginning to get nervous about what remains of Rick might actually be left in the stable.

The first floor was clear, and Eric began to hobble up the stairs to clear that as well. The house was completely empty of everything. The upstairs windows were smashed out, and not even a shred of clothing existed in any of the cabinets or drawers.

He came downstairs, defeated. "I think we may want to look at moving to one of the other houses. It is going to get awfully cold here tonight."

"Where do you think your boss could be?" Sam asked Eric.

"He might be in the stable?" Drew answered for him, and Eric nodded in agreement to his response.

"Someone came through this house already, taking basically everything they would need or want. I can probably guess it was someone from one of those new houses," Eric responded.

"Do you think we should go to one of them?" Naomi's voice was asking, but in reality she was mentioning their next action.

"I don't really see what other choice we have. We can't stay here; it's going to get cold as hell. We need to go somewhere we can at least close a window," Eric said as he began to walk out of the house.

There was a house at the end of what Eric believed to be Rick's property. It was a large house with bright, white, brand-new siding that shone in the noon sun. As they walked up the long, newly-paved driveway, they were able to make out a body lying in the doorway. They saw two bare feet and a pair of blue jeans caked with dried mud and blood hanging halfway out of the house.

Eric pulled the pistol and hobbled up the steps to the door. He pushed the light-green door open and glanced at the wooden plaque that hung from a green wreath under the door's window. The plaque read, *Welcome*. The smell of rotten flesh smacked him in the face like a wave as he pushed the door open the rest of the way. The formerly-undead ghoul was lying face down, and the back of its head had been blown open by what could have only been a large shell from a shotgun. Inside the living room, another ghoul was lying on the ground in the same condition as the one in the doorway. In the corner of the room were scattered innards and body parts, probably chewed off the body of the defender of the house. Strewn across the living room amongst scattered and smeared blood trails were green shotgun shells from a pair of blood-drenched blue jeans. Eric looked behind him as he stepped farther into the house and saw that black blood splatter from multiple shots to several undead speckled all four walls opposite from the dried blood pool; a black shotgun lay in the blood of the user. Eric turned to the curtains and pulled them to get more light and then proceeded through the rest of the house.

Drew stepped on the corpse after Eric walked deeper into the carnage, releasing pent-up gas that had sat in its decomposing stomach since it had turned. The women gagged from the added putrid smell and backed away from the house as Drew quietly laughed and ran into the living room, carefully trying not to step on any of the dried ghoul parts scattered on the bloodied carpet.

"Get your fucking ass out here and take that with you." Pointing down at the rotting zombie, Naomi whispered as loud as she could, so only they would hear but her point would be made.

Drew stepped on the ghoul again, expelling the rest of the gas, and he began to laugh even harder until the smell hit him. When he experienced what they had smelled, his face turned red and he gagged as he ran from the house and rolled on the snow-covered grass of the front lawn. Then it was the girls' turn to laugh at him.

Drew and Sam were pulling the undead over the door jamb when Eric came out. "Well, if we can deal with the smell, I think we may have found home for a while."

Naomi looked at him, dumbfounded, not knowing really how to respond. She had thought about where they were going to stay, but had never imagined living in a farmhouse in Maryland. She kind of had thoughts of going back to her home in South Carolina.

The winter chill roared over her, and she was not pleased about staying, but Maryland did have its benefits, especially in the winter.

"The guy who lived here has a huge stock of canned foods. He or she, or whatever that was," Eric pointed over his shoulder with his thumb. The girls had not looked inside due to the gas cloud Drew had released, so they did not know exactly what he was talking about, but thousands of pictures of twisted corpses popped into their minds. "He must have raided all the houses around here, because he has all kinds of stuff in the kitchen. Look, this is probably the best place we could possibly be right now. Food to last us through the rest of the winter, and an underground spring feeds the farm, so water is not an issue. There's a fireplace to cook and heat up the water." A thought popped into his head. "You could take a warm bath."

That was the winning statement. Naomi and Sam both were ready to pack it up and set up camp. "Drew can help me pull this carpet up, and that should eliminate the smell," Eric said, and Drew appeared not to have a problem with it.

****

Within a few minutes Drew had pulled the other zombie's remains out onto the front lawn and begun collecting the shotgun shells. Eric had told the ladies how to find the well and had begun to make a fire in the fireplace so they could heat up some water and take a bath. The thought of staying here was beginning to sound better, with each uneventful passing moment, to all of them.

Naomi and Sam walked across the overgrown, dead, brown grass and onto the dirt road that passed Rick's house, toward the barn and stables. Just as Eric had described, next to the white stable was a pipe wrapped with black pipe insulation and ending in a red pump spigot. Naomi was the first to grab it and pulled up on the handle. She got excited when the sound of running water could be heard flowing up the pipe. Sam was more focused on what was moving inside the white stable.

She walked over toward it. The sun was beginning to rest over the trees and created a long shadow of her body that climbed the length of the building. Something was moving inside the stable and she could not help but look inside. There could be horses in there, after all—it *was* a horse stable.

The windows on the double doors were too high, and she could not get a clear view of the inside. There were windows on the sides of the barn, but a good distance away from Naomi. Sam began to make her way toward the first one, but her mother called her back because she was wandering off too far, and this caused something to stir inside the building. There was no growl or moan, just the sound of shuffling, as if someone or something was dragging their feet or something in gravel.

The office door had a long, vertical, narrow window over the door handle, and she cupped her hands around her face, blocking the sun's glare on the glass. The office was a mess, but not because someone had destroyed it. It was a mess because whoever was in charge of the office had poor organizational skills. Stacks of paper lay on the desk haphazardly, and a brown leather saddle leaned on a chair in front of the desk. The office had a door with a large window in it that led to the stable. Sam stared at that window, hoping to see a large beautiful horse walk past, but none did. She squinted her eyes to get a clearer look as the sun squeezed through the cracks of her fingers, when she saw something move past the window, only further away, in the shadow of the setting sun. It looked like a girl, a girl about her age and height. She could not make out much, but she saw golden blond hair that was kept in braids that ran down her back. "Mom, I think there is a girl in here."

"There might be, but we aren't going to find out today,"

Naomi said as she pushed the lever down, stopping the flow of water, and replaced the bucket with the second one. "You have to carry one of these buckets, so don't think about going anywhere."

"I know, but she's not like any of the other ones." Sam ran back to her mother.

"Eric will come with us tomorrow, and if it is one of them, he'll kill it." Naomi wanted nothing to do with killing any zombies, especially if she was going to be the one that provoked it. "They'll be frozen in the morning. Less risk."

They carried the two buckets back to the house, and for the first time in months ran warm, wet washcloths over their skin. Eric agreed he would find a hose tomorrow and they would run it from the spigot to the house. Since the hose would be downhill anyway, the water should have no problem getting to them. They would just have to shut it off when they were done filling up the buckets so the hose did not freeze. Tomorrow they would take their first warm bath.

****

When they removed the covers, cold immediately replaced their warm layer of comfort. Eric and Naomi lay close together, but the pain in Eric's foot throbbed with each beat of his heart.

"Did you see any antibiotics or peroxide or anything in the stable when you were in there last night?" Eric said, nursing his foot.

"We never went in, but Sam said it was a mess in there," Naomi responded, putting on her clothes. She had rummaged through the previous owner's dresser drawers and was able to fit into a pair of the woman's black sweatpants. The woman that had lived here was obviously a smaller woman, compared to Naomi's full figure and height.

"Well, my foot is killing me, so I need to find something." He stood up and almost fell when he put weight on his left foot. Eric fell back to the bed and picked up his foot. "I can't go anywhere right now."

Naomi turned to him. "I'm not going alone."

"I can't make it. I just can't do it. My foot is killing me."

"Well, good luck. There's something in that barn, and I'm not going in there."

Eric lifted his foot, and Naomi cringed at the sight of it. The entire outside of his foot from his small toe to his heel was blood-red, and the middle of the gash was covered with a yellow scab. "I can't make it. Naomi, I'm sorry, but it's not going to happen."

She turned and walked out of the room in frustration, but she could not blame him. "I'm taking the gun, then," she hollered back.

Naomi and Sam walked out the front door, and the outside greeted them with a Maryland winter. They recoiled back into the house. Eric pulled his coat tight around him, but stepped out as something caught his attention. Drew saw it, too, and followed him out into the yard.

At the end of the driveway, two figures stood motionless. Drew began to walk toward them, and Eric stopped when he got to the edge of the porch. "Sam, come on," he turned and hollered to her. Drew had an aluminum bat at his side and waited for Sam.

They walked down with Naomi following behind. She carried the black pistol in her cold hands, and Eric was left at the porch, sitting on the step with the twelve-gauge resting on his lap. She had an empty camouflage backpack strapped over her shoulders to gather whatever supplies she could.

The two undead were standing straight up with their feet shoulder-width apart, one just slightly in front of the other. The one that was in front was wearing a loose orange hoodie and looking straight down at the ground, and the one behind held an endless stare straight ahead, a cream-colored snowboarding jacket zipped all the way to its chin. Both of them were grown men who must not have turned too long ago. Their skin was still intact, and they did not appear to be decomposing as fast as the other undead had during the summer.

Drew put the bat between the rear one's eyes and pushed it back. It fell straight back like a flat board. He then took the bat to the top of the front one's head. It was looking straight down, so his swing came down directly on the back of its skull, causing it to split down the middle and then fall to the side and onto its stomach. He kicked it over to its back and used the end of the bat to separate the two sections of skull. "I split its head."

Sam looked away in disgust, but curiosity took hold of her and she watched as Drew slowly opened its skull in two complete frozen pieces, revealing the intertwining brain of the ghoul. She had expected the brain to be what she had always seen on T.V., red and shiny, but that was not what she saw. The brain was covered in a thick black mucous, and the red intertwining pieces of brain were replaced with a grey substitute. "You have to kill it."

Drew pressed on the brain with his bat, but it was hard. He pulled his sunglasses over his eyes, stood over the body, and swung down again. The bat sent shockwaves through his hand and up his arms, and the brain stayed intact. He shook off the shock and came straight down on the top of the brain again, only this time he smashed down on the brain with the end of the bat instead of swinging it high over his head. He repeated this motion over and over again until the head was only an empty cavity of crushed grey brain-ice. After taking a quick break and regaining his breath, he performed the same act on the zombie's partner.

The sun was shining on the other side of the stable, forcing them to lower their shades until they entered the long shadow of the building. The plan was for Sam and Drew to open the double doors and Naomi to shoot whatever came at them, but Drew and Naomi were able to see inside the windows of the stable doors. On the other side of the stable, beams of light shone on a small lone figure sitting against a stall pillar.

"I think there's only one of them in there," Naomi said.

"I could go in and take care of it. If you want me to?" Drew sounded excited about it and his grip on the bat said he was looking forward to it.

"Do you not care that at one point in time, these things were living, loving people?" Naomi was disturbed by his lack of sympathy.

"It's only one of them, and it's frozen just like the other ones." He looked back through the windows, and the lone figure was now looking in their direction. Drew almost fell over in shock and let out a nervous chuckle. "This one's not so frozen."

Naomi looked back inside and saw it press down on its hand, then lean to the side to try to stand. It was moving slowly, so Naomi hurried and opened the door. "Drew, go get it before it stands."

The door swung open and dust from the sitting straw twisted in the fresh air as the stable breathed it in. Drew stepped hesitantly as he passed over the threshold and looked to his sides nervously. The closer he got to the ghoul, the more detail began to appear. The undead was a small boy, dressed in blue overalls and a white crew t-shirt that was covered in dried blood.

It crawled to its hands and knees and began to stand. Drew ran in quickly, not looking to either side, before it could look up, and took the bat to the back of its skull. It dropped flat to the ground, but began to writhe its body, trying to regain its composure. He brought the bat to the back of its head again. This time it lay still.

Happy with this outcome, Drew watched for just a second and then skipped backward toward the open stable door. "Oh my god, that was intense."

"You're sick. Let's just get what we came for," Naomi said as she walked through a freshly-painted white door, just inside to her right, that led to the office.

He was smiling at Sam, but she paid no attention to him. She walked into the stable, kicking up dust as she walked. She stood over the boy and tapped its head with her black sneakers. After she was positive it was dead, she grabbed hold of its shirt and rolled it to its back.

The boy's face was smooth. He had been very young when he changed; he had to be younger than seven or eight. His blond hair was parted on the left side of his head, and black veins stretched up his neck from a wound that was hidden under his overalls.

Just then, Sam heard shuffling directly across from her. A figure began to emerge from the dark stall. This figure was just a little taller than the boy and was moving toward her. Drew stood with his bat drawn.

He gripped the bat and stood in front of Sam in a defensive posture, waiting for this ghoul to enter the light. A black dress shoe was the first thing to appear, and then the frill of a dress, and then a hand stretched from the shadow, spreading its long fingers. Drew raised the bat, ready to swing, when Sam grabbed the end. Looking at her, confused, he lowered his eyebrows. Sam shook her head and whispered, "Not yet, I want to see it."

A clean blue frilled dress, and then long, flowing golden hair entered the main path of the stable. This ghoul was a girl the same age as Sam. Her face entered the sunlight, revealing beautiful blue eyes and perfectly clear skin. Her face was perfectly draped by her clean, curly, golden-blond hair, and her face showed no emotion as she walked forward. Even in the afterlife this ghoul was as beautiful as before it had died, and the emotionless features entranced them both.

"She is pretty," Sam said quietly, and Drew just nodded in agreement.

Drew pulled the bat from Sam, but she grabbed hold of his shoulder. "You can't kill her."

The sound of a cabinet closing made Drew do some quick thinking. He took the end of the bat, pressed it hard against the girl's chest, and pushed hard, forcing the ghoul to trip backwards. "We'll kill her tomorrow," he said. Sam agreed and then ran to the office.

"I hope this shit doesn't kill him." Naomi held up a bottle that read *antibiotics*. "Good thing is, if we ever need anything for worms, his old boss has a medicine cabinet full of stuff to get rid of them."

Drew locked up the stable and they began looking for a hose to hook up the well. They found one coiled in a bathtub, hooked up to a black float like the ones used in the backs of toilets. As the water level got low, the float would energize a pump to fill the bathtub for the horses, and as it rose, the float would shut the pump off. The hose was stuck in a thin sheet of ice, so Drew commenced freeing it by crushing the ice.

Naomi caught a glimpse of something as she watched the young boy beat the ice. She looked to her daughter, and a dark spot looked as if it were seeping through her blue pants just below her butt cheek.

She walked toward Sam and turned her around, but Sam pulled away from her. "Turn around, girl, let me see something." She turned hesitantly, and Naomi knew exactly what the stain was. "Come with me," she told her softly, and they walked away, but not too far from Drew.

After Drew broke the hose free, he dragged it back to the house. Sam and Naomi walked into the house without saying a word and went straight upstairs and into the bathroom. After what felt like forever they came out and took Drew by the arm. "You're coming with us," Naomi demanded, and they walked out. Eric remained quiet, but very confused, so he lit the wood in the fireplace and began to warm some food over the fire.

They went to the closest house and Drew was the first to enter this time, carrying the pistol. The house was clear of undead and also food, but Naomi was not looking for food. She went directly for the bathrooms and found what she was looking for.

That night Naomi taught Sam how to keep herself clean, and Drew brought a few lengths of hose in from the barn and laid them next to the fire to thaw. They ate another warm meal and Eric took half of a pill from the mysterious bottle that read *antibiotics* in black permanent marker. He figured if these were literally strong enough for a horse, less than one would do the trick, so he took one half early in the morning and the other half after dinner. As darkness set in over the house, so did the boredom, and everyone called it an early night.

Eric and Naomi lay in each other's arms, absorbing each other's warmth. "I got a feeling it's going to be real cold tomorrow," Eric said.

"God, I hope not, but it is pretty nice not having to worry about any of them running up on us." A slight pause and then she continued. "Oh, by the way, we may have to tread carefully with Sam." Naomi said.

"Okay?"

"Sam became a woman today."

"Not following," Eric stated with a confused expression on his face.

"She got her first period today."

"For the first time, like ever?"

"Yeah, like ever." She didn't find his statement humorous. "You're an idiot, you know that?"

Eric didn't know how to respond, but felt he had to say something. He couldn't sit in an uncomfortable silence at this point in time. "So you helped her and told her what to do?"

"Yeah, but we are going to have to get some stuff. I wanted to go into some of the other houses and see what they had. I don't have enough for two of us right now."

Eric had always known why she wanted to go searching through the medicine cabinets of the houses they went through on their way here, but he had never imagined it would be such a big issue. Then again, he was not a female and had never cared to know anything about this kind of thing. "I don't think anyone will fight you on that. Can't you just use toilet paper?"

"You truly are an idiot. You know that!"

"What? It was just a question. I don't know these things."

She turned away from him, annoyed. "I'm going to bed."

Eric decided to cut his losses and just give up.

****

First thing in the morning, Drew was ready to go back to the stable and start hooking up the hoses, and Sam couldn't stop thinking about the female zombie with the golden hair and blue eyes. Eric dreaded waking up and dumping half a bottle of peroxide onto his open wound. After he soaked his foot in a tub of peroxide, the white foam from the infection started to calm.

The morning was incredibly cold, and billows of smoke rose with each breath, fogging their sunglasses. As Sam and Drew walked to the stable, frozen grass crunched beneath their feet. "I'm going to hook up the hoses before we kill the zombie," Drew said as he shook off the cold.

"Won't the hose just freeze?" Sam said, being the pillar of wisdom.

"I have to find a valve for the end and then we can let it trickle out."

"Does that actually work?"

Drew shrugged, "How the hell should I know? Eric said it would work. He said if you let water run out, it won't freeze."

"I don't think it'll work."

Sam walked toward the stable, but Drew began to walk toward

the well. She didn't turn around and was completely focused on the white building, and Drew began to think about her going in there without a weapon. He dropped the length of hose and then called out, "Do you want me to go in with you?" He didn't want her going in unarmed, and he was the one holding onto the bat.

Sam thought about it for a second and then shook her head in approval. She opened the door, and the undead stood in the middle of the stable facing away from them. The sun was shining through the windows in the double doors across from them, and square beams of sunlight shone down around her black shoes. They approached her slowly and cautiously.

Drew took his bat and tapped it on the top of her head. He let out a laugh. "She's frozen stiff."

They walked in front of her, but they were unable to see through their sunglasses in the dark stable. Sam opened the double doors the ghoul faced, allowing the sun to fully enter the stable and create a wind tunnel that blew hard through the aisle and caused them to pull their jackets tight against them. Sam quickly ran to the other side and closed the opposite doors.

As she walked toward the ghoul, she saw Drew looking at it closely. He was standing in front of her, examining her. Sam stood next to him and studied her. "She has no sign of a bite or those black veins that run up their neck or anything," Sam said, examining her, flipping up her hair.

"I've never seen one with such pretty eyes," Drew said. He rubbed his fingers over her cheeks. "You are a pretty one, aren't you?"

"You got a thing for dead girls now?" Sam said and pulled his hand down from her face.

"Yeah, that's it." He handed her the bat. "I'm hooking up the hose." He walked out without saying anything else to her.

The ghoul's eyes drew her closer, and she caught herself gazing into their still orbs. She stood directly in front of her now, very close to her cold, pale face. Sam whispered, "You *are* pretty." Her heart started to beat a little faster and a little harder. "You're so fucking pretty, aren't you." Her body became warm and her sunglasses started to fog. "You're fucking dead," she said a little louder, and then jumped back, startled by her own excitement. "You want to eat me, don't you, bitch? You want to fucking bite me. Bite this!" She let her anger out and swung the bat at the undead girl's left leg. The bat moved freely into the thick frill of her blue dress and then struck her solid leg, causing the ghoul to fall to its left. Sam was surprised at the shock that went through the bat, and she alternated hands, holding onto the bat as she opened and clenched her free hand, working the shock from them.

This is what Sam wanted. She wanted to hurt one of them and this was her chance. The undead girl was face down, but she swung the bat again at her legs. She wanted to look at her face as she beat her, so she rolled her over. The blond-haired girl was stiff, but now her hair covered her face. Sam used the end of the bat to move the blond strands that hid her beautiful young features. Moving the hair revealed those striking eyes that made Sam hate her even more. She beat on her hips and stomach, taking pleasure in the shock that she received from each blow of the bat. She watched her emotionless face with each hit, and with no emotion, Sam was not getting the satisfaction of inflicting pain on her. She wanted the satisfaction of getting revenge. She wanted revenge for everything they had taken from her.

She heard footsteps moving around the stable, and then Drew appeared. Sam stopped hitting and stepped away from the ghoul. "Hey, I need to look for that valve and don't really want to go without something like a bat." He pointed to the one she had in her hand. "Did you kill it or what?"

"I think so?" she said, lying. "I'll be out in a second. I wanted to cover her up."

"We should probably pull them out eventually, because as

soon as it gets a little warmer they're going to start stinking." He walked toward the zombie and looked down at her. "She's not dead. You didn't hit her in the head. You want me to do it?"

She held onto the bat and pulled it from his reaching fingers. "Nah, I'll do it, just not now. Let's cover her up and we can do it when we pull them out."

Sam grabbed hold of her hair and tried pulling her into one of the stalls, but her hair pulled from the scalp, causing Sam to fall backward into a pile of hay. Drew laughed out loud and Sam covered her embarrassment by cursing and then throwing a grey wool blanket over the creature's body.

"You want her to be comfortable while we're gone?" Drew said mockingly.

She began to walk out. "I'm going to get something to eat first. Fuck your valve." She began to close Drew in the stable, but he jumped out before she latched it closed.

Drew began to mock her. Sam closed her mouth and tried to ignore him, but he began to press on her last nerves and she took a slow swing at him with the bat that he easily dodged.

"God, no wonder that thing in there isn't dead yet." He was jumping around her, laughing. "If you are going to swing at her like that, she'll thaw out, take the bat from you, and beat you with it before you do any damage to her."

"If I wanted to hit you I could. Stop being such a dick." She walked in silence the entire way back to the house, fighting her urge to scream at him.

****

Breakfast turned into a late lunch and a search through two other houses not far from their new home, looking for tampons and other women's toiletries. Naomi didn't find exactly what she needed, but was able to find some of the things she felt she could not do without. On the way back to the house, carrying paper towels, toilet paper, and body wash, Drew realized by the setting sun that night would soon be on them, and he still had to find a valve to attach to the end of the hose. Getting the opportunity to clear a house like Eric used to had made him forget all about finding the valve.

As soon as they walked through the front door, Drew stopped Sam. "So, you ready to go?"

Sam was looking forward to going back, but not for a valve. She wanted to go and see that undead ghoul. "Yeah, sure, let's go."

Naomi overheard their conversation and turned to them. "Where are you going?"

"We've got to find a valve to put on the end of the hose," Drew said excitedly. "I'll take the pistol, so we'll be alright."

Sam nodded her head and smiled. "I'll take the bat."

Drew was walking fast, and Sam was traveling right along with him. "I'll clear that overhang with all the heavy machinery, and then we'll start looking for what we need."

"I'm going to the stable," Sam refused, having her own agenda.

"We've got to find the valve before it gets dark." Drew could not believe what he was hearing. He had believed she wanted to fix the hose just as much as he did, but this was obviously not the case. He had to complete this mission. Finding this one valve was completing something that he could take pride in. Finishing this hose would mean just taking a short couple steps out of the front door to get water. This mission was important to him. This was his contribution to his new family.

"Drew, I have to kill that girl."

"What if I just go in there and shoot her?" he said, aiming the pistol.

"No, I'll do it. I really want to do it."

"Will you be okay by yourself? She's probably still frozen."

Sam really didn't want him in the stable when she was in there with her. She didn't want Drew to see her anymore. The girl was pretty–Sam believed the ghoul was prettier than she was. "Yeah she's probably frozen anyway, like you said. I'm going to go in there and bash the back of her skull."

They came to the overhang that stored the tractors and other heavy equipment, to their right as they walked the main path from the house. The stable was directly in front of them, and the sun was to their backs, casting long shadows before them. Drew stopped. "I'm going to be right in here. If you need anything just holler and I'll be right there."

"I've got to go in through the back. I locked the front doors and left through the back ones, remember?"

"I can walk you there."

"I'll be fine," she responded and started walking, finishing their conversation.

Sam walked slow, listening to the birds and other sounds that surrounded the farm. The singing of birds chirping in the distance was more now than in the morning and the wind picked up as the day went by, but something was different. The sound of grass cracking from the morning frost was missing. As the sun rose and beat on the farm, the temperatures had risen enough to melt the small puddles of water and dry up the moist earth.

Sam began to think that maybe she wasn't going to be lying under that blanket, and as she walked up to the front window, she stood on her toes to look in. She leaned the bat on the door and cupped her hands to block the sun so she could see into the stable. The blanket was balled up in the middle of the aisle between the stalls.

Sam began to walk around the stable and opened the double back doors. Sun shone through the front windows, and the smell of old manure and death was strong. The cold morning air had masked and hidden the smells, but the smell of rot now assaulted her nostrils. She stood in the back entrance and waited for the ghoul to come, but nothing moved. She took a few cautious, uneasy steps and raised the bat over her shoulder. "Hey, bitch." She wanted to say it a lot louder, but it came out as barely a whisper.

A few steps deeper and she was looking at the dead boy in the blue overalls, imagining it rising up and reaching out for her. As she watched the boy, movement from the stall directly in front of her made her jump back and hit her back against a pillar on the opposite side of the stable. A silhouette was moving toward her, and as it crossed the barrier of the stall, hands emerged from the darkness and grew into arms.

She took a hard swing at the emerging hands and made contact with the left one. The swing felt good, making solid contact with her target. The sound of a crack from the ghoul's wrist filled Sam with confidence. The creature slowly walked from the shadow and was revealed as if the darkness were a thick blanket slowly rolling off her smooth young features.

Sam wanted to hit her, but could not. She was moving slowly, as if she were not completely thawed. Something inside of Sam could not kill her, but that didn't keep the ghoul from coming at Sam. One clawed hand grabbed at her, and the other, mangled hand attempted to. Sam stretched out the blunt end of the bat and pressed it against the girl's forehead. She pressed hard on the bat, pushing the undead back, making it stumble to the side, and she repositioned herself so that her back was to the open door.

The ghoul's face didn't change. No expression, just a drive to reach her, shone in its blue eyes. It continued to take slow, steady steps toward her. Sam raised the bat and placed it on its face. She bumped it slightly against its cute nose. The ghoul's head was pushed back, but it kept moving forward. She bumped it a little harder, rocking its head back a little more. Sam had to step back from the approaching ghoul, and she tripped, forcing her to spin around to regain her balance.

She did not fall, but she had to move quickly to maintain her balance. The bat went back up and she struck the creature hard with the blunt end, this time ripping its cheek and revealing black blood that leaked from a loose piece of skin. Now it was no longer a cute girl. Now it was no longer this adorable, unfortunate little girl. Now it was just an undead zombie, and Sam began to feel as if she really could do this. With the sun behind the ghoul, it turned into a dark silhouette moving toward her. She pushed her sunglasses onto the top of her head so she could see the creature better.

The bat swung hard into the hip of the undead girl, making it fall flat to the ground. It began to crawl on its hands and knees, and Sam swung down on the top of its head, right at the base of the neck. The creature's head snapped down and smashed into the earth. The ghoul began to press itself up, and it looked up at Sam. A golf swing to its face snapped its head around, knocking it off its kneeling base.

Sam stood over the zombie. It wasn't pretty anymore, and now she could kill it. As it began to roll, Sam raised the bat and came down on the back of its head a second time. This time it lay still with its face flat in the dirt. Sam took the bottom of her shoe and kicked its head to the side so she could look at her one last time. Black smears of blood leaked from her wounds, and dirt and pieces of straw from the aisle stuck to her skin.

"Who's pretty now?" Sam said and raised the bat to smash the ghoul one last time. The bat sunk deep into its face and Sam was forced to look away when she felt something splash onto her face and into her left eye. She dropped the bat and rubbed her eye with the back of her hand. Dark black fluid smeared on her hand, and she could feel her eyelashes sticking together as she batted her eyes.

Oh my god, she thought, *What did I do?*

"You sure are taking a long time," Drew said as he walked to the open door.

They'll kill me. I know they'll kill me. I'll be just like this girl and Drew will want nothing more than to kill me. "Give me a second," she said as she stood up and turned her back to him. She rubbed her face with the inside of the fleece inner liner of her coat. Black, thick blood smeared the inside of her jacket. She rubbed vigorously until her face began to burn.

"Are you okay?" Drew began to walk toward her.

Sam acted as if she was laughing. "I killed her. We should get them out of here before they start to really stink."

Drew stopped, sensing something was wrong. "It's going to get dark soon. It could probably wait till the morning."

Sam looked to the windows, and the sun was no longer shining through. Drew was right, and as long as she didn't look directly at him, he might not notice the blood on her face. She walked by him quickly, not saying a word.

Drew quickly followed behind her. "Sam," he called to her, but she never turned. "Sam, what's wrong with you?"

Sam wasn't feeling sick, but she wanted to be left alone. She thought back on her mother's and her conversation when Naomi had noticed her coming into cycle. Her mother had told her that she might start to experience cramping, and that is what she told Drew. "I'm not feeling good. I have cramps real bad."

"Oh, you have women issues, then?" Drew left it at that. Rod had always grabbed him and would take him to the beach or the mall when Julie got her period, so that is what he related this to. He would just leave her alone.

As they walked into their house, Sam ran straight upstairs to her room. Naomi and Eric were sitting at the dining room table talking when Sam ran past them. Naomi was getting up to go after her when Drew explained she didn't want to be messed with because she was getting cramps, but that did not stop Naomi.

Naomi knocked on the closed door and let herself in. Sam was already tucked under the new pink covers they had found from one of the other houses, facing away from her. "Are you okay, honey?"

"I feel sick and just want to be left alone." Sam pulled the covers up tighter around her face. She didn't feel any different, but just wanted to hide and be left alone.

"I'm so sorry, honey. Tomorrow I'll go into town and get you some medicine." Naomi rubbed the blankets around her shoulder. "There's medicine out there that will take away your cramps." She leaned over and kissed the top of her head. Naomi noticed a strong iron smell coming from her and decided, *Before she wakes up, I'm going to make her a warm bath.* "I'll bring you up dinner when it's done." She got no reply from Sam but the covers being pulled tighter around her.

"She must be feeling real bad," Naomi said to Eric, but Drew heard her. Drew and Eric were sitting at the table with a deck of cards. "So what happened down there?" she addressed the young boy.

Drew didn't want to get Sam in trouble, so she kept the girl a secret. "Nothing, really. She started to complain about her cramps or something like that when I was hooking up the valve."

When dinner, which consisted of pork and beans and beef stew, was ready, Naomi dropped it off on the table next to Sam's bed. Naomi sat on the edge of the bed, but Sam hollered something to her that she was not able to make out and then a very clear, "Just leave me alone, please."

Naomi and Eric lay in each other's warmth, and concern for Sam weighed heavily on the mother. "I have to go out in the morning and get her what she needs."

"I am so sorry I haven't been able to help out as much and go out more."

Naomi understood why he couldn't. Every time he put pressure on his foot it would rip open. The infection appeared to be clearing up, but every time he would walk, winces of pain shot across his face. "There's nothing you can do right now, anyway. Maybe Drew can pop the clutch in one of those old trucks back there and you could tag along for the ride, since you know where you're going."

"Yeah, we could do that." He held her closer. "You know, I am so happy we found each other."

"I'm happy you saved us from my house."

"God, it feels like it has been forever, doesn't it?"

"Well, it was a couple months ago. It's not like it was just yesterday," Naomi said and then laughed. "If it wasn't for you and Drew, Sam and I would be dead by now."

"You know, you are the closest thing I have ever had to a relationship," Eric said, trying to swing her back into a romantic mood. "Some things just happen for a reason."

Naomi squinted her eyes. "You think all this happened so fate would bring us together."

"Yes, that is exactly what I mean," Eric responded smartly. "The world went to shit so we would meet."

Naomi just laughed and kissed him and then crawled on top of him, straddling his waist.

****

Eric ripped his foot back open when he tried to take control of Naomi and roll on top of her. He was able to fall asleep, but only in brief increments. He knew his foot was bleeding, but didn't want to crawl out from under the warm covers to put a new bandage on his wound. He tossed around the idea of getting up, but could not find the will to do it. Then something fell in the hallway, causing him to jump.

He reached under the covers and felt Naomi's warm hip to ensure she was still sleeping. Knowing someone else was out there gave him the motivation he needed to get out of bed. He hobbled out the bedroom door and closed it behind him. He began to make his way to the stairs down into the kitchen. From a bedroom down the hall walked the silhouette of a slender figure. Eric recognized it was Sam by the way her braids hung down, like dark fingers waving freely in the shadows.

Eric was happy to see her up and whispered very quietly, so he did not wake anyone else, "Hey, how you feeling?"

The silhouette froze and quickly jolted her head toward him, sending the braids jumping and twisting. Eric's good feeling drained from his body as the dark figure turned toward him. Long, dark-shadowed fingers like sharp daggers stretched from her sides, and then she took a step closer.

Eric's heart jumped up into his throat. He didn't know what to do. His legs didn't want to move, and all he could think about was Naomi and Drew. Then the ghoul that had been Sam let out a long and piercing screech and ran toward him.

Eric forced his legs into action. This was his little girl, but he knew there was no hope for her. As she took off toward him he ran toward her. He wanted to get past Drew's bedroom so he could escape without having to walk close to Sam and risk getting attacked.

They met past Drew's door, but not past the stairs. Eric crouched down low and pushed the frenzied ghoul up and off her feet, driving her back to the other side of the second floor.

"Get out of here!" Eric screamed, but he was not sure if they would be able to make out what he said over Sam's screeching.

She scratched at his arms and ripped at his face. Eric felt her dagger-like claws tear into his cheeks and neck. He closed his eyes to protect them as her fingers raked his face. "Get out!" he screamed again.

He didn't have to give them warning, because Drew and Naomi were already watching him drive Sam's body against the hallway walls. Drew turned to Naomi and saw her run back into her room. He ran to help Eric, but Sam's arms and legs clawed, kicked, and wrapped around Eric all at the same time, as if she were a wild animal backed into a corner.

Drew didn't know what to do. There was no way he could help without injuring Eric. Just then, a shot was fired and chunks of drywall and dust flew into the air next to Eric's head.

Naomi had run back into the bedroom to get the pistol and attempted to fire a shot at Sam, but could not find the strength and courage to pull the trigger on her daughter. Eric felt the debris hit him in the face and hollered again. "Get out! Get out of the house!"

Drew looked to Naomi and then to the gun as she dropped the pistol to the wood floor. A loud thud forced Drew's attention back to Eric and Sam. The ghoul had kicked off the wall and forced Eric against the opposite side. Sam let go of Eric and looked to the two at the opposite end of the hall. She began to run at them, but Eric reached for her, found a handful of braided hair, and pulled her to the floor. He got to his feet and pressed her head to the ground, but with her immense strength and absent of sense of pain, Eric knew he would not be able to hold her for long. "Get out!" he screamed again in the brief second Sam was not bellowing out the horrid screech they all had learned to fear.

Naomi stood screaming, not in fear, but for the loss of her daughter. She was not moving, and Drew knew he was going to have to force her. He grabbed her hand and pulled her toward the steps. As they started down the steps Naomi faltered and fell to her butt, the entire time screaming Sam's name.

She fought Drew's hands from hers and tried to climb back up the stairs. "Sam, no! Not my baby!" she cried.

They were halfway down the stairs when Naomi started to regain her composure and Drew could no longer overpower her in her hysteria. He didn't know what to do. He was losing her to the stairs, and he was being dragged back up to the fight. He began to cry from panic. "Mom, I can't lose you," he said, crying. "Mom, I can't lose you too." He felt his grip pulled away and Naomi advancing up the steps, crawling. "No! Please no! Mom, I can't lose you!" Tears rolled from his eyes from fear that he was going to be alone, but then Naomi stopped.

She turned to him, seeing him kneeling on the steps, begging for her to come back in sheer helplessness. Naomi turned to him. Then she made her way down the stairs and grabbed him. They ran from the house with nothing but what they were wearing. Neither one wore shoes, and the cold from the snow bit at their toes as they crushed the layer of ice under their feet. The wind blew hard, throwing ice from the snow-covered ground, causing chills to force their way into their clothing. They ran as fast as they could to the abandoned farmhouse and wrapped themselves with the old torn blankets that covered the old broken beds and anything else they could find to shake off the chill from the ice.

The back bedroom window had a view of the house they had just left and they could still hear Sam's screeching from across the snow covered fields, over the strong wind, and through the old house. The night was cold and the wind blew hard, but that was only a mild distraction from the sound of Sam screeching. Madness and chaos continued to encompass both Naomi and Drew.

Naomi could not shake the thought of her daughter being one of *them* and could not help but wonder what she was going to do if Eric couldn't fix this. She didn't have an answer. She didn't want an answer.

Then a loud bang, and silence was restored. The chaos was over with the single shot of a gun. The wind died down as if it were nonexistent, and even the cold chill of the melting snow on their clothing no longer mattered. The bittersweet of not having to interact with the undead version of Naomi's daughter was replaced by the remorse of knowing her child was no longer with them.

Naomi turned from the window and sat on the corner of the old bed, covered her face with her hands, and then cried into her lap.

Drew watched the open front door, expecting Eric to walk from it. He watched as the wind appeared to die completely and small snowflakes fell gently to the cold earth. The moon shone brightly on the dark house, illuminating all the magnificent features of every frame and the icicles that hung from the gutters.

The sound of another gunshot echoed over the fields.

Naomi got up and held onto Drew, knowing that from now on, it was just the two of them.

The End

Jason Deyo

CPSIA information can be obtained
at www.ICGtesting.com
Printed in the USA
LVHW051755171220
674450LV00013B/1154